# IT'S N[...] I KNEW HER

## A Novel

## PAT SPEARS

Twisted Road Publications LLC

Twisted Road Publications LLC

Copyright © 2016 by Pat Spears
All rights reserved
ISBN: 978-1-940189-12-3
Library of Congress Control Number: 2016930449

www.twistedroadpublications.com

# IT's NOT LIKE
# I KNEW HER

## Summer 1963 - Catawba, Florida

## One

Jodie Taylor hesitated beneath a canopy of sweet gum, hickory, and beech trees, and squinted into the sun's white glare. Ahead, the familiar clapboard house, bleached the color of oak ash, straddled the ridge like a well-worn saddle. In the dappled sunlight, the porch appeared to slouch away from the main house, evoking memories of the rank contrariness that had dwelled there. She picked up the battered suitcase and stepped from the shade's relief onto the lane's hot sand.

A murder of crows cawed down at her from their perch along the power line. The more curious birds swooped closer, appearing to memorize her face, and she wondered by what name they might call her. Crows as messengers of death was a superstition held by some, but not her.

She peered through the porch's rusted screen door and called his name, not in the hard-earned voice of the woman she'd become, but in a small way, borrowed from her childhood. As though neither the departure of Miss Mary nor the passing of time and distance had made her anyone other than his curse.

Hearing not as much as a guttural whisper, she walked to the edge of the porch and stared back along the empty road, her will trapped between her impulse to flee and her need to own the consequences of the way she'd run seven years ago.

She stepped across the scarred threshold and into the front room, a soft swath of sunlight falling across the heart of pine floors, dust particles swirling about her swollen ankles. The close room had retained its tight-fisted bearing and it was as she remembered. The maroon couch and side chair that had felt like sandspurs caught in a dog's fur against the backs of her youthful bare legs stood as they had, facing off against Red's radio/record player console, an identical twin to the one he'd given her mother. In Miss Mary's shrill madness, she had avowed that Ernest Tubb, Kitty Wells, and Hank Williams were merchants of evil, their honky-tonk lyrics of sex and hard living depraved messages from Hell. Red had turned up the volume and resettled, his forbidden shoe heels defiantly propped on the arm of the couch, mindless of the fresh doily.

Jodie tiptoed down the narrow hallway to the bedroom Red had shared with Miss Mary and pushed open the door. She peered into the near darkness, struck by the room's smallness. As a child she'd thought of it as huge and forbidden, filled with quarrelsome marital secrets.

The air hung stale, trapped in sweltering heat, and she covered her mouth against the sudden bitterness that swirled in her stomach, biting down hard on her determination. From the floor next to Red's bed, Buster got up on stiff joints, his large box-like head swaying on his thick neck. He came closer, sniffed her outstretched hand, and began licking her fingers. The pair had spent too many terrifying moments hiding for either to have forgotten the other. Red had called the breed mostly bulldog, and had justified the dog's presence as an obligation. She believed he'd done the same at her arrival.

Red lay still as death beneath a soiled sheet marked by overlapping circles of urine, a naked pillow drawn beneath his sweaty head. He was little more than a skeleton laboring to breathe, a mockery of his former self. The stroke's fury had split his face and slammed it back together in a bad realignment, his left eye rimmed in pus and the right lifeless, the color of congealed oatmeal. She worried it was he, and not the dog, who was blind.

"Red, it's me." Her words came out thin, as if her voice box suffered a leak.

He stirred.

His left eye fluttered behind a thin, bluish eyelid and he looked beyond her toward the hallway as though she was a stranger and he waited for something or someone who might explain her presence.

"It's Jodie, Red."

He struggled to rise onto his elbow, but sagged back onto the bed, a useless right arm curled at his side. He closed his eyes, and his raspy breathing and her hammering heart were the room's only sounds.

Damn Red Dozier. It had taken her seven years to build a new life in which he no longer counted. Now, it was the very putrid scent of him, his weak, pathetic, wasted body that trapped her.

She pushed back hard against what she feared would become her undoing, and although she could not say why exactly, she decided to do what she could to ease his going out. But what did one do for a dying man?

She remembered the clean, white shirts and pressed trousers he'd worn daily. She would clean him up, do what she could to return him to his pride.

She went into the kitchen and put on a kettle of water to heat. When she'd gathered a chipped enamel washbasin, a bar of Ivory soap, and a washrag and towel, she returned to the bedroom.

Over his silent protest, she gritted her teeth and set about removing his soiled clothing, and when she'd washed away the worst of his stench, she changed him into clean pajamas. Rolling him off the bottom sheet, she stripped and remade the bed with fresh sheets she located in a hall closet. When she was done, she bundled the soiled bedclothes and pajamas, leaving him to rest.

She stood at the kitchen sink, running cold tap water over her wrists until her newest wave of nausea lifted, but she needed fresh air. She poured herself a double shot of bourbon from Red's stash of Ancient Age she found in the cupboard. She smiled, remembering Red had told her that if she was going to drink, she should drink good whiskey. Claimed it would never hurt her, but he'd been mostly wrong about that.

She took a seat on the back stoop and peered into the gathering darkness. The air was sweet with the fragrance of the tea olive shrubs at the corners of the stoop and, except for the scurrying retreat of a critter from the direction of the fire drum, the evening was still.

She cursed Silas straight through two quick cigarettes and a second drink before accepting that nothing he could have said on the telephone would have prepared her for the way she found Red. Silas had said he believed Red was knocking on death's door, but she'd known him since childhood as one whose words were often half or twice as much, his particular circumstances striking the balance. Still, in fairness to Silas, it was she who had taken solace in the absurd notion that Red would never die before having the last word between them. She'd always meant to come back, try settling things, but in her own time. She feared that she'd waited too long.

The liquor she'd drunk on an empty stomach fueled a return of her nausea, and she remembered she'd had no food since the stale donuts she'd eaten at the Selma bus station while waiting for the outbound bus. Red had to be hungry as well, considering the plate of uneaten, fly-infested food she'd emptied.

A more thorough search of the kitchen cupboards turned up a sack of grits, two cans of pork 'n' beans, a quart jar of peaches, and a sack of bug-infested flour. If Red still kept hens, then eggs were her best bet for a meal. She located a weak-beam flashlight and made her way along the overgrown path to the chicken yard. She gathered four brown eggs from the nests, counting on them being fresh and not some hen's notion of a setting.

Grits and eggs weren't much of a meal, and when she offered them to Red, he motioned toward Buster and turned his face to the wall. He still had not spoken a word.

The dog followed her into the kitchen and she fed him Red's rejected supper. Silas had lied when he said the old dog was unwilling to take food from anyone other than Red, but he hadn't exaggerated Red's condition.

When she had washed, dried, and put away the few dishes, she returned to sit in the rocker at the foot of Red's bed, and although he made no attempt to speak, she thought of herself as keeping him company. Again she wondered whether his silence was caused by his anger or the stroke had robbed him of his ability to speak. She considered asking, but right now she was unwilling. Instead, she felt it best she rely on their shared memories.

"Red, you remember the time that wild boar lit into Buster?"

He reached a slow hand and traced the jagged scar that ran the width of the dog's broad chest, and she wondered if he remembered the event the way she did.

He'd dragged the bleeding dog home on a rig fashioned from his best winter coat and two green saplings, and she'd held the lamp while he stitched the open wound. He'd bedded the dog down next to the kitchen's wood heater. She'd stayed, keeping him company through the night, while he tended the fire.

Red closed his eyes, his breathing still raspy, but slowed, and she believed he slept. When she had straightened the bedcovers, she went to sit in the swing on the front porch, the dog following her.

The scent of the honeysuckle growing along the fence hung in the humid air and mosquitoes droned. Back of the house, down along the creek, frogs croaked and rat-faced bats darted back and forth across the yard. From a distance, the clear yodel of a lead hound rode the wind currents, and the dog rose and sniffed the air. He eased down the porch steps and disappeared into the heavy broom sage, and her thoughts returned to the night she and Red had tended the injured dog, and a part of the memory she'd long denied herself.

She'd awakened to discover that Red had pulled her close, and with her head pressed to his chest, she listened to the sound of his big heart, wishing she might will her own heart to beat in rhythm with his.

She felt tears building behind her eyelids, and for the first time since beginning her homeward journey, she understood she was here because of that moment. For now, it was enough that he'd come for her when news of her mama had reached him. She'd stay and care for him. She owed him that much.

# Eufaula Alabama – Summer 1948

## Two

Ten year-old Jodie ran in the direction of the roar of a diesel engine. Back over her shoulder, she saw Ginger moving toward the highway, but she knew Ginger would watch from a safe distance. She ran to the center of the narrow bridge, the metal grating bruising her bare feet. Thirty feet below, the shallow, sandy-bottom creek took no notice of her damnable foolishness, and in spite of her fear of heights, she climbed onto a cross rail. Balancing there, she gripped an upright and raised her fist in the air, signaling the driver of the approaching semi, and he blasted his air horn.

The tractor-trailer pressed so close she could see the driver's eyes popped wide with disbelief. The backdraft sucked at her body, threatening to snatch her from the rail. Her shirt snapped like a flag caught in a high wind, her teeth clattered, and her knee joints locked.

The roar of the huge engine and the pounding rotation of its eighteen wheels deafened her. The bridge shuddered under its power, and Jodie clung to the vibrating rail with all her might. But she didn't dare close her eyes. As the semi passed, she watched Ginger's small face, stricken with terror, mouth caught open in a silent scream.

Jodie climbed down from the railing, her legs wobbly, strangely gratified by Ginger's fear. She walked to where Ginger stood looking at her in a way that felt brand new. Jodie inhaled sharply, believing she meant to hug her. But she only touched her lightly on the forearm.

"Oh, Jodie, I could never do that. You're so ... so courageous." Ginger liked big words. Courageous felt even bigger coming out of her mouth.

"Ain't special. Just something I like doing." She flushed with pride at having shown Ginger Sutton that Jodie Taylor was braver than any boy on the row could ever be.

They turned toward home, careful to keep out of sight at the edge of the woods. Approaching the rutted clay road that fronted the row of weathered shotgun shanties, they skirted the stench of a bloated dog, green-headed blow flies working its corpse. Ahead, white heat waves jitterbugged across the sun-bleached landscape in the direction of the vast cotton fields, stretching as far as Jodie could imagine; its entirety conveyed an emptiness she could not yet name, but one that stayed with her, as real as her very skin.

Ginger turned to her and Jodie's heart quickened in the odd way it could at the nearness of her. Neither girl flinched, Ginger lingering a beat longer before turning and walking away.

Jodie held her breath, her stomach fluttering with what, exactly, she wasn't sure. Ginger slowed, turned, and looked back in her direction, but she didn't wave. Yet Jodie allowed herself to believe it was a true sign that she, too, had liked their closeness. She waited until Ginger had disappeared inside her house before stepping from the cover of the trees.

Jodie eased into the kitchen through the back door, mindful of the penalty for waking her mama before she was ready to emerge from the bedroom, expecting supper to be on the table. Her trip to the bridge with Ginger meant she'd need to take care not to give her mother any reason to get her nose out of joint.

She filled a kettle to warm the water Jewel would want and set yesterday's leftover coffee on to reheat. Her mother liked it strong and bitter. Anything less and she'd bitch that she could get plenty of piss-poor coffee on the road. Jodie brushed crumbs from the faded oilcloth and searched the cupboard, choosing stewed cabbage over boiled potatoes. She removed the cheesecloth from the dwindling slab of white meat and sliced four even pieces.

At the sound of a chair scraping across the worn linoleum, Jodie turned from the pan of frying meat. Her mama had come into the kitchen and collapsed onto a chair. She didn't speak but gave Jodie a groggy nod.

"Ready in a jiffy." She measured cheerful against hurried.

Jewel sighed and raked her long, slender fingers through her hair.

Jodie admired the way her mother's black hair hung long and straight nearly to her waist, and her olive skin was smooth as a drawn bed sheet. Red had said Jewel's eyes held womanly mysteries. Jodie hadn't known what he meant, but she liked the promising sound of her mama's name on his lips.

Jewel lit a cigarette and nodded toward her shiny red stilettos on the kitchen chair where she'd placed them on her return. "These babies may be just the ticket for lifting tits and ass, but they're hell on feet." She drew nicotine into her lungs, slowly exhaling. "Singing's natural as breathing, but standing all night ain't as easy as it once was."

"Yes ma'am, they're sure to. Uh … hurt your feet, I mean." Jodie had believed Red when he said her mama would stand knee-deep in pissed off rattlers as long as there remained one person sober enough to call out her name.

The shoes had cost a month's worth of tips from the truck stop café where she'd worked as a waitress for as long as Jodie could remember. She spoke of café work with the same loathing she reserved for coming up short on rent day. Claimed that her very pores had begun to ooze rancid hog lard and that no amount of bathing and cheap perfume could take the odor away. Said it was the way old women smelled before they died.

Jewel wore her nylon stockings rolled down around her ankles, and she gently pulled them off her feet as if they were soiled bandages. Jodie tested the temperature of the water in the kettle, and after cooling it down, she filled the chipped washbasin, adding two tablespoons of turpentine, meant to take away the soreness. She set the pan on the floor before her mama, who slipped her feet into the hot, oily water.

Jewel sighed. "Lord God, baby, that's good. These feet of mine are going to be the death of me."

Jodie turned back to the stove, thinking her mama talked a lot about dying, but it was more likely her fear of wearing out before realizing her dream of appearing onstage at the Grand Ole Opry.

Jewel reached for her pocketbook and poured a double fistful of coins onto the table, along with a few wadded bills. She held up a lone five.

"If I'd been of a mind to, I could've just as easily gone off with this one as not." She arched her back, her firm nipples pushing against the thin robe she wore.

Red had bought his way into Jewel's favor, but Jodie was careful to never mention him. It soured her mama's mood, sometimes causing her to take to her bed for days.

"Go on, girl, hand me the bank. This pitiful pile ain't going to grow no matter how much I handle it." She snorted a surly laugh.

Jodie retrieved the Luzianne coffee can from the icebox and set it on the table. Jewel pushed the coins, separated and stacked by denomination, over the edge of the table. The room filled with the sound of them dropping into the can.

"Bet your sweet ass Kitty's got men with nothing to do but count her take."

"Not fair. It's just that she gets to sing on the radio. Wait till people hear you. We'll need to buy a second icebox just to hold all the money."

"Icebox, be damned." Jewel smiled. "Someday I'll swish my fine ass into the biggest bank in Nashville and open an account. And pour so much money into that account we'll need to open a second." Jewel laughed, and Jodie did the same, although she worried that Jewel's laughter could sometimes trigger her blues.

She'd believed Red when he said Jewel's singing brightened her in the way color dye transformed an ordinary hen's egg, causing lesser women to move closer to their men. Jodie didn't know if it was still true since her mama had stopped doing gigs for Red months ago and hooked up with Troy, Jewel's so-called manager-songwriter, and his band of half-assed musicians. Still, she lifted her gaze to the water-stained ceiling and wished she trusted God or even Oral Roberts. Her mama could use a first-class miracle.

Jodie poured Jewel's coffee, taking only a half cup for herself, and doctored her own with PET milk and three heaping teaspoons of sugar.

"You sure as hell know how to ruin a good cup of coffee." Jewel smiled, though it wasn't one that reached her eyes. Still, Jodie liked her mama's teasing, even about the sissy way she drank her coffee.

"Way better than that jacked mess you drink."

Jewel snorted. "Gal, where'd you get that damn sassy mouth?"

"Some say I take after Jewel Taylor." Jodie grinned.

"Hear tell that one's a half-breed bitch in high heels. She's said to carry a twelve-inch prick-sticker strapped to her inner thigh."

"Yeah. And if you mess with her, she'll cut your throat and watch you bleed out."

"Lord God, girl." Jewel shook her head and smiled the one that lifted Jodie, making all the dark times bearable, and she hoped it would stay.

Jewel didn't offer to make her customary pitcher of tea, and it was just as well, since Jodie had forgotten to put the ice card in the screen door. The ice man wouldn't be back until Tuesday.

"Jesus, it's too damn hot to live." Jewel opened her robe, flapping the front halves like a fan. "Wish to hell I was straddling the North Pole."

At the sight of Jewel's full breasts, the circle around her nipples brown as tree ripened figs, Jodie felt her heat rising, and she turned away, confused and shamed by her desire to know how it would feel to touch breasts like her mama's. Could Jewel know her secret thoughts? Was this the reason she never included her in stories about leaving with strange men who left five-dollar tips?

"Unless you intend to burn down this sorry excuse for a house, you'll need to drag that rancid grease off the burner."

She pulled the smoking pan off the stove. Behind her, she heard the slapping sound Jewel's slippers made against her heels as she left the kitchen.

Jodie cringed.

There was no breathing easier at the familiar, bittersweet lament of Bessie Smith's *Down Hearted Blues*. It was certain to fan her mother's smoldering bad mood.

Jewel returned to the kitchen and sat with her back pushed up tight against the chair spindles. Jodie braced against her dread.

"What'd you do all day?"

"Me? Nothing." Jodie busied herself at the stove.

"Damn it, Jodie. Look at me when I'm talking to you."

Jodie concentrated on the dangling ash from Jewel's cigarette, avoiding the storm she knew was gathering in her mama's dark eyes. One slip from her and things were bound to go from bad to worse.

"That nothing didn't have to do with that little gal next door, now did it?" She flicked ashes onto the floor.

"Played ball." Jodie was careful to always hold ready an elaborate story, one she could detail without stammering. "Roscoe was short a decent fielder, so he sent Rabbit to get me." She had played earlier before going to the bridge, and a sin of omission was better than an outright lie. Her mama hated liars worse than axe murderers.

Jewel squinted against the heavy blue smoke, her head tilted in the way she had when she wasn't buying. It meant Jodie would need to keep talking until her mama heard something that satisfied her.

"I'm a better hitter than any boy on the row, except for Roscoe." He claimed to hate tomboys worse than Negroes, and to make his point, he'd sometimes send for Alvin instead. Then, it wouldn't do to mention Alvin.

Jodie wished she could tell the whole truth and that Jewel would understand why she'd become such a liar. But her gut told her she was to trust no one, not even her mama.

Jewel picked bits of loose tobacco from her teeth while Jodie prayed that whatever had fed her mother's bad mood would fade with the same mystery of its sudden onset. She lifted the dancing lid on the steaming pot, stuck a fork in the over-cooked cabbage, and turned off the burner.

"Lord God, Jodie, put a damn lid on that pot. Whole house smells like an overturned outhouse." Jewel waved a dishrag as if it could make a difference.

"Bring something home that don't smell like shit and I'll gladly cook it."

She'd crossed the line, and braced for Jewel's flashing anger, but she only glared, leaving Jodie to think her mama was either too tired or too fragile to put up a fight.

Jodie took plates from the dishpan of cold water, a greasy scum floating on top, and ran cold water over both. She placed white meat, cabbage, and the last slice of stale Wonder Bread onto a plate and set it before her mama.

"Not much to get up for." Jewel pushed the plate aside.

"But I thought you liked stewed cabbage better than boiled taters." Jodie hated the whine that had crept into her voice.

"Damn it, Jodie. I hate both, and if you cared you'd know." Jewel pushed up from the table and rushed out of the kitchen, slamming the bedroom door behind her.

Jodie added cane syrup to the cabbage to take away the bitterness, and when she'd eaten, she scraped Jewel's plate into a bucket for the three hens—Sadie, Sybil, and Shirley—Red had given her one Easter as fluffy biddies. She piled the dishes into the dishpan and filled it with hot water from the kettle.

The same Easter Red brought her the biddies, he'd hung a tire swing in the chinaberry tree next to the house. She remembered the sound of his big laughter each time she squealed for him to push her higher and higher. With him she'd felt as if her pointed toes could touch the sky. After he stopped coming, she could never send the swing as high as he had, no matter how hard she pumped her legs. She wanted to believe Jewel was wrong about Red never coming back. So much so that after six months, she still stopped whatever she was doing to watch slow-moving cars approaching the row.

After his last visit, she'd awakened not to the sound of his big laughter but to a heavy silence that hung over the house as though it had taken on a shape of its own. She first wondered if his visit had been a trick of her mind, so she searched the house for signs. Like all the times before, he'd brought her favorites: Rice Krispies, Del Monte ragged peaches, strawberry Jell-O mix, and animal crackers. She went outside and walked the tread marks left by the big Dodge. She didn't know whether they marked his coming or his going.

She'd known to look for Jewel sitting alone on the back porch steps. Smoke from the tip of the Chesterfield dangling from her lips rose to join the vapor steaming from the cup of coffee she cradled. Jewel's face, red from crying, held something much deeper than the sullen anger Jodie had come to expect with the departure of other men.

"You might as well know. He's not coming back."

"Why? I thought he liked us. You, I mean." She hadn't heard harsh words coming from the bedroom before she fell asleep, only their low voices. Now she thought their voices had been strained, but she wasn't sure.

"God, girl, it's never been about that." Her jaw was set against whatever it was and the hurt it caused.

She shrugged. "I don't care. He was never my daddy, was he?"

"Maybe he's got a whole other life, but Red Dozier's your daddy all right. Same as if he got mail delivered to that box there." She jerked her head in the direction of the road, and that was all she said.

Jodie felt better knowing her mama, at least, thought of Red that way. But her story didn't change "bastard." For that to happen, Red would need to come back and stay steady, like Ginger's daddy next door. He came home evenings, except for those times he was in trouble with the law, to sit on the porch, sipping whiskey. When he was in a good mood, he pitched for Roscoe to practice batting, and Jodie and his younger brothers ran down fly balls.

If she was man-smart like Jewel, she'd take her knife to the swing's rope, learn to forget Red Dozier. Then, Jodie believed him different from the other men Jewel brought home on the occasions of her highs—men who watched her with eyes she distrusted. The same men she'd learned to walk wide circles around, making herself into a ghost.

A timid moon slipped in and out of cloud cover, and Jodie eased to Jewel's door and tapped lightly, quietly calling, "Mama, it's time."

She listened for the slightest movement on the other side of the door, her only answer a heavier silence. She worried that Jewel had had what her boss called her final warning.

Again, she dared. "Mama, it's time to leave for work."

"Get the hell away from my door."

It was these times when Jodie wished Red had brought her a dog rather than pink biddies. She could pet a dog, talk to it, and never need to lie.

# Three

A light tap sounded on the kitchen door, and Ginger peered through the screen. The fading light cast a halo effect around her fair hair and pale, round face. Jodie wished she believed in angels, because Ginger would certainly fit the bill.

"Hey, you're not supposed to be here. You're gonna get us killed."

Ginger whispered, "You didn't tell her about yesterday? Our going to the bridge?"

"Hell no, I'm no fool."

"What, then?"

Jodie shrugged. "She's just in one of her snits. But I can't go as far as the creek and chase minnows. Besides, you've gotta know by now they won't live in fruit jars." Ginger wanted goldfish and a bowl she'd seen at the dime store in Eufaula, but since Red stopped coming, Jodie's pockets held nothing but red dirt.

"No, it's not that. Mama's visiting Aunt Trudy and she left me with a hamper of peas to shell. Won't you come help?"

Jodie couldn't be sure Jewel was sleeping. If she was drinking, her blues only worsened, and her snits could turn mean. Still, she followed Ginger across their adjacent yards and onto the Suttons' back porch.

The late summer purple hulls were dry and brittle, better suited for cows and hogs at this stage. Then, Ginger's family ate what they had when they had it, the same as she and Jewel.

"I wish we had the grape Kool-Aid you like. But there's leftover tea."

"Don't drink it after it gets syrupy." She liked that Ginger remembered her favorite, even if she had none to offer.

The worst of the day's heat had lifted, and a welcome quiet stretched up and down the row. They sat on the porch swing, each bent over a pan of unshelled peas. Neither spoke, but the easiness Jodie always felt with Ginger returned as they fell into the rhythm of shared work. The pile of hulls on the floor between their bare feet grew and their separate pans began to fill.

Ginger paused to point out the flittering fireflies, sprinkling what she liked to call magic dust across the back yard. She spoke hopefully about catching a few and putting them in a jar.

"If you ask me, there's no point in that." Catching critters and holding them in jars till they died was senseless, even mean.

"I only want to hold them closer. Make things brighter." Ginger's small voice carried a wistful tone. So much so that Jodie set aside what she knew of hope as a poor excuse for truth.

Rufus, the Suttons' three-legged coonhound, came from beneath the house, barked, and limped across the side yard toward the road. Jodie tensed. She glanced in the direction of Jewel's bedroom window and listened hard for sounds of her mama's disagreeable stirrings.

"It's nothing. That danged old hound will chase a shadow quicker than a cold biscuit."

"Where'd you say everybody was?"

"I didn't. But Roscoe's gone to Eufaula to take Daddy clean clothes. He ain't due back till after dark."

Normally, Ginger's daddy didn't stay locked up long enough to need clean clothes.

"What about Rabbit?" He didn't taunt her as much as Roscoe, but he was two-faced, bad to snoop and tattle.

"Him, too. There's just us." Ginger smiled shyly.

Ginger's smile was soft like a kitten's paw, and Jodie leaned into its warmth. She knew Ginger wasn't that crazy about shelling peas, which likely meant she'd bribed her mama in order to stay behind. The notion of Ginger bargaining time to be with her made Jodie giddy. She stared into the pan of peas, hundreds of eyes staring back at her, and although she saw Jewel's threat in each, she relished the good she felt more than she feared Jewel's wrath.

"Jodie, why don't you have a daddy?" Ginger didn't look at her.

"Don't you think that's a question better put to my mama?"

"But are you … a true bastard?"

"What if I am?"

Ginger's tone was nothing like the high-pitched chants of "whore brat" and "bastard" Jodie had settled on as hateful, but words that connected her to Red on those occasions when he came and stayed for a time. But "bastard" out of Ginger's mouth felt worse than a thousand wasp stings.

"Please, Jodie, don't get mad. But is that why mama says I'm to play with nice girls?"

"I don't know. Why should I? She's your damn crazy mama."

The back door hinges squealed like a doomed hog, and Mrs. Sutton burst onto the porch. She stood, bug-eyed, rage distorting her features, and she screamed, "Filthy bastard, I'll teach you to sneak around on my back porch," in a voice Jewel was bound to hear. She slapped Jodie, her rough handprint burning into her cheek like a branding iron.

Jodie jumped to her feet. The shelled peas spilled across the floor as if they were running for their lives. Ginger screamed but Jodie was too shocked to cry out. She leaped off the porch and ran past Roscoe and Rabbit as they rounded the corner, demanding to know what had happened. Mrs. Sutton hurried after Jodie, her furious name-calling echoing up and down the row.

Jodie stumbled onto her and Jewel's front porch, her chest pumping like a smithy's bellow at the sight of Jewel staggering bleary-eyed through the door.

"What the hell's all this racket about?"

Jodie opened her mouth to speak but her throat seized.

"I'll tell you what it's about. I caught that … gal of yours on my porch. And I want to know what you mean to do about her."

"Jewel, please. It wasn't like that."

"Shut your mouth, Jodie. I'll get to you."

Jewel looked straight through her as if she were a stranger before turning her full fury on Mrs. Sutton.

"It's not her you need to worry about, but that wormy, peckerwood husband of yours I keep having to chase away from my back door." Jewel's voice was deadly calm. Her hands rode her hips, her bare feet firmly planted, and her strong legs spread. "You need to take your tight ass out of here before I come off this porch and do harm we'll both regret."

Whatever Mrs. Sutton imagined in Jewel's threat had her gathering her boys and hustling back across the invisible property line that Jodie believed was certain to become an impregnable wall.

Jewel turned to Jodie, her face pained, as though she'd suddenly bitten into something too bitter to swallow. "Lord, baby girl, it's starting to look like you're going to need to take up far less space in this world. Double up on them clever lies you're so good at. That's if you figure on staying alive."

Jewel's shoulders slumped as though her strength seeped like rosin from a freshly scarred pine; she turned and staggered back through the door without another word.

Jodie continued to sit, long after the sounds of Mrs. Sutton's fury and Ginger's pitiful pleading had ended. Up and down the row, a sense of normal returned: windows framed in soft light, and cicadas, crickets, and frogs serenaded. Yet Jodie knew that here on the row, and maybe even beyond, Jewel's warning had set her apart in some peculiar way. A deep sense of aloneness washed over her, and she wrapped her arms tightly about herself. Unable to abate her tears, she sobbed.

# Four

The screen door slammed, and Jewel came onto the porch wearing her red backless sundress. The smoothness of her bronze skin caused good men to stare in a way that made Jodie proud, while she'd learned to hate the looks from men whose eyes burned with lust. Townswomen like Mrs. Sutton shunned Jewel and swapped slanderous stories behind her back. If Jewel was bothered, she hid whatever she felt behind her best kiss-my-ass smile.

Jewel came to the edge of the porch and called to Jodie.

"Get down out of that swing before you kill your fool self. Ought to cut the damn thing down." She shaded her eyes against the sun's glare. "Fixing to go to the store. Get something decent to cook. I'm thinking pork chops." She paused. "Come along if you want."

Troy came onto the porch, puffed like a strutting rooster, and said to Jewel, "Come on if you're coming. I don't have all day."

Jodie hated that Jewel was willing to spend money they didn't have just to please Troy. After sleeping until noon, Troy would stretch out his long legs beneath their kitchen table, bragging that he could open doors. The more he talked, the more Jodie felt her doors to her mama closing. Jewel's dream of the Grand Ole Opry was bigger than any truth.

"Well, get on in here. Wash that nasty face. And for God's sake, take a hard brush to that bushy head." Jewel hadn't said as much, but Jodie knew her mother sometimes hated her dark curls. In better times she'd spoken of her curls as a gift from Red, and had washed and brushed it out for her. Jodie now believed Jewel's ambiguity was like what she felt for the swing.

"God, baby, we don't have time to wait on her."

Jodie watched her mama like a junkyard dog. Lately, her moods were more fleeting than ever.

"Girl, if you're coming you'll need to shag ass."

Jodie ran past a pissed Troy and whispered, "You ain't the boss of me."

Troy now parked his bus full-time in the overgrown field behind the house. Jewel had never once bothered to ask her about him taking her place in the big bed. The makeshift cot in the kitchen was hers full-time. She slept among the odors of onions, potatoes, whiskey, and sweaty men who sprawled about the front room on made-down pallets, their drunken snoring every bit as pretty as their playing.

Jewel's words scattered like a flock of jabbering blackbirds, and Jodie caught only the part about their leaving. Based on nothing more certain than a month of Troy's boasting, Jewel quit her job and sold her prized phonograph, removing the last vestige of Red Dozier from their lives. She sold the double bed, their kitchen table and chairs, and the rusted ice box for fifteen dollars to a new couple who had nothing but their love, the stringy-headed, pregnant girl had exclaimed. Jewel tossed the balance of their meager belongings, including her scratched Bessie Smith records, into an old trunk Troy lashed onto the back of the made-over school bus.

The morning Troy picked to pull out left Jodie barely enough time to risk a stolen good-bye with Ginger. She crouched in the tall weeds at the edge of the Suttons' cluttered back yard, waiting until Hattie Sutton had taken a bucket in hand and gone into her garden before knocking on the back door.

"Oh, Jodie, aren't you afraid?" Ginger looked in the direction of the garden. "What's all the commotion at your house? Who's that skinny man with whiskers?"

.

"Never mind about him. Jewel's moving us. We're leaving right now." Jodie's words came thick to her throat and she swallowed hard.

Ginger's small hand flew to her mouth and she stammered, "Oh no, Jodie. That's not fair."

"No, it's not. But I can't fix unfair, now can I?"

Jodie ignored the blaring horn and handed Ginger the two crinkled dollar bills she'd stolen from Jewel's coffee can.

"This dollar's for them goldfishes and that bowl you want. The other's for chicken feed." She'd said an earlier good-bye to Sadie, Sally, and Shirley. A dollar wouldn't buy much feed, but Jodie knew those three old gals were destined to find themselves floating in a sea of dumplings before the bus reached the hard road.

She dared not say more, or even look at Ginger's tear-stained face. Instead she studied the intricate pattern of a cobweb hanging overhead, glittering more brightly in the early morning sunlight than any jar of fireflies might.

Jewel came as far as the property line, threatening to leave without her.

"I gotta go." Jodie turned away from Ginger, walked off the porch, and got into the bus.

Through a cloud of swirling dust, Jodie looked back in the direction of the tire swing that hung limp from its rope like some dead thing. Ahead of her was the unknown, and in the absence of anything more, she'd need to trust Jewel's dream.

Five

After six months on the road, traveling through south Alabama, Georgia, and north Florida, the band was still playing music's bottom rungs: small juke joints and local county fairs. The crowds were small and Jewel's take, after Troy's tally of shared road expenses and his fees, wasn't enough for three square meals a day for the two of them between gigs. Yet Troy never tired of boasting about doors only he could open.

Whenever the bus passed a school yard filled with kids, Jodie worried that she'd grow up dumb. Maybe she couldn't list the major agricultural products of Brazil, the way she imagined other fifth-graders doing, but she could follow the band's routes on a road map. She read new comics on those stops when a store clerk looked the other way. When there were no new comics, she read the white on red Burma-Shave signs, making up her own slogans. Randy, the band's bass player, bragged that her slogans were good enough to pass as song lyrics. She knew better than to share her made-up stories where she was Wonder Woman fighting crime with her best girlfriend, Glory Gal. Her stories were about a place where big, strong women fought against evil and were loved for their heroics. When she wasn't staring out the window, reading, or making up stories, she slept. It helped to avoid the escalating fighting between Jewel and Troy over the songs Jewel was to sing.

Jodie sat up, startled, her legs cramped. The bus had no heat and she was cold, even beneath the ragged quilt. The band had left Nashville, Georgia, late last night. It was the closest they'd come to Ryman Auditorium and the grand stage of country music.

She hated waking hungry. Her last meal had been a soda and animal crackers. She couldn't remember the last time she'd felt really full.

She watched Randy pump gas and pour three quarts of oil into the engine block. He'd warned Troy plenty of times that the engine needed an oil change, but the boys barely scraped up enough money among them to fill the gas tank. Troy declared that they weren't to bitch. Good money awaited them down the road in Crestwood, Florida.

"Here, kid." Randy slipped Jodie a Baby Ruth from his jacket pocket and shivered, drawing his skinny neck into his dungaree jacket. "The bastard who said come on down to the Sunshine State where it's summer year-round is a liar."

"If you ask me, Florida's built on lies." She took the candy bar, thanked him, and crawled beneath her tarp. She'd swiped the smelly, half-rotten tarp from behind a filling station, and Randy had helped her anchor it over two rows of seats to carve out her own space.

She didn't believe the showy billboards that promised her in Florida she'd see Ross Allen milk rattlesnakes and alligator farms where gators ate roadkill right out of your hand. If that wasn't enough, there were warring Indians taking white scalps, and beautiful mermaids who blew kisses underwater. But these exotic places were always miles ahead in a part of the state that, as far as she knew, didn't exist.

She bit into the Baby Ruth, not caring it was stolen. She and Randy were a better team than Randy alone. While storekeepers watched her, believing only kids stole candy, he filled his pockets with candy and gum they shared.

On Christmas Eve the bus rolled on toward Crestwood, Florida. Jodie huddled beneath the tarp, her hands over her ears. But neither that nor the roar of the bus engine could drown out Jewel and Troy's fighting. He claimed Jewel had screwed up the words to his newest song, and maybe she had. Not even Jewel's voice could make music out of what he wrote. Just now he accused her of screwing up the play list, while the band boys were just as likely to mess up as Jewel. The presence of whiskey before, between sets, and after the shows was as common as missing meals.

Back on the row, Jewel's moodiness had come and gone, but what she'd once laughed off, calling cases of the mulligrubs, arrived more frequently and stayed longer. The white powders Troy now gave her for headaches did little more than get her out of bed and onto the stage. She'd grown thinner and worried less and less about how she looked.

Jodie didn't have a name for what she feared was happening to Jewel. She heard it in the sound of Jewel's voice, drifting from the stage with a sadness that didn't match the up-tempo songs Troy insisted she sing. Of late, not even the band boys' incessant clamor that a big-shot record producer was in the joint, a contract awaiting their signature, could lift her spirits.

When they reached Crestwood, a nervous fat man in a fringed Buffalo Bill jacket met them, complaining about their running three hours late, and pointed them to a back entrance. The boys griped that there was nothing to eat before starting to haul band equipment.

Because Troy never tired of yelling that she was to stay the hell out of their way, Jodie gained the freedom to walk wherever she pleased with only her tangled thoughts as company. But tonight she had a bad feeling about Jewel and stayed in the bus. She sat behind the steering wheel and watched as the grassy parking lot filled with junk cars and old pickups. One man came riding a farm tractor.

The band's late arrival meant less time for Jewel before her appearance on stage. It was normal for her, the star of the show, to stay behind the curtained-off section of the bus she shared with Troy until show time. She had only to get herself sober and pretty.

Jodie wasn't surprised to see Randy loping toward the bus, his big hands jammed deep into his pockets. He claimed the cold made his fingers stiff, affecting his playing. Truth was, hot or cold, Randy played as though his fingers were sausages.

Randy stood in the door of the bus and nodded toward the curtain. There had been no sound from Jewel's side of the curtain for some time, and Jodie prayed hard before peering in.

Jewel sat slumped, near-naked, an empty glass in her hand. Jodie shut her eyes against what she saw and snapped the curtain closed.

"Damn, we've gotta get her on her feet. If she can stand then by God she can sing." Randy leaped up the steps. "She drunk or doped? Mixing that shit's gonna kill her someday."

"Just drunk." There had been no money for the white powder. Jodie bit her bottom lip until she felt a bigger pain.

"Jesus, kid, don't go pussy on me. Not now. You've got to get her drunk ass up. Make her presentable. Them people paid money to hear her. She don't sing, we don't eat."

"It ain't that. Got something in my eye, that's all."

"Yeah, I know. You've got a fucking right. Her, your mama and all. I'll tell Troy she's on her way. The boys and me will stall. But you've got to hurry." He jumped from the bus and ran toward the sound of the band.

"Jewel, it's me."

"Jodie, baby? Go find your mama another bottle." Jewel turned the empty upside down and shook it. She tried sitting upright, but failed, slumping back onto the makeshift bed.

"You'll want to know tonight's crowd is bigger. Everybody's waiting to hear you sing. And the band sounds … good. Can you hear them?"

"Screw 'em. And screw you if you don't get me that damn bottle."

"Out cold," Jodie said to Randy when he returned. It was better that way. She sure didn't need Troy's rant.

Jodie could hear the fat man onstage, pleading that Jewel was too sick to perform and assuring the angry crowd that their ticket stubs were good for the next show. But there was no second chance for the band. They broke down equipment, loaded the bus, and left town. Their first stop the following morning was a pawn shop where Troy hocked a piece of sound equipment. Money enough for a couple of meals and gas to make the next gig.

Jodie felt a new ending coming, and she worried what it would mean for her and the woman she called Jewel, although she didn't think of her mama that way.

# Dothan Alabama – 1950

## Six

On a spring morning, ripe with the scent of gardenias, Jodie stood next to Aunt Pearl, her mother's only sister, whom she'd met for the first time last evening. She struggled to make sense of Jewel's rant about her biggest stage yet.

"Playing Jacksonville's everything." Jewel worked her painted nails up and down the tiny pleats of her lemon yellow skirt. Her red-veined eyes remained dry, as though tears had no part in what she said. Maybe the real divide between Jewel admitting the truth and blindly clinging to wishful thinking was the fine line of headache powders Troy had continued to supply when her will failed and she needed a little something to help her move from behind the curtain and onto the stage.

"Okay, but why can't I go?"

"You know the road's no decent place for a kid. Here, with Pearl, you'll have a normal life. Get back in school. Maybe even start church."

"I hate school. And I'm not normal. You said so yourself." She hated Troy. Blamed him for Jewel's choice to leave her behind. "Please, Mama, I promise I'll be nice. He won't even know I'm around."

Jewel grabbed Jodie's shoulders and squeezed. "Good God, Jodie, I thought you were smarter than that."

Jodie's silent anger made her dizzy, and she ground her words through her teeth, "I hate him. I want him dead."

"Jodie, Jodie, he's nothing. I've never cared about him." Jewel glanced in the direction of the idling bus. "Picture me swishing my fine ass onto that stage." Jewel's hand now gently cupped the back of Jodie's neck. "Me singing my way straight into a miracle." She smiled briefly in the way she might at the fading of a pleasant image.

"Yes'um, I know, but who's going to take care of you?"

Jodie clung to Jewel with the same might she'd used when she held to the bridge railing. Biting into the flesh of her forearm wrapped around Jewel's neck, she accepted that her mama had always lived inside her dream, and that the woman she'd loved was already gone.

Troy sounded the bus horn and Jewel pulled free of Jodie's grasp, stepped back, and although her eyes were full of uncertainty, she turned on a quick heel and walked off the porch, her resolve set in the tightness of her thin shoulders.

Standing next to the stranger she was to come to know as Aunt Pearl, Jodie watched as the bus bounced over a slight rise and disappeared in front of a whirling cloud of dust.

Later, her aunt asked how she got such a nasty bruise, a purple-blue oval against her buttermilk skin, and she'd answered, "It's a little something to remember Mama by."


At first the postcards came once a month, the hurriedly scribbled message always the same: *Miss you. See you soon.* Still, Jodie looked forward to the next, and continued to go daily to the mailbox until even a fool would have known better.


After her Saturday morning chores, Jodie made two grape jelly sandwiches and filled a fruit jar with sweet tea. She climbed the giant oak that had become her best friend and hid among its massive branches. Slouched against the tree's rough, dimpled trunk, she pitched bread crusts in an attempt to bait a male cardinal to come closer. She admired the way he flitted about, flirting with his mate, and she attempted to imitate his calls, if not his haughtiness. But the bird only laughed and did what she couldn't do; tired of his stay and flew away.

An approaching car caught her eye, and she stared toward the street. A sheriff's cruiser slowed; the officer stared at the mailbox lettering and drove the cruiser into the yard. A slight man stepped from the cruiser, settled a big-brimmed Stetson atop his head, and studied his image in the side mirror. Jewel would have mocked him as looking like a piss-ant under a collard leaf. The officer squinted into the bright sunlight, and Jodie wondered just what evil he expected to find lurking in the yard. He carried a package clamped beneath his arm.

He walked onto the front stoop directly below Jodie's perch and knocked on the door. He removed his hat and stood, twirling the Stetson like a windmill caught in a storm, until Aunt Pearl opened the door.

"Morning, ma'am. I'm Officer Howard Shuler from Montgomery County." He cleared his throat. "And, ma'am, if you're Pearl Taylor, you're the very person I was sent to find."

Although his tone made it sound as though Aunt Pearl had won some kind of prize, dread had begun to drain the sap from Jodie's legs. She leaned as far as she dared to learn his reason for coming. She worried that whatever brought him to Aunt Pearl's door couldn't be good. Jewel had warned that the law never came bearing good news to folks like them. But Jodie thought her aunt was different.

Aunt Pearl's pale face contorted with alarm, and she answered, "Yes, officer, I'm Pearl Taylor."

"Ma'am, do you … what I mean is, did you have a sister named Jewel Taylor?"

Aunt Pearl clutched her hand to her throat and spoke so softly Jodie couldn't hear. What had the deputy come to say about Jewel? Her grip slipped and she felt she'd fall before she caught herself up.

"In that case, ma'am, I'm sorry, but I bring you bad news." He cleared his throat a second time. "There was a terrible wreck, first of the month, on the Birmingham highway. A semi loaded with hogs was struck by a made-over school bus. A bunch of them hogs died. But that's not really the worst part." The officer put a hand to the back of his neck and rubbed as if he might spare himself whatever else he'd come to say.

Aunt Pearl uttered a mournful sound, followed by words Jodie couldn't make out. She gulped air and clung fiercely to the tree. The officer was wrong. He'd made a big mistake. Taylor was a common name. He had the wrong Jewel Taylor.

"Oh, no ma'am. For some reason, your sister was riding with a load of band types." He paused as if making space for Jewel's deliverance. "The men were drunk as river cooters. Likely never knew what hit them." A faint smile played at the corners of his mouth and he lifted a quick hand, rubbing it away.

He may have intended sparing her aunt the birds of a feather, but it was too late. Still, Jodie believed he was wrong. Drunk or sober, Randy was a good driver. He'd never killed as much as a raccoon or even an armadillo. Maybe he wasn't much of a picker, stole stuff, and drank too much, but when Jewel came back for her, she'd need Randy as her friend. If Aunt Pearl's God would only make the policeman a liar, she'd promise to give up stealing, even against road hunger.

Aunt Pearl stumbled back against the door frame, and the officer reached to steady her, speaking quietly. "We found a note in your sister's purse, naming you her next of kin. Took some time to track you down. Ma'am, the chief sent me to find out what you want done." He studied the porch boards between his worn boots.

"Oh, no ma'am. You're not gonna want to see her."

The door opened wider and the officer disappeared inside. Jodie's eyes burned like fire ant bites as she scampered down the rope ladder. Her feet touching shaky ground, she ran, a guiding hand scraping the length of the neatly trimmed holly hedge. She entered the house through the kitchen door and collapsed onto the floor, out of sight of her aunt and the officer. She peered around the door frame and saw the officer handing her aunt a sheet of paper.

"In that case, ma'am, I'll need you to sign here on this line."

Aunt Pearl signed the paper and the officer folded it into neat quarters, placed it in his shirt pocket, buttoned the flap, and patted his pocket.

"I'm truly sorry, ma'am. Untimely, the way it was. There must've been a time when your sister was real pretty. It's a shame when the pretty ones die young."

"Oh my, yes, Jewel was the pretty one. Always had the boys she wanted." She giggled in a strange way that didn't seem right somehow, but her tone held no malice.

They rose from their chairs. The sound of her rustling skirt, the cracking of her arthritic knees joints, and her slow footsteps as she ushered the officer to the door roared in Jodie's ears like the sound of the diesel engines she once invited. She leaned back against the wall and clutched her stomach.

Aunt Pearl came into the kitchen where Jodie had continued to hide. She put on a pot of coffee and took a seat at the kitchen table, her wet face cradled in her palms.

Jodie stood.

"Oh God, Jodie, you heard?" Her face was drawn, white as a bleached bed sheet, and her eyes stretched in something akin to panic.

"It's not true, you know. Law's not the final word."

"Your mama was such a sweet child. But from the time she was your age, she sought the hard-eyed boys who only knew how to live on the edge of destruction."

Jodie needed no reminder of the kind of men Jewel had brought home, but she didn't believe her mama had been fated to die among a truckload of hogs.

"When're we going to get her? Bring her here?"

"Jodie, your mama's gone."

"You don't know that. I want to see the woman he claimed is Jewel. He never one time mentioned me. She'd have put my name next to yours." Her voice had weakened with each denial, her last squeezed from her heart.

"No, child, it's too late. I signed over her remains to the county. I don't have the money for a cemetery plot." She handed Jodie the brown package the officer had delivered and turned away, her thin body racked by spasms.

Jodie stared at the package, traced its edges with her wet fingertip, and dared to tear away the blood-smeared wrapper. It held Jewel's Bessie Smith record, broken into two perfectly matched halves. Jodie sat, cradling the broken remains to her heaving chest. She'd known all along her mama wouldn't last without her to care for her. Still Jewel would have laughed at the irony in dying on the road, and in death she would have despised charity. Jodie wanted to blame her aunt for Jewel's final shame, but she knew better. She knelt next to her.

Her aunt embraced her for the first time since she arrived and whispered, "God knows I tried, but I couldn't save your mama." She released Jodie and said, "I can't promise that you'll end better."

Her voice had grown resolute, and Jodie understood that whatever she believed Jewel needed saving from, Aunt Pearl attributed the same to her.

Long after her aunt had gone to bed, Jodie sat alone in the kitchen listening to late-night radio. She wanted to hear her mama's voice. Have her say that she had a good girl back in Dothan, and that her next song went out to her. For the first time ever, Jodie prayed hard, although she didn't believe God answered prayers for those like her and Jewel. If the officer was right and her mama was dead, it was up to her to mark her passing.


Jodie rose in pre-dawn darkness, dressed in clean jeans and shirt, and brushed the night tangles from her hair. She slipped out the front door and stooped at the edge of the woods to pick a handful of wildflowers.

The faintest light of day appeared as a jagged scar, and Jodie imagined the row's narrow clay road, snowy-white cotton blooms sparkling like fireflies of an evening. In that moment, like all the times before, her mama stepped from the bus and smiled at her. *Hey, sugar, Mama's home.*

Jodie released the wildflower petals, and Jewel Taylor's sarcastic laughter rose to gather them. She was at last to sing the blues.

## Seven

Aunt Pearl's months of diligent letter writing to north Florida county sheriffs, inquiring as to the whereabouts of Red Dozier, finally paid off in the form of a phone call. Over supper, she offered, "Mr. Dozier has agreed to come for a visit. And he sounded real nice on the phone."

Jodie shrugged.

Aunt Pearl fidgeted with her spoon, her brow gathered. "Soon, I believe. Though he didn't say exactly."

Red had his certain charm with women, but if her aunt had bothered to ask, she could have told her he was plenty good at showing up, but even better at disappearing. It was all right with her if Aunt Pearl meant to squeeze money out of Red. She fretted often enough that her weekly pay of thirteen dollars as a telephone operator wasn't enough to cover their expenses.

Three months later, Aunt Pearl returned from the mailbox, a one-page letter clutched in her hand. She stopped beneath the oak and called up to Jodie.

"Letter says he'll be here Saturday." When Jodie didn't answer, her aunt continued on into the house, pulling the door closed between them.

Living with Aunt Pearl was as boring as Lawrence Welk's accordion solos, but she'd grown to welcome its predictability. For that reason, Jodie had gritted her teeth against boredom, done her chores without bitching, and kept her mouth shut. She gave up baseball for basketball, a game she could play alone, shooting baskets at a clay court whenever she could avoid the older boys.

However, she'd continued to steal comics, and had become even bolder, stuffing pulp detective novels into the waist of her jeans whenever the half-blind storekeeper was distracted. Aunt Pearl couldn't know Jodie projected herself into the fictional heroics, imagining the pleasure of winning the favors of beautiful girls. About the same time she began touching herself in ways that caused her breath to come rapidly and her body to convulse in strange pleasure. These feelings, while thrilling, left her confused, even ashamed in those moments when her aunt insisted she must grow up differently. She took differently to mean she wasn't to take up what Aunt Pearl hinted were Jewel's "whorish habits." Yet nothing she said was enough to cause her to stop what she was doing.

Aunt Pearl got up from the supper table, scraped her untouched food into the bucket for her neighbor's backyard chickens, and turned back to Jodie.

"My goodness, child. Aren't you one bit happy? Don't you want to see your daddy?"

"He's never claimed as much. And just because Jewel accused him doesn't make him guilty. He wasn't the only big, curly haired man she … she screwed."

"Sweet Jesus, Jodie Taylor. Hush your shameful mouth." Her voice dropped to a whisper as if she feared eavesdroppers. "You must not vilify your poor dead mama that way."

"That's not what I did." She'd never run Jewel down, but the truth about Red was anybody's guess. How many times had her mama laughed and teased, "Tom, Dick, or Harry," to efforts at pinning her down. She'd gone along with her mama, though not knowing felt nothing like a joke. It was only after Red stopped coming that Jewel had branded him guilty. Then, it was clear Aunt Pearl wasn't interested in knowing the truth.

"Lord, child, your mama bragged that you're his spitting image. All that fuzzy hair, and those big hands and feet. She claimed nobody with eyes to see would think otherwise."

"Does that include his wife, you think?" Jodie leaped to her feet, the chair slamming hard onto the floor, and Aunt Pearl screamed for her to sit back down.

Jodie stood on the opposite side of the bedroom door, inches from the sound of Aunt Pearl's pleading, "I swear it's only a visit. I don't mean for you to be hurt."

Jodie kept still. How was putting her off on a man who refused to admit to being her father not supposed to hurt?

The day Red was to show, Jodie climbed the oak and sat silently while Aunt Pearl called up to her, insisting she come inside and get ready for his visit.

Jodie Taylor had no intention of prettying herself for the likes of Red Dozier. Hadn't it taken him three months to show up? It was clear he had no burning desire to take her off Aunt Pearl's hands.

It was afternoon before the big Dodge pulled into the yard. Red stood next to the car, raked a slow hand through his curly red hair, and settled his hat back onto his head. Jodie compared the curl of his hair to her own and stuffed her shaggy bangs beneath her baseball cap, pulling the bill lower.

Red stepped onto the path and approached like a man marching to the hangman's scaffold. He knocked, removed his hat, and squared his wide shoulders.

Aunt Pearl opened the door, and he leaned toward her, an ass-kissing smile warming his way.

"Afternoon, ma'am. You must be Miss Pearl. I'm Red Dozier. It's a pleasure."

Then—damned if he didn't have the smoothness of a Bible salesman—he even made a show of scraping his big shoes clean before entering the house. Jodie slid down the tree rope and hurried to the kitchen door. Inside, she crouched near the cupboard, out of sight and where she had a clear view of the parlor.

Red sat upright and attentive. Aunt Pearl perched on the edge of the sofa across from him, her back ramrod straight. She poured tea from her best pitcher and he nodded politely, taking the sweating glass into his big hand. She poured a second glass for herself, and when she'd touched it to her lips, he drank deeply, declaring the tea to be the best he'd ever drunk.

Jodie placed a hand over her mouth, smothering a snicker as her aunt tried to excuse her absence. He nodded, but anyone who knew her knew she wasn't attending Saturday afternoon Bible drills. Aunt Pearl tearfully recounted the details of the deputy sheriff's visit, omitting the fact that Jewel had died in the company of drunken men she'd earlier condemned as wild and horny. Surely she didn't think Red was fooled. He only needed to look in the mirror.

"I pray God's forgiveness that my poor sister was buried at county expense." She shed a few more tears.

Red's shoulders rounded. "I'm truly sorry. If I'd known …." His last words trailed off, and Jodie wanted to know if he was lying about sparing Jewel the indignity.

"She left nothing behind, except for that poor child. She's twelve now. Advanced for her age, and I might add quite cunning. Even a bit peculiar, I fear."

Red's head tilted slightly, and Jodie wondered if he'd heard something in peculiar. Was it the warning Jewel had meant? Had Aunt Pearl known all along what she did when she was alone? Did that mean Red now knew? She drew her legs in tighter, folding her body into itself, an attempt at making herself smaller.

Aunt Pearl laughed nervously. "How silly of me. Of course you'd know the child's age." She glanced down at her hands folded in her lap.

Red shifted and his Adam's apple danced in his throat.

"Please tell your fine Christian wife I tried putting her in Sunday school. But she kicked up such a fuss. I'm sorry to say, I gave up."

"Ma'am, I do appreciate the fine job you're doing. But about me taking her off your hands ...." He paused, and the air went out of Aunt Pearl in a deep sigh. "I'll need to talk more with my wife. Maybe come again before the next school term."

Jodie bristled at his bald-faced lie. Since when did he talk with his wife where she or Jewel were concerned?

"Mr. Dozier, please understand that I never meant for her stay to be anything but temporary. If she's to ever make a proper young lady, she'll need a firmer hand than mine."

"Yes'm, I understand. But, there's the balance of the school term to consider." He tapped his hat against his knee and glanced toward the door. He'd had his say, but her aunt wasn't ready to give up.

"Sir, that's not exactly the problem it might have once been." She bit her tongue. "But, yes, you're right. School's end would be a better plan."

Jodie exhaled, relieved that her current school suspension hadn't become part of their bargaining. Red didn't need to know she'd pulled her knife on Tommy Lee. If she had it to do over, she'd do the same. No boy was ever again going to pin her and feel her up.

"Ma'am, if you're strapped for money, I'll gladly pay." Red stood and handed Aunt Pearl a crisp bill from his wallet. "And I'd appreciate you passing along these funny books." He smiled sheepishly. "Her favorites, I believe."

"I'm sorry, Mr. Dozier. I must ask that you not leave those." She stared at his big hands as he rolled the comics into a tight tube.

Too bad he'd wasted his money. Aunt Pearl had set down the rule of no comics as punishment for what happened with Tommy Lee.

Concealed behind the hedge at the corner of the house, Jodie watched as Red crossed the yard, the rolled comics clutched in his hand. Reaching the car, he turned and squinted back in the direction of the house. He bent and placed the comics on the ground, got into the Dodge, and drove away.

Why had he bothered if he was just going to drive away like all the times before? She got a sinking feeling that after hearing *peculiar*, he was gone forever. Then it suited her fine that he'd come only to hear about Jewel. Let him stop by the cemetery, put flowers on her grave. Not that it could make a tinker's damn to her now.

She walked to where he'd stood, picked up the comics, and glanced back to see if her aunt was watching from the front window. She'd take his damn funny books, trade with one of the kids on the block. That way, it didn't have to mean she'd ever expected anything from Red Dozier.

The last day of the school term came with no word from Red, and it pleased Jodie that Aunt Pearl had stopped repeating the certainty of his return. In her book, he was no more dependable than her mother had been, although Jewel had the better excuse. Rather, she believed her best bet lay with the envelopes that arrived monthly. Jodie had to hand it to her timid aunt; she was a damn sight better at squeezing money from Red than Jewel had been. She had begun to relax, believing Aunt Pearl had come to view her staying as profitable, if not ideal.

Jodie's end of the year report card sat propped against the salt and pepper shakers in the center of the kitchen table, along with a vase of mixed flowers from the yard. The aroma of chicken, deep frying in the big Dutch oven, wafted through the house, and supper promised to be as close to a celebration as Aunt Pearl permitted.

Jodie scrubbed her face and hands and stared at her image in the cloudy mirror. She had none of her mother's good looks, and any similarities ended with their tar black hair, hers impossible to drag a comb through. Aunt Pearl had said she had her mama's way of looking on others with suspicion. She straightened her rumpled shirt and shrugged, her reflection frowning back at her. She'd at least go to the table dirt-free the way Aunt Pearl expected.

"Oh, there you are. And don't you look … clean. Chicken's ready to take up. Go ahead and sit down."

"Sure smells good. I believe I could eat a whole fryer."

"I'd give anything if your poor sweet mama could know how well you've done during your time here." The grave had served to soften Aunt Pearl's recollections of Jewel. Her mama was never sweet, and she wouldn't want to be remembered that way.

"Sit, child, and eat. It's your special night." Her tone had the ring of a once in a lifetime happening, even though her aunt had begun to harp on the perils of her getting fat, warning that boys didn't like fat girls. As far as Jodie was concerned, big wasn't the same as fat, and big was her equalizer with bullies like Tommy Lee. Besides, she didn't give a damn what boys liked or didn't like. The prettiest girls liked having a big, ugly girl as company, although she was never among those invited to their sleepovers.

Jodie filled her plate, her attention giving way to the pleasure of stuffing herself. While Aunt Pearl wasn't a big eater, she'd hardly touched her food, and she'd done that odd thing of patting down the right side of her heavily sprayed hairdo, a habit she had when perplexed, causing her head to appear tilted.

"Why aren't you eating? Chicken's the best. Taters melt in my mouth like ice cream."

"Thank you, shug. I guess I grazed too much while fixing supper." She smiled, but in a way Jodie knew was forced. "Go on and enjoy your food. But save room for my twelve-layer chocolate cake."

Jodie turned back to her plate, thinking of the thin-layer chocolate cake, her absolute favorite. Yet, the more Aunt Pearl picked at her food, the more Jodie wished she hadn't eaten so fast.

The big hand on the grease-spattered clock hanging on the wall above the stove clicked slowly toward what Jodie felt was some impending doom. She swallowed hard, forcing the food to stay down.

"All right, what are you not telling me?"

Yesterday she'd stolen two new comics, and although old man Pepper, the storekeeper, had taken her dime for the RC Cola, she wanted this to be about him having noticed the bulge under her shirt. She'd return the slightly used comics, cry convincingly, and offer to sweep out the store for a week. Lay low for a time, and all would blow over. Stealing was fixable.

Aunt Pearl put down her fork, the deep lines of her worn face etched in dread. She gathered their plates from the table, plunging them into a cloud of sweet-smelling suds. She stood staring out the kitchen window before turning back to Jodie's question.

Jodie pushed up hard against the back of her chair; she knew what was to come was much bigger than stolen comic books.

"I washed up your clothes, and you'll want to pack them in that old brown cardboard suitcase you came with."

"Why? Are we going someplace?" She and her aunt had never as much as gone to a picture show together.

"Mr. Dozier called yesterday. And he's agreed to take you to live with him and his family in Florida." Aunt Pearl's fake cheerfulness was lost in the tears she wiped away on the back of her soapy wrist, lather running down her forearm, dripping onto her clean kitchen floor.

"Agreed? No damn way. It was settled." Had Red stopped sending the envelopes?

"He's insisting." She glanced at the floor. She was a terrible liar.

"So what? There's no law against me being here." Still she clutched thin air.

"I know, but you're wrong. If put to a judge, he'd say you belong with him." Aunt Pearl paused, as if searching for a higher reason.

But whether she stayed or went with Red didn't feel to Jodie like the kind of decision the law should make. "No, here with you is where my dead mama wanted me. And what she wanted can't be changed by God, or no judge, and least of all Red Dozier." Her lungs collapsed like a pricked balloon, her voice thinned, and she pleaded, "Please, you don't know anything about where he means to take me."

"He can give you a real family. And that's something you and I can never be. He's got a good Christian wife and a … daughter. Be grateful she's willing to take you in."

"But, you're a Christian." Jodie had heard in Aunt Pearl's hesitancy the truth she could not escape. No matter how hard she tried to become someone worthy, she was *peculiar*.

Jodie, I'm sorry. I know you don't understand. But I'm doing what I think best for you." Aunt Pearl dropped into a chair, her forehead resting against her palms.

"You're wrong. I do understand." Jodie rose from the table and walked out of the kitchen.

When she'd packed all she owned in the tattered suitcase, she lay down on the bed, fully dressed, to wait out the night. She had no choice but to go with Red Dozier, wherever he meant to take her.

# Eight

Red arrived early, declining to stay for the meal Aunt Pearl offered. Jodie refused to hug her tearful aunt and walked to Red's car without looking back. If she ever stopped feeling betrayed, maybe she'd get around to thinking of Aunt Pearl more kindly.

The Dodge smelled of spit and polish, and Red wore starched and ironed khaki pants with hard creases and a long-sleeved shirt bleached whiter than what Jewel had called the underside of death. Jodie sat up straight, tugged at the short hem of her dress. Her school shoes pinched so her toenails rolled under.

It hadn't taken long for the two of them to become strangers. They rode the first hour or so mostly in silence, neither seeming to know what to say to the other. Then he turned to her, surprising her with his question.

"What ever happened to those Easter biddies we fixed the pen for?" He smiled slightly. "They didn't stay pink, did they?" His smile widened.

"Them? No way. They turned out to be Rhode Island Reds. As to what happened, they stayed behind with a friend when me and Jewel went on the road."

"Did that last long? Traveling with the band?" He frowned.

"Not really. After a while, I begged Jewel to leave me off at Aunt Pearl's. I was missing too much school." She looked away, pretending sudden interest in the stiff corpse of a raccoon picked apart by buzzards.

"How was it there with your Aunt Pearl? She seemed nice enough."

"Like watching a hen set eggs. But I got used to steady. Never went hungry and never slept cold. Aunt Pearl was always home before sundown."

After that, conversation dried up. Jodie covered her growing uneasiness by faking an interest in the Bible Aunt Pearl had given her as a going away present. In the front of the Bible, she had neatly written *Frances Josephine Taylor*. On a second page, decorated in fancy curvy lettering and titled "Family History," she'd written *Jewel Faye Taylor* above the line denoting mother. Above Jewel's name was written the names *James Franklin Taylor and Frances Josephine Ayers, Grandparents*. Was she named for a woman Aunt Pearl claimed was her grandmother, a woman Jewel had never as much as mentioned?

The line naming *Father* was blank, and Jodie decided Aunt Pearl's certainty was no more solid than her own.

Slipped between the pages, she found a faded picture of two young girls. The older wore a worried look, her arm shielding the younger. On the back of the picture was written *Pearl Mae Taylor, born 1911 and Jewel Faye Taylor, born 1921*. Her mama had been sixteen the year Jodie was born. All the times before when she'd asked about family, Jewel had only shrugged, as if they had crawled fully formed from some slimy place like slippery toads.

"Read the Bible a lot, do you?" Red glanced at her with the playful twinkle she remembered.

"Can't say I'm altogether faithful." Jodie closed the book and watched cotton bolls escaping from the bed of an open trailer ahead, swirling in the hot air like popcorn.

"I've never been much for reading the Bible. But I've always liked the story of that kid, David. It says he brought down a giant with one smooth stone, using a little bitty slingshot he whittled while tending his daddy's sheep." He kept a straight face, and Jodie decided that Red Dozier was likely good at poker.

"Yep, I'd say he got off a lucky shot. Then, I'm partial to a pig sticker." She'd never heard the story of David, but she liked his guts, although the boy could not have been too smart.

"That right?" Red smiled, and she was sure he was onto her lie, but he seemed to lighten up all the more.

"Play the radio if you want. Might pick up a decent station out of Pensacola. It's not all that far now."

"Did you ever hear Jewel sing on the radio?" Maybe he had and she'd somehow missed it.

"No, I never did. Don't think that radio deal panned out." There was a hint of regret in the slow way he shook his head.

There was never a deal. Just Troy's bullshit. Had Jewel fed Red the same line? If so, was that why he never bothered coming back? She'd ask, but she really didn't want to know.

"Why do you call your mama Jewel?" His forehead wrinkled and his blue eyes searched hers.

"She said calling her 'mama' made her feel old." But now that she'd never get any older, what she called her couldn't matter.

He nodded, but his frown stayed.

"What am I to call you?"

"Red will do fine. And where we're going it's just as well you don't talk about your mama. It'll go easier on you." The big vein in his neck popped blue under the red splotching of his skin.

"As far as I care, you can tell your fine wife any lie you want. But Jewel Faye Taylor was my mama. I bet you didn't even know I·was named for my grandma. Says so right here in this Bible. You want to see for yourself?" She waved the book at him in the way she'd seen Aunt Pearl do. "And I'm not pretending otherwise. If you don't like it, you can stop this car and let me out." Choking back tears, she grabbed the door handle.

He reached across, laying a firm hand on her shoulder.

"No doubt she's your mama." For an instant, a faint smile played at the corners of his mouth. "And you can forget what I said. You're right to stick up for her."

His admitting to being wrong didn't mean she forgave him. But for now, her choices were Red's place or the state orphanage. She'd take her chances with him.

An hour or so later, Jodie got her first look at Catawba, Florida. It was a pitiful looking town: five blocks of nothing to brag about buildings facing off along Main Street, including a Western Union, dry goods store, hardware, grocery, feed and seed, filling station, café, brick schoolhouse, and two churches. A heavy veil of putrid smoke nearly blocked the sun, and Jodie pinched her nose, breathing through her mouth.

"That stink's the paper mill located over in the next town. On a good day, when the wind's just right, it stinks up our town only half this bad. You'll get used to it. Everybody does."

Jodie was certain she'd never get used to living in a town that smelled like rotted eggs and pine rosin. It was just as well that Red had never tried bringing her and Jewel here to live. Catawba was in no way a place of deep breathing.

Red pointed out a grassy square and the two-story, red brick building that occupied its center. "That's the county courthouse. Some of the state's biggest crooks operate out of there." His sternness led her to take him at his word. Two old men dressed in bib overalls and white shirts sat on a green bench near the courthouse. One leaned and spat a stream of brown tobacco juice onto the manicured lawn. On the far side of the green, two boys about her age chased each other in hard play. They reminded her of black Alvin and white Rabbit, boys from the row. A long-legged, brown dog barked and chased after them.

"Those two boys, there." He pointed. "The towhead's Silas and the other's Little Samuel. Samuel's daddy works there at the A&P. And Silas," he paused, "let's just say he's figuring on how to get along without one. They're good boys." Red sounded the horn, and the two stopped long enough to wave.

"That so?" She had drawn the boy's piss-poor luck times two. And she was yet to know a boy she thought much of.

"There on the corner, that's the elementary school. What grade you in?"

"Seventh."

"Then you'll go to the new junior-senior high. History teacher's a fine lady and a damn good teacher. You'll like her. Name's Miss Ruth O'Riley."

Jodie hated history, and the teacher he was so sure she'd like sounded like an old maid. They made the worst teachers.

Several miles out of town on a county road, Red turned the Dodge onto a sandy lane, and at the top of a rise she got her first look at the clapboard house. An array of ramshackle outbuildings dotted the yard cluttered with junked farm equipment.

The late afternoon sun reflected off the tin roof, the house appearing to be ablaze. The house was even smaller than Aunt Pearl's, and only slightly bigger than those on sharecroppers' row. If the entire house and its outbuildings burned to the ground, Red wouldn't be out much. Nothing about what she saw made her want to stay.

He shut down the engine and turned to her.

"There's bound to be a bit of friction. But I'm counting on you being gritty like your mama." He paused and glanced toward the house. "Things will work out. You'll see." He showed her his best poker face, but the circles of sweat at his armpits told a different story.

She followed him through the sagging picket gate. The day's heat, trapped beneath the tin roof of the porch, shimmered like Christmas tinsel. He stepped onto the porch, his lanky frame casting its long shadow across the lye-scrubbed boards. Standing next to Red, Jodie clutched the brown cardboard suitcase, glad Aunt Pearl had insisted she wear her best school dress, although it was badly wrinkled, and splotched with yellow mustard from the hotdog she'd eaten on the road.

A stout, hard-eyed woman sat in a straight-back chair, cutting sweet corn from the cob. A shy, pudgy girl peered from behind her. Neither lifted a hand or spoke, the only sound that of Jack Bailey's booming question: *Do you want to be Queen for a Day?* The shrill voices of desperate women erupted, shamelessly pleading to tell their stories. Jodie hated the show, believing pity shouldn't be put to a contest.

Red nodded to the silent woman and ignored the girl. He jammed his big hands into the pockets of his trousers, rocked heel to toe, as if he meant to gather momentum, and cleared his throat. Overall, he struck an odd if not downright silly pose. Jodie ground her teeth and waited.

"This is Jodie Taylor. Like I said before, she's to live here. And there's nothing more to be said." He placed a hand on her shoulder, nudging her forward. His manner reminded her of all those times she'd gone to Jewel, ready to take her punishment, but not seeking forgiveness.

"Jodie, this lady's Miss Mary, my wife. You're to call her Miss Mary. And you're to do as she says. The girl's Hazel. You can call her whatever you work out between you. And you two are to get along."

He took a clean white handkerchief from his pocket and mopped at the sweat rolling down his temples. There was a rank odor about him that Jodie hadn't noticed earlier.

Miss Mary drew the skirt of her cotton print dress across her knees, binding her short thighs in a vise. Her stout fingers worked through the chalky-white kernels as if she meant to separate Red's words into truths and consequences. Her puffy, dough-like face was drawn and pale, and she glared at him from where she sat, her dark eyes wet, fired stones.

The girl, crouched next to her mama, stared, saliva trickling down her chin as her stubby fingers worked like tiny shovels inside her chapped cheek. Jodie believed her to be a year or so younger, and she looked as if she knew to fear what was to come.

Jodie gripped the suitcase more tightly. It held all she possessed: her link to her past—the busted seventy-eight, carefully packaged, and the Bible—along with two pairs of jeans, three shirts, a pleated green skirt, a white blouse, two school dresses, three changes of underwear, her Wonder Woman comics, and the three detective novels she'd stolen.

"Hazel, you're to make room. Now show Jodie inside."

The girl looked to her mama, but she was too busy glaring at Red's back as he turned and walked off the porch. He stood in the yard, whistling for a dog he called Buster.

Jodie had no choice but to follow the mute girl into a tiny bedroom furnished with a double bed, home to a collection of stuffed animals, a scarred chifforobe, and a three-legged stool painted bright yellow.

"Now, this is what I call damn pitiful. Barely room enough to cuss a crippled cat. And that mess of kid toys piled there has got to go." She gave Hazel her best Jewel stance.

Hazel moaned, a hand to her mouth, and she backed away, bumping into the near wall.

"What's the matter with you? You retarded or something?"

Hazel ran from the room, crying, and Jodie stared after her. Maybe she was a bit unfriendly, but now was the time to settle things between them. If she stayed, she'd have her hands plenty full with the old woman.

She didn't bother unpacking but shoved the suitcase under the bed. She lay on the bed, curled into a defensive ball, and in the moment she hated Red Dozier, her Aunt Pearl, and most of all Jewel.

At the sound of footsteps approaching, Jodie sat up on the side of the bed and squinted through her grogginess. She'd fallen asleep.

"My daddy says you're to come to supper." Hazel turned and hurried back down the hallway.

"Wait. Is there a bathroom in this place?"

Jodie glanced at her reflection in the cracked mirror hanging above the bathroom sink and ran wet fingers through her snarled curls. When she entered the kitchen, Miss Mary slammed a dish of macaroni and cheese onto the table and stomped out.

"Go on, Jodie. Get to the table." Red sat at the head, his face flushed, and he appeared to grind his teeth. He motioned for Hazel to sit. She glanced over her shoulder as if confused as to which parent she owed her allegiance.

Jodie took the chair nearest Red, her back pressed up hard against the chair spindles, so much so she was certain of grooves. Red sighed and called upon Hazel to pray.

"God is great. God is good. Let us thank Him for our food. Amen." Hazel raised her head and smiled so sweetly pious, Jodie was sure sugar wouldn't melt in the girl's mouth, proving she wasn't dumb after all.

Jodie pushed the yellow, brick-like macaroni and cheese around on her plate, fearing she'd gag if she tried swallowing it. Meals in this house weren't going to be Aunt Pearl's; supper was skimpy and cold.

Red cursed, slammed his plate into the sink, and went to the pantry. He came back with a quart jar.

"You girls like peaches?" He winked at Jodie. He knew they were her favorite. "Grab those leftover biscuits out of the safe. We're about to eat our fill of Red's famous peach cobbler."

They added milk to the crumbled biscuits and peaches, finishing off the entire jar.

Red leaned back, patted his belly, and said, "What'd ya'll say to a game of Chinese checkers? I'll play two colors. Double my chance of winning." He stepped to the stove and poured a cup of coffee.

"Can I get a cup of that?" Aunt Pearl had forbidden coffee, something about coffee stunting her growth. Jewel had told her it would turn her black. Both were lies.

Red poured a second cup and set it on the table next to her. "You gonna want sissy mess in that?"

"Nope, drink my coffee black."

He looked at her, and slowly nodded. "Figured as much."

Jodie studied his face, his expression giving away nothing of what he felt.

Hazel had retrieved the game board and set it up on the kitchen table.

"All right, young ladies. You're about to get yourselves dry-gulched."

Hazel giggled. "I'm playing red, Daddy."

"Dang, girl. You know red is my color." He poured a double shot of whiskey in his coffee and sat back at the table.

"No, you had red last time, remember?" She gathered the marbles and began filling the spaces on the board.

"All right, Jodie, I guess you get to pick next." Black was her lucky color.

The three played as if the headwinds of an impending storm weren't swirling about in another part of the house. When Hazel began to nod, Red sent them off to bed.

Being with Red and Hazel had helped to settle her nerves, and sleep came easier than Jodie expected. She slept hard until startled awake by strange voices. At first, she was confused, believing she was back at Aunt Pearl's. A whimpering Hazel lay next to her, curled into a tight ball, her fists covering her ears. Jodie strained to hear what she now knew was Red's checked voice, coming from the other side of the house.

"Girl, shut your damn blubbering." It wasn't her they fought about. Jodie heard *whore's bastard* in Miss Mary's shrill voice.

"She won't have her back."

"Then send her to a home. Anywhere. I want her gone from here."

"No, she stays. That's final." Red's anger ricocheted off the walls like the blasts of a scatter gun. Miss Mary wailed as if he'd shot her. His fury driving his heavy footsteps across the parlor, he slammed the front door back on its hinges.

Jodie jumped off the bed and hurried to the window. Across the ridge, the moon shone brightly, and she saw him as clearly as day. He kicked open the gate and crossed to his car. He got into the Dodge and sped away. No chance he'd seen her timid wave.

Jodie got back into bed, her eyes squeezed tight against what she knew was her fate. Jewel had once warned that if they were to make it in this world, they'd need to butt with their own heads. They were not the type to be rescued. Before Jewel had fallen under Troy's dark spell, she'd had a way of being right about hard things. Red came for her, but she was to be alone in this house.

# Nine

Jodie pulled at the long strands of cobweb tangled in her hair and scrunched next to a foundation post. Buster rose from the pit he'd dug next to the fireplace footing and crept closer. She wrapped an arm around the dog's thick shoulders, and he licked her sweaty face. Both hid beneath the house from Hazel, her mother's dutiful spy.

A pair of dirty feet appeared at the outer edge of the porch, and Jodie scooted further toward the center of the house. Hazel squatted, peered beneath the house, and grimaced. Jodie counted on the girl's fear of all things that crawled, and the glare of the mid-morning sun, to shield her.

"Jodie, I know you're under there. Mama don't like the way you hung the wash." Her sing-song cadence put Jodie's teeth on edge.

It was on the line, and just how many ways were there to hang a wash?

"If you know what's good for you, you'll get out from under there."

"Best stay put, dog." Miss Mary had a way of catching Buster in her circle of rage. She crawled from beneath the house and went to stand on the back steps, Buster slinking at her heels. "Damn dog, told you to get."

Miss Mary came onto the porch from the kitchen and glared at Jodie. "I see that whore mama of yours never bothered teaching you to hang a proper wash."

At the sound of the hated word *whore,* Jodie's scalp tightened as if it had shrunk too small for her skull, her fury trumping smart. "My mama wasn't like that. And she taught me plenty."

Red had said she was right to take up for her mama, but he wasn't here, and she was helpless against Miss Mary's cunning trap. Behind her, Hazel gasped, backing away, afraid of standing too close to their heat.

"Get your sassy butt back out there. Take that wash down. And I want to see towels with towels, sheets with sheets, all down the line. Dinner's on the table and it looks like you won't be done in time."

The hot sun hung midday and Jodie looked down the long line, gritted her teeth, and started anew, her stomach growling.


Red continued to stay away, convincing Jodie that Jewel had been replaced. Only the discovery of a small creek offered her refuge from Miss Mary. She whistled to Buster and the dog trotted along, wagging his chopped tail in what she took as dog gratitude.

They walked along an animal trail that led through an overgrown field to where the ridge fell gently toward a narrow strip of old stand longleaf pines. Beyond stood large tupelo gum and bay magnolia. A bald cypress grew at the edge of the meandering creek that was fed by natural springs bubbling up through limestone beds. She imagined herself Tarzan, running wild and free, living in harmony among herds of white-tail deer, flocks of wild turkey, feral hogs, and a friendly black bear that ate berries from her hand.

She sat with her back propped against a willow and watched a tag match between two squirrels chasing along the branches of a water oak. She didn't hear the boy's approach until he'd flopped onto the ground next to her as if invited.

She jumped to her feet and cried, "Where'd you come from? What if I'd been swimming naked?" She sputtered, her hands punching the air.

The knotty-kneed boy didn't speak but thrust a fistful of ironweed at her.

"What am I supposed to do with these weeds?"

He shrugged.

"You got a tongue, boy?"

"Yep, I'm Silas. Live the next place over, where the creek takes a sharp turn west." He pointed to the creek, as if she didn't know it existed, and it clearly in sight.

"That right? And what brings you over on Red's place?" She believed this Silas was one of the boys Red had pointed out the day of her arrival.

"Miss Maggie sent me. Said I should come and get acquainted. I think Mr. Red would've said the same if he hadn't left in such a hurry. But she never warned you'd be so contrary."

"I do believe you can talk. And just so you know, I'm not one bit contrary unless first pissed off. And who's this Maggie?" She smashed a yellow fly perched on her elbow, flipping the corpse his way.

"She's not like any woman you've ever seen. Drove an army ambulance right into the thick of Hitler's war. Now she doctors those who don't have time off or money to see the real doctor."

"You don't say? Since when did women get to be in the Army?" She plopped back onto the ground but kept her distance.

"Every word's the truth. She wears pants and curses like a hussy. People say things, but I don't care. She and Miss Ruth are my best friends. And Miss Ruth don't cuss or drink. She's always home before dark."

"Is that a fact?"

He nodded repeatedly as though he'd spoken the truth on female respectability.

"You wouldn't think so highly of this Maggie if you'd known Jewel."

"Uh-huh, and if you had half a boy brain, you'd be grateful to Maggie." He tugged on Buster's ear and didn't look at her.

"Watch your mouth. I don't have cause to be grateful to nobody. Least of all a woman I've never laid eyes on."

"It figures Mr. Red wouldn't have let on, since she scalded his dog."

"Boy, what the hell are you talking about?"

He picked up a sweet gum ball and tossed it hesitantly at a cluster of pitcher plants growing along the creek, as though he was making up his mind about saying something he'd likely been told to keeping under his hat.

"Well, I'm waiting to hear whatever it is you're too chicken to tell."

"You're not going to like it."

"Try me."

"Miss Maggie told Mr. Red she didn't give a good gosh dang about his woman troubles. Called him a lily-livered coward. Said he was to fetch you back here or he'd answer to her." He paused. "Don't nobody but her get away with talking to Mr. Red that way."

Jodie needed time to gather herself, and she stared in the direction of noisy chatter. If it was true Red never wanted to bring her here, she didn't want to hear more from this boy.

He followed her gaze and they both watched.

"That big one's a boy squirrel. He wants to make babies with that girl squirrel." He spoke in the same certain tone and he'd started to piss her off.

"Oh, yeah, and I guess you've seen a grown man and woman do it."

"No, I ain't had a decent chance. Lost my daddy to Roosevelt's CCC for the promise of what he called a dollar a day, three hots, and a flop. And since my mama's a Christian widow, she refuses traveling men."

"Boy howdy, Jewel sure didn't. She was so pretty. She had a new man every night. They all wanted to marry her and be my daddy." Jodie waited for him to run like a turkey, but he only blinked hard, leading her to believe she'd outdone him.

"My daddy helped build a big dam till a dynamite charge went off in his hand. The others looked for him, but they never found parts enough to send home. That's why Mama got a check for fifty-seven dollars and a letter telling her about daddy's bravery, signed by nobody other than President Harry Truman." His eyes narrowed in a challenge.

"Jewel died in a head-on collision with a semi loaded with hogs. Law swore folks stopped to butcher dead and crippled hogs. Blood and guts ran in the ditches steadier than water in that creek."

His face puckered and he looked as if he might puke. She'd outdone him, all right, but her stomach felt queasy, and she wished she'd left out the part about blood and guts.

"This Jewel, she was your mama?"

"Didn't like for me to call her that. We were more like sisters."

"Mama said Daddy died a no-account drunk. But I miss him just the same."

Silas had ways Jodie had never known in a boy. Without really trying, he made her feel better about the way her mama had died.

He pulled a book from the bib of his overalls and held it up to her.

She looked away. It wasn't a book she recognized. Besides, there was a boy pictured on the cover.

"No, it's a real good book. About a boy named ...." He paused and squinted at her. "Jody's a boy's name. How come your mama gave you a boy's name?"

"What my mama did is none of your business." She stood, her hands jammed in her pockets, and she glared at him.

"You a tomboy?" There was no meanness. Only his question.

"So what if I am? I'll gladly take it over sissy bookworm."

"You ever heard of Abe Lincoln? He read every book in the library. And look where it took him." He glared back, and she was starting to feel better about him.

"Oh, so someday you're growing whiskers and living in the White House?"

"Maybe, but first I'm taking over my uncle's shop. Mean to fix people's cars and trucks. Then I'll see about the other."

"I got news for you, sucker. No grease monkey's ever made it that far. Generals get to be President. And you don't look like general material."

"Miss Ruth says there's a first time for everything. And besides, if you're so dang smart, what're you planning on?"

"I haven't decided. But for sure I'm not fixing busted cars." Right now, staying a step ahead of Miss Mary's strap was using up her best wit. Beyond that, she wasn't sure.

He'd sat calmly through her tirade, his slow hand working its way around the binding of the book he held. "If I had a knife I'd cut fronds from that palmetto," he pointed, "and we'd make a flutter mill like the boy Jody did in the book."

She took her Barlow from her pocket and held it out to him.

"Dang, girl." His eyes flashed with admiration.

She didn't know if she wanted to be friends with a boy who read books and failed to carry a knife. She admitted to her insides calming, but she couldn't be sure it had anything to do with this strange boy.


Silas had a fascination with other people's junk, and she'd agreed to spend another hot morning scavenging the county dump. Her decision came only after he'd promised she would finally meet the infamous Maggie, who would give them a ride back and haul his treasured cast-offs.

They'd taken turns riding the bike he'd acquired from an earlier trip to the dump. He declared it to be as good as new, although it was short a seat and both fenders. He argued that only lazy riders sat to peddle, and the absence of fenders caused the bike to go faster. Silas had a special knack for explaining away all things contrary to what he wanted to believe. Given his pitiful station in life, she'd decided that his doing so served him well.

Silas piled the last of his treasures, a twisted tongue and front axle from what had been a kid's red wagon, next to the road. He wiped sweat from his eyes on the tail of his nasty shirt and grinned as if he'd bagged gold.

"What're you going to do with that?" Jodie shaded her eyes from the sun's glare and wished they'd brought water.

"Don't know yet, but something useful." He stood staring at the pile, and she believed he was reconfiguring scrap.

"How much longer we got to wait?"

He squinted up at the sun. "I've never known Maggie to be late for a meal. Don't worry. She'll be along."

He'd brought along his Roy Rogers BB gun, and they went back to targeting rats until the clatter of an approaching truck had Silas scurrying. He shouted, "It's her all right. Dead on the dime."

The truck slid to a quick stop and Jodie got her first look at the woman he so admired. Her sunburned face wasn't altogether unfriendly, but there was a sternness about her that put Jodie in mind of Jewel.

"Get that mess loaded, boy. My dinner's getting cold."

"Yes'm. You bet." Silas grabbed up the bag and, with Jodie's help, heaved it and the bike into the bed of the truck. He scampered around the truck and held the door open. "Boys ride shotgun."

"Slide on in, girlie. You must be Jodie Taylor."

Jodie stared at the woman. Her hair, the color of Spanish moss, was cropped just below her ears, and she wore a white shirt, open at the collar, sleeves rolled above her elbows.

Silas gestured that she should answer. She jabbed him a sharp one to the ribs and he drew back, looking both surprised and anxious.

"I'm Jodie Taylor, all right. And don't call me girlie. It's meant for sissies, and I'm not one."

Silas gulped air like he'd stepped on a rattler.

The big woman smiled. "You may survive after all. I'm Maggie, Jodie Taylor, and I'm pleased to meet you." There was no sign of Jewel's brooding, only a hard playfulness in Maggie's manner.

"Plenty of starch, all right." Silas nodded like a bobble doll, his tone one of relief, as if he'd set aside some personal dread.

Maggie turned the truck around and sped back onto the highway as if the devil gave chase. Jodie studied the woman's relaxed, one-hand grip on the steering wheel.

"You drive like a man."

"No, Jodie Taylor, I drive like a woman with somewhere to be."

Jodie settled back against the scratchy wool blanket covering the seat. For reasons she couldn't fathom, she felt more at ease, squeezed between Silas and this strange woman, than at any time since leaving the row.

# Ten

Jodie and Silas sprawled on the front porch, intent on playing a mean game of checkers. They played with two sets of caps, Silas insisting that RC caps were luckier than Aunt Jemima syrup bottle caps, although she still beat him seven out of ten games. If Silas was anything, he was loyal to a fault. They stopped their play and watched the approach of a delivery truck.

Miss Mary hurried onto the porch, flashing a rare smile. Her plump hands clasped beneath her double chin struck Jodie as an oddly prayerful pose. In a display of what Jodie viewed as downright silliness, she flitted about the small, over-crowded front room, directing the reluctant delivery men in multiple arrangements of the new furniture into what she must have imagined as fashionable. Jodie was sure Jewel would have gotten the arrangement right the first time, saving the backs of the delivery men and shaping a better looking room.

Jodie pondered the price Miss Mary had extracted from Red for trips to the row. Surely Jewel had cost him more than an ugly couch and chair. The more she saw of Red dealing with Miss Mary, the more she considered the radio/record player console Jewel had prized a similar act of appeasement.

Dressed in his customary starched khaki pants and long-sleeved white shirt, Red came onto the porch. He watched their play, and Jodie, feeling the nearness of him, leaned back against his leg. He bent and with his strong fingers gently kneaded her scalp, his whiskey-flavored breath brushing her cheek.

She pushed into the pleasure of his touch, remembering those late nights when he'd lifted her into his arms to the sound of Jewel's soft laughter and carried her to the makeshift cot in the kitchen where she'd slept the balance of his visit.

Silas scrambled to his feet and asked, "You want us to stop this game? Get the Chinese checkers out so you can play too?"

"Naw, boy, you kids are having too much fun. Besides, I've got me a strong hankering for strawberry cream." He walked down the steps, rattling the loose change he always carried in his pocket.

"No you don't. Wait for us." She, Silas, and even Hazel, chased after him, Hazel looking relieved when her mother didn't call her back. It seemed she, too, was to reap the reward of a temporary ceasefire between her parents.

They piled into the Dodge and headed for Gaskin's Drugs. Jodie and Silas hung out the passenger side window, hot air rushing into their lungs, and sang *She'll be coming around the mountain* loud enough, Red joked, they were surely heard in China. She wanted Red to say she sang good like her mama had, but it wasn't true. Still, she was disappointed and puzzled by the way Red picked truth from among so many lies.

Red followed the three of them into Gaskin's, a haven from the blistering heat. Its wagon wheel–sized overhead fans cooled the black-and-white tiled floor, and Jodie took care to step only on white squares. There was a part of her that still wanted to believe in good luck.

Red handed each a dime. "You kids take these before they rub a hole clear through my pocket."

A car trip into town with Red, double scoops of strawberry ice cream, and a comic was more than Jodie had hoped for, the true makings of a perfect day.

On their return, Jodie sat in the porch swing, her new Wonder Woman comic, and Hazel's silly Archie, hidden inside her shirt, tucked up tight against the bib of her overalls.

"Jodie," Hazel whispered. "It's my daddy's sin that me and you got funny books, right?"

"Damn, girl, they're *funny* books. Don't that tell you something?"

"But I think God's against fun."

Hazel chewed her bloody cuticle, a habit she had when faced with the prospect of her parents' fighting. She was too dumb to know Miss Mary didn't give a big rat's ass about God, the Bible, or Satan's part in who read comics.

"I know." Hazel's face lit up with her perceived cleverness. "We could hide them in his car."

"And what happens when he takes a notion to drive off in the middle of the night?"

Hazel sucked blood from her torn cuticle.

"Damn, that's nasty. You some kind of girl vampire?"

Jodie had removed the stashed comics and flashlight from the wooden box with busted hinges that she and Silas had dragged from the dump and hidden beneath the house. When the light beneath Red and Miss Mary's bedroom door disappeared, she retrieved both from under the bed.

Cocooned in the wraith-like glow of the flashlight beam, they scrunched beneath the sheet, Jodie quietly reading the forbidden Archie comic, Hazel having reaffirmed that her just listening surely carried a lesser penalty. Jodie knew Hazel's thinking was flawed and that the spineless girl was never in any real danger of the lash. Still, she liked the conspiratorial feel of their doing so. It was, after all, their one act of shared defiance.

Miss Mary's squeals shattered any semblance of balance, giving ground to the certainty of doom. Jodie felt the air rush from her lungs, her words frozen, left unspoken. Yet she made no attempt to conceal the comics. She accepted that only Miss Mary's sudden death, or her own, could forestall the inevitable. She pressed Wonder Woman to her chest and imagined the day she'd find her strength and wrestle the strap away, and she, not Miss Mary, would rule in Red's absence.

Next to her, Hazel curled into a tight ball and whimpered.

Jodie wrapped her arms tightly about herself and held her breath against the certainty of Red's heavy steps crossing the front room, the slamming of the door, the pitch of sand beneath the Dodge's tires as he made his escape.

She stood, her calves pushed up tight against the bed, her thighs straining to flee, but she could not summon the will to resist. Revenge approached: one, two, three—fourteen angry strikes against the splintered floor.

Miss Mary stood in the doorway, her feet spread, her wide girth blocking the room's only escape.

"How dare you disobey me? My word's law in this house." Her loathing regurgitated from deep within her bloated belly.

Hazel screamed, "No, Mama, please. Daddy ...."

Miss Mary never as much as looked at her daughter. Her wrath was focused solely on Jodie. It was never about the deed, but the bargain Red had struck. The truth of his betrayal burned through Jodie like venom, and every good she'd ever felt for Red Dozier was poisoned.

A cornered, animal-like hissing forced open Miss Mary's hard mouth, and a scream of pure agony escaped. Jodie believed she heard an echo of her own pain—the absence of love suffered each time Red bargained her to Miss Mary's rage. Her full vengeance fell across Jodie's right shoulder, and fire spread along the strap's bloody path, Jodie writhing in pain. Slumping onto the floor, she crouched next to the bed. Her arms shielding her face, she squeezed her eyes shut against her fate. Miss Mary gathered her strength, her unabated fury lashing out again and again. Jodie closed her mind, absenting herself from the pain and humiliation, her psyche transcending the moment.

At first, Jodie did not recognize the voice that called to her, her consciousness returning only in her memory of the strong arms that lifted her. Her mama's laughter comforted her, bidding her return from the enveloping darkness that had swallowed her, and only just now spit her back into full awareness.

Red stood over her, and he glared at Miss Mary, each poised in mortal combat. The old woman's mouth gaped as she sagged back against the doorframe, her arms limp at her sides, and she leveled no resistance as he took the strap from her and wound it around his fist.

"Use this again and I swear to God you'll go early to your grave." His voice was chilling, his eyes flashing a deeper burning, and Jodie shuddered. Still, she questioned what Red professed to know of God.

"Lie still. I'll get something for those welts."

For the first time since her arrival in this house, Jodie believed she heard pain in his voice equal to her own. He straightened, stepped past Miss Mary, and Jodie listened for his footsteps until they'd faded. She heard what she thought was water filling the kettle, and maybe she only imagined the scent of sulfur.

Miss Mary's words were barely audible above her raspy breathing. "He'll never own you. I'll see to that. You'll never be more than his wretched whore's bastard." Her words were eerily calm, but Jodie felt their certainty. Red's flagging will was no match for her vengeful cunning. The beatings might stop, but the hate would stay.

## Eleven

Jodie took the flat envelope, addressed to Red in Aunt Pearl's neat handwriting, from the mailbox on the road and worried what Miss Mary labeled as her "sassiness" had convinced Red to go back on his word. She was wrong to defend her mama against Miss Mary's slander, and he now intended to force her back on Aunt Pearl. Months earlier she would have been grateful, but now things were oddly different. She had Maggie and Miss Ruth, and even Silas, and giving up what was beginning to feel like a make-do family would be hard.

She'd ripped open the letter and read Aunt Pearl's seemingly dry-eyed explanation that county officials intended to relocate the pauper's cemetery where Jewel was buried to make room for the ever-expanding county dump.

It was Maggie and Miss Ruth who drove Jodie to her mama's gravesite. Red had claimed urgent business elsewhere. The crude, hand-drawn map Aunt Pearl included in her letter led them to an overgrown cemetery seventeen miles north of Ava, Alabama.

"Damn his rotten hide straight to hell." Maggie pulled Red's Dodge to a jerky stop and sat pounding the steering wheel, ignoring Miss Ruth's quiet pleading that "Red's salvation is in God's hands," and not hers.

Jodie thought about the kind of God Maggie might be, and figured her heaven would be populated by a very different crowd than those of Ginger's mama's stripe.

"Merciful Jesus, Ruth." Maggie lowered her voice. "It's not like the child doesn't know." She stared ahead at nothing in particular and then back at Miss Ruth. "Maybe if I didn't always cut the sorry sapsucker so much wiggle room, he'd straighten up and do right."

"No, Maggie. I understand that you're disappointed in Red and that you hurt for Jodie, but you aren't making this any easier."

Jodie and Silas sat in the back seat, Silas shaking his head, as though he meant to defend Red, believing Maggie was unfair. But even blind, faithful Silas knew Maggie didn't lie, and deep down he had to know the same could not be said for Red Dozier.

Silas rolled the cuffs of his Sunday pants to his knees, and they picked their way through patches of sandspurs, prickly pear, and beggar lice. The worrisome weeds stuck to Jodie's shoestrings and socks, and even to the hem of the new dress Miss Ruth had sewn, insisting Jodie should dress appropriately in honor of her mother. Had Miss Ruth known Jewel, her tone would not have been so confident.

Jewel's grave—an elongated indention in the red clay, marked by a weathered card inside a clear plastic holder fastened to a metal stake—was located at the back corner of the cemetery. While Miss Ruth cried openly for a woman she'd never known, Jodie felt Maggie's heat beside her and heard only the sound of her breathing as she stooped and began snatching weeds from a grave that would soon disappear, as though Jewel Taylor had never as much as drawn a deep breath. Jodie, Miss Ruth, and Silas joined Maggie, and they didn't stop until the gravesite was clean. Jodie wanted the county to know she was no fool. She knew they lied about moving remains. They'd put up new markers all right, but her mama's bones were destined to lie beneath mountains of other people's garbage.

Back in the car, Jodie glanced back at the cemetery, and there was nothing left to do but to pack her grief deep down inside her.

Sunlight crept toward the tidy row of rusted cans filled with blooming pink and red geraniums, and Jodie stared in the direction of the road. But there wasn't a person or vehicle in sight. Maggie was adamant about their being on the river by sunrise, and starting late meant they'd need to fish the deeper pools rather than the shallows. She glanced back at the road, and still no sign of either Silas or Maggie.

Lying her way out of church had been as easy as claiming her habitual Sunday morning bellyaches. Miss Mary's abhorrence at being seen in public with her made Jodie's dishonesty pointless, and she wasn't sure why she kept up her side of the pretense. Miss Mary wasn't saved from the tight-lipped old women, claiming pity for her shameful burden, while whispering "his bastard daughter" behind blue-veined hands.

From the direction of the road, Jodie heard the clicking sound Silas's junk bike made with playing cards clipped to its spokes. She shaded her eyes against the sun and watched his approach. He rode the pedals hard as though the devil chased his tail. He slid to a stop at the gate, his cheeks flaming red, and he puffed like a horny toad.

"Jodie, get down here, right now."

"What's the big hurry? Can't you see I'm just fine? Sitting here, minding my own business? You could take a lesson."

"Maggie ain't going to be in a mood to wait. She was up most of the night at Mr. Samuel's, birthing Pokey Dot's litter."

In the distance, they sighted Maggie's GMC pickup speeding toward them. The battered truck was sixteen years old, but Maggie referred to it as a coming-undone miracle machine with heart. Her proudest possession, a brand new super-powered twenty-five horse Wizard outboard, bounced from the rear of the green bateau in the back. A clutch of fine cane fishing poles whipped like switches from the tailgate. Maggie stopped at the bottom of the lane and lay down on the horn.

She leaned out the window and shouted, "You young'uns get a wiggle on. We're burning good daylight."

"Told you so. Now come on." Silas dropped his bike and Jodie sailed off the porch, running hard to overtake him. He was a sprinter and she was built for distance. He faded before reaching the truck.

Jodie slid across the seat and sat next to Maggie.

"Look out for that sack of hot biscuits and ham you're about to set your nasty butt on." Maggie's bark rarely vanquished the twinkle in her blue eyes.

They spent what was left of the morning fishing the steep banks of the Apalachicola River that formed the western-most edge of land that had once been a part of Maggie's family's ancestral cotton plantation. When they'd caught enough for dinner, Maggie ran the boat onto a sandy beach, and they began to unload what they would need.

"Take this hatchet, boy. Cut lighter wood off that pine stump. Enough to get this grease hot. And while you're about it, try your damnedest not to piss off old grandpappy rattler."

"Dang, Maggie. You didn't have to say that." Silas stomped off, watching his bare feet.

"No, I didn't. But now maybe you'll look where you're going and go where you're looking. Jodie, you start in on cleaning fish while I get us set up to cook. Then I'll come help you."

Silas claimed Maggie's habit of giving orders she got from her army days. But Jodie believed Maggie was born to boss.

The fish were nearing ready when they heard the clatter of a vehicle approaching from the direction of a clearly marked private road. Maggie stepped away from the sizzling pan to stare toward the sound. A flatbed loaded with well drilling equipment pulled into the clearing.

"Damned if it ain't that no-account Samuel." She waved him over.

He got out of the truck and hobbled toward them. He favored a twisted right foot. Odder than his bum foot were his eyes, set deep into his brown freckled face—eyes that were every bit as blue as Maggie's.

"My nose led me here." He flashed an easy smile.

"You've never been a slouch at rooting out a ready meal. Take a load off. Just now taking it up."

"Don't mind if I do. Where'd ya'll fish at? Water's down a mite for backwater fishing." He removed his wide-brimmed straw hat with the built in green visor strip, and ran a slow hand over his balding head.

"Uh-huh, and on top of that, we got a puny start. Some contrary old hog farmer wouldn't be satisfied unless I hung around and drank bad whiskey while his sow dropped her seventh litter. Never needing help doing any of it."

"Now ain't that a shame?" His booming laughter echoed across the water and skipped merrily back to them.

Jodie leaned and whispered, "She delivers pigs too?"

Silas replied, "Sure, babies, foals, calves, whenever she's called on." He spoke with a certain pride as if her status included him.

"Morning, Little Red." Samuel was the only one who called her that, and although she liked that he did, it always caused her to blush. Maybe he knew of a confession she wasn't privy to.

"Hey, Mr. Samuel."

When they'd eaten their fill of bluegills, fried crispy-brown, along with hushpuppies and canned beans sweetened with molasses, Mr. Samuel stood and rubbed his belly, his face serious as a gravedigger.

"Mighty proud you kids came along with this old woman. Would've hated sitting down to sardines."

"I do believe I was the very one who taught you not to eat the worms, but bait the hook for something better."

He chuckled. "Now that I've raised her hackles, I'll take my leave. Catch me a string before sundown." He walked away, got into his truck, and drove back in the direction he'd come.

"Sure wish we didn't have to go just yet." Silas gazed toward the broad river and back at Maggie, a boy's pleading in his tone.

"Who said anything about going? Let's pack up, stow away, and get back on the river. There's fish to be caught."

Jodie jumped up and began tossing sand on the coals. Their staying meant dinner on the grounds and an afternoon of gospel singing at Miss Ruth's church.

"Yeah, another Sunday afternoon lost to God's selfishness."

They giggled at Maggie's blasphemy, and Jodie liked the way she swore in their presence. It made her feel grown-up, and Silas always sat a little taller and fished harder. But the day either could out-fish Maggie would be the day Maggie shaved her underarms.

# Catawba Florida - October 1954

## Twelve

The first break in the summer's heat came the third week of October, the day the much-anticipated carnival caravan approached Main Street. Only the arrival of the new football season could equal opening night at the county fair. It was a throwback to the times of bountiful harvests, Red had said, and although there was now little to celebrate, it seemed everyone still welcomed a measure of fun.

The customary fire drill emptied the student body onto the sidewalk to cheer an assortment of thrill rides, sideshows, wagering attractions, and caged animals creeping into town atop flatbeds. Exotic, dark-skinned men and their hard-edged women of the same hue waved from last-breath vehicles towing travel trailers.

Jodie stood aloof from the rest of the junior class on the pretense of watching the parade while she stole glances at Clara Lee Adams, the object of her secret crush since ninth grade. While she had always scoffed at the notion of love at first sight, the first marks she'd made in her new Blue Horse notebook that year were the initials C.L.A. written inside a lopsided heart.

Jodie glanced back at Clara Lee, who drew attention like bees to honey. Not only was she the school's smartest, she was hands down its prettiest. Her soft brown hair fell smoothly to her shoulders, not a strand out of place, even in the slight cool breeze of summer's relief.

Her pleated skirt and sweater set were the same deep blue as her eyes. Her saddle oxfords still looked new, not as much as a mark on the toes.

Jodie wiped sweat from her temples on her sleeves and rubbed her scuffed oxfords on the backs of her sock tops. Polished shoes were easy, but shoe polish would not straighten her fuzzy hair, shrink her waistline, improve her social ineptness, or raise her average grades. Except for her infatuation with Clara Lee, she didn't give a damn about anything more than the accuracy of her jump shot. But best girls' basketball player in the county went unnoticed, except for the crude jokes about the certainty of her being queer—a word she now knew, replacing her earlier vocabulary for what it meant to be *peculiar*. In frustration, Jodie turned back to watching the parade.

"I love opening night at the fair. You are going, aren't you?"

The alluring voice Jodie knew with every fiber of her body and mind was that of Clara Lee Adams. It was her chance, and if she didn't faint, she'd say aloud the line she'd practiced.

"Yeah, I guess so." She actually shrugged. "Opening night, sure. Why not? That's if you'll go with me … what I mean is, we could go together." She felt a bit dizzy, and stepped back from Clara Lee's heat. Her dopy performance nothing like the cool, nonchalant Jim Stark character she'd wanted to imitate. She prepared for a swift and solid letdown.

"Yes, I'd like that. I think it would be fun." Clara Lee smiled, and a wave of electricity shot through Jodie's limbs, settling in her crotch like a brush fire. Nothing less than a grand realignment of the cosmos could possibly account for the unlikely shift in her fortunes. They agreed to meet near the Ferris wheel and settled on a time.

Jodie would finally have what she thought of as her first date with Clara Lee.

Stuart Walker headed in their direction, his swagger leading his way. Jodie watched Clara Lee and wanted to believe she read annoyance in the slight resistance of Clara Lee's body at his approach.

"Come on, baby." His tone carried ownership, and he gave Jodie a hard look. "Unless you'd rather be seen hanging out with weird gal, here."

Clara Lee looked to Jodie with something like an apology, but she still walked away with Stuart, his arm firmly around her waist.

Jodie watched from a safe distance as the light-hearted crowd moved with the certainty of a river current toward the carnival's entry gate. Opening night, and she'd spent the day wrestling with her angst as to whether or not Clara Lee would show. She'd refused Silas's invitation, telling him she hated the noise and smell of fairs and had other plans. When he pushed her, she lied, saying she was going to the drive-in movie.

In conjunction with opening night, Red had arranged for an assemblage of home-bred musical groups, and each took their turn performing on a flatbed Red bargained from the owner of the local feed and grain by heralding the benefits of free advertising to a man who had no competition.

His rallies were popular with locals, and he claimed that free food and toe-tapping music persuaded the gullible to hear more promise in the words of politicians than they ever intended to deliver. He set events up so local politicians got their crack at the crowd between musical sets, and in that way the entire shindig was paid for by obliging traffickers in illegal liquor, gambling, and prostitution. Red joked that it was smarter for the poor to sell their vote rather than squandering it on empty promises. The secret ballot made any double-cross profitable.

Jodie crouched behind a vehicle, her attention focused on the approach of the carnival rover. He drew nearer, his muscled arms the size of stovepipes, and he wore a full black beard. He patrolled the flagged rope that encircled the midway, his target gate crashers like her. He twirled a three-foot baton, and Jodie imagined he enjoyed the authority it afforded him. Still, she considered those who paid the fifty-cent entry fee suckers. The carnies would get plenty of her hard-earned savings once she was inside. She got lower, the knees of her new blue jeans soaking up the fresh night dew. She held her breath waiting for him to pass.

He stopped, pulled a half-pint bottle from his hip pocket, clamped the cork between his teeth. She was close enough that she heard the gurgling sound he made downing the whiskey. He slipped the bottle into his pocket, slapped the baton against his palm, and squinted in her direction. She tried making herself smaller, but doing so would mean she'd need to disappear.

Terrifying screams erupted from those slung into space by the centrifugal force of the Hurricane, splitting the brightly lit night like a warning. Sweat ran along her temples, and Jodie began to second-guess her will to defy. Still she stayed down.

Perhaps satisfied there were no rope jumpers further down the line, the rover turned and walked back in the direction he'd come. Jodie exhaled but stayed put, watching his back until she felt sure his reversal wasn't a trick to draw would-be gate crashers from hiding.

Convinced, she crept beneath the rope and scurried onto the midway from the position of the last gaming stall. Its attendant was busy stealing dimes from a wad of giggling boys attempting to hook yellow rubber ducks to win big-bosomed Kewpie doll showgirls.

The midway was a kaleidoscope of color, tinny music, and the aroma of fried foods. Jodie was hit with a strong whiff of the pitiful menagerie of caged animals: a pacing black bear, a pair of disgusting baboons picking at each other's genitals, and an aging male lion. Jodie drew near the lion's cage, and the animal raised its massive head, its matted mane tangled and grey. He seemed sad and compliant, bearing no resemblance to the mighty beast he was born to be, and Jodie felt a strong urge to comfort him.

"Do that, and Brutus will make you supper." The warning came from a boy only slightly older than her. He was dressed in a threadbare costume of red balloon britches and a black embroidered vest over a tattered shirt. He sat astride a hobbled camel, a needless whip in his hand.

As she walked further along the midway, the clamoring of men and boys caught her ears and she slowed. A stooped man, his skin pitted, barked the marvels of nature's most wondrous freaks: a genuine two-headed chicken, a sow with three rows of twelve teats each, and a six-hundred-pound woman in the raw. Rattled by the unbridled glee of those jostling to be among the first to witness nature's handiwork gone mad, Jodie shivered at the thought of what these men and boys might pay to gawk at a queer girl.

She rushed along the midway toward the soothing sounds of children riding brightly painted ponies. What Jodie needed was to find Clara Lee and be reassured that she waited for her. She rushed in the direction of the Ferris wheel.

"Damn her," Jodie muttered aloud and pulled up abruptly. What she saw was Clara Lee with Stuart Walker. Her anger flashed like a gasoline fire, and although she wanted to choke the smugness from Stuart Walker's face, it wasn't as though she had suitor's rights, only Clara Lee's broken promise.

As she watched Clara Lee, Jodie couldn't be sure he wasn't forcing his attention. He was laughing, maybe bullying her toward the Tilt-A-Whirl. His two lackeys, Billy and Jake Timmins, snickered right on cue.

"Hey, what are you doing here? Thought you weren't coming." The agitated voice at her elbow belonged to Silas.

"No, I said I wasn't coming with you." Jodie continued to watch Clara Lee sidestepping Stuart Walker's attention. Her frustration mounted and her muscles grew spastic from holding back.

Silas followed her hot glare. "Damned if that rich boy don't mean to pop that sweet cherry." Silas hooked his thumbs in his belt loops and Jodie knew he'd given the same lust plenty of thought.

"Damn your ass straight into hell, Silas." She'd loved and hated him in the same breath for so long that her emotions kept them both off balance.

"Whoa down, girl. You're not her mama, now are you?"

"No, but I figure to even things up a bit." She decided Clara Lee wasn't with Stuart, and had intended to wait for her. "That is, unless you've grown squeamish. Too afraid to spend a night in Daddy Walker's jail."

Silas grinned, and for the moment she was back to loving him.

"My lead or yours?" The skin beneath his eyes quivered a bit and she remembered old scores between Silas and Stuart Walker, and wondered how far settling up might push Silas.

"All right, you take the lead."

He nodded, and they walked toward the sound of Stuart's come-on and Clara Lee's weak resistance.

"Howdy, Stuart. You boys having fun?" Silas balanced on the balls of his feet before settling into the stupid hip hitch thing he did. With his bright yellow hair swept back in a ducktail, he looked more like a pale Woody Woodpecker than James Dean.

"What's it to you, Mister One-in-Three."

Ouch! Jodie frowned. Stuart had landed a gut punch. The football team's start was nothing if not miserable, and Silas could get down on himself by shouldering too much of the blame.

"Plenty, since it's your candy ass collecting splinters on the bench." Silas turned his hard stare on the brothers, and they stepped back. As quarterback of even a losing team, Silas had clout.

Clara Lee looked to Jodie, her eyes weepy, and Jodie stepped forward, bumping her way between Clara Lee and Stuart.

"Damned if it ain't the Amazon freak." Stuart looked Jodie over in the nasty way he had, but when she stared down at his crotch without flinching, he looked back at Silas. "She what you've got as backup?" He glanced at his boys, who gave him half-assed grins but stayed where they were.

"Truth is, Stew Meat," Silas lingered over the hated nickname like it was nine inches long, "you might say I'm tagging with her. She's short on warning. Just comes on you like a pissed off cottonmouth."

"Screw you." Stuart lowered his voice, likely not wanting to attract more attention from the carnival goers who had slowed, their interest pricked.

A devilish grin spread over Silas's sweaty face, and Jodie realized he was about to get really playful. Slipping her hand into her pocket, she tightened her fingers around the smoothness of her knife, the same knife that had once before delivered her from evil.

"Damnit, Jodie, you promised to keep that pig sticker out of this. Give me a chance to reason with these boys before you set about castrating."

"Shit, what's the point unless I get a little blood on my blade?" Jodie experienced a quick shot of adrenaline, momentarily finding the best of her Wonder Woman, her strength expanding in rhythm with her challenge, and it felt as good as any memory.

Clara Lee moaned, "Oh, Jodie, please don't make trouble." She moved nearer to Silas.

Stuart's eyes stretched to the size of half dollars, his round cheeks flushed. The hollow-heads stepped further away, and Jake's big hand flew to cover what Jodie imagined were his shriveled balls.

"Now, Jodie, stop and think. Are you ready to live with these town folk pouring out of them titty shows to watch you carve up old Stew? Personally, I think he's got it coming." He turned to Stuart, his voice dropping. "It's your call, Stew. God knows, I've tried."

"You damn crazy bastard. I don't fight girls." Stuart's demeanor, stripped of its earlier bluster, carried the full weight of his defeat.

"I'm hearing you say she's back to being a regular girl? That's quick thinking. Oh, but Cinderella boy, I want you on your knees." Silas glanced about at those who'd stopped. "Begging apologies right here before the good citizens of Catawba."

Stuart stood motionless, as if rooted to the ground, and in that instant Jodie remembered the hobbled camel and the boy's pointless whip. She was satisfied to have shown Clara Lee that she'd stand up to bullies, but Silas wanted more. He wanted to humiliate Stuart Walker. Not for what he'd done alone, but for who he was.

Jodie placed a hand on Silas's forearm. His skin was hot and his muscles tense. "That'll do, Silas."

Silas looked at her and then at Stuart. "Get, boy, while the getting's good."

Stuart turned away from Silas's murderous glare, quickly disappearing among the sights and sounds of the crowded midway.

Silas leaned, his hands resting on his knees, and moaned. "Jesus, I wanted to hurt him. And I wanted to hurt him bad."

Jodie nodded. "I know. But you didn't." His tension lessened, he straightened, and she studied his drawn face. What she believed she saw was confusion, but maybe shame as well.

"Oh, Silas, I'm so sorry to have been the cause of such trouble." Clara Lee placed a lingering hand on Silas's forearm and he blinked hard. His male sap rose, hastening his recovery.

"Aw, forget it, Clara Lee." He exhaled and squared his shoulders. "It's not like you can help being the prettiest darn girl in the county. Maybe even the entire state of Florida." Delivered with less than his normal bluster, his flattery still brought a cherry-red blush to Clara Lee's cheeks. Jodie shot Silas a look to kill. But he was much too busy wooing Clara Lee to notice.

"What do ya'll say we give that bad boy there a test run?" Silas nodded toward the Tilt-A-Whirl and pulled three quarters from his pocket.

Clara Lee looked to Jodie with new found excitement. "That would be great fun. Wouldn't it, Jodie?"

"If Mister Big Britches wants to throw his money away, then I'd be a fool to stop him." She rammed her hands into her pockets and glared at Silas.

He frowned. "What's wrong? I thought …."

"Nothing, that's what." He was no better than Stuart.

She followed Silas and Clara Lee onto the Tilt-A-Whirl. Silas squeezed in between her and Clara Lee, and just like that she was back to hating him.

# Catawba Florida - November 1955

## Thirteen

Jodie stopped on the sidewalk outside the A&P and stared in disbelief at the poster taped to its door. Did she dare believe her own eyes? The so-called famous Texas Cowgirls basketball team, featuring ten of the tallest, most beautiful redheads Jodie had never imagined, was coming to Catawba. Did these women truly play full-court basketball against men and beat them eighty percent of the time?

She'd played varsity basketball since ninth grade and piled up better numbers in points scored and rebounds than any player on the boys' team. Since her play was against girls, her record was simply dismissed, while the county weekly touted Silas as a dribbling, passing, and scoring machine.

Girls' games were considered amusement for the fans arriving and settling in before the boys' games. No one seemed troubled that the assigned male coach spent the second half of the girls' games in the boys' locker room to assist in readying the boys to play.

Red had always arrived for the tipoff of her games and had not stayed for the boys' games. He never spoke of finding fault with how things were, but she chose to believe his leaving was a form of silent protest. When Silas complained of Red's slight, she'd shown him his picture in the local paper. Because he was the only one who said it was unfair that her picture never got in the paper, she worked at not ripping the paper to shreds.

Jodie sighed and stomped away, deciding these women were not for real, but only pretended to play—were laughingstocks. She'd heard enough of that crudeness. She refused to pay good money to hear more.

But wait, fool, she reasoned. What if the Cowgirls were for real? Did she dare risk missing her one chance to watch these women play? She'd buy a sucker's ticket and take her chance. She could always walk out.

She ran back to the store, glanced up and down the block, and noted that the store clerk was occupied slicing bacon while gossiping with a customer. Jodie eased the door open, reached a hand inside, and ripped down the poster. Her loot concealed under her shirt, she ran.

The night of the game, Jodie walked into the packed gym, bursting with noisy excitement. She looked for Clara Lee among those crowded onto the top bleachers and glanced about for Stuart Walker, relieved to find him nowhere in sight. Clara Lee, wearing the pink sweater Jodie liked, stood and waved.

The rumble at the fair had put an end to Stuart's public bullying, but not his pursuit of Clara Lee. He'd gotten way smarter: he now bargained his family's wealth and social position with Clara Lee's status-conscious parents. They were now invited to social events at the plantation-style home of Judge and Mrs. Walker, Stuart's grandparents. Pressure from her mother meant Clara Lee wore Stuart's class ring on a gold chain around her neck. When Clara Lee was with Jodie, she slipped his ring into her purse, and they pretended she wore the ring Jodie hadn't been able to afford.

Out on the court, a team of Catawba's best former high school stars horsed around, taking wild shots, playing to the crowd's smug certainty of their victory. Yet the uniforms of the players were drenched in sweat and, in spite of their clowning, Jodie sensed they were nervous.

"Hey, Jodie, what's so funny?" Clara Lee looked around.

"You'll see soon enough." She took the seat next to Clara Lee, their thighs intentionally touching.

"Did you get the car?" Clara Lee blushed.

"Said I would, didn't I?" Jodie wished the anticipated pleasure of being with Clara Lee in the back seat of Red's Dodge didn't always make her feel lightheaded. Clara Lee had allowed their kisses, and tonight she'd promised more.

"Mother thinks I'm going to the Dairy Queen afterwards with Stuart."

"If that's what you want, I can't stop you." She hated the sound of his name in Clara Lee's mouth. There was something troubling in the way Clara Lee bitched about having to see him while arching her back and thrusting her breasts forward the way she did just now.

"No, Jodie. You know it isn't. Why are you always so jealous? It isn't as though I can tell Mother the truth about us. Please don't be mad."

The heat of Clara Lee pressed against her was too much. "Okay, okay, but don't talk to me about him. Not now or ever. I don't want everything spoiled."

It was true that Clara Lee couldn't tell her mother about what they did whenever they were alone. But why not stop pretending? Give that dickhead, Stuart, back his damn ring and tell him to his face that he should peddle his family's money and reputation elsewhere.

Clara Lee didn't have the nerve to stand up to her mother, and that bothered Jodie. In her most judicious moments, she feared Clara Lee didn't have what it took to be full-time queer. Unlike Clara Lee, Jodie accepted being queer. She was all in, and for her there was no taking it back.

Jodie leaned forward in her seat, and what she heard and saw made her eyes sting with more than excitement. Male dominance in the game of basketball was about to be tested, and Jodie Taylor would be a witness to its demise.

The loudspeaker blasted "Orange Blossom Special" in breakneck tempo as ten redheaded wonder women ran onto the court. In addition to their flaming hair, the women wore boleros, western hats, and holstered pistols over their skimpy uniforms. Jodie swelled with newfound pride, feeling as though she, too, took the floor to the jeers of the crowd.

On the other end of the court, the men watched, jaws dropped, as the women shed an article of western fashion with each spectacular shot. The stunned crowd sucked the air from the gym and exhaled in unison, the place exploding in wild cheering. Jodie stood with the crowd, her eyes filling with tears. No doubt these women were physical marvels—but would they play?

By the end of the third quarter, the men's team was up fifteen points on the Cowgirls. Jodie's earlier hopes had sunk with each uncontested layup, and when the taunting began, she thought about leaving. But she worked to push her doubts to the outer edge and wished for a miracle.

At the start of the fourth quarter, Jodie saw the big center signal the team, and the Cowgirls picked up their defense to a mind-boggling level, getting turnovers and storming back on fast breaks, demonstrating incredible stamina and skill. The shocked men lagged, stopping to grab the cuffs of their shorts on each made Cowgirl shot. They could only watch as the women closed out the game, dribbling and passing the ball to open shooters who made shots Jodie had never imagined possible. They soundly whipped the exhausted and humiliated men by eighteen points.

The dumbfounded crowd filed out of the gym, some shaking their heads in amazement while others claimed the Cowgirls were men dressed as women. Others mocked the women as freaks of nature, and Jodie swore she'd never again succumb to the false notion that strong women were not true women but nature's botched creation. Her proudest moments came from the bitterly angry, who mumbled *damn queers*. She prayed it was true.

"Jodie, come on. We have to go. Stuart's walking this way," Clara Lee pleaded.

"Yeah, okay, in a minute." Jodie watched until the last woman ran off the court, ignoring Clara Lee's urging, savoring the sweetest moment of her life.

"Jodie, aren't you coming?" Clara Lee's impatience grew, but Jodie had made a decision.

"You go ahead." She didn't know how to tell her, or even how to go about doing, what she was thinking, but she was sure it was her only shot.

"Go without you?" Clara Lee's mouth set in a hard pout.

"Please, I've got to do this thing. Can't you just wait in the car for me?"

"But, do what? Where are you going?"

Stuart Walker crossed the gym floor on forbidden street shoes, and he called to Clara Lee.

"Jodie Taylor, you come with me now … or I swear I'll go with him." She reached into her purse, and maybe she searched for his ring.

"I can't, Clara Lee." Jodie leaped down the bleachers and headed for the women's locker room. She'd patch things up later.

She stationed herself outside the locker room door, and within the hour, the door pushed open. The team's center and best player emerged. She'd shed her uniform, and her face was wiped clean, her hair in a ponytail. She wore jeans and a red team tee. Jodie approached and opened her mouth, but none of the smart words she'd practiced came out.

"Hey, sugar. You enjoy the game?" The big woman looked Jodie over, not in the way she was accustomed to, but in a way that made her proud.

"Yes'm, I sure did. I've never seen anything like you ladies. Your playing, I mean. I'm going to learn that fade-away hook shot." She wanted to speak the lingo, impress the star. One big woman to another.

"Where'd you get all them pretty black curls?"

"The black is surely from my mama. And, uh, the curls … I'm not all that sure." She shrugged, "Daddy, I think. That's if he's really my daddy." Jodie felt the back of her neck burn, and she stared at her high-tops.

"Had me one of those daddies. But my hair's out of a bottle." She laughed easily.

"I want to join up. Be a Cowgirl … for real, I mean. Don't wear makeup, but I would if that's what it takes. Anything to be one of you." She thought about the skimpy uniforms and swallowed hard.

"You're a little young, aren't you?"

"No. I'm seventeen, but easily pass for older."

"You any good?"

"Yes'm, the best. Around here anyway." If tooting her own horn was what it took, she'd do that too.

"That right?" That her tone wasn't mean gave Jodie courage.

"I know you've gotta hear that a lot. But I'm not blowing smoke up … ah, hell. I mean, I'm sorry. Guess I'm too nervous to make sense." Jodie stood like the fool she was.

"What did you say your name is?"

"Jodie. Jodie Taylor."

"Well, Jodie Taylor, why not take that big foot out of your mouth and let's go back in the gym. Show me what you've got."

"Yes'm. You bet." Her throat swelled with all the tears she swallowed. Her world had spun about, and every wrong she'd ever felt got itself righted.

She took to the court, fixed her sight on the rim, and drove hard to her right hand. In the blink of an eye, the lane closed, and she extended straight into the big woman's armpit. Her thunderous block sent the ball flying out of Jodie's hand and into the bleachers.

Jodie scraped her injured pride off the floor, and someone tossed her the ball. She walked to center court, gritted her teeth, and again dribbled hard to the basket. When she sensed the big woman's powerful body coming strong to her right hand, she cross-dribbled to her left and the path to the rim opened, not like the Red Sea, only barely enough. She laid a sweet spin off the board at a perfect angle. The ball dropped through the net, and cheers rang out from other players who'd drifted into the gym. Jodie felt her knees give a bit, but she stayed upright.

The big woman slapped her on the back. "Damn, Jodie Taylor. I do believe you've got game."

Jodie gushed, "Then you're saying I'm good ... good enough?"

The woman sighed, stepped back cradling the ball on her hip bone. "You're good, kid." She paused, shifted her weight, and added, "Maybe even good enough. But the odds of you making it ... well, that's a long shot."

"Yes'm, I get that and I thank you for your time." Jodie turned to walk away, fearing if she tried to say more, she'd go sissy, embarrass herself further. She felt the pain of every time she'd had to hear "not good enough."

"Jodie, hold up."

Jodie turned back.

Lou Palmer reached into her back pocket and handed Jodie a tiny card. "Should you ever get to Dallas, look me up."

Because there was no one to share her triumph, Jodie sat alone in the Dodge, and from the glow of the dashboard lights, she read over and over the business card clutched in her hand. Someday she'd play for the Cowgirls.

# Catawba Florida - June 1956

## Fourteen

The mid-day heat had sucked the last of the overnight relief from the tiny bedroom, and Jodie, stripped to her underpants and a white tee, kicked at the limp sheet entangling her long legs. A slow smile formed on her lips as she remembered.

Tonight, she and Clara Lee would graduate from high school, Clara Lee as valedictorian, Jodie distinguished only by her height, second to Alfred, a gangly boy of odd proportions. Her first pair of glaring white pumps, a formidable dare to her clumsiness, teased her from atop the chifforobe. The white cap and too-short gown hung from a door nail.

A timid knock signaled Hazel's dutiful summons, and she called through the closed door. "Mama says you're to get your trifling ass out of bed." Giggling, she whispered, "Her words, not mine."

"You can tell her I'm not picking peas today." Jodie had long suspected that Hazel got off on repeating their insults.

"I bet you're doing that nasty thing." Hazel whispered.

"And you'd better not bring your hoity-toityness in here. It's catching, you know."

"Oh ... you're ... you're a sinner, Jodie Taylor. And God punishes the wicked." Her footsteps sounded her rapid retreat.

Jodie smiled, picturing Hazel's pudgy cheeks burning with forbidden excitement. She flipped onto her back and stared at the stained ceiling, a canvas of overlapping water marks, her thoughts turning to those she was never completely without—her impending escape with Clara Lee.

By summer's end they would have earned enough money to buy bus tickets out of Catawba to Dallas, where she believed a spot on the Cowgirls' basketball team awaited her. There, they were certain to find other girls they'd dare to trust with their secret.

She drew the pillow between her legs and drifted into a dream-filled sleep, only to be jarred awake by the deep-throated roar of Clara Lee's mama's big Buick. At first she believed it was part of her dream, for neither she nor Clara Lee ever visited the other. Their love was a secret from everyone.

She hurried to the window and peered out toward the road.

"Holy shit." The Buick was coming, and coming fast, Clara Lee behind the steering wheel. It could only mean trouble, but of what stripe?

Jodie pulled on yesterday's jeans, grabbed a cleaner shirt from the bedpost, and scrubbed the night sweaters from her teeth with her finger. She retrieved her high-tops and sweat-stiffened socks from beneath the bed and ran to answer the urgent rattling of the screen door.

Clara Lee stood on the opposite side, her eyes beet red, and she wore yesterday's wrinkled white blouse, its row of tiny pearl buttons unevenly matched.

"Oh God, Jodie, we have to talk." Her words were barely audible between deep sobs.

"Okay. But tell me what's wrong." Jodie pushed open the door and reached for Clara Lee's hand, but she stepped back, clutching her slender white throat. Right away, Jodie noticed Clara Lee was back to wearing Stuart's ring rather than her heart-shaped necklace.

"What's with that damn ring?"

"Jodie. Don't you see? None of that matters anymore."

"No, I don't. Tell me. Whatever it is, I promise we can fix it."

"Please, don't argue. You're making everything harder." She turned and walked off the porch, straight to the car, and got behind the steering wheel.

Jodie's temples pounded and her head felt like it would explode. Still, she followed Clara Lee to the car. Clara Lee ground the gear shift into reverse and spun the rear tires through Miss Mary's prized daylilies. She pulled forward, and two sets of car tracks divided the huge bed of hybrids into four sections, two smashed flat on the ground. Jodie glanced toward the pea patch, and Miss Mary was hurrying toward the house, Hazel running ahead.

"Shit, you've plowed up half the yard."

"I'm sorry, but I can't worry about that."

Clara Lee drove the sedan onto the county road, rapidly gaining speed, her reckless driving propelling the car back and forth over the center line.

"First the flowers, and now you're set on killing us."

"I can't talk now." The car accelerated. The roadside a blur.

"Okay, okay. But you've gotta slow down." Jodie stared ahead, swallowing her anxiety until her belly swelled.

Clara Lee turned onto the narrow logging road that led to their secret place. When she reached the high bluff overlooking the sluggish river, she pulled the car to a quick stop.

Clara Lee turned to Jodie and whispered, "Jodie, Mama knows." She buried her damp face in the curve of Jodie's neck.

"Knows? Knows what? That you've lied about being with me?" While imagining the worst, Jodie sought a lesser threat.

"No," Clara Lee whimpered. "She knows what we do." Clara Lee's terror reverberated against Jodie's collarbone, her fear contagious.

Still Jodie managed, "Hell, no. She's bluffing. How could she?"

"No, it's true. And it's my fault."

"How's it your fault?"

"Mother asked questions about the necklace."

"What kind of questions?"

"At first I lied. Said it was a gift from Stuart."

Jodie felt her blood start to boil.

"I thought that would satisfy her. Make her happy."

"And?"

"I know we promised to never keep anything that could be used against us. But I couldn't bear to part with your pretty Christmas card. I was sure Mother would never find it."

The card had accompanied the necklace, and she'd dared to write *My Love Forever* and sign her name. Jodie felt as though her windpipe had shattered, and she struggled to breathe.

"Please say you don't hate me."

Regaining her breath, she forced her words. "No, I could ... never hate you." Didn't they have every right to hold onto scraps of paper that had passed between them? "But we've got to know what she means to do next."

"She said that if I ever again as much as speak to you, she'll tell my father everything. Oh, Jodie, I'd die if he knew."

Her father was a damn bank clerk. What made him so special? Then, he wasn't their immediate problem. Jodie sat apart from Clara Lee. Clear thinking was hard with her so close.

Clara Lee watched her. "What are you thinking?"

"That she won't tell. And that we're okay. But we've got to leave Catawba. We'll drive to Panama City, get the first bus out. From now on she'll be watching our every move. If we don't go now, we'll never get away."

"But Mama says we're an abomination. And our leaving won't change that. I'm so afraid." She looked beyond Jodie as though God hovered nearby.

"You've got to forget all that Bible bullshit." It was unfair that she'd dealt God into the mix, like some ace in the hole.

"But Mother said …."

"Stop and think. God's got a shitload of troubles. Starving kids in Africa. Lepers. Hurricanes. Famines. North Korea. He doesn't give a rat's puny ass about two ... *homosexuals* in Catawba, Florida." She used the word they'd only recently learned from the school's main dictionary.

Clara Lee blinked hard, as though she'd heard something she could accept. Maybe she favored *homosexual* over *abomination*.

Still, she asked, "But how can you be so sure?"

"I don't know. I just am." It was somewhat more settling to know a smart word.

"Holy shit. Wait a damn minute." All of a sudden the word wadded in Jodie's craw like yesterday's oatmeal, and she remembered the dictionary's directive to *see mental illness*. In her way of thinking, being called crazy was a far more immediate threat than God's abomination. But who had the legal say in questions of *homosexuals*?

"What? You're confusing me."

"If we're fruitcakes? And we stay here? Sheriff Walker can lock us away in Chattahoochee. He's the one we've got to stay in front of." She meant to scare Clara Lee into leaving before she could argue the finer points of such a plan.

Clara Lee gasped. "He'd never do such a thing."

"Maybe you've got a bargaining chip with Walker Junior's old man, but I sure as hell don't."

She pulled Clara Lee into her arms, intending a Wonder Woman kiss that would erase both their fears. Instead, their front teeth banged, and Clara Lee recoiled.

"But what about my valedictory speech? I've work so hard."

"Damn, Clara Lee. It's a twenty-minute speech to a bunch of half-wits. What I'm talking about is the rest of our lives."

"Jodie, I can't go with you. I promised Mother I'd get engaged. Marry Stuart, if it comes to that." She pressed her palms to her face and sobbed.

Caught between her mother's anger and her own failure of will, Clara Lee had surrendered. Jodie held her breath against her anguish and realized she was once again alone. She threw herself against the car door and ran from the sound of Clara Lee calling her name.

Reaching the main road, Jodie lay hidden in the underbrush and watched as the big Buick passed and disappeared into the blinding sunlight. She was certain Clara Lee's mother would find a way to spare her daughter's sterling reputation, but her own transgressions would give Miss Mary the leverage she sought, that which would surely force Red to choose. She wouldn't stay and suffer his choice.

# Fifteen

Jodie walked the blistering asphalt, trying to imagine her next move without Clara Lee. She failed to notice the approaching car until the driver slowed and pulled to a stop next to her. Roy Dale Pitts leaned through the open window of an ancient Hudson Commodore, but Jodie walked on.

"Whoa down there, gal. Where 'bouts you headed in this heat?" He propped a sunburned arm on the metal window frame, then drew back, swearing.

"Where I'm going's not one bit your business, now is it?" Jodie kept walking and he followed.

"All right, Miss High and Mighty Jodie *Taylor*. No skin off my nose if you die of a heat stroke. Then, that'd be a pity since I'm going right by Mr. Red's." He grinned like the fool she remembered from junior high.

She didn't like that he'd slurred her surname; too much of a claim of peas from the same pod. She remembered him: dull as a butter knife, known to be a self-made loser, a sure-fired bust at all things requiring steady doses of brains and sweat. He'd dropped out of school the year she'd passed to senior high. Then, it didn't take much schooling to be Roy Dale Pitts.

"Last chance. I got way better things to do than worry about your sassy ass." He raced the engine, his foot riding the brake, playing her.

"You can forget the ride. But I'll take water if you got any."

"Nope, but I got a real cold beer." He gave her a cunning look.

It was five long miles to Red's, and on top of hot and thirsty, she felt so rotten that she set aside knowing better. Let him think what he would. She got into his car and gulped what turned out to be lukewarm beer.

When they reached the lane he slowed the car, looked over, and winked. "What you say to me and you taking a little ride? Finish off them beers. Have us a little homemade fun."

She shrugged, and he couldn't know it wasn't his promise of a good time that made up her mind, but rather the sight of Miss Mary and Hazel stooped, rows of unpicked peas stretched before them. She wouldn't open herself up for more misery, not now, not after losing Clara Lee.

He drove them to Scott's Ferry Landing, twelve miles west of Catawba, and they sat on a downed bay magnolia beneath the shade of a water oak. Behind them, dark clouds were building toward an afternoon thunderstorm, and the air was stifling.

She sat in silence while he lied about one stupid boy stunt after another, and they finished off the remaining beers. He seemed to figure his beer had earned him the right to meddle, because he asked what had her hot-footing it along the county road when he happened along.

"Not that it's any of your business, but I'm headed to Dallas." The beer had loosened her tongue, but no amount of beer could cause her to say why she travelled alone.

"Dallas? You're messing with me, right? What's Dallas got that here don't?"

"Less of here and more of there."

Roy Dale couldn't have pointed out Dallas on a map of the United States, but his eyes lit up like Times Square, which she knew was not in Texas but New York City.

A flash of lightening, followed by a sudden downpour, forced them back into the car where water dripped around the dash and onto the floorboard. Mosquitoes swarmed against the roof, and Roy Dale bragged that he'd burned his last mosquito coil while screwing Bonnie White.

"Hear she'd give it up for a Tootsie Roll. Must have cost you an even dozen."

He laughed as if he thought she meant to slur Bonnie.

Jodie stared through the fogged window and felt an odd kinship in the way he deflected her insult. Roy Dale had clearly had his own lessons in dodging sticks and stones.

"Shit, girl, let's me and you go. Nothing here to hold me. My mama's the only family who'd notice."

"Roy Dale, they likely don't grub earthworms in Texas. What other line of work you got, besides that and stocking shelves at the A&P?"

"Don't, but I'll figure something out. You'll see."

The river's cypress-stained waters had turned from the color of day old sweet tea to a dull green. The last of the hurried fishermen slid their boats into the beds of idling pickups and hastened to tie down bundles of fishing poles before making wild dashes. The boat landing was steep and slicker than boiled okra when wet. Roy Dale had wisely parked on the river's bluff.

Jodie stared at the rain pelting the river like tiny silver bullets, twisting her thoughts, and what she said next surprised her as much as it did him.

"Okay, by damn. I'll do it."

"You mean it?"

"Said so, didn't I? But you've got to know I wouldn't be caught dead with you on the road if I wasn't desperate for a ride out of here."

In the moments that followed, it took all the grit she could muster not to back out. But she'd always been more stubborn than smart. Roy Dale cocked his head, as though he was making sure in his own mind what she meant to place off limits. Whatever he thought, he kept between his ears.

"Gal, we're as good as gone." He started the engine and they headed back in the direction of town.

He stopped at his folks' place first and threw a handful of clothes onto the back seat. When they reached Red's, she directed Roy Dale to stop short of the lane, calculating that Miss Mary and Hazel would be sitting in the kitchen shelling the peas they'd picked. Neither had planned to go to her graduation.

She slipped through the front door and into the bedroom. She poured her savings—from the coffee can she'd hidden between the walls—into the toe of a sock, tied it off, and crammed the sock into her pocket. She packed Jewel's record, her souvenir poster, and the Bible Aunt Pearl had given her, along with jeans, three shirts, socks, and underwear. It would be awkward to carry, but she picked up her basketball and penned it beneath her armpit. She took a last look around the room. There was nothing she'd miss. She had arrived light and would leave the same.

As she eased back through the front parlor, there were muted voices coming from the kitchen, but it was Jewel's voice she heard: *Baby girl, the fat's in the fire now.*

## Sixteen

Roy Dale drove them back into the teeth of the storm and onto Main Street. Suddenly, he swung the car about and backed into the dead-end alley between the A&P and Gaskin's Drugs.

"What the hell?" One more delay and Jodie feared she'd come to her senses and back out altogether.

"Sit tight. Old man Golden owes me wages. I mean to get what I got coming."

He hurried out of the car, grabbed a tire iron from the trunk, forced open the back door of the A&P, and disappeared inside. She picked at a bleeding hangnail, sorting through what he meant.

At the street end of the alley, a car approached, its bright lights reflecting off the rain slick walls. The driver came to a full stop and sounded the horn before moving through the intersection. She exhaled, her hot breath forming a perfect circle of relief on the windowpane.

Roy Dale was a damn fool if he thought his declared intention would cut it with the law, and her staying in the car made her an even bigger fool. He'd land his puny ass in the slammer, and if she was to avoid the Ocala Reformatory for Girls, she'd need to drag his pokey ass back through that busted door before it was too late.

Grabbing the door handle, she laid a shoulder into the frame, and in that instant a crash of lightening split the sky like an executioner's axe, the alley flashing a bluish-white light. Her scalp tingled and the trapped air in the Hudson smelled scorched.

The sound of heavy boots sucking mud grew loud behind her and she turned to see Roy Dale. He was high-stepping his way toward the car while stuffing something shiny into his belt. The wet paper bag he clutched ripped apart, spilling Tom's peanuts, Juicy Fruit gum, and assorted candy bars onto the ground. He crouched, stared at the busted sack, his mouth forming curse words, then he slogged on toward the car. He snatched open the door, jammed his boney hip hard against her shoulder and shouted for her to move over. Rainwater poured through the open door and her instincts told her she was about to be sucked along by an undertow not entirely of her making.

"Drive, damnit." He leaned, inches from her face, his eyes stretched wide in his ghostly pale face. Droplets of rainwater ran along his temples and dripped off the beak of his nose. He was soaked through to his skin and he reeked.

Caught up in his panic, she turned the ignition key. The engine caught, sputtered, and died. "Carburetor's flooded."

"No, stomp it. Stomp it harder."

The engine roared and she ground the gear into first, the car jerking forward. The front tires slammed hard onto Main Street, and she pointed the hood ornament toward the town's single traffic light, swaying in the wind like a tethered ball, blinking its amber caution. Through chattering teeth, she asked for directions.

"Haul ass out of here." His high-pitched tone was chased by crazed laughter, and he slid something under the edge of the passenger seat before flipping onto his knees and grabbing a dry shirt from the pile he'd stashed earlier. He wiped his face and arms, shivering.

The wiper blades squeaked with each pass, and she strained to gain a guiding glimpse of the center line. He dropped onto the seat, yammering that her pussy driving would get their asses snagged.

"What's the hurry? There's no crime in our leaving." She squinted at him, but there was nothing in his paddle-shaped face but a mix of fear and excitement. She knew if she could see her own face, it would look the same.

"Yeah, you're right. Two losers ain't a loss." His right eyelid fluttered, and she hated that he was more right than wrong.

By the time they had crossed into the neighboring county, they had outdistanced the westernmost reaches of the storm, and Roy Dale's earlier hype had gone the way of a slow tire leak. He retrieved a quart jar of 'shine from beneath the seat, taking a long pull. He squeezed his eyes shut and shuddered, then pushed the jar toward her. When she waved it off, he screwed the lid down tight, shoved the jar back under the seat, and settled his long frame, all the time bragging on the roomy, step-down body of the old Hudson. Folding his thin arms across his sunken chest, he laid his head back, his oily hair damp and matted, and in no time he slept. A perfect picture of what Maggie would have called rotten-boy innocence.

Fragments of regret pierced Jodie's thoughts like fine shrapnel, and she doggedly rubbed tears away with a clenched fist. Just how hard would Red search before welcoming the conclusion that she'd left of her own will? His womanizing hadn't started with her mama, nor had it ended with her. Still, Jodie knew the lack of her presence as a daily reminder of his infidelity meant he was certain of an easier go with Miss Mary. Red's serial cheating left the old woman little more than her denial, never mind its hollowness.

Miss Ruth held her worries close, while Maggie raged—swearing and threatening whomever she thought to have dirty hands. Yet Jodie counted on Maggie to know she'd played the hand that was dealt her, and that alone would eventually earn Maggie's forgiveness.

Thoughts of Clara Lee brought wave after wave of pain, and Jodie's chest felt as if it would collapse inwardly upon itself. She gripped the steering wheel tighter and sucked air into her deflated lungs. Pushing upward into a new determination, Jodie swore she'd leave Clara Lee Adams—and her broken promise—behind.

Then, Silas was a much harder worry.

Roy Dale stirred, glanced at her, and retrieved the jar. He tilted it, whiskey dribbling from the corners of his mouth. He wiped it away on the sleeve of his shirt and resettled.

She remembered the summer Silas submitted a story to the publisher of the *Grit* newspaper, believing it was his ticket to a scholarship to the university. He'd met the empty-handed postman daily for the balance of the summer. His dream of college was just that, and nothing more. Then, Silas always had a backup plan. Shade-tree mechanic wasn't Mark Twain, but he'd sworn he'd turn the shed bearing his uncle's name, situated under a huge live oak, into the best auto shop in the county.

He had plotted her future as well as his own. She'd clerk at Gaskin's Drugs until they'd saved enough money to marry. He'd done so in spite of her adamant rejections of his advances, choosing to interpret them as virtue while it was nothing of the sort. He'd planned for the two of them, while she and Clara Lee had plotted their escape.

Now, she rolled westward along a deserted highway with the likes of Roy Dale Pitts, the whole of her plan a destination and a dream. She'd need to take to heart Jewel's notion that regrets stole dreams, and that where she was headed, a belly full of stoked fury would serve her better. Still, she wished she'd taken time to say a few good-byes.

Roy Dale sat upright, squinting as though trying to remember why he agreed to leave town on nothing more than her exaggeration. If he wasn't, then he was a bigger fool than she remembered.

He wallowed his tongue across his yellow-stained teeth, his liquored breath foul.

"What's the time? Where the hell are we?"

"Hour hand there on that clock is stuck. My best guess is about eight, maybe earlier." She wasn't sure where they were, but she'd driven in the direction of Mobile. She'd pick up a road map on their first stop, but for now, she'd follow the swirling glow of headlights west along Highway 98.

Roy Dale slammed the dashboard a hard blow with his fist; the minute hand dropping, both hands now settled on six.

"Damn this piece of junk. If I'd known, I would've stolen us something better."

"What the hell? You said it was yours." She let up on the accelerator and glared at him.

"It was fixing to be till you showed up." His right eye fluttered, and she now knew it was a dead giveaway. Her gullibility was about to suffer yet another spike.

"I was headed back from what you might call a test run. Aimed to strike a nickel down and nickel a week deal with old man Stone when I caught up to you. Hell, you know the rest."

"Jesus, Roy Dale." She was driving a stolen getaway car from what was likely a robbery. While her only crime was grand stupidity.

"Remember, it was you who was hot to trot."

"Did I say steal a car? No, hell, I didn't."

"You're driving. I'm along for the ride." He looked like a slinking dog, caught sucking eggs. "Hell, forget it. Old man Stone's plumb addle-brained. He won't remember diddly-shit."

"And that makes it all right? Damn your rotten hide, Roy Dale."

He shrugged and turned his attention to the radio, running the full band before settling on a station, grinding out blips of "Yakety Yak" between longer runs of static. He pounded the dash in time with the music, and she cringed at Webb Price's rendition of "In the Jailhouse Now."

She didn't feel any better about what Roy Dale had done, but he was right that the old man's pathetic condition went in their favor. What was done was done, and there was no easy way of turning back. Still, she meant to know the full extent of her troubles. She reached across and slapped Roy Dale's shoulder a hard lick.

"Roy Dale, you're coming clean, or I'm wrapping this heap around the nearest light pole." She jerked the steering wheel, the car swerving.

Roy Dale scrambled to right himself, his arms flailing as if he fought off a swarm of pissed off yellow jackets.

"You stole this car and flat out robbed the A&P." From the moment he'd taken the tire iron to the door, she'd known the truth.

He shrugged. "So what if I took a little extra? Stingy Jew bastard never paid me what I was worth."

"If he paid you a cent, he did."

"Are you saying it was right he paid that old blue-eyed sambo more than a white man?" He bristled with what she recognized as a common mix of unfounded pride built on willful ignorance.

"Yeah, I am. Mr. Samuel works hard. Never missed as much as a day."

"You'd be wrong on that. After the dent I put in his wooly head." His eyes flashed mean, and she saw him clearly, and what she saw scared her.

She slammed on the brake and struggled to steer the speeding car onto the rough shoulder. The car slid to a stop, the engine stalling.

"Holy shit. You set on killing us?" He wiped blood on the tail of his shirt from the cut that had opened above his right eye.

"We're turning back to that town we just passed. Find a pay phone. If he's hurt, he'll need help." Jodie felt she might get forgiveness for leaving the wrong way, but not for going on, knowing Mr. Samuel was hurt. She attempted to restart the engine.

"Ah, come on, gal. I didn't hit him that hard. How'd I know that old spook would get between me and the cash box?"

It was like Roy Dale to misunderstand an act of loyalty.

"Reckon I should've used the barrel end." He reached beneath the seat and pulled out a Browning snub-nosed .22-caliber handgun, rusted with age and neglect. "Passed down to my pa from his pa. Mine now, I reckon."

It had been the gun he'd put into his belt as he ran from the store. She'd underestimated Roy Dale Pitts. She grabbed for the door handle, meaning to take her chances at flagging down an approaching vehicle.

He reached, grabbed her hair in his big hand, and snatched her head against his chest. With his sweaty face pressed close, he put the gun to her temple, a nervous laugh on his tight lips. She felt the round coolness against her hot skin, her flesh filling the inside circumference of the barrel. If she gave into her fear, she was certain she'd pass out.

"Listen, and listen smart. What got done back there's on you, same as me. Now drive. The further we get, the less likely the law will come after us."

"All right, but take that gun out of my face. It could go off." He might use it, and if he did, it wouldn't be an accident.

Roy Dale squeezed the back of her neck, and she bristled at the touch of his hot fingers on her skin. When he figured he'd made his point, he let go and looked as if he believed he'd drawn an inside straight. But he was dead wrong.

She restarted the car, drove back onto the highway, and stared into the darkness ahead. She'd need to stop thinking regrets and start thinking smart. The road ahead would be what she made it.

They entered a south Alabama town, a near replica of Catawba, and Jodie searched the street for a cop car. Roy Dale yawned and stretched as though nothing had ever gone wrong in his entire sorry life.

"Pull over at that filling station. My tank's way over on empty. I need to grab a candy bar or two."

Jodie stopped the car at the gas pump. "Send the attendant out."

He nodded toward the restrooms.

"No, you go ahead. I'll wait."

He grabbed the keys from the ignition. "Jingle-jingle, gal. You stay put unless you figure on walking to Dallas."

She showed him submission, the kind she imagined he'd learned to expect from women, while counting on him to still be pumped after his earlier stunt. Roy Dale walked into the station and pointed toward the Hudson. A teenage attendant nodded and headed toward the pump.

Roy Dale walked around the corner of the station toward the bathrooms, and then popped back, a fool kid grin on his ugly face. She expected him to be satisfied with his game of "gotcha," and as soon as he was out of sight, Jodie grabbed her suitcase. She paused to consider her basketball, but decided to leave it behind and take Roy Dale's gun instead. She slipped the gun into her belt, punctured a front tire with her knife, and ran full out into the path of a semi pulling away from the diesel pump.

She waved and shouted at the confused driver. He couldn't possibly hear her over the noise of the engine, but neither could he mistake her panic. She looked back over her shoulder. Roy Dale hadn't emerged from the bathroom, but it wouldn't be long before he discovered her attempt to escape.

The driver brought the tractor to a stop and leaned out the window.

"Little lady, what the hell's got you playing wrinkle-fender with a semi?"

"I've gotta have a ride out of here." She fought back tears.

"I can see that, but that's no good reason for me to break my road rule."

"I'm headed to Dallas, Texas. Trying out with the Cowgirls." There was no recognition in his gathered brow.

"Can't help you, even if I was of a mind to. I'm headed north."

"Don't matter. I mean to go as far as you'll take me. Go on from there."

The driver looked back toward the station where Roy Dale now leaned against the Hudson. He wore the arrogant grin he'd perfected; one that said he considered her shit-out-of-luck with the driver.

"What's that boy to you?" He looked down at her, and only the truth could save her.

"Nothing. A ride, that's all." His question was about ownership; he wasn't a man who'd interfere with another man's rights to a woman.

He looked again at Roy Dale.

"I was traveling with him, and he turned … rough."

"You live around here, do you?"

"No, sir. I'm from Florida." She'd be from anywhere that suited him.

"And does your mama know you're out here thumbing?"

"She died a long time ago." If he didn't shut up with the questions she was sure she'd croak.

"And how old would you be?"

"Twenty, next month." She didn't hesitate. It was a convincing lie, and she felt the driver's disposition shift, like momentum in sports.

Roy Dale must have sensed it as well. His slouched posture coiled into that of a man of action, but he didn't advance.

"Like I said, I don't make a habit of riding gal hitchhikers, but I can't say that I like that feller's manners. Go to the other side and climb in."

She scrambled into the cab ahead of Roy Dale, who was now running flat out toward the semi, shouting and waving the way she had. The driver pulled the semi onto the highway, and Roy Dale leaped back from its path, shaking his big fist in the air. She felt blessed that was all he could do.

The driver stared straight ahead, accelerating and working through the gears, and if he regretted that she'd talked him into breaking his rule, he didn't show it. She watched for Roy Dale through the side mirror, fearing she'd see the Hudson speeding after her.

"Don't worry. No man's willing to tackle a speeding semi. Unless you stole his money. And if you ain't lying about the other, he's got no smart reason to come after you." He squinted over at her and then back at the road.

"Like I said. He's nothing to me. And I'll have you know I'm not a thief or a liar." She guessed that he figured her both. "Okay, so I took his gun. But where I'm going, I might need it."

"Yep, you just might at that. But a little advice."

"What's that?" He was starting to make her squirm.

"Don't point that thing unless you intend to use it. And understand it's a piss-poor excuse for a gun. It's not about to stop something thick as a man with evil intent unless you luck up and hit a vital part."

"I'm not planning on shooting anybody."

"That's likely good. For now, I recommend you take it out of your belt before you shoot yourself another butt hole."

Embarrassed, she nodded. She removed the gun from her belt and put it inside the suitcase, snapping it shut.

Too exhausted for more talk, Jodie stared out the window, and the driver didn't seem to mind. He hummed to himself, doing no more than occasionally glancing in her direction. The trees along the roadside began to blur, and her eyelids drooped.

"If you're a mind to, you can climb back there and pile up a few Zs." He nodded toward the sleeper. "Go on now. But take care you don't piss off that old tom. His name's Buddy Highway, but that don't mean he'll take a shine to you. Then, he'll let you know. He ain't a bit bashful."

She took a bet with fate that she could trust a trucker who rode with a fussy tomcat and climbed into the sleeper. It smelled of old sweat and recent sex, the way Jewel's bed had after one of Red's longer visits. A gray cat opened a lazy yellow eye and closed it without complaint. She took that as a good sign, and she, too, closed her eyes and slept.

Sometime later, she was jarred awake by the pitch of the big rig coming to a full stop. Buddy lifted onto his haunches, blinked hard at her, as though he didn't remember going to bed with a stranger.

"Hey, kid. Here's where you get off," the trucker called to her.

She climbed down from the sleeper and sat rubbing her eyes, her thoughts scattered.

"You're in downtown Selma, Alabama."

"Where?"

"Little darling, Selma ain't the end of the earth, but you can sure make it out from here. If you're hungry, go in there." He pointed to a café. "Ask for Sally. Tell her Buddy sent you. He runs a tab there." He grinned for the first time.

She wasn't sure why she hesitated, just that she did.

"Go on now, girl. I've got a load to drop."

"I'm grateful to Buddy." Most of all, she was grateful to him, but not sure how to thank him for not hitting on her for no reason other than he could. She climbed down out of the truck and reached back for her suitcase.

"You stay low, you hear?"

She watched until the semi rolled through the second traffic light, and although she didn't know the man's name, she felt a strange sense of loss. Her empty belly pinched through to her backbone, and the promise of a free meal had her crossing the street. Whatever awaited her would be easier on a full stomach.

# Selma Alabama - 1956-1963

## Seventeen

Sally, a plump woman Jodie guessed to be in her late forties, didn't ask how she knew Buddy Highway, though the question appeared lodged behind dark eyes that didn't match the dullness of her hair; it was piled high and sprayed into a hardened shell, giving her a rigid yet unsettled presence. She glanced at the suitcase and sighed, then led Jodie to the table nearest the kitchen. Most likely she wasn't the first girl to arrive hungry, carrying a battered suitcase.

"Where you headed, shug?" Her curiosity was laced with pity, and Jodie considered walking out. But her rumbling belly trumped her pride.

"Dallas, Texas, ma'am." Her sagging confidence rallied at the sound of certainty in her own voice. Maybe she'd arrived in Selma through ill-fortune, but she had a plan for moving on. She wanted Sally to know that she was no hard-luck case.

"All right then, what're you gonna have?"

Jodie liked that Sally's earlier hint of pity was somewhat tempered, although her doubts may have lingered.

"I'll have a cheeseburger, double fries, large fountain co-cola, and a piece of that lemon pie." The thought of food had caused her to drool.

"Lord, child." Sally laughed. "It's eight o'clock in the morning."

Unlikely or not, Sally called across the café to a colored man the size of a bear, his hair big as a smutty wash pot.

"Arthur, give me a cheese with double fries." She leaned and whispered. "If he weren't the best cook in all of Dallas County, I'd never put up with that mess of wild hair. Ain't it just awful?" Shaking her head, Sally walked away.

Sally's problem with her help was none of Jodie's concern. What mattered was taking full advantage of Buddy Highway's generosity and getting back on the road. She stood and crossed the room to a public telephone hanging from the wall in a dimly lit hallway. She pulled the sock from the pocket of her jeans and counted out ten dimes, cupped the grease-smeared receiver in her hand, and pressed it to her ear. Line static sounded like a hive of angry bees.

The long-distance operator asked for the name of a city and a number. Jodie's anxiety swelled in her throat, choking her voice, and she hung up. She dropped into a squat. Dimes rolled across the dirty tile floor, spun on ends, and flopped.

"Hey, kid. You all right? You sick or something?"

Jodie looked back along the hallway where a second waitress stood at the far end, a steaming pot of coffee clutched in her hand.

"Yes'm, I'm fine. Dropped some change." Jodie began gathering the coins, and the woman watched until Jodie turned back to the phone and lifted the receiver. She gave the operator the number she'd memorized and leaned against the wall.

"Yeah, yeah, I'm busy here. Make it snappy." The speech Jodie had practiced for months was never intended for the gruff male voice at the end of the line. She'd imagined Lou Palmer's friendly greeting. Jodie froze, turned stupid and tongue-tied.

"Out with it. You're wasting my time."

"Hey, yeah, sorry. I'm Jodie Taylor from Catawba, Florida."

"Speak up, kid."

Jodie believed she heard the sound of balls bouncing and the high-pitched chatter of women. "Mister, I don't know who you are, but Lou Palmer's expecting my call."

"Palmer ain't on the team no more. Broke her contract. We don't need her kind. What's this about?"

"Trials. She said I should come try out. Said I'm good enough." It wasn't what she'd said, but she had given Jodie her card.

"That right?" His tone carried a load of sarcasm, and Jodie wanted to blame him for her shitty luck.

"Yes, sir. I'm headed your way now. Can be in Dallas in a day or two." Thumbing a ride was chancy. Maybe it was best she sacrificed, bought a bus ticket. A sure arrival time would mean she'd hit Dallas nearly broke, but she'd only need to hold on until her first check.

"Look, doll, I don't know a damn thing about a Joanie whoever you said …."

"It's Jodie, Jodie Taylor." Had *Joanie* made her sound like a sissy?

He paused. "Look, you're too late. I'm set here."

She slumped against the wall. "Then at least tell me when trials come up again."

He laughed. "Ten months. But unless you've got an invite, you can forget it. We get girls like you all the time, wanting to catch on. Forget basketball. Marry some shoe salesman and squirt out babies."

"No, sir. I'm not interested in that. I'll call back."

He laughed. "Yeah, you do that, kid." The man slammed the phone.

Jodie felt weak. She'd need to eat, and soon, or she'd surely faint. She walked back and sat at the table. Her entire body felt numb, her brain on fire. Roy Dale's crimes and her idiocy had likely made her a fugitive. Even if she wanted to go back to Catawba, she didn't dare.

Struggling to check her near panic, she forced herself to focus on the café. The place smelled of years of grease and sweaty men who chain-smoked. Its patrons were mostly blurry-eyed laborers, along with a few white-shirt store clerks. Swap overalls for heavy denim work pants and khaki shirts, and they were the same dull-witted men she'd known all her life.

The café was roughly the size of a half court, barely room for a short-order grill, a counter with ten tarnished chrome stools, and the same number of tables, four to six metal chairs at each. A full-color, autographed picture of Governor "Big Jim" Folsom hung from a back wall and on the center wall, behind the counter, an unsigned picture of Coach Bear Bryant. Jodie knew nothing about Governor Folsom, but it figured a coach's autograph was harder to come by than a politician's was.

A clean-shaven young man, his upper arms heavily tattooed, looked Jodie's way and winked. She turned away, focusing her attention on the approach of the waitress who'd called to her moments ago. She twisted her way to the man's table, and his face brightened with something far different than the lust she'd known in the eyes of the men her mama had bedded. Yet their exchange held familiarity of a kind she couldn't name.

Jodie overheard "Hey, shug, you gonna have your usual?" He smiled and nodded. The waitress poured coffee and called across the café, "Arthur, give me a full Ted." The bear of a man nodded, but never as much as looked up.

Sally returned with a platter of food and a tall, frosty glass of Coke and set both before Jodie. "There you go. Eat up."

"Thank you. Looks mighty good." Jodie lifted the hot burger and her stomach romped and stomped.

"What's your name, honey?"

Jodie put the burger back onto the plate and considered her answer.

"Well, you've got one, don't you? Nobody here's got much, but at least we all got names." She waved the hot pot of coffee, meaning to take in the curious, their forks suspended in the spaces between mouths and their next bites.

"Jodie … Jodie Smith. And you're every bit the kind of boss I favor." Where was her mouth taking her? "And believe me, I know plenty about café work. My mama owns one down in Florida. You might say the café trade's in my blood." Feeling she would drown, she paused, sucking air into her burning lungs. "And I can see my stopping in here is about to work out good. I mean for both of us."

"And just how would that be?" Sally shifted her weight, and maybe she'd gone back to thinking *free-loader*.

"I've just now decided to settle in Selma for a time. And, I need work. I figure me and this place fit together smooth as slip and slide."

Jodie sat back in the chair, her chest pumping like the gills on a dying fish, and Sally looked as if she'd heard the whopper of all whoppers. But to Jodie's amazement, her face broke into a slow smile.

"Well, Jodie Smith, it just so happens today's our lucky day. I'm short a busboy. The job's bussing tables, along with cleaning the toilet, vacuuming, and hauling garbage to the alley after closing." Sally looked again at the suitcase, and Jodie wasn't sure how much it played into her next offer. "The job comes with a room upstairs, the blue-plate special twice a day, thirty-five cents an hour, and you share tips with the waitress."

"That's kind, but bussing is a bit of going backward. What I mean is, I'm used to waiting tables." Shocked by her own bluster, Jodie felt to hurry what she figured was her last meal at the Red Wing Café.

"Now, is that a fact?" Sally grinned and glanced toward the door.

"Yes ma'am." Jodie scrambled. "But I tell you what. I'll take it, and if you're happy with my work, then maybe you'd consider a promotion."

"All right, that sounds fair. Job starts soon as you clean your plate." Sally called across the room, "Crystal Ann, get over here and meet Jodie Smith, our new bus*boy*."

Jodie flinched at *boy*, but got what Sally likely meant as a joke. Then Sally turned conspiratorial.

"That one's a mite slow of a morning. And if you ask me, it's too much late night partying." She nodded toward the young man.

Jodie hadn't asked, and she read in Sally's face a replica of the nosy slander her mama had known. On the spot, Jodie decided to trust Sally only as far as the job dictated.

Crystal Ann took her time pouring refills before strolling over, her chin a bit in the air.

"Jodie Smith, welcome to paradise. You can start by clearing table six." She pointed. "And watch out that you don't pocket my tips."

Jodie stuffed the last of the French fries into her mouth and stood. With that, Buddy Highway's generosity was extended, and Jodie Smith was born.

# Eighteen

Jodie Smith had mostly stopped looking up at the sound of the café's door, expecting a cop asking about a fugitive named Jodie Taylor. But after six months of bussing tables at the Red Wing Café, she still worried that crazy Roy Dale Pitts might somehow track her down, stroll into the Wing with his ignorant boyish bluster, and blow her carefully constructed cover.

There were plenty of slow times when Sally and Crystal Ann had managed to squeeze every ounce from local gossip, and one or the other turned to her with a meddling glint in her eyes. While Sally's prying had the potential for exposing Jodie Smith as a liar and a fraud, Crystal Ann had Jewel's suspicious eyes and possessed the same cleverness at peeling back layer after layer of her best sidestepping, half-truths, and bold-faced lies. Jodie worried that Crystal Ann's probing carried the greater consequences.

There were times when Crystal Ann had her pinned in one lie or another, and then simply backed off, leaving Jodie to believe she'd heard traces of melancholy in Crystal Ann's voice, as though she had her own pocket of stones. Still, she was at a loss to know what lay behind Crystal Ann's probing, especially after the incident that had shocked her and left her even more baffled.

Crystal Ann had straightened from refilling sugar shakers, her hands pinching into her lower back, and she'd asked, "You ever hear of a tourist attraction down your way where specially endowed women dress as mermaids and swim underwater in a big-ass tank?"

Jodie slowed her pace at rolling breakfast setups and stared at Crystal Ann while weighing the risk of divulging any part of her past, especially a trip with Red to world-famous WeekiWachee Springs. She'd been thirteen and credited the scantily-clad mermaids, gracefully poised behind the glass wall of a giant fish tank, with her first arousal not caused by her own hand. Miss Mary and a disappointed Hazel had waited impatiently in the hot car beneath a noon August sun while she and Red viewed a second show.

"Was that a puny-ass yes?" Crystal Ann showed impatience.

"Yes ma'am, I did once. WeekiWachee Springs, I think it's called."

"Good, 'cause I'm thinking seriously about getting out of the café trade and moving on up to the titty business." She'd arched her back, thrust her ample breasts forward, and shook wildly.

Jodie had looked away, blushing.

"Well, what do you think? Am I mermaid material?" A scathing laugh escaped her lips.

Jodie had been speechless, and although she'd felt a jolt pass between them, Crystal Ann turned away abruptly and rushed down the hall, slamming the bathroom door behind her. Jodie believed she'd heard in Crystal Ann's laughter the kind of despair she remembered from her mama's darker moments.

Jodie's cheeks still flushed with thoughts of how good it might feel to touch Crystal Ann's breasts. Hers were womanly, in full bloom, while Clara Lee's had been girlish buds. Still, she couldn't shake her fear that should she ever as much as think such a thing in Crystal Ann's presence, there would be an awful price to pay. The coffee can hidden upstairs held a mere forty-nine dollars and forty-three cents: her savings for a bus ticket and living expenses when she reached Dallas. In an emergency, it wouldn't take her far, but there was enough for a ticket should she need to escape Selma.

On the sidewalk, two Negro women hurried toward the corner bus stop, and Sally stared after them, her jaw set firm.

"Wish the city would relocate that stop. With all that colored mess stirring in Montgomery, it's bound to spread." Sally sighed heavily and looked to Jodie, for what exactly she wasn't sure. "They'd better stay the hell out of here. There's plenty of our regulars who'd go to their vehicles and bring back guns."

The two watched the crowded bus pull onto the street.

"I sure don't want no kind of trouble. Barely keeping the doors open as it is."

"No, ma'am," Jodie muttered. She now understood that Sally wanted nothing more from her.

Sally flipped the card that hung on the door to *CLOSED*. She then stepped onto the sidewalk, locking the door behind her. With the aid of the corner streetlight, Jodie watched as Sally rushed to her car and drove away. Jodie believed she'd seen fear in the way Sally had hurried past the alley and continued to glance over her shoulder as if she expected an attack.

Jodie hauled the carpet machine from the storage closet and began to vacuum the tattered carpet that no amount of effort could ever again make clean or smell different than a wet Buster. She thought of the dog and hoped he'd taken up with Silas. When she'd gathered and dumped four loads of garbage into the overflowing drums in the alley, Arthur called to her from the kitchen door.

"I'm out of here. And if I see the light of day, I'll be right back here tomorrow." Arthur laughed, and just that quick, he was through the door and into the alley. Minutes later his Chevy sped onto the street to the thunderous roar of its rebuilt engine.

Her third week at the Wing, she'd heard Arthur bragging to someone over the phone that there wasn't a cracker in all of Dallas County with engine enough to run him down. At the time, she'd wondered how his fast car connected to his rant that Atlanta had failed to send a real teacher. He'd slammed down the receiver, turned, and stared at her from across the diner, his eyes burning with instant suspicion.

She meant to keep her head down and stay out of his business. She'd shoved the vacuum into storage and turned to leave when he yelled that local calls didn't cost extra and Sally was a stingy racist. The veins in his neck bulged against his dark skin, and his anger scared her.

She'd never before heard a Negro speak that way. The sentiment was as old and thick as time, but the word *racist* was new to her. Then, she knew him for a liar, at least about the forbidden use of the phone. Just the day before, she'd heard Sally wrangling with the telephone company about false charges. She'd declared the café's phone was off-limits to her colored help and that none had gumption enough to make a long-distance call.

Jodie had managed to mumble that his personal dealings with Sally were no skin off her nose either way. He slowly nodded, and maybe he suspected her a liar as well, but appeared to accept what neither could undo. He walked past her into the kitchen, leaving her to sort out Jewel's harsh warning that she was never to trust a Negro. Still, she'd decided to watch and wait before making up her mind about Arthur. She was still watching.

Pocketing a handful of saltines and a newspaper left by a customer, Jodie braved the growing chill of the evening and hauled her exhaustion up the alley steps to the room above the Wing's kitchen. The room had no heat of its own, but it stayed warm most of the night from the heat that had built below during the day, summer and winter.

Outside the door, she prepared for yet another round of the welcome home "game" she'd invented. She rolled the newspaper, clasped it weapon-like, and gripped the wobbly doorknob. Drawing a deep breath, she snatched the door open, flipped on the overhead light, and the horrors of the game were on.

She chased down and swatted as many startled roaches as she could before the escapees gained cover between the walls. The carnage past, she swept dead roaches into a neat pile in a corner of the room as a warning to those who dared venture from cover.

Because she'd eaten her free blue-plate special late and was in a hurry to leave for the park, she took a single can of sardines from her stash above the enamel sink. Holding the can over the sink, she twisted the key, bracing for the rotten fish odor. She bought cans of sardines at ten for a dollar and splurged on fruit cocktail at twenty-three cents a can.

She plucked the tiny fish from the oily liquid and dropped one at a time into her mouth. When she was done, she washed the fishy oil from her hands, changed into jeans and a tee shirt, and retrieved her high-tops from beneath the cot. She frowned at the sweat-dried socks. She slipped on her hand-me-down jacket and grabbed the basketball she'd bought with her first pay.

Running down the outside stairs into the alley, she cross-dribbled the eight blocks to the outdoor basketball court she'd discovered her second Sunday in Selma. It was an asphalt surface that held two courts, and the outdoor lights stayed on until ten o'clock. There had been no such courts in Catawba.

She entered the sagging chain link gate, ignoring the three teenage boys who'd looked up from their game of HORSE. Her routine was to warm up by shooting free throws. She shot, rebounded, taking as many shots as needed to sink fifty baskets.

At around twenty made baskets, the boys stopped and stared in her direction. She'd learned to ignore the gawking of jealous boys with far less skill. After making her next shot, she moved to shooting layups, noticing that the interest of the boys had picked up, and the usual name-calling set in.

"Hey, biggun, you a real girl?" The boys stopped playing and took up the game they were better at: harassing her.

"Hell no, girls can't play. This one's one of them queer gals." Their laughter grew meaner, and they crossed the narrow strip of ground between the two courts. They stood less than thirty feet away and watched her.

"Hey, girl, prove you ain't one of them."

"Show us your tits," a second called, the other two laughing.

"Damn, boy," the first turned and said. "You some kind of fool? Their kind's got tits. They want other girls to suck on them. Ain't I right, dyke?"

Jodie stopped, put the ball on the ground next to her jacket, and turned to face them. She'd hoped they'd be satisfied with harassing her, that there wasn't enough juice among them to do her real harm. Still, there were three of them, drawing macho from their numbers. She reached into her pocket and folded her sweaty hand around her switchblade.

The leader, an older and bigger version of Tommy Lee, closed the space between them, his features twisted, his pitted face glistening under the lights. She was taller, but he was built sturdier and was likely stronger. The middle boy looked toward the gate as if he'd just as soon end things, but the smaller boy had something to prove. Yet neither boy advanced. She counted on them being no more threat than the Timmins boys were. The kind to stand back until she was down before piling on, claiming their share of her. She'd need to stay on her feet or fall victim to their malice.

She pulled the knife from her pocket, cradled its deadly menace in her palm, and with her thumb, she summoned her will. She heard only the soft swish of cold metallic precision as the razor-sharp blade released and locked into place.

"Shit, Roger, the bitch's got a knife," the middle boy shouted. His eyes bulged, and he took a quick step back.

Roger blinked hard, his nose flaring like that of an aroused animal, and although she saw fear in his eyes, he had a reputation to uphold. He wasn't backing down. Did he think the knife was for show, that she was easy prey? She glanced at the other two, judging their will to face the knife. Both stayed put, and she focused her full attention on Roger. He hesitated, his breathing coming in quick gasps between parted lips. His eyes narrowed, and he shifted his weight onto the balls of his feet.

He was coming.

She gripped her knife and crouched. Striking the first blow was her best chance. If he wrapped her up, succeeded in putting her on the ground, the other two would attack. She swallowed hard and fought back her raging panic.

Roger lunged, landing a solid blow above her right eye. Her head snapped back, and a bolt of electrical-like shock charged through her, nearly blinding her. She dropped onto one knee, feverishly rubbing her eyes, the smell of blood oozing from her right temple.

Wild laughter exploded all around her, the ringing thrill of first blood sighted.

"Get the fuck back. I got her first," Roger screamed.

The two stayed back.

He came at her again. His scream rose from some dark, primordial place of evil.

She struggled, miraculously regaining her feet, and managed to sidestep just before he lunged, so he grabbed her by the arm instead of the full takedown he had intended. She swung wildly, landing a glancing blow to his right, cheek. Momentarily stunned, his hold on her relaxed, and she fought to gain separation. She slashed out at him, catching him across the forearm with the blade, opening a six-inch gash.

He screamed in pain and caught his arm, staring wildly at his blood oozing between his fingers.

"You crazy bitch. You cut me." His face glistened stark white beneath the light, and he wrapped his bleeding arm in the tail of his tee.

If she was to survive retaliation, she'd need to build on his fear.

"I'm picking up my basketball. Walking through that gate." Her hands trembled, though her voice was deadly calm. "If either of you move, I'll take my gun from the pocket of that jacket there on the ground. And I swear to God, I'll blow your puny peckers to Abilene."

The boys froze in place, watching her with scared eyes, and a strong sense of pleasure swept over her. The park lights flickered; she had three minutes before darkness fell over the court. She turned and walked though the gate on knocked-out legs. Reaching the sidewalk, she dared not look back but ran full out until reaching the alley.

Inside her locked room, she sat cross-legged on the cot, drawn near the window. In the darkness, she pressed a cold washrag to her swollen face. The street below was empty, except for the crippled gray cat she knew to be a regular alley scavenger. It sat back on its boney haunches at the street corner. Its drab coat flashed alternately pink to green in the glow of the traffic light.

Beyond the narrow window, she heard squealing tires laying down scorched rubber, and a clunker slid into view. The noisy chatter of its engine, together with the nervous giggles of a girl, punished the quiet below. The light changed and the car sped away. The crippled cat was nowhere in sight.

# Nineteen

Jodie woke late to the right side of her face throbbing. She'd lain awake much of the night debating the possible consequences for what she'd done. She hoped Roger wouldn't admit to being bested in a knife fight with a girl. If she was wrong, and the cops came for her, then an investigation could possibly turn up a Florida warrant.

She stripped and washed in cold water, using soap she'd taken from the bathroom downstairs. She drew the hand-me-down nylon uniform over her head, frowning at its odor. No matter how many times she washed it, the scent of fried foods stayed in the fabric.

She hurried down the stairs and joined Arthur, who stood smoking in the alley outside the kitchen door. He winced at the sight of her bruised face, but didn't ask the obvious.

"Can I get one of those?"

She drew the nicotine deep into her lungs and slowly exhaled. Lord, she hated how good fire in her lungs felt. She nodded her thanks.

"You're good for it, aren't you?" His eyes narrowed, but with far less of his earlier distrust.

"Yeah, I am. That's if you're willing to wait till my gravy boat docks.

Arthur laughed. "Figure I'm not out anything yet." He continued to study her for a moment longer, as if he was making up his mind about something important. Then the sound of brakes squealing from the street caught their attention, and both turned.

"Maybe you ought to know that a white boy, driving a Hudson older than my dead granny, pulled into the alley a day or so ago. And damned if the fool didn't stand up on the running board like some old-timey gangster, yelling what he must've thought was scary." Arthur shook his bushy head and chuckled.

She shrugged, swallowed hard, and squinted back at him. "And why exactly are you telling me? I don't know no gangster white boy."

"Claimed a big dark-haired girl's dying daddy sent him to fetch her home. Mentioned some hick town in Florida, likely not even on the map."

"That's home, all right. But if that boy knew me, he'd know my old man's dead. And I don't have a brother who gives a big rat's ass about ever seeing me again."

"All right, Miss Jodie Smith." Arthur wasn't one bit fooled.

"What you plan on saying should that boy come back this way?" Now it was her asking that he keep a secret.

"Not a damn thing." He paused. "I don't mix in white folks' messes." He flipped the butt against the brick wall and stepped back through the kitchen door.

She drew the last of the nicotine into her lungs, dropped the butt onto the ground, crushing it with a twisting step, and cursed her bad luck. Damn Roy Dale Pitts's cunning hide. Snooping, figuring his pitiful show of *white* could threaten Arthur. Why was he dead set on finding her? Did he figure to have something big enough to press her into leaving Selma? If he did, he was sure to come back around. Whatever his warped notion, it could not be good for her.

Jodie delivered cups of fresh-made coffee to Arthur and Bo, his helper, and returned to the dining room. She sat with her first cup, welcoming the calm before what promised to be another long day. Out on Water Street, early morning traffic built, and Jodie watched for Crystal Ann's battered Nash Rambler.

"Holy crap," Jodie swore, pushing up from the table.

Roy Dale was slumped behind the steering wheel of the Hudson, staring at her through the Wing's plate glass window. She was trapped, like the frantic minnows she and Ginger had placed in fruit jars. He made no move to exit the car, yet she knew he'd come prepared to wield whatever leverage he believed he had. Nothing left for her but to face him head-on.

Crystal Ann appeared at the door, her shoulders drawn into the warmth of her heavy coat, her head wrapped in a green scarf. She banged on the locked door Jodie had failed to open earlier.

"Good Lord, girl, you trying to freeze my big ass? It's colder than a witch's brass tits. Or haven't you noticed?" Crystal Ann stood shivering before the nearest gas heater. "Can you believe twelve damn degrees? I need gallons of hot coffee in more ways than one."

Crystal Ann poured a steaming cup and took a half-pint of Four Roses from her purse. "Oh, stop your damn frowning, Sister Jodie. I get bitching enough from Sally. Besides, a little Irish never hurts on a freezing morning." Topping off the coffee, she put the bottle back into her purse, stashed it under the counter, and squinted at Jodie.

"Just who the hell pissed in your oatmeal? You look like you've wrestled the devil."

"It's nothing. Just a first day of cramps, that's all. You got aspirin?" She stood with her back to the street.

"Uh-huh. Those cramps got anything to do with that ugly boy sitting in that old car with expired Florida plates?" Crystal Ann glanced toward the Hudson, but Jodie was careful not to follow her glaze.

"What boy?"

"Sweet Jesus, Jodie … Smith. You're one more stubborn gal."

"And I guess you know every boy with expired Alabama plates?"

"You can bet your sweet ass I know all who might have cause to look me up." She retrieved her purse. "Here, down this BC powder. But it's not about to get that boy off your ass." She sighed.

"I swear, it's nothing like what you think."

"Girl, don't pretend to know what I think." She grabbed her purse and started down the hallway, disappearing into the bathroom.

Standing on the sidewalk, arms bare and teeth chattering, Jodie watched Roy Dale's approach. His face was thinner and he wore a too-large pea coat he'd probably stolen. He looked as though he might blow away in the icy wind.

"Hey, gal, how you been?" A sudden shudder shook his upper body, and his lopsided grin slipped from his haggard face. For sure, Roy Dale hadn't eaten regularly.

"Fine till about three minutes ago." She tucked her red chapped hands inside her armpits, determined not to think about any hardship he may have known, but rather that she wanted him gone, forever out of her life.

"Never was this cold down home. You want my coat to stay warm while we talk?"

"No, we're not talking that long." She glanced toward the Wing and shivered in spite of her best effort.

"All right, but ain't you even curious about how I found you?" He wanted to gloat, but his slouched stance gave his uneasiness away.

"No, and whatever you did, you wasted your time."

"Used my manly charm to sweet-talk a pissed off waitress. Your trucker friend jilted her back up the road in favor of some woman or another who works there." He nodded toward the café, his shaggy eyebrows touching as if he imagined he had cause to judge her unfaithful.

"Roy Dale, how you did it doesn't interest me." She'd have known if the trucker had come anywhere around the Wing. Then, she didn't know a thing about Sally's personal life, other than Crystal Ann's hints that Sally had a trucker she met at some all-night diner on the eastbound highway.

"Yeah, but you gotta know I've searched every café between there and here." His voice was almost whiny. Then he smiled. "Maybe you heard about me coming up here a day or so ago? Squeezing the truth out of scared kitchen help ain't all that hard." He nodded toward the alley.

He couldn't mean Arthur, but she wasn't sure about Bo. Still, she said, "I can tell you there's not a soul here scared of you, least of all me. So if you've had your say, I'll go on back to work." She turned to leave.

"Damn, Jodie. I put my ass on the line with the law to come here and warn you. And that's the thanks I get?"

She faced him. "Warn me? About what?" Damn him.

"Law down home's still hunting us. Got it straight from my momma, and you know she don't lie." He drew his hands into the coat sleeves.

"No disrespect to your momma, but even if you're telling the truth, I'll go to jail before I'll go a block with you."

"Not when you see what I've got. It can take us slap to California."

He dug into his pocket, pulled out a wad of cash, and thrust it at her. A sudden gust of frigid wind snatched a twenty from his hand and carried it into the gutter. He looked at her with boyish bewilderment, making no move to retrieve the bill.

"Jesus, Roy Dale, who'd you beat and rob?"

"Ah, come on, Jodie. Maybe I was a bit rough with you. But you'll see I've changed. Didn't you promise me a good time?"

He and his supposition was so damn pathetic she should hate him, but she pitied him more. Yet his play at pity was a trap. She stepped back from him.

"Roy Dale, I never came on to you and you know it. And for the last time, I'm not coming with you to Dallas or California or any place else."

He slumped as though she'd punched him, his breath coming in puffs of warmth, captured and frozen in midair. Instead of anger, she saw pain stenciled on his ashen face.

"You gotta know I've always liked you." He paused, kicked at the crack in the sidewalk, and muttered, "Just wanted you to like me back. That's all." He turned and walked slowly away in the direction of the Hudson.

She remembered burning the hand drawn "HapyValintime" card he'd given her in seventh grade and felt a flush of guilt, accepting that he would have never made the decision to leave Catawba on his own.

She watched as he steered the Hudson into the morning traffic and pointed it westward. Maybe she'd seen the last of Roy Dale Pitts, but his threat had pushed her into an even more troubling decision.

# Twenty

Jodie hurried to the public telephone across from the park where she had continued to play basketball, loose change stuffed into the pocket of her jacket. She'd need to make her call and return to the Wing before the start of business. She pulled the door closed against the chilling wind, and with stiff fingers she stacked coins on the booth's metal shelf before giving the long-distance operator the location and number for Silas's shop.

Silas yelled into the phone, and in the background she heard the muffled voices of men known to gather on cold mornings around the shop's one kerosene heater—workers soaking up the last bit of warmth before heading to jobs that would require they spend the balance of the day outdoors.

"Silas, it's me, Jodie." The air went out of her lungs, her nerve undermined, and her impulse was to hang up. Who'd know to look for her in Selma, a place she'd never imagined when she and Clara Lee had planned their escape?

"Good God, Jodie. Where the hell are you? Are you all right?" He forced his words through clenched teeth.

"I am. All right, I mean. But I've got to ask you if the local law is looking for me." She pictured Silas tightening his grip on the receiver and walking the length of the tangled cord, his back turned to any eavesdroppers.

"Just like that." His voice was wet with constrained emotion. "Our living without knowing whether you were dead or alive." He ground his teeth, a habit he had when biting down hard on his mounting anger. "Do you even care that Red accused me of keeping your whereabouts from him? Hell, he drove clear to your Aunt Pearl's looking for you still believing I'd lied. Maggie dogged Clara Lee so bad, her daddy threatened to get the law if she didn't back off. And all you can say is some bullshit about the law looking for you?"

"Silas, please, I know I was wrong leaving the way I did. Then nothing turned out the way I planned." She hated admitting she's been such a fool. "Do you mean to tell me or not?"

"Jesus God, Jodie. The law's got no interest in pursuing an eighteen-year-old runaway. At your age, stupid is perfectly legal."

"But can you tell me about Mr. Samuel? Is he …?"

"Mr. Samuel? What's he got to do with any of your mess?"

"Uh … nothing. It's just that he's … old, and you've talked about everyone else. I just wondered." She pressed the receiver to her ear, fearful he sensed her dishonesty as clearly as she felt her hot blood pounding at her temples.

"Maggie tells me he's had it pretty rough since he quit the A&P."

"Why'd he do that?" He'd said *quit* not fired. Was she to believe he'd voluntarily left a job he'd held for decades?

"I'm guessing he got tired of kissing white ass and getting paid peanuts for his trouble."

It was true that pistol-whipping an old Negro man may not have concerned the local sheriff, but a store robbery was different. How had such a newsworthy event gotten past Silas's notice? It was clear Silas had not connected her leaving to the time of the robbery. She couldn't know whether or not Roy Dale was lying without asking if he was a suspect in any unsolved crimes of robbery, assault or car theft.

"Silas, I'm sorry, but I've got to ask if the law's looking for Roy Dale Pitts."

A gust of cold air shook the booth, and Jodie drew her jacket tighter, her upper body bent to a deeper freeze. She trembled inside and out, waiting for Silas to absorb the meaning of what she'd asked.

"What the hell? Are you telling me you ran off with that low life?"

"It was nothing like that. Listen … I can explain." In truth there was nothing more she could risk telling him, the deeper truth being all the more damaging. The line went to static, and the receiver slipped from her stiff fingers. The stern voice of the operator shifted in and out of her consciousness.

Jodie stepped from the booth into the frigid cold, shivered hard, and with her back to the wind she walked in the direction of the Red Wing Cafe. Christmas promised to be colder than any she'd known.

Crystal Ann hung the last of the tarnished red and green ornaments on the stumpy tree and stepped back, her hands riding her hips in harsh judgment.

"Should've known a string of colored lights and a few glass balls wasn't going to make things one bit normal." She turned and glared at Jodie. "And you've got nothing worth saying?"

Jodie figured anything she said was bound to turn up the heat on whatever threatened to boil over from inside Crystal Ann, and right now she didn't give a big rat's ass about some god-awful tree. Still, she muttered, "Just that it's … not half bad, considering you started with so little … the tree I mean."

"God, Jodie, you're as uplifting as a blind bat." Crystal Ann tossed a final fist of drab icicles onto the tree.

Christmas Eve was too late to expect anything special from a wilted cedar that had been wisely rejected. Compared to those she and Maggie had cut the first Saturday of December and hauled home for Miss Ruth to decorate, Crystal Ann's tree was pitifully ugly and twenty-three days overdue.

Arthur's deep voice blasted forth from the kitchen and Jodie abandoned Crystal Ann to her unnamed misery, joining Arthur and Bo for their daily pilfering in the kitchen. Crystal Ann declined, but kept their secret. It was likely the size of her daily hangover, rather than any personal quarrel she had with stealing.

Jodie bit into the hot biscuit and slice of pink ham the size of a flying saucer. Streams of hot butter ran between her fingers, and she licked it away.

"Lord, girl, your mama never bothered you with learning no table manners, now did she?" Arthur grinned, shaking his head.

"Would've needed practice at eating regular," Jodie quipped, her mouth full.

"Christmas is on us." He paused, his brow gathered. "Tell me you're not spending it alone."

"Oh, no, I got nearby kin coming for me. What about you?" They'd never spoken of families, but somehow Christmas gave them permission.

"Oh, I'll gather at Mama's. Ten of us children, counting wholes, halves, steps, and then there's my brother, Shad, and me. He's soldiering in Korea." He paused again as if he weighed something further. "Family jokes me and him was Mama's last fling." He laughed softly.

She nodded, not fully understanding his meaning.

"Word is our daddy went up north, worked in the steel mills. Sent Mama a little all along …." For an instant the muscles in his face tightened, and she decided that pilfering might not be all they had in common.

"Ya'll need to get done in there. Boss is headed this way," Crystal Ann called.

Sally came through the door in a puff of cold air, more haggard than usual. She glanced around the near-empty café, and Jodie decided it was money worries that had worked Sally's face into a fixed frown.

"That's a damn poor excuse for a tree." Sally poured coffee.

"Ten-year-old decorations can't save an ugly tree. If you weren't so tight with a dollar …." Crystal Ann scoffed.

"Christmas Eve don't exactly set aside rent due or the death rattle in these old appliances. But you know what? I wish to hell it did.

We'd all go bat-shit crazy. Shut the door and stay gone for as long as it pleased us. Hell, we just might all decide to move out to California for a suntan."


By midday business had picked up; late shoppers joined the regulars for the fast and cheap blue-plate special. Jodie was hard-pressed to clear tables fast enough to keep customers from backing up at the door. Sally's face brightened with each crank of the cash register, and it was two o'clock before the last of the lunch crowd drifted out.

Among the regulars was Ted, and although she'd never asked, Jodie had decided he was Crystal Ann's man. He chain-smoked, and unlike the tattooed, tough guy who roared through the streets of Selma astride his customized Harley, Ted now looked like a man carrying a shitload of grief.

Crystal Ann came from the bathroom, took one look at Ted, and grabbed a fresh pot of coffee, ignoring another customer's call for a refill. She poured a cup and slid onto the seat opposite him. He leaned and whispered, and her fingertips flew to her mouth, her anxiety mirroring his.

She reached across the table and took his unusually small hand in hers, and there was no mistaking their feelings for each other. Crystal Ann talked and he nodded, saying little more, and finally he dropped change on the table and left the café. The street filled with the loud fury of his speeding away.

Four regulars Jodie had learned to despise lingered over one cup after another of coffee, spiked from a bottle the man called Chief pulled from his coat pocket. Crystal Ann signaled Jodie, silently pleading for a hurried trip to the toilet. Jodie nodded, picked up a fresh pot of coffee, and approached the men.

At the sound of Sally's high-pitched rebuke, the men went silent, their attention focused. Arthur's bulk filled the space that served as the pass-through from the kitchen into the dining room—the color line he wasn't to cross.

"Hell no, ain't you already got Christmas day?"

It was true. They had Christmas day off, although, of course there was no pay. But Arthur knew that. What more was he asking from Sally, and why? Jodie watched the table of men, and what she saw worried her. She wished Crystal Ann would get back on the floor.

"But, Miss Sally, like I said, Bo's agreeable to staying over in my place. Ask him. He'll tell you." Arthur's voice was strained, but controlled.

"That'd be just fine and dandy if staying or going was left up to you two. But it ain't."

"Yes'm, for sure, Miss Sally. But I promised my soldier brother I'd fetch his wife and kids home from the army base in time for the family tree. As it is, I'll already need to drive through the night."

"You and your damn kin ain't my concern. Now get back where you belong."

Arthur stood for what seemed like an eternity, his huge fists flexing at his sides, his frustration so palpable it appeared to Jodie he'd lift off the floor.

Tension mounted among the four men. Their bodies coiled as if they readied to spring into action, their hatred so barefaced it fouled the air. Jodie bit down hard on her bottom lip and watched Arthur. He was no fool; he dared not look in the direction of the men lest they take it as a challenge. He turned back toward the kitchen.

Sally let go a nervous giggle and looked toward the men.

"If that boy wasn't the best cook in all of Dallas County, his uppity ass would be out of here." She walked to the counter, took the bank bag containing the day's receipts, and grabbed her coat. Reaching the door, she turned back to the men. "If that young one don't take good care of you boys, I'll expect to hear about it." She winked and left, the bright green deposit bag clutched under her arm.

To her credit, Sally had attempted to play down the incident, but Jodie worried that these men wouldn't be easily placated. She refilled their cups and stepped back, but not beyond Chief's reach. He grabbed her around her hips and drew her to him. He smelled sour from the whiskey, reminding her of all the men Jewel had brought home and the gut gripping sickness she'd felt when they'd put their hands on her. Maybe little girl Jodie had hoped to find a daddy among them, but she was all grown-up now. She knew Chief as one of their kind, and she distrusted them down to a man.

"You heard the boss." He squeezed her butt cheek in his big hand.

She pulled away and glared, too angry and humiliated to think smart.

"Better look out, Chief. She's a big'un." The man, his round cheeks flushed, belly pushed up against the table edge, laughed like a marauding hyena.

The second man chimed in. "Then, she ain't exactly too pretty to mess up." The third, a pimpled-faced boy her age, blushed, pretending sudden interest in the empty sidewalk.

"Aw, come on, gal. Forget those fools." Chief waved a dismissive hand. "I favor my women big. Come on over here. Show me some Christmas spirit."

"In a pig's eye." Jodie took a firmer grip on the handle of the steaming pot, her rage making her dizzy. She wanted to cut his throat and watch his blood pool on the nasty carpet.

Chief's eyes went a shade darker and icy cold. The others held a collective breath. From behind her, she heard footsteps. She glanced around to see Crystal Ann hurrying toward the table.

"Sweet suffering Jesus. What do you call yourself doing? These big boys are mine, so back the hell off." She bumped her round hip against Chief's shoulder. "Forget her. She don't know a stud from a damn horny toad."

Chief was too damn dumb to hear the loathing behind her words.

Crystal Ann turned to Arthur, who was again straddling the line between black and white.

"You better be back in here to tell me my turkey and dressing's ready."

"Yes'm, Miss Crystal Ann, that's what I've come to say."

"All right, you've said it. Now get your black ass back behind that line."

Arthur turned on a quick heel back toward the kitchen.

"Girl, you've got tables to clear."

Moving to the farthest table, Jodie began to pick up dirty plates and cups. The sounds of chairs scraping, men cajoling, and the closing of the cash register drawer passed before Jodie dared to look toward the street. The four stood on the sidewalk, leaning in tight, Chief gesturing, the others nodding. They got into a dark green '57 Chevy and sped away.

"I hate those mean sonsofbitches. I wish they'd all drop dead."

"Yeah, well we know God don't exactly play fair."

Jodie hung her head.

"Girl, I'm here to tell you, you're gonna need to learn that you can't fight every asshole that crosses you. You've got to outsmart 'em. It's not all that hard."

"But I can't do what you do."

"If you think sucking up to that bastard doesn't turn my stomach, then you're not smart enough to survive our world." Crystal Ann glared.

"I'm sorry. I know what you did. But I'd rather die first." *Our world* had not gone unnoticed. But which world? There were so many from moment to moment. Yet she knew in her gut that she wanted to be in whatever world Crystal Ann occupied. The very thought made her blush.

"Living can come down to choosing. And I can tell you, this mess is far from over."

Sally came bursting through the door, shouting, "Big day at the bank, girls," and when neither joined her celebration, she exclaimed, "And just what the hell's the matter with you two? Ain't your apron pockets jingling?"

It was half-past nine before Crystal Ann took her purse from beneath the counter and tucked a quart jar of leftover coffee under her arm.

Sally looked up from the inventory records. "Merry Christmas. Hope Santa didn't mislay your address."

"Haven't you heard? It was all over the radio."

Sally's neck stretched, her full attention captured.

"That fat fart died. The clap, I think it was." Crystal Ann stepped through the door, and Jodie stared after her as she hurried along the sidewalk, her body bent against the bite of the raw wind.

"Jodie, get busy. Clean up this mess. My boys are expecting Santa, and I'm not ready." Sally walked back into the kitchen, and Jodie heard her yelling at Arthur.

Jodie had gathered the first of the garbage and started for the alley when an unexpected gust of cold air hit the backs of her bare legs. She turned toward the sound of the door, expecting a street bum hoping to buy a fifteen-cent cup of coffee and get warm. Instead, Crystal Ann walked back through the door, and Jodie remembered the turkey.

"You forgot your turkey and dressing."

"Naw, I don't need a bunch of turkey and dressing." She paused. "It being Christmas and all, I thought you might want to come home with me. Place ain't much, but it's a far sight better than that roach palace you call home."

Jodie's tongue lodged in the back of her throat, her relief so complete she felt tears building behind her eyelids.

"Girl, I'm not standing here all night. You coming or not?"

"If you're worried about me here alone, I'm used to it." She'd hated the thought of Crystal Ann's offer as mere pity. More than that, the thought of Crystal Ann and Ted together.

"Hell, it's not about that. I figure we both deserve better than to wake up alone on Christmas morning." She shrugged.

"No. I mean, you bet I do." Hearing "waking up alone," Jodie's world flipped. Then she remembered the remaining garbage, and she hadn't started vacuuming.

Sally came into the dining room and stopped short.

"Caught a case of the holiday spirit. Figured it can't hurt that me and Jodie keep each other company."

Jodie gave Sally a pleading look.

"All right. But get the balance of that trash out so it don't stink up the joint. Vacuuming can wait. That is, as long as she promises to get you back in time to do it before opening."

Jodie hauled the garbage to the alley, rushed upstairs, flipped on the lights, and slung clothes around on the cot. After changing into jeans and her best flannel shirt, she took the coffee can from beneath the cot and stuffed her entire savings into the pocket of her jeans. She never again wanted to feel the shame that came with the charity boxes of canned food and hand-me-down toys that were left on her and Jewel's front steps. She grabbed the winter jacket that Sally's oldest had outgrown, and hurried downstairs.

"What you want I should tell them poor disappointed kin of yours, should they show before I go?" Arthur chuckled.

"Tell them I got a better offer."

Jodie burst into the café, her jacket tucked under her arm, thinking that Arthur would make a perfect department store Santa. But the image of his black face behind a snowy white beard set her to wondering what Negro kids believed about a white, cherry-cheeked Santa. On those Christmases when Santa hadn't shown, her mama sought to blunt her disappointment with a story of Santa's obligation to fill the wish lists of rich kids before dividing the remains among kids like her and those on the row. She would have likely said that Negro kids deserved to come last, or not at all, but she would have been wrong. Santa had everything to do with privilege and nothing to do with deserving. That much she knew.

Crystal Ann led Jodie across the street to where she had parked her car. Gripping the driver's side door handle, Crystal Ann delivered a solid hip bump, forcing the door open. The passenger door, wired shut, had a diagonal crack in the glass, and Crystal Ann motioned for Jodie to slide in under the steering wheel.

Alternate coaxing and cursing had the vehicle leaping like a tipsy frog into the intersection. Crystal Ann hung a wide left into the path of an oncoming car. The driver laid down some serious rubber, avoiding a head-on collision. Crystal Ann gave up a tight laugh, swore at the gesturing driver, and pushed the Rambler westward out of Selma.

She looked at Jodie, who was cowering. "You haven't been in a car lately, have you?"

"Not with the likes of your driving." Jodie smiled, prepared to take her chances with a wild woman behind the wheel of a last-gasp car.

# Twenty-One

Crystal Ann drove in silence, and Jodie stared ahead into the whirling tunnel the headlights cut through the darkness. Jodie chose to believe Crystal Ann's silence was the result of exhaustion, and not that she regretted her hasty decision.

Over the car radio, Bing Crosby sang of a white Christmas, and Jodie turned to Crystal Ann and asked, "Did you ever see one? White Christmas? Like the song says?"

"Did once, right here in Selma." Crystal Ann frowned. "Was the same year I started working at the Wing. Can you believe twenty years ago come January? Minus six months spent in Waco, Texas." Her laughter was thick with regret.

Desperate for more talk between them, Jodie asked, "What'd it feel like? Snow, I mean." She sat back against the torn seat, a cushion spring jabbing into her shoulder, prepared to wait out any silence.

"Wet, cold, and short-lived."

Jodie sat forward, fervently nodding, and she must have looked like a puppet tangled in its strings.

"I did like the way ice hung in the bald trees like tiny fairies, dancing in the wind." Crystal Ann paused, glanced at Jodie and back at the road. "Then, pretty don't last."

Crystal Ann could be hard to follow, but Jodie recognized talking in riddles as a way of staying away from the hurting parts of her story.

After miles of more silence, Crystal Ann's mood seemed to turn a page the way Jewel's could, and she began to hum along with Andy Williams.

"Don't you just love his brand of holiday? It's so fucking perfect."

They turned onto a bone-jarring dirt road and after a mile or so arrived at a Pepto-Bismol pink trailer, raised on cinder blocks, situated in a small clearing cut from a withered corn field. A string of colored lights hung from the roof's edge, giving the tin box a false gaiety, akin to a made-up, but not made-over, aging woman.

"Those lights … they're from a better time. But they're kind of nice. Like a welcome home you can count on."

Jodie nodded. More riddle talk, she decided, and she followed Crystal Ann along a weedy, trampled path and into the trailer.

"Place ain't much, but it's always better after I've shed my girdle and thrown back a few." Her tone was one of getting her through the door. "Don't know why I bother. Damn thing pushes my belly fat to where I once had a waist."

Crystal Ann slipped off her white oxfords and walked stocking-footed into an alcove that served as a one-butt kitchen. Jodie watched as she poured a double shot of Four Roses, the cheap whiskey the band boys had drunk. Jodie imagined it burning its way down her throat, making her braver.

Crystal Ann downed the drink, then tossed Jodie a box of matches and told her to light the kerosene heater in the hallway. When she had a fire going, she glanced about the shoebox shaped room, bare except for a lumpy brown sofa, a coffee table made from a wire spool, and a television with splayed rabbit ears wrapped in foil chewing gum wrappers. There was no Christmas tree.

"Go on, girl, take a load off." Crystal Ann poured a second drink.

Jodie took a seat on the couch and stared at the cover of the Sears Roebuck Christmas Wish Book, romance and movie magazines, and an ash tray running over with dead butts. Along with a couple of bad habits, Crystal Ann appeared to have more interest in wishful thinking than housekeeping. There was no evidence of Ted or his belongings in the room. Then, she hadn't seen the bedroom.

Crystal Ann's brow gathered. "You want to know why there's no tree?" She came from the kitchen to stand next to the wire spool table.

The question took Jodie by surprise, and before she could respond, Crystal Ann added, "Came home from work one day last spring to find her side of the closet cleared out. No note. Nothing, mind you—just an empty closet."

Jodie had clearly heard *her* when she'd expected *his*, for she had decided the absence of his belongings could explain Ted's last visit to the Wing, and the hushed exchange that appeared to have to do with something neither of them wanted. Maggie had claimed that a hen's craw held the stories she'd swallowed while some rooster crowed, but that didn't appear to match Crystal Ann's story.

"The next morning, that creep, Buck, who'll never do better than pump gas, strolled into the Wing, wearing his normal stupid grin. Sally asked if he'd had a better night than he deserved, and he blurted out that she was going to be a gal short." Crystal Ann got up and brought a box of Kleenex back to the couch. She dropped back down, honking into a tissue.

"That's how I learned for certain that Brenda had left me. Standing like a fool in the middle of the Wing, loaded down with a tray of hot food, my legs nearly buckling from under me." Crystal Ann wiped at her tears. "And you know the worst? If she showed up here tonight, begging me to take her back? Against everything I know about her, I'd do it. I'd take her back." She sobbed. "She promised we'd be family."

Crystal Ann rested her head against Jodie's shoulder, and although Jodie had no notion as to the nature of a family of two women, Crystal Ann's painful loss was nevertheless real. But how did Ted figure into her story?

"Sweetie, tell me I'm right about you."

The muscles in Jodie's shoulders twitched and she stared at the space above Crystal Ann's head. "There's nothing more to tell. You know what there is to know."

"Did you understand anything I just said?"

"What if I did?" She stood and glanced toward the door. She'd walk back to her room over the Wing if she had to.

"Jodie, don't be afraid. I've known about you for some time. But I need to hear it from you." Crystal Ann reached a hand, guided Jodie back onto the couch.

"Okay, so what?" Her relief was sweet terror. "How did …?"

"I know? Maybe it was the way you never flirted with the young guys. And there were the times you stared at my prizes when you didn't think I noticed." She laughed softly, and Jodie felt her face flush hot. She swiped her sweaty palms along her thighs and stared at her shoelaces.

"Aw, sweetie, I think we somehow know each other. While straights miss what's right under their noses. That is, unless we slip up and say something honest." Crystal Ann laid a warm hand on Jodie's knee.

She hadn't known there was a word for the others. She felt let down. *Straight* wasn't hateful enough to balance the names she'd been called.

"What about Sally? Does she know?"

"Hell no. Considering she's blind to Arthur's doings? If she knew he was mixed up in that civil rights mess, he'd be fired before he could boil a pot of grits."

"What's that mean, exactly?"

"He goes nights to citizenship school. Means to learn enough civics to pass a test to vote. Then, nobody in Alabama's fixing to give Arthur the vote. If they intended to, they'd throw out them arbitrary tests and poll taxes."

Crystal Ann looked at her. "Let's forget about him for now. I want to know more about you."

"Got nothing more to tell." Her breath got short, and she felt the walls of the trailer pressing in on her.

"I already know you're a runaway, plain and simple. Figure you may have left a mess behind. But I don't need to know about that."

"What then? You already know about … the other."

"But, you're so young. Are you sure?"

"I'm older than you think. And yeah, I'm sure."

Crystal Ann smiled. "What'd your mama have to say?"

"Not a lot. I guess she figured a hard warning was all she owed me."

"Aw, baby, that's awful." The toughness Crystal Ann showed at the Wing melted, exposing a vulnerability Jodie had not seen from her.

"And the girl who broke your heart, sent you running?"

"We were going away together—to Dallas so I could try out for the Texas Cowgirls basketball team—but that didn't work out. Never meant to land in Selma. I'm putting money aside, leaving again for Dallas in about six months."

Jodie felt emboldened, which maybe explained her reaching for Crystal Ann's hand. It was bigger, rougher than Clara Lee's, but warm and strong. Crystal Ann didn't resist, and Jodie felt her heart accelerate.

Crystal Ann's body tensed and she grew quiet. The only sound was the popping of the trailer's thin walls contracting from the cold.

"You've got to know I'm a drunk. But I like the word *alcoholic* better."

"No way. If you can haul out of bed at dark-thirty, six days a week, and drive twenty miles to work, hung over or not, you're neither. I've known my share of drunks, and trust me, you're not one." If Crystal Ann sought a contradiction she could hide within, Jodie meant to give her the benefit of her talent for lies and half-truths. There had been no good way to think about her mama's blues or the whiskey and drugs that pushed her down one wrong road after another.

Quiet returned.

"Jodie, have you thought about moving out of that nasty room? Rent here's cheap, and half wouldn't be but fifteen dollars. Best of all, it's a place where you won't need to live a lie."

"Are you saying I should move in here with you?" Doing so would mean less for the coffee can, but she believed she'd heard more than charity in Crystal Ann's offer. Jodie glanced toward what she thought was the bedroom.

"Uh, that's if you don't mind sleeping on this couch." She squeezed Jodie's hand. "Let's say I'm not over Brenda just yet."

Jodie pondered her future, deciding that Crystal Ann would grow tired of being alone. What did she have to lose?

"I'll be fine here on the couch. I've known worse."

"Okay, that's settled. Now, Jodie Smith, let's cut us a tree. I've had my eye on a pretty cedar out beyond the clearing.

"It's Taylor. Jodie Taylor." She owed Crystal Ann that much.

"You had the entire phone book to pick from, and you chose Smith?"

"I was jammed in the moment."

Crystal Ann laughed softly and Jodie Taylor breathed deeply.

## Twenty-Two

Christmas morning arrived on the back of a hard freeze. Cold had penetrated the thin trailer walls and now hung damp, the smell of it strong in Jodie's nostrils. She moaned, threw back the quilts, and hurried off the saggy couch. She fumbled with stiff fingers to ignite the kerosene heater, and stood before it, shivering.

The cedar they'd decorated late into the night stood in a corner of the room, and Jodie felt blessed that she hadn't woken to the misery of the room above the Wing's kitchen. Still, she felt badly that she had nothing under the tree for Crystal Ann.

At the sound of water running in the bathroom down the hall, she decided to dress and go for a quick run. She pulled on yesterday's jeans, a double layer of sweatshirts, and two pairs of socks. She thought about leaving a brief note, but where would she find paper and pen? Still, it felt good to have someone who might question her absence.

After what she judged a brisk two miles, Jodie turned back for the trailer. Nearing the clearing, she made out the approach of a vehicle and wondered who it might be. She sprinted the last quarter mile and upon reaching the outer edge of the clearing she leaned, her palms braced on her knees, and sucked cold air into her lungs. An apple red Studebaker coupe, the ugliest car ever built, idled in the clearing.

A smiling Crystal Ann came from the trailer, and it was clear the passengers were welcome. The driver shut down the engine and the car belched, sputtering to a stop. Crystal Ann hugged a petite woman while a second woman got out of the car, frowned, and kicked a front tire.

There was much about her stocky, muscular body and cocky, one-sided grin that reminded Jodie of someone she'd seen. But she was certain she didn't know the woman.

"Jodie, come on over. We have company." Crystal Ann motioned her closer.

Jodie's pulse rate had leveled out, but for some reason she couldn't fathom, her flight reflex kicked in. Crystal Ann reached and put an arm around Jodie's waist, drawing her closer.

"Jodie, these are my dearest friends, Maxine," she giggled, "and I do believe you know Teddy. She's the handsome one there, punishing faithful Bertha."

The three smiled at her, and Jodie struggled to hide her bafflement. She felt the fool—the butt of their shared joke. She swallowed hard and tried speaking, but her astonishment left her tongue out on a limb. Inside her head, she sorted pronouns: he/she/Teddy—she/he/Ted. Nothing she'd ever experienced helped her to make sense of what she saw.

"You're one damn lucky stray, kid." The woman's grip was strong, and she squeezed hard, making her point. "How's the training going? Crystal Ann tells me you've got big-ass plans." Teddy looked Jodie over, an appraisal behind her hard stare.

"Just fine … ma'am, and I do. Did … have a plan. Then it got waylaid a bit." She hated her hesitancy. She'd need to learn to own up, speak out, even in those moments when self-doubt undercut her resolve.

"That's fine. Plans are good," Teddy's cockiness taunted. "And I may be ten years your senior, but I'm not your damn granny, so lose the cracker politeness."

"Oh, baby, hush your rudeness." The one Crystal Ann called Maxine gave the big woman a playful slap on the shoulder and turned to Jodie. "Sweetie, don't mind her. Reared by a mean cave bear. Resulted in no social skills of note." She flashed the purest smile Jodie had known since saying good-bye to Ginger Sutton.

"You know you like my cave bear." Teddy leaned and nuzzled the back of Maxine's neck, kissing her there.

Enthralled by Maxine's feminine appearance, Jodie riddled as to whom Maxine imagined during sex: Ted or Teddy? She'd never before seen such intimacy pass openly between women. While it felt forbidden, it carried an equal weight of liberation, excitement, and a strong sense of pride she had nothing to compare to, other than the exhilaration she felt when lifting off the gym floor and reaching the ball beyond the outstretched fingertips of an opponent, followed by nothing but the sweet swish of net.

"I've got sweet potatoes ready to go into the oven. Ham hocks and turnips ready for the pot."

"Teddy roasted a turkey, and I made Mama's cornbread dressing. And of course there's pumpkin pie."

"Teddy is as good with meat as Arthur," Crystal Ann declared, smiling at Jodie. Teddy beamed.

Maxine and Crystal Ann took the picnic basket from the car and entered the trailer, leaving Jodie alone with Teddy. She had no idea what was expected in the way of conversation.

Teddy crossed her arms, leaned back in a stance that spoke brazenly of challenge. "If that old rusty rim there on that tree's not just for show, what'd you say to a little wager on a game?" Teddy grinned as though the pot was hers to claim. She took a scuffed basketball from the car and pulled a fist full of dimes from a pocket of her jeans, laying them on the car fender.

"Since we just met, and that ball's yours, it's only fair that I warn you …." Jodie matched Teddy's stance.

"Uh-huh, we'll just see about that." Teddy tossed Jodie the ball and dropped into a crouch.

Jodie rested the ball on her hip and gazed at Teddy.

"But first, I gotta know."

Teddy straightened, and at her full height she was three inches shorter. "All right, spit it out. Let's get it over with."

"Why? Why do you …." Air squeezed from Jodie's lungs.

"Pass … as a man, sonsofbitches that they are?"

"No, forget it." Jodie bounced the ball. "Let's play."

"No, girl, let's put it behind us. Besides, it's easy. Auto mechanics make ten times what harder working women make. Men don't hit on me. I'm not expected to bend over for every low-life with nothing going for him but his pitiful dangles."

"Is it hard, what you do?" Jodie felt her face fire, and she looked away.

"Nah, it's not hard if you're of a mind to forget the part where I get found out and get gang raped and dead. Then there's sterilization. Or worse—Maxine loses her babies on account of me."

Jodie saw genuine fear in the big woman's eyes.

"Now, if that don't satisfy you, then picture me flirting with any woman I like." She winked, her fear only slightly dissipated.

Jodie had tried imagining the lives of others like her, but she'd never dreamed there were women like Teddy. Nor mothers with children at risk. Clara Lee's fear of God's abomination felt inconsequential—cold and distant as the stars. Maxine and Teddy's fears were immediate and constant: damnation and death real. Jodie felt ushered into a new world far more complicated and more dangerous than she'd ever envisioned.

Teddy now sprawled on the hood of the Studebaker, her powerful arms folded across her breasts. Her sly smile spoke to her mocking wit.

"One more question, kid. Then school's out."

"Who did you say I'm playing? Not that it matters."

"Girl, you're dropping coins to Teresa Granger. I'll see she get them."

Teddy wasn't bad for a slow, flat-footed shooter. Move her off her sweet spot and her shots bonged off the rim seven out of ten times, but she hustled, played a dirty black-and-blue game, using her superior lower body strength to block Jodie's approach to the basket. Then, she was a sucker for a quick jab step, getting her back on her heels, creating space. When they were called to dinner Teddy's bank was bled dry, and Jodie's pockets jingled. Teddy copped to an off day, and bragged that Jodie should save her money for a rematch. Jodie decided Teddy was someone she could learn to like.

Dinner conversation turned to Maxine and Teddy's sadness at not having Maxine's kids for any part of the holidays. They were with their alcoholic father and his live-in girlfriend.

"Asshole refused the Santa Claus I got them unless Maxine agreed he got to put his name on everything."

They sat silently, their shared pain and anger seething, threatening to set aside the good they'd felt, until Teddy reached and patted Crystal Ann's forearm.

"Sorry, shug. I'm gonna need a new fork if I'm to have any of that pumpkin pie." Teddy squeezed the bent prongs of her fork between her thumb and index finger. "Some better, but it's bound to stay a cripple."

Jodie couldn't imagine the secretiveness that went with such a union. Teddy was Ted to Maxine's kids? How could that possibly work? Left alone to make sense of Jewel's lies, even the purposeful ones, Jodie had created her own versions of the truth. Surely Maxine's kids were doing the same.

Late afternoon, when it was time for Maxine and Teddy to leave, Teddy placed the overflowing basket of leftovers in the trunk. She and Maxine got into the car and drove away, everyone waving.

Jodie watched until the vehicle disappeared from sight, and she was acutely aware of a change, a new sense of self. A lightness of spirit she'd not felt before. Maxine and Teddy, with all their heartaches, had shown her a glimpse of what she wanted to believe queer love could be.

Crystal Ann sat on the trailer steps and patted the space next to her. Jodie sat, and Crystal Ann placed her hand on her knee.

"I know today was a lot to take in. And that getting comfortable with our lives is never easy. It takes living queer to understand who we are."

Jodie nodded.

"You're not to trust every queer woman you meet. There's meanness and betrayal among us as with everyone else. Choose carefully, but know those two are good clear through to the bone. I trust my life to them."

"How's that?" She wanted to know more about what Crystal Ann expected from those she trusted. Had she thought of Brenda that way?

"Those you decide to trust," she paused, "they'll have your back. Keep your secrets to their graves."

Jodie considered all she'd heard and seen from Maxine and Teddy and slowly nodded. She favored Maxine's gentle ways over Teddy's explosive nature, yet Teddy reminded her of Maggie's gruffness, and there was no one she trusted more.

While Crystal Ann napped, Jodie prowled the nearby woods, returning at sundown. Crystal Ann had warmed leftovers, and when they'd eaten, Jodie offered to do the few dishes.

Crystal Ann disappeared into the bedroom, and when she reappeared, she had changed into a body-hugging skirt and a gypsy blouse, and she wore heels. She swirled about, giggling and showing off her good legs.

"How 'bout it, Jodie Taylor? You ready for your first visit to dyke paradise?" More nervous giggles escaped Crystal Ann's brightly painted lips.

Likely she had her own doubts, Jodie decided.

"Given my acquaintance with those who believe their tickets have been punched, I'll need to know more about this paradise before I can decide." Her hands had begun to sweat, and it was clear her stab at humor stunk. She jammed her hands beneath her armpits, her body swaying in rhythm with her mounting anxiety.

"Aw, baby, come here." Crystal Ann reached for Jodie's hand, and drew her down to sit next to her. "A first glance, it's nothing more than a bar populated only by women."

"I've never been to a bar of any kind. But I've been around lots of drinking. Don't much care for how liquor smells."

"Think of it as a secret gathering place for women seeking other women. There is drinking, and for some far too much. Then we laugh, cry, comfort, flirt, love, fuck, break hearts, and plot revenge." She smiled, "And if that elusive bitch, Lady Luck, smiles on us, we find a good woman who plucks our magic twanger. Then we pair up, lay claim, and hold on for dear life. Which doesn't make us all that different."

Jodie felt a surge of the purest exhilaration wrapped in a blanket of nearly unbearable panic. While she could not imagine approaching a woman for more than conversation, she wanted to become one of the brave women she only imagined who sought and won the favors of beautiful women.

"It's all of this, and much, much more." Crystal Ann stroked Jodie's forearm. "It is a sacred trust."

"Does that mean this place is safe?"

"No, and you must bear that in mind. Safety is just the risk we accept … woman to woman."

Crystal Ann stared into Jodie's eyes, and maybe she saw what she needed to believe. Jodie knew that she did.

## Twenty-Three

A series of backcountry roads took them north out of Dallas County, and Jodie listened as Crystal Ann told of the fabled Gabby, the owner of the Hide and Seek. She described her as a big butch with the arm strength to ass-whip Tarzan and the smoothness to win Jane's heart. After a decade in New Orleans's French Quarter, she returned home to claim her inheritance: eighty acres of virgin timber and a dilapidated building.

On the third Saturday of each month, the Hide and Seek became the destination of queer women within a hundred-mile radius.

"Rumor is Gabby buried her grandpa, the old geezer she'd called the grand son-of-a-bitch, in his Klan garb, sniping that it was only fitting that he arrive in Hell suitably attired."

Jodie could not know whether there was an ounce of truth in what she'd heard. Still, she marveled at such a feat, choosing to believe the story in its entirety.

They left the highway and drove on an unmarked, jaw-jarring dirt road for several miles before making a hard left onto a barely discernible tire-worn trail that ended in a small clearing. A squatty cement block building stood partially hidden beneath the sweeping branches of an ancient live oak. At the outer perimeter of the clearing, Crystal Ann backed the Rambler into the underbrush, declaring it reduced the chance of getting boxed in by slow moving escapees should a sudden need arise.

If Crystal Ann intended her remark as reassuring, it wasn't. Until now, worries about how she would fit in had dominated Jodie's thoughts, but Crystal Ann had given her a much bigger worry.

Crystal Ann downed a hefty slug of Jim Beam and tucked the bottle back beneath the seat. "Hard liquor's not allowed inside. Somewhat of a drawback if you ask me. Then, nipping doesn't count, as long as the nipper comes and goes under her own steam."

Crystal Ann stared into the mirror, reapplied her bright red lipstick, fluffed her unremarkable brown hair, and frowned at her reflection. She turned to Jodie, her smile strained.

"Okay, sugar, let's me and you rock and roll."

Jodie got out of the truck. A quick sniff of her armpits, and she wished she'd had a cleaner shirt. She ran her fingers through her hair, and the cold air felt good on her flushed cheeks.

There were no outdoor lights, and they made their slow, deliberate way along a footpath among an erratic formation of vehicles whose owners didn't appear to share Crystal Ann's inclination toward a quick getaway. The path led them to a purple door, its paint blistered and flecked off in chunks. A single yellow light hung over the entrance.

Jodie noted that the glass panes of the windows on the building's front were painted over in black, permitting only the slightest light framing the window's edges. The low rumble of pulsating music was audible from inside the building.

Crystal Ann rang a bell and stepped back, tugging at her tight skirt. Frowning, she grumbled, "This damn thing's not one bit happy unless it's crawling up my ass."

Jodie hoped Crystal Ann's frown was all about the hitch in her skirt and not that she was second-guessing her decision to bring along a first-timer.

"Gabby bribes county officials. Then, she can't rule out locals stumbling onto the place, figuring to crash the joint, forcing their own sick brand of fun." She patted her heavily sprayed hair. "But it's all right, you'll see."

Jodie peered into the darkness, listening for sounds that didn't belong. Her muscles tensed, but she heard nothing over the music and the tempo of her racing heart.

The door opened the width of a short, heavy chain. Light and the sound of music poured through the opening, and a partial face appeared.

"Hey, darling, it's Crystal Ann. And I've brought along a friend."

The single eye disappeared. The sound of the chain disengaging, and the heavy door flew open.

"Hey, there, pretty thing. Who's your young rooster?" The woman had a face that would scatter little children.

Crystal Ann embraced the woman. "Her name's Jodie. She's good." The woman looked her over, head to foot, and Jodie felt as though she'd had her tires kicked, hood raised, and was about to be taken for a test drive.

"Good and lucky if you ask me." She turned to Jodie. "Come on in, gal, and grow your young self a wattle."

The woman winked at Crystal Ann, and she squeezed Jodie's hand, her expression reminding Jodie of the uneasy way Ginger's mama had smiled when the preacher came for Sunday dinner and Ginger's daddy had gone early to the sauce.

They picked their way among tight groups of women seated at mismatched tables—more women than Jodie had imagined in her wildest dreams. For the first time ever, she saw women dancing together. She feared her intense staring would pop her eyes clear out of their sockets. She felt a bit unsteady, and squeezed her eyes shut.

Crystal Ann paused to hug one woman and yet another, and clutched Jodie's hand, encouraging her along, shouting her name over the noise. Most nodded nice enough, but there were those who stared the way Teddy had, sizing her up, for exactly what she wasn't sure.

"Hey, sweetness." A woman, her pink scalp showing beneath her cotton candy–like hair, grabbed Crystal Ann around the waist, drawing her to sit across her thick thighs. Jodie judged the woman to have done her share of heavy work.

"Got you a young one, but is she naughty enough to satisfy your appetite?" She buried her face between Crystal Ann's breasts.

Crystal Ann threw her head back, pretending a sensual moan, and cradling the woman's washboard face between her palms, she kissed her.

"No one does it better than you, Miss Doris."

"Oh, baby girl, you'll always have a place in my old heart." The woman's voice was wet with emotion.

Those nearby cheered and clapped, and Jodie felt an odd bout of jealousy toward the old woman's intimacy and those who'd cheered her. Still, she didn't know what to make of what she'd witnessed: women openly engaging each other, easily joking about their sexual desires. She was both astonished and aroused by their brazenness.

They made their way across the room to the bar, Crystal Ann explaining, "The woman back there is seventy-nine. Poor thing lost her soul-mate of forty-seven years last September. She isn't likely to get over it in this lifetime."

Jodie understood Crystal Ann's comment to mean Miss Doris, like Maggie or Miss Ruth under the same circumstances, would run out of time before she ran out of grief. Jodie was embarrassed by her earlier jealousy.

They reached the bar fashioned from the ripped length of a half-inch sheet of plywood and supported by carpenter's sawhorses. Crystal Ann leaned across it and called to the woman elbow deep in a washing machine tub filled with chipped ice.

When the woman straightened to her full height, Jodie pushed back on the bar stool, unable to conceal her amazement. She could be none other than Gabby, a full six feet or better, weighing at least two thirty, maybe more. She was the second woman, after Lou Palmer, to cause Jodie to feel normal. The breadth of her smile matched her size, and when she opened her mouth to speak, Jodie braced for a voice equal to the roar of a hurricane.

"Hey, gal, damned if I hadn't started to worry you'd jilted me for some skinny bitch." Her voice was gentle as a receding tide licking sand.

"No, darling, you're the only woman for me." Crystal Ann's face brightened, her come-on playful.

"Uh-huh, I know that's right." Gabby slid an icy Pabst along the bar into Crystal Ann's open hand. "That one you got there with you even old enough to drink?" She placed a bowl of freshly popped popcorn in front of Crystal Ann. "Reckon I could gig around in that damn ice long enough to turn up an RC."

"Not necessary. I'll have what she's drinking."

Crystal Ann cut Jodie a look.

"It's not exactly like I got raised by church-goers." The swagger she'd intended fell limp like bird shit on her shoulder.

Gabby cocked her head to one side and a slow smile spread across her face. She reached and pulled a second beer from the tub and slid it along the bar. "First one's on the house."

Jodie fumbled a clean catch, recovered, and mumbled her thanks.

The big woman laced six beers between her broad fingers like cheap glass jewelry and walked toward the sound of her name.

Jodie sat, drinking the bitter beer in slow, measured swallows. There was everything soothing about the closeness of other women that slowed her heart rhythm, and she took her second deep breath since leaving Catawba.

When she'd begun to feel less conspicuous, she noticed the crowd noises building behind her and swiveled about, daring to search among the women for the one she'd imagined since arriving in Selma. She saw no one she preferred over Crystal Ann.

Jodie followed Crystal Ann to a table where they joined Teddy and Maxine. Jodie tried not to stare at Teddy, but she couldn't get over her transformation from Ted to the Teddy sitting across from her. While Teddy wasn't a woman Jodie could ever think of as pretty, just now she was softer, less harsh. Maybe what she saw were glimpses of Teresa, and Jodie contemplated the extent of Teresa's compromise in becoming Ted.

Jodie watched as Teddy and Maxine took to the crowded dance floor. She envied the familiar way in which Maxine slipped into Teddy's arms and Teddy's surprising grace as she guided Maxine across the floor.

"How 'bout it, Jodie Taylor, you want to dance?" Crystal Ann leaned and placed warm fingertips on Jodie's cheek. Her closeness was such that Jodie felt the heat of her stronger than ever. She felt dizzy, deciding it was the effect of the beers she'd drunk.

"With you? Oh, no. I couldn't." Her face caught fire. "What I mean is … I don't dance. Never learned."

Crystal Ann stood next to Jodie, her hand extended. The women at the next table stopped talking among themselves and stared.

"Hell, gal, forget that pup. I'll dance you right out that door into the back seat of my car."

Crystal Ann twisted her butt at the woman. "Lord, darling, how many times I gotta turn you down? That bucket of bolts you call a car hasn't even got a back seat."

Their good-natured laughter spread to the next table, and Jodie eyed the door. She'd never danced with anyone other than Silas, and only when he'd gotten crazy and insisted on thinking of her as his girl.

"I'm not asking twice."

"Okay, I'd love to, but I swear I don't know how."

"If you've got two good legs, and you do, then you can dance."

Jodie stood, and Crystal Ann led her through the snickers and onto the dance floor.

"Forget them and follow me," Crystal Ann whispered.

Jodie's stiffness began to melt, and her two left feet found their rhythm. Dancing with Crystal Ann felt far more natural than she'd ever managed with Silas.

When they weren't dancing, the four of them sat, polishing off pitchers of cold beer and consuming plates of barbeque. Jodie learned that Gabby's famous pork had found its way into the governor's mansion. Jodie laughed at the notion of a crowd of straight politicians chowing down on barbeque shared by women they would surely have arrested and thrown into jail. She remembered Sally ranting that Arthur's uppity black ass would have been gone from the Wing if he were not the best cook in the county. Then, targets of hate made no sense.

Jodie pushed back, looked across the room, and soaked up the good she felt. Was she to find her place among these women? There was so much they could teach her about staying alive while living queer.

## Twenty-Four

Jodie woke to her first alcoholic fog and fumbled her way into her uniform while Crystal Ann poured one cup of coffee after another. They reached Selma at five-forty, a virtual ghost town, streetlights weakened by the density of the fog. Crystal Ann parked the overheating Rambler and sighed relief at the old car having made it this far. Nearing the Wing, Jodie noticed that there was no light streaming into the alley from underneath the kitchen door, and Arthur's car wasn't parked in its usual spot.

"What do you think?"

"I'm thinking we're not the only ones who had ourselves a little too much Christmas cheer," Crystal Ann cracked, shoving her hands deeper into her coat pockets.

Jodie slowed. "Could be, but I've never known Arthur to be late."

"He's not exactly late. We're a mite early." She frowned.

Jodie vacuumed the ratty carpet while Crystal Ann made the day's first coffee. Arthur still hadn't shown, and Jodie began to worry until she remembered his trip to Albany, deciding he'd been delayed.

At six, Sally came charging through the door, the craziness in her eyes at a fever pitch. Jodie had never seen her wound so tight.

"Whoa down, boss lady," Crystal Ann joshed. "What brings you in at this hour in such a state?"

Without looking her way, Sally yelled for Jodie to shut off the machine.

"I've got a shitload of trouble, that's what." She glared at Jodie, her eyes flinty, although she'd spoken directly to Crystal Ann.

"Uh-huh, and would that be ongoing trouble, or maybe you're just pissed at Santa?" Crystal Ann glanced over at Jodie, and if she had a notion as to what had put Sally into such a nasty mood, she didn't let on.

"Jodie, just what the hell did you call yourself doing, pissing off Chief? Raining grief down on me?" Sally's eyes bore into Jodie.

"Wait a minute. I never invited that mess." Jodie pressed her fists at her sides, her anger firing, overtaking her caution. "And … and if kissing his ass is part of this job, then I'm not your gal."

Sally collapsed into a chair, her face resting in her hands, and mumbled between her fingers, "Lord, don't I wish that was all there was to it."

"What? What are you saying?" Jodie dropped the vacuum.

"Arthur's dead. That's what."

Acid from the coffee Jodie had drunk backed into her throat, and she gagged, choking out any words she might have spoken.

"Dead? Just like that?" Crystal Ann's voice was eerily calm. "No damn way." She dropped onto a stool, her stark features awash in the intermittent flickering of the overhead row of dying lightbulbs.

"Chief and his bunch caught up to him on the Albany highway. The four bragged that they'd beaten him to death. Claimed it was a favor to me." The dark circles under Sally's puffy eyes were magnified against the pastiness of her skin. "They never even said what he'd done so wrong."

"He got born black. That's what he did. And you know that's all he did. Why are you just now telling us?" Crystal Ann glared at Sally.

"Had no way," Sally pleaded. "Got no number for you."

At the sound of the front door, they each looked up. Bo stood in the doorway, his solemn face ghostly gray, and he glanced nervously behind him at the traffic moving along Water Street. He mumbled something about opening the kitchen door.

"God help us. I guess I will." Sally started toward the kitchen, and Bo ducked back through the door, disappearing into the alley.

"Sally, wait. Bo knows something he isn't telling." Imbedded in Bo's uneasiness, Jodie believed, were details about Arthur that Sally didn't have.

"No, Jodie. You stay the hell out of this. You're already way too deep as it is. Chief would be within his rights to demand I fire you for that fool stunt you pulled."

"I mean to talk to Bo."

"Do and you're fired." Sally's eyes brimmed with tears, but there was no doubting her words. She'd chosen to side with Chief to protect her own interests.

"If that's the way it's got to be, I quit."

"Then get out. And stay the hell away from Bo. Two women alone can't run this place." Sally hurried from the dining room toward the kitchen.

Jodie turned and started for the door. Her only thought was to get to Bo before Sally.

"Wait, Jodie. Take my car. I'll get the last of your stuff from upstairs. Come for me at quitting time." Crystal Ann handed Jodie her key ring. "Meet me in front of the dime store. Those bastards don't need to see us together outside of work." Her voice shook. Crystal Ann hugged her. "Now go."

Jodie entered the alley and slumped behind a stack of delivery crates. She lit her last cigarette and thought about all the smokes she'd shared with Arthur. Tears fogged her vision, but she was counting on her grief fueling the anger she'd need to get through whatever lay ahead.

It was first light before Bo stepped into the alley. He took one look at her and headed back through the door. She followed him into the kitchen.

"I don't know anything." His fear was as palpable as hers.

"Yeah, you do, and you're going to tell me."

"She'll set them men against me. They'll kill me, Miss Jodie. I'm not strong like him." Bo's hands trembled.

"Strong? You saying—he's not dead?" Her heart slammed into her throat so hard she felt she'd choke on her relief. "Jesus, Bo, I know you're scared. I'm scared. But I'm not budging a step till you tell me what's happened to him." She stood so close to the trembling man, she smelled his terror. Or was it hers?

"Some say they took what was left of him to the Catholic hospital."

"His brother's family? Were they with him?"

"Ain't heard about nobody but him."

"Good. That's real good." Footsteps sounded in the hallway and Bo paled fair as an Easter lily. Jodie ducked through the door and took the alley to Crystal Ann's car. She started the Rambler, pulled onto the street, and accelerated. She had no real plan. But she'd learn Arthur's fate or die trying.

## Twenty-Five

Jodie approached the hospital and turned onto a driveway with signage denoting the emergency entrance. If Arthur had survived the beating, and Bo was right, he would have entered the hospital through the set of double doors. She'd find him and do whatever he needed. She owed Arthur that much, and after the way in which she'd failed Mr. Samuel, she owed herself a second chance to be more.

The double doors swung open, and a young, slender woman with blonde hair exited. She descended the ramp at a quick pace, hurried into a late model green Chevy, and drove toward the exit. She glanced in Jodie's direction for only a second, but long enough for Jodie to note her red, tear-stained face. She turned onto the street and drove east, away from downtown.

Jodie got out of the Rambler and walked up the ramp, stopping at the double doors. She rang the doorbell marked for emergencies only and listened for movement on the opposite side of the door.

A short, middle-aged man with a round, boyish face and a woman's wide hips appeared in the doorway. He wore a priest's collar and a wrinkled black gabardine suit.

"Good morning. I'm Father Francis Dean. May I be of service?" He looked past her, his face expectant.

"I'm alone. Here to see ... a friend."

"I see." When she wasn't more forthcoming, he said, "Then you'll want to enter through the front. This is the emergency entrance." Once again he looked over the parking lot and then back at her.

She studied his kind face and risked that if he knew Arthur, he'd take her to him.

"I'm here to see Arthur Washington." When he hesitated she added, "Please don't try stopping me. I intend to see him, come hell or high water."

His face muscles relaxed. "Do come in." He stepped aside, making room for her to pass.

They entered a dimly lit hallway. The strong odor of disinfectant rose to meet her. She followed him down two narrow flights of stairs to what she believed was the hospital basement. He stopped before a double door.

"No damn way. I'm not going in there." Bo had said Arthur was alive, but the priest had led her to the hospital morgue. Her pulse raced and the back of her throat was parched. She backed away from the door, prepared to run back the way she'd come, but her leg muscles failed her, and she leaned against the wall to steady herself.

"Good heavens, young woman." Father Francis reached an arm around her shoulders. "I sincerely apologize. It's much safer if he's kept separated from other patients." His round face was earnest.

"He's not dead? He's alive?"

"Oh yes, my dear. He's alive. A lesser man would not have survived the brutal beating he took, but it seems God has a bigger plan for our friend Arthur." Father Francis gently squeezed her elbow.

Sickened by the thought of Arthur's horrific suffering at the hands of Chief and his goons, Jodie was unsure how God's hand could have been in both. Her relief was so complete, she wanted to share Father Francis's vision of Arthur's future, but she understood that God could not be counted upon to blunt the hatred she'd witnessed at the Wing— and that Arthur was a dead man if he stayed in Selma.

Father Francis eased the door open, sending a narrow path of light streaming across the floor. At her hesitation, he gently nudged her forward.

Inhaling sharply, she stepped deeper into the cavernous room, reeking of formaldehyde that stung her eyes. In the room's dimness, she bumped into a gurney. She gasped at the sight of ten stiff, chalk-white toes, tipped with claw-like, black fungal nails, pointing skyward.

She glanced back toward the open door, and Father Francis was barely containing his amusement. He pointed in the direction of a curtained-off area in a far corner. Jodie soothed her embarrassment with the notion of Arthur's big laugh, enjoying the irony of sharing the morgue with a white corpse.

At the sound of the hooked curtain sliding across the metal bar, Arthur turned his head ever so slightly, and Jodie flushed with new anger. His face was bruised and lacerated. He wore a patch over his left eye, and his right had been reduced to a narrow slit. His ribs were heavily strapped and his right arm, wrist to shoulder, was in a hard cast. His pulpy, swollen lips parted and he spoke her name, his raspy voice barely audible. The deep bruise on his neck matched the shape of a boot heel. Her grief, caught up in a maddening whirl of rage, took her breath.

Still she managed to whisper, "Your redneck roommate could use a longer sheet. He's got some damn ugly feet."

"You're not safe here." His speech was labored.

"Tell me where it's safe, and we'll both go there."

"You're a fool." His chest rose and fell with his effort.

"Maybe, but at least I got a friend out of it." Her instinct was to touch him. Instead, she shoved her hand deep inside a pocket. Shaken with shame, she prayed he hadn't felt the moment. But he had.

"No meanness in it," he said. "More of what we all got to unlearn."

She sat with him late into the afternoon, leaving his bedside only to join Father Francis for a bowl of soup. Arthur slept and woke, only to look over at her and then drift back into what she hoped was the power of sleep to restore.

When it was time for her to leave, she whispered, "Arthur, it's me, Jodie. I've got to go. But I'll be back."

He turned toward the sound of her voice, but he didn't speak.

Evening had descended, blanketing Selma in a cold, wintery darkness. Jodie turned the Rambler onto Seventh and spotted Crystal Ann pacing, her hands jammed deep inside her coat pockets. Jodie pulled to a quick stop, and Crystal Ann hurried into the car.

"Where the hell have you been?" She shivered, her shoulders lifted into her coat. "It's not exactly a night for strolling."

"I've been with Arthur. He's alive, but hurt real bad."

Crystal Ann buried her face in her hands and moaned. "Thank God. But why didn't you call me?"

"Afraid to. Sally's not to be trusted."

"Tell me he's safe."

"For now …."

"Teddy heard Chief and his bunch showed up at both colored funeral homes asking questions. And after you left, Sally went back to the kitchen, found a pot of grits boiling, but no Bo."

"Figures if he's got somewhere to go, he'll haul ass out of town."

Crystal Ann blew her nose. "I'm a damn mess. Pass me that bottle there under the seat."

Jodie retrieved the bottle.

"We'd just closed when Chief came banging on the door, calling Sally out. They talked, and after he left, she ran back inside, grabbed her coat and purse, and lit out."

"Did she say anything about me?"

"No. Said nothing more than I was to lock up."

Jodie reduced speed, testing the driver of the pickup truck who'd been following them for some distance. She'd need to keep her movements secret until Arthur was safely out of Selma.

## Twenty-Six

Dawn had come as a bloody stain on the distant horizon when Jodie dropped Crystal Ann three blocks from the Wing, then drove to the nearest filling station. She purchased a full tank of gas, mindful that she and Crystal Ann might need to leave town in a hurry. She placed eighty dollars in the carton of Lucky Strikes she bought, leaving it under the car seat. It was most of her savings, which meant she'd likely miss basketball trials in the spring, but wherever Arthur was headed he'd need cash.

Father Francis met her at the emergency entrance, wearing the same wrinkled suit that looked as though he'd slept in it. He didn't offer to follow her downstairs, explaining that he was busy making arrangements to move Arthur.

"Where?" she asked.

"New Orleans. A convent there has agreed to take him under their care until he's well again." Father Francis grimaced and rushed back along the hallway.

Jodie entered the morgue, the scent of formaldehyde still strong, and drew back the curtain that barely separated Arthur from the dead. He attempted to raise his broad shoulders, but groaned, clutching his bandaged ribs, and eased back down onto the bed.

"It's early, but I brought along Crystal Ann's chicken soup."

Jewel had never made her soup, not even the time a case of German measles drove her fever to what the doctor had called brain-boiling. She had no faith in the heralded powers of soup to heal, but hoped Arthur had better memories of his mama's chicken soup.

Adjusting the pillows beneath his head and shoulders, she spooned the broth between the pulpy rawness of his swollen lips, his body quivering with his effort. With less than a fourth eaten, he waved the spoon away, his breathing labored from exertion.

"Preacher's moving me." She thought he may have been searching for an answer as to her involvement in the decision. "Don't cotton to running." He turned his face away.

She set the thermos cup on the bedside table.

"I hear New Orleans's got some real fine jazz. And plenty of fancy cafés where a good cook can find work."

"I got work here." He watched her from behind the bandages.

New Orleans wasn't Harlem, any more than Selma was Dallas. Then, lives lived at the bottom got remade by circumstances they were more often than not powerless to change. There were times when running was all they had.

Late afternoon, Jodie joined Father Francis on the bench outside the morgue, the weight of securing Arthur's safety bearing down hard on each of them.

"What does his family know?"

"They'll be told that he survived the beating. But oddly enough, Arthur insisted that, with the exception of his nephew Ben, his family not be told where we're taking him."

Jodie nodded, knowing Arthur's demand was not odd. Family couldn't let slip what they didn't know.

"When will you leave?"

"Tomorrow evening. I trust God grants us that much time. Ben heard from a woman who cleans for the wife of one of those godless men that they had learned their shameful deed failed."

"How long ago?"

"Earlier today, I believe Ben said." His eyes narrowed with sudden recognition.

"Don't mean to discount God's hand in Arthur's future, but we've got to get him out of Selma today."

"You may be right. But what if he isn't strong enough to travel?"

"He'll have to be."

The priest took a silver flask from his inside coat pocket. "Are you a drinking woman, Miss Jodie?"

She took the flask from his hand.


Ben had worked into early evening removing the back seat and trunk panel from Father Francis's Oldsmobile and cutting and fitting a sheet of half-inch plywood into the space, fashioning a makeshift bed. Jodie, Father Francis, Ben, and two stout nuns used a bed sheet to draw Arthur onto a gurney. The bigger job was passing him through the trunk opening onto the plywood bed. It took several brutal attempts before they maneuvered his bulk into the space, and the five stood back, gasping.

Had Sister Mary Alice not administered a double dose of pain medicine, Jodie was sure Arthur would have passed out. The sister placed extra bandages, iodine, and pain medication on the front seat with instructions for what Father Francis was to do should any of Arthur's stitched wounds start to bleed.

To Arthur she said, "Dear man, I'm so sorry, but there's nothing more I can do to protect your fractured ribs against the jarring." She placed a hand on his shoulder. "God willing, in time your bruised kidney will mend."

Arthur called to Ben. "You're the man now. It's up to you to get your grandma, mama, and those little ones to your Uncle Willis down in Florida. Them crackers stole my car, so you need to borrow from some of the family."

"You can count on me." Ben looked as if he'd choke on his held back tears.

Jodie stepped to the car and handed Arthur the carton of cigarettes.

"Don't owe me. You're all caught up."

"Naw, go on. Take 'em. I've quit."

Sister Mary Alice handed Father Francis a urinal, a bed pan, and a roll of toilet paper. He looked at Arthur's bulk and grimaced; his round cheeks blushed rosy.

Arthur clutched his ribs, his muffled laughter racking his tortured upper body, and the laughter of those gathered built, rolling back their shared fears, momentarily lifting their spirits.

The car eased onto the street, and Jodie watched until its flickering taillights disappeared. She had never heard of a friendship between a white woman and a black man, but if there was such a thing it was what she felt just now.

## Twenty-Seven

After several failed attempts at finding work, including a job gutting chickens on an assembly line, Jodie gave in to her despair, complaining to Crystal Ann.

"That sonofabitch, Chief, dropped a dime on me. Nobody within the sound of his nasty lies is going to hire me. What am I going to do?" If she didn't find work soon, she'd need to leave Selma to look elsewhere.

Crystal Ann shrugged. "Can't say he did. Can't say he didn't. But either way, you're going about this thing all wrong." She walked out of the kitchen, clutching her second double shot of bourbon.

"Don't just lay down something and walk the hell off."

"Girl, when's the last time you knew a hiring man you'd trust with the truth?" Crystal Ann turned on her Sunday night show, *The Defenders,* and flopped down on the couch.

Jodie poured her first drink of the evening and slammed out the door. She sat on the steps, swatting mosquitoes and grappling with what to do next. What had been Crystal Ann's point? Lying was no problem. Everyone she trusted was a liar. *Which* lies was the question that stumped her.

In spite of Teddy's warning that the blue jean factory was a hellhole of female slave labor, Jodie was desperate enough that she'd try anything. She shucked her pride and walked back inside, accepting Crystal Ann's earlier offer of help.

"First off, you'll need to invent a man in your life. One who'll vouch for your female respectability." Crystal Ann chuckled.

"Respectability, my ass." Teddy had claimed that the factory hires were a gaggle of all-around female misfits: aging singles, girls with bastard babies, divorcées, and abandoned wives with broods of hungry kids. What kind of respectability went with that crowd?

Crystal Ann walked to the stove, stirred a pot of rice, and growled. "You sure you want to work in a snake pit of straight women? You'll have to keep your mouth shut and your hands in your pockets. Teddy claimed to know a young dyke that didn't, and she hasn't been heard from in over a year."

Jodie had heard the same story, but her determination was hard set. She needed work, any work, short of selling her body on the corner of Sixth and Middleton.

"Okay, but about a man vouching for me—Arthur Washington's not around anymore, and if he was I don't think his recommendation would exactly cut it. And I'm not about to ask Teddy to do anything like that. It's too dangerous.

"Dangerous? What the hell do you think she does every time she walks into that garage pretending to swing a dick?"

"No, and that's final."

"Ah, here's where brains and grit kick in." Crystal Ann smacked her lips, and Jodie knew she was hatching some wild scheme.

Sessions over the balance of the evening were equally grueling and humiliating. Jodie stood before the bathroom mirror, fabricating a life story, while Crystal Ann barked instructions from a seat on the toilet. She was a natural at playing the asshole hiring man.

The morning of the interview, Crystal Ann insisted Jodie wear the one skirt and blouse she owned, forcing makeup and whorish styling on her bobbed hair.

Jodie swore, "Oh, God. With my face, it might as well be Halloween."

Crystal Ann blasted back, "Forget showing a little cleavage, but would it kill you to smile?"

Nerves sharper than barbed wire, Jodie parked the Rambler in the factory lot, and the engine sputtered to a stop. An array of junked cars and trucks told the tale of flat pay envelopes. But she wasn't here to get rich. Rent and food money would be good. She followed the sign to the front office, her confidence so low she feared tripping over it.

Approaching the woman seated behind the front desk, Jodie said, "Hey, I'm here about a job. Do I tell you?" She'd meant to sound smarter, but it would have likely been lost on the woman.

"Yes, I'm Mr. Jackson's secretary."

Jodie took her superior tone as one aimed at separating her from the women on the floor.

"You here about the inseamer job or the ticket-tacker?"

Crap, it already felt like a shell game. Maybe she could work a little arm around the shoulder, gal-to-gal humor.

"Now on that," Jodie paused. "Hellfire, to us working gals, a job's a job, right?"

The woman's dismissive stare told Jodie all she needed to know about her pissy start.

"What I mean is, it don't really matter. I need work."

"I see. You've got no experience." Her second shot of superiority.

Jodie glanced at the door, considered walking. But she swallowed hard and offered the best she had. "Not exactly. I'm considered a quick study."

Forty-three minutes later by the agonizing tick of the clock on the wall, a man shouted, "Sugar, send that gal on in here."

*Sugar* wiggled her sweet little ass, the whole of her redeeming value, into the office, and announced, "She says she's Jodie Taylor, and she's got no experience." She turned and walked out, the man never looking up.

The office smelled of the cigar butts that overran the bear claw ashtray at the man's elbow, and his bald head shone pink as a newborn's under the overhead light. He looked up, his gaze traveling the length of her body, and in spite of Crystal Ann's efforts, it was clear he saw nothing that interested him. She instantly despised him—and every circumstance of her miserable life that had her at his mercy.

"Well, go on, sit down." He removed a nubby cigar from the corner of his mouth and spit into a Del Monte pineapple can.

The odor wafted across the desk, and Jodie willed her disgust from her face, fighting back her desire to run. Then she remembered nights on the row when she'd gone to bed with her belly cramping so that sleep wasn't an escape. Instead of flight, she planted her feet on the floor, pinching her knees together in the fashion Crystal Ann declared lady-like, her self-image enough to gag a goat.

"I'm Jodie Taylor and I'm here about any job you got. Know that I'm not afraid of work." She wished she remembered the job titles the woman had used.

He squinted across at her. "You're not from around here, are you?" His tone carried the message that outsiders weren't hired.

"No, sir." Jodie pictured Crystal Ann screaming, her hand pressed to her forehead. For sure, she'd stumbled coming out of the gate, and she worried that the job was already lost.

"You'd be married? A house full of sickly babies, I'd wager."

"Married? Oh, yes sir." She smiled sweetly, dropped her tone into syrupy sadness. "But there won't be any babies. You see, I got kicked by daddy's mule." She placed a hand to her lower stomach.

"Got nothing but the graveyard shift. And your husband's gonna want a young thing like you around nights." He gave her a knowing wink.

She lowered her eyes, her fingers laced. "Yes sir. But, he's in bed early. And all such as that comes before."

She hoped he'd mistaken her disgust for shyness. He chomped down hard on the cigar nub, causing her to believe he'd heard something that wrongly tipped the scale. She'd need to shift to the bigger lie, the one Crystal Ann swore would land her the job.

"Like I said, I'm not from around here. But you might know my Aunt Sally. She offered to come here and personally vouch for me." She felt she'd gag on her own sweetness.

He sat upright, glanced toward the open door, and leaned across the desk. "That'd be Sally at the Wing?"

Jodie nodded vigorously, still smiling.

The yellow pencil he held snapped in half. Blood drained from his face as if a vampire had sucked him dry. He shouted for the woman.

"Get ... what'd you say your name is?"

"Jodie Taylor."

"Get Taylor signed up." He turned to her. "When can you start?"

Jodie walked out of the building with orders to report to the night supervisor at ten-thirty. Crystal Ann had sworn he wouldn't dare check her story, and had giggled, adding details about an incident at the Paradise Motel and Mrs. Jackson's solemn oath, backed by a double-barreled shotgun. It would appear he'd taken his wife's threat to heart.

Crystal Ann brought supper from the Wing, wrapped in waxed paper, and cleared the kitchen table of accumulated junk. She set the table with a tablecloth, placing a single candle in the middle, and had changed out of her uniform into a floral smock Jodie liked. It had a scoop neckline trimmed in pink lace. Jodie studied Crystal Ann's face in the soft glow of candlelight and considered that she'd once been pretty.

"Go on, sweetie. It's your celebration."

Jodie's last celebration hadn't gone so well. Then, Crystal Ann wasn't Aunt Pearl.

"These pork chops sure aren't Arthur's. Then, we get plenty of idle time."

"Sally still blames me, right?"

"She does, but let's forget about that. I'm so proud of you. You've outgrown the scared runaway who stepped into the Wing collecting on a handout."

"Couldn't have done any of this without you."

Crystal Ann reached across the table, squeezed Jodie's hand, and smiled. Jodie sensed an opening, and she dared.

"What do you hear from Brenda?" She knew of the letters that came occasionally to the mailbox on the road.

Crystal Ann withdrew her hand. "I've heard nothing new. Only good intentions served up as empty promises. But it's sweet of you to ask."

"I'm not asking to be sweet. I'm asking for more."

"And I've thought about you and me. But I'm not ready. I don't want to promise what I can't deliver. Neither of us deserve that kind of hurt."

Jodie nodded. She'd wait. Should Crystal Ann ever let go of Brenda, she felt her stay in the pink trailer would change for the better.

## Twenty-Eight

Jodie arrived thirty minutes early and sat in the Rambler, watching the shift workers arrive and disappear through a side door. She gathered her scattered Wonder Woman and followed the last of the stragglers through the same door.

"Hey, you the new girl?" The question came from a woman half Jodie's size, and one she guessed to be a few years older. Her stringy brown hair was twisted into an unruly pile caught up by a bright red ribbon, her look that of a festive porcupine. She sported a fresh shiner that she made no attempt to hide. She chewed bubble gum and stood so close Jodie could smell the gum's strawberry flavor.

"I'm not so new. But I am here to start work."

The woman tilted her head and grinned. "You're a smart-ass, ain't you? I'm Bitsy Whogivesaflyingfuck. My mama swears the name's Comanche, but she'd rather lie than suffer the truth."

"I'm Jodie …."

"Well, *just* Jodie, you're in for a big treat. That old hag standing over there next to the time clock is the super-bitch. You're bound to hate her guts by sunup. She ain't met you, but she already knows you're white trash. A born whore, and too damn sorry to work."

"Well then, I guess I'm off to a better start than I figured."

There might be something to reincarnation. If so, Jodie believed she'd met the remake of Jewel Taylor. She smiled, in spite of her rule about straight woman, admitting to liking the broomstick with the sassy mouth.

A horn blasted, and Jodie watched gaggles of clucking women break ranks and move to positions along the rows of machines. She covered her ears as the cavernous room exploded with a deafening mix of machine noises: clatters, clangs, and deep hums. How was she to fit into this breakneck-paced assembly of machines and women?

Spotting the supervisor moving in her direction, Jodie worked to steady her nerves. The woman appeared to be middle-aged and walked with the stiff gait of a woman with worn knees. Her hair was teased and sprayed into the shape of a school globe, the entire western hemisphere flattened against the right side of her head. She put Jodie in mind of Aunt Pearl.

"You Taylor?" Her tone, more an indictment than a question, did nothing to contradict Bitsy's remarks.

"Yes, ma'am, I am for sure."

"Well, come on. Let's see if you've got sense enough to run one of these machines. Looks like you've got the back, all right. Then, you big gals are the first to wear down. It's all that extra weight on these concrete floors that does it."

"Yes, ma'am," Jodie echoed.


Six months on the job, and Jodie had advanced five stations on the assembly line, but it hadn't taken her that long to learn that piecework was rigged to reward nimble fingers and dulled minds. Arthritic hands that slowed or active minds that wandered contributed to failed production quotas and flatter pay envelopes. If a woman's work didn't rebound, she was let go without ceremony.

Jodie's extra pay over her quota was enough to keep her on the job, but she was more determined than ever to refill the depleted coffee can and take her leave. If the backbreaking work wasn't enough, the daily stories of these women fed her determination.

Yolanda Yates, bleached white as an albino from fifteen years of sleeping days and working nights, was a pure marvel: a long time in piecework yet bright as a button, and she held her own against younger women. Still, she'd tell anyone who cared to listen that a fifteen-year pin, stirred in a meatless stew, was a meal that hung in the throat.

Jodie and Bitsy sat together at supper break. Hard-eyed Sybil, three-times divorced, sat at the next table.

"If you ask me, they're breeders and leavers. Ain't worth the little effort I'd use stomping their balls to jelly."

"That sour bitch is at men again. I've loved every man I've bedded." Bitsy shrugged. "At least for the duration."

Sybil's harsh words had a way of spooking the timid, but not Bitsy. "And how come you don't use that mean mouth of yours to complain about two toilets for thirty-five women pissing on the whistle?" Bitsy slammed her meal bucket shut.

"And why don't you sit your skinny ass down?" Sybil was a woman Jodie wouldn't choose to tangle with.

Yet Bitsy, thin as a hoe handle with an edge as sharp, shot back. "'Cause we've got a so-called ventilation system that don't do nothing but circulate clouds of lint. That blue crap sticks to every inch of our bodies. Clogging our noses, filling our throats, and stinging our eyes. If that don't kill us outright, then we survive it to push out monster-like babies."

Bitsy had insisted that they should confront the manager, and if he turned a deaf ear, they should walk off the job like mill workers up north.

Sybil harrumphed through her flat nose and drawled. "And that one's going to make this shitty job sweeter with tough talk. Her no bigger than a bloated tick."

Jodie watched in silence, as though she had no stake in the argument. Teddy had warned her to keep her head down and her mouth shut and not get close with anyone. What Teddy discounted was the fact that Jewel Taylor had raised her from the crib with the same warning. She needed no reminder. Secrecy was as much a part of her as whatever bad shit she breathed in the moment.

## Twenty-Nine

The letter Jodie had dreaded for nine months, since moving in with Crystal Ann, arrived on a Saturday. Crystal Ann sat at the kitchen table late into the night, swigging whiskey and reading the one page written with a blunt pencil, letters shaped like those of a kid, over and over, tears streaming down her swollen face.

"How can you be sure? You're leaving on nothing more than that? It doesn't make sense." Jodie worked at keeping the anguish out of her argument.

"I can't be sure. And I know it doesn't make sense. It's not meant to make sense. I feel what I feel. She swears leaving me was the worst mistake of her life. Promises that if I'll come to Mobile, everything will be good again."

Jodie didn't argue further, although she'd heard plenty of doubt in what Crystal Ann didn't say.

"You think you might get back this way someday?" Jodie was unwilling to say *if it doesn't work out.*

"No, I hear Mobile's real pretty and warm year round. I think I'm going to like it there on the Gulf of Mexico. Should you ever come that way I hope you'll look me up."

"I'll do that." She said what Crystal Ann wanted to hear, but the offer that Jodie should look *her* up didn't go unnoted. She'd hang her hope on nothing more than its vagueness.

By the scant light of the setting moon, Jodie helped Crystal Ann load what little of her possessions the Rambler held.

"Please tell me you're going to be okay. You've got your job, this place, Teddy and Maxine, and the women at the Hide and Seek. Your truck should get you to Dallas for the tryouts next spring. You'll be okay. Please tell me you understand."

"It's all right. Don't worry. I'll be fine. Send me a pretty postcard, and I'll write you back."

She drew Jodie close, held her tight, and whispered, "If I'd only met you first, you know I could've loved you the way you wanted."

Jodie blinked hard and stepped back. Just maybe, Crystal Ann doubted the promise of love as much as she did.

Crystal Ann gave her a pained smile, got into the Rambler. "You promise to feed the stray cat until he decides to go elsewhere?"

Jodie nodded.

She watched as Crystal Ann drove out of the clearing onto the dirt road. She swore at having failed to remind Crystal Ann to have Teddy fix the Rambler's busted taillight. Right along with other things she hadn't found a way to say. She took a seat on the top step, and the air smelled of the damp leaves that now covered the ground in the nearby woods. The half-moon had disappeared behind a flurry of clouds, and Jodie felt that old ache of aloneness.

From the field of withered cornstalks, the stray entered the clearing on stiff legs, his tail arched, tip end swishing like an antenna.

"Damn, cat, where'd you come from?"

The cat walked a measured distance and stopped.

"You here for a handout?" She stepped inside the trailer, leaving the door ajar.


Jodie sat with Rose, a woman she knew but was in no way attracted to, apart from Rose's willingness. Rose had peppered her with a steady stream of questions that Jodie took as a way of judging her intent, until she grew weary of either side-stepping or outright lying.

"Jesus, Rose, stop with the damn questions. I'm not here to spill my guts; I'm here to get laid." A quick apology did nothing to change the outcome, and Jodie found herself sitting alone.

Gabby leaned across the bar. "What do you hear from our gal in Mobile?"

She frowned and shook her head. "Not a damn thing. You?"

"Nothing." She wiped beer mugs and glanced out across the near empty barroom. "Had hoped she'd finally ditched that religious nut and would stay put."

Jodie nodded. "Yeah, well I guess I'll shove off. See you."

"Hold up a minute."

Jodie turned back, and Gabby came from behind the bar.

"If you're damned determined …." She nodded in the direction of a skinny bottle-blonde dancing alone on the empty dance floor.

"Her? What makes you think …?" Jodie rammed her hands in her back pockets, swaying a bit. One rejection an evening was her limit.

Gabby frowned. "Hell, do you think she came here to dance alone any more than you want to go home to your own hand?"

Jodie weighed the emptiness of the long drive and, against her better judgment, crossed the room and took the woman, who called herself Star, into her arms. She was certain Gabby had called her Betty June.

They made their drunken way to a late model ragtop, Star confessing to having paid top dollar for a convertible without working hydraulics. Jodie asked what she was thinking.

Star shrugged. "And who's going to know it don't work?" She smiled conspiratorially, as if she'd somehow outfoxed the envious. The irony wasn't lost on Jodie, but it wasn't Star's brain that had her caught up in a reckless mood.

"It's not far. Leave your old truck for now." Her nose wrinkled, and typically a put-down of her truck would have pissed Jodie off. But she caught the keys Star flipped in her direction and slid behind the wheel.

They roared onto the highway, the radio blaring. Star sat close, her hand on Jodie's upper thigh, and such was the pity that roadside parking on a public highway was off limits.

The sky ahead was a washpot black, threatening to unleash a downpour. Jodie licked her fingertips and rubbed her stinging eyes, and in spite of the rain that began to pound the canvas top, she drove on at a reckless speed.

Star's head sunk onto Jodie's shoulder and she either slept or passed out. Jodie turned up the radio static and drove on through the downpour in search of a place Star had only vaguely described.

The car lurched. The steering wheel jerked from Jodie's hand; the sound of sand and gravel pounded the undercarriage. She fought to regain control of the speeding car, and ahead through the darkness she made out the bridge railing racing toward them.

She pressed the brake pedal in rapid repetitions. The car fishtailed and struck the bridge railing a glancing blow. It spun and bucked its way back off the bridge onto the muddy shoulder, landing right side up in the water-filled ditch on the opposite side of the highway.

Jodie remembered her head striking something, but it was her right leg, jammed beneath the steering column, that sent wave after wave of excruciating pain all the way into her hip. She put a hand on her leg and felt the stickiness of blood and smelled its coppery scent. She gagged and her vomit was sour, smelling of beer, and she was sure she'd pass out.

Rain pelted her, and water from the overflowing ditch rushed into the car. Star lay crumpled on the floorboard. Jodie struggled to reach her but remained trapped, managing only to grab a hunk of hair and to hold her head above the rising water.

A searing flash of lightening lit the roadside, and Jodie's scalp tingled, the scent of pine tar exploding in the air.

## Thirty

Jodie woke to a set of false teeth smiling at her from a glass container. She attempted to move, but the pain in her right leg was so intense she moaned and dropped back onto the pillow.

"Shug, you ain't gonna want to try nothing like that." The slack-mouthed warning came from a woman Jodie took to be the owner of the teeth.

"Where am I? How'd I get here?" Her throat was parched and her focus blurred.

"Deputy brought you here to County. But don't worry, they take charity cases." To her question as to how long ago, the old woman answered more or less twelve hours. "You're here for a stay."

"What's wrong with me?" Her right leg was wrapped thigh to calf, and it hurt to as much as wiggle her toes.

"Likely I ain't supposed to tell you. But I overheard the doctor say a bit more and you'd have woke up peg-legged."

The old woman went on with bits of something about a ripped leg and enough stitches to make a good-sized quilt. "But other than being scarred, and a real bad limp, I'd say God's been good to you."

There was nothing about her situation that made her feel blessed. She pictured the Cowgirls streaking up and down the court and knew there was no place for a gimp in their game.

"That pipestem-sized, stringy-headed blonde gal, who claimed you stole her brand-new car …." The old woman smacked her lips in what Jodie took to be puzzlement. "Now she claimed she dragged you out of that sinking car just in the nick of time, you up to your chin in filthy ditch water." The woman paused. "You know, she never said exactly how all that happened."

"Got run down in a high-speed chase. Shoved off the road into that ditch." Sweet Jesus, if the old woman didn't shut her mouth, Jodie felt she'd drop dead here and now.

"Goodness, you don't say." She squinted at Jodie, appearing to search for something she might believe. "Just the same, she said I should tell you she won't be back."

The door pushed open, and the face of Jodie's hottest dreams appeared in the space between the door and frame. Though brain-warped on pain killers, Jodie still had enough juice to imagine the Marilyn Monroe body that matched the woman's perfect face.

"Well, God bless you, Sister Sarah. Ain't you just the sweetest thing to visit an old, dying woman?" The woman grabbed her teeth and popped them into her mouth with the resolute click of a bullet forced into a chamber.

"Good afternoon, Mrs. Hansford. I do believe the rosiness has returned to your fair cheeks. I trust this means you're feeling better."

The woman's schooled enunciation was precise, and her accent meant she wasn't from Selma, maybe not even the South. She wore a dark rose-colored, two-piece suit with a sheer white blouse ruffled at her pale throat, her posture erect and balanced on open-toed pumps. She was a stark contrast to the haggard, dull-eyed women who'd come into the Wing, and her appearance on the floor of the jean factory would stop the machines from spinning. Operators would stand idle, mouths gaped wide, as they stared at everything beautiful in a woman they were never born to become. Everything about her spoke of birth and life-long privilege.

The woman looked over at Jodie, a slight smile on her full, red mouth. Embarrassed at being caught staring, Jodie turned her gaze away. An odd hint of detection had passed between them: one both dangerous and forbidden. Yet overriding her fear was Crystal Ann's claim that somehow *they* could know each other. During the brief conversation that ensued between the old woman and the visitor, Jodie savored the woman's every word, holding each in her mind, committing them to memory.

At the sound of the door opening and closing, the sharp clipping of heels as the visitor made her retreat down the hallway, Jodie felt a sense of loss she could neither explain nor deny.

Jodie woke suddenly, and she couldn't be sure how long she'd slept. The door opened back forcefully, and Ted stepped into the room. The old woman smiled and turned away.

Teddy winked and Jodie got a much-needed jolt of amusement at the notion that the old woman likely meant to give her and her sweetheart suitable privacy. Teddy drew the curtain closed, stared, and turned a bit pale. She gripped Jodie's shoulder in her strong hand, leaned, and smacked her on the cheek.

"Damn, girl. You look like warmed-over death." Teddy frowned and drew back the top sheet, getting a look at Jodie's heavily bandaged leg.

"What do you think?"

"That at least it's still attached." She shook her head in disbelief.

"Aren't you just a shitload of cheerfulness?" Jodie tried deflecting, but Teddy's honesty was too much to overcome.

"Maxine sends her love. Along with decent pajamas, toothbrush, paste, comb—you know, the stuff of a stay." She set a brown bag on the bedside table. "They said how long?"

"No, unless I'm to believe her." Jodie nodded toward the old woman. "I haven't seen a doctor."

"I'll buttonhole a nurse on my way out."

"God, Teddy, this isn't the stay I'm worried about. Am I going to jail?"

"Cop kept saying how lucky you were the railing wasn't concrete." She paused. "Damn, girl, I can't believe you decided to go back to the Hide and Seek on the night both kids were down with the shits. And then you leave with that crazy broad? You need something steady. That bitch changes lovers like me and you change our socks."

"Never came to that."

"Then you are lucky."

"Yeah, well forget about her. Am I going to get charged?"

"Too much bother, I'm guessing. Considering nobody got hurt but the drunk driver."

"Love me a lazy cop. And that heap of a car?" She worried she was responsible for removing it, and the repairs.

"Far as I know, that shit's totaled and right where you parked it." Teddy snorted. "I'll get the shop boy to haul it to the salvage yard."

"Thanks. Guess I am lucky. But my leg's a damn mess." Jodie shoved her knuckles in her mouth, fought back tears.

"Yeah, well, someday I'll show you my motorcycle scars." Teddy leaned and whispered, "And don't you dare start up with some kind of self-pity bullshit. You'll heal in time for the trials."

Jodie searched Teddy's eyes for the slightest indication that she believed what she'd said. She read a world of improbable hype.


Mrs. Hansford checked out the following week, and there had been no more visits from Sister Sarah. Jodie's stay stretched into a third week, during which time her leg healed well enough for her to master the use of crutches. She limped out of the hospital with Maxine, who drove her home with her. She stayed with Maxine and her two kids her first week out of the hospital. The bill put her into debt to Teddy for two hundred dollars. The entire ordeal left the coffee can empty and her with a noticeable limp the doctor claimed—with luck, and her staying off her feet for a few months—would lessen but likely never completely disappear.

If that wasn't bad enough, she developed a nasty habit of nipping a little all along, straight through the day and late into the night. She was learning that pain coupled with self-pity were two of the main ingredients for the kind of blues Jewel had sung.

## Thirty-One

Week six and Jodie was back on the job as a new hire. The steady pain in her leg slowed her production pace to one that got her regular hard looks from the super and little extra in her pay envelope. After meager expenses and paying down her debt to Teddy, there was nothing to deposit in the coffee can. The odds of her putting aside enough money before trials grew slimmer with each passing day.

Still, most Saturdays, when Ted wasn't repairing some woman's car in Maxine's back yard, Teddy was badgering Jodie into shooting baskets, her enticement Maxine's fine home cooking following workouts.

Jodie and Bitsy emerged from the plant into a welcome Saturday morning, blinking against its brightness like two blind armadillos. As they made their bone-weary ways to their vehicles, Jodie spotted a late model green Oldsmobile. The driver slowed the car, appeared to fix her attention on her and Bitsy, and then sped away.

"Reckon how it is that rich bitch strayed from her side of the tracks?" Bitsy lit her last cigarette. "Don't figure her kind's looking to get on the graveyard shift." Bitsy puffed a cloud of smoke into the frosty air.

"What do you know about someone like her?" Jodie grinned.

"Her?" Bitsy snorted smoke. "What I know is, the uppity bitch's old man preaches at that big-ass church downtown. And Bess says she's too proud to mix with the ladies of the congregation. On account of she went to one of them fancy Yankee schools just for rich girls. They may've taught her how to talk pretty and which fork to use, but I figure she don't look no different from any other woman flat of her back with her legs spread."

"Why do you say shit like that?" Alarmed by her unchecked outburst, Jodie walked on.

Bitsy called to her, "Now, I'm just asking. Wouldn't such a school be the absolute pits?" Bitsy shook her skinny ass like a mare in heat.

"Maybe, but don't you sometimes think about doing better?" Some days it was hard to remember if she'd ever believed in her chance at playing ball with the Cowgirls.

"Girl, you're crazy. My mama jerked my dumb ass out of sixth grade and stuck me in the cotton fields. This shitty job's a sweet deal compared to chopping cotton in July. Hell, I got plenty of picking scars." She held out her hands for Jodie to see.

"Yeah, but I'm thinking about enrolling at that new junior college. Pay for my wild-eyed fantasy with wishful thinking. What you think?" Jodie ached for better, an ache so real she felt her breathing had shut down.

"Go on with your damn foolishness. I got hungry kids waiting for breakfast. See you back here Monday for more of the same." Bitsy's bitterness was the kind that destroyed dreams. She hung out the car window and waved, the cigarette dangling between her tar-stained fingers.

Jodie headed the truck in the direction of the A&P, intending to restock her fridge and maybe cook herself a decent meal. Patting down her hip pocket for her wallet, she walked into the store. It smelled of rotting bananas and cabbages. She wanted the shopping ordeal over and to get home to collapse into bed.

At the meat counter, she ordered a pound each of ground chuck and sliced bacon, then caved to the overpriced pork chops, ordering two. The distracted butcher pushed her three brown packages across the counter and called an earnest greeting to an approaching shopper. Her order in hand, Jodie turned to leave.

"Good morning, sir. It is indeed a fine day. And good morning to you, miss."

At the silky-smooth sound of her voice, Jodie stood fixed to the floor, her words stuck in her throat, and she stared.

The preacher's wife stared back, then turned abruptly and hurried toward the door. Jodie watched as she rushed from the store, got into a green Oldsmobile Ninety-eight, and sped away.

The butcher muttered, "Strange, mighty strange, that pretty one." His tone was not one of ridicule, but of mystery. He sighed and returned to slicing prime cuts from the hindquarter of a perfectly marbled beef.

Jodie cut her shopping short, and after stashing her few bags, she swung the truck onto the street and headed downtown.

The billboard in front of the large brick church read James R. Curtis, Minister. If her instinct was right, Mrs. James R. Curtis was hiding behind a respectable marriage. Clara Lee may have married Stuart Walker Junior, but Jodie believed the girl who'd moaned under her touch was the true Clara Lee. She pulled the bottle from beneath the seat, took a generous pull on the whiskey, its fire burning its familiar way through her, and pointed the truck toward the pink trailer.

For two straight Saturdays following her chance encounter with Sarah Curtis, Jodie went to the A&P, buying groceries she didn't need. Finally, rather than continuing to leave the store disappointed, she stopped going, except when she actually needed to restock the fridge. But she still went on Saturdays, even though it meant the store was more crowded.

Jodie made a quick stop at a well-known filling station to purchase gas and a fifth of the cheaper, label-free bootleg whiskey sold there. Reaching the dirt road, she glanced into the rearview mirror and swore. She waited next to the mailbox, but the green Oldsmobile she believed she'd seen following was no longer there. Her growing obsession with Sarah Curtis, an untouchable, was downright stupid.

## Thirty-Two

A week's worth of pressed jeans and flannel shirts hung in the bedroom closet. An overflowing sink of dirty dishes had been washed, dried, and put away, garbage burned in the drum out back, and a pot of ham hocks and lima beans simmered on the stove. Jodie's restored sense of order had earned her a long Saturday afternoon nap.

She dropped onto the couch, a glass of cold milk and a stack of two-day-old donuts within reach. But before finishing either, she drifted into a restful sleep, only to be startled awake by the sound of an approaching vehicle.

She swung her sock feet onto the chilly floor and eliminated a visit from Teddy. Bobby had a tag football game, and she knew Ted straddled *his* machine out of sight of Maxine's mother, who sat with Maxine in the section of the grandstands meant for family. The old woman despised Ted, thinking *him* crude—beneath her daughter and unfit to be around her grandchildren. She'd threatened to file for custody in her latest attempt at cutting Teddy out of the lives of Maxine and her kids.

The timid knock on the door most likely belonged to the Jehovah's Witness who called herself a disciple. She was a tight-lipped woman of few words, and Jodie had decided her silence came with all that she knew but left unsaid. Jodie took her doomsday pamphlets and pressed dimes into her outstretched hand for no better reason than the woman's blind allegiance to duty. At the second light tap, Jodie slipped on her work shoes, crossed the room, and opened the door.

"Oh, Jesus Christ, it's you!" Jodie blushed so, she was sure she smelled her own scorched hair.

"I'm sorry to have startled you. I'm intruding." Mrs. Curtis turned away, hurrying back toward the idling car.

Jodie called, "No, Sarah, wait. You just got here." At the sound of her voice calling Sarah's name, Jodie's stomach lurched, and it was as though she actually knew her.

Sarah Curtis turned back. Her shallow breath pushed through her parted red lips, her reticence betrayed, igniting in Jodie a sense of her own vulnerability, and she struggled to regain some semblance of control.

"Unless you've come to invite me to church, you're welcome."

"No, I'd never do that. Invite you to church, I mean." Sarah's lip quivered.

"Then why are you here?" Jodie ran her fingers through her cropped hair. Every fiber of her body warned against her willingness to become this woman's ticket to the wild side, if that was what she wanted from her.

"I hoped you might take a drive. With me, that is." Her voice shook and she clutched a slender hand to her throat. She wasn't wearing a wedding band.

Jodie turned the fire off from under the beans, pulled the door closed behind her, and got into the car. They drove an unfamiliar back road into the next county, and Jodie gave little thought as to where they might be going. She'd stopped caring the moment she saw Sarah at the hospital.

"How'd you find me?" Maybe she knew already.

"Forgive me, but I followed you home from work one day last week."

"Just so you know, I kept going back to the store for a time."

"Yes, I know. I saw you there from across the street."

They turned off the highway onto a dirt road that ended at a green metal gate. Jodie took the key from Sarah's hand, got out of the car, and unlocked the gate, careful to secure the lock behind them. The fence enclosed a collection of six cabins arranged in the shape of a horseshoe, a larger building at its open end. Beyond these cabins, they ascended an incline into a heavily wooded stretch of a narrow lane. She stopped the car in front of an isolated cabin that stood beneath a canopy of naked trees.

The cold pricked Jodie's flushed cheeks as she waited while Sarah Curtis fumbled a second key into the lock. The one-room cabin was bare except for a double bed and a lone, green, straight-back chair, its paint chipped. Above the bed, a picture of a crucified Jesus hung crooked from the wall.

Dust motes and lint fibers floated upward from the worn chenille bedspread when they sat, and Jodie's heart pounded with an even mix of desire and fear. She reached and took Sarah's moist hands in hers. While Jodie's hands were rough, nails worn jagged, cuticles stained blue from denim, Sarah Curtis's were deathly pale with long, tapered fingers and palms smooth as ice. Her near-perfect face was adeptly fashioned into what Jodie imagined was the feminine ideal. Jodie's hands trembled, but she took the woman's face between her palms, and with her thumb she gently wiped Mrs. Curtis's painted mouth.

"I want to taste you. The real you."

She lifted her gaze to Jodie, but she didn't speak.

"You don't need to be afraid. You're safe with me."

Jodie's sought her own courage, courage enough to act blindly, and with only her desire fueling her boldness, Jodie drew Sarah Curtis down next to her on the bed. She brushed her thick hair back from her face, and the darker flecks in her irises flashed some terrible memory. She pressed Jodie's fingertips against rough patches of skin at her temples, her one imperfection, it would seem.

"The electric shock treatments were supposed to cure me of my sickness. I pleaded with the doctor that if God created me, then Jesus Christ embraced me. But he shouted me down, insisting that such an absurdity was further proof of my insanity." Her tears reached Jodie's fingertips.

The State of Florida had "Old Smokey" to punish murderers, but she'd never heard of electricity curing anything. If this all-important Jesus had come to establish goodness, then such cruelty had silenced any such intentions. She recalled the directive that she and Clara Lee should *see mental illness*, and what should have terrified her in this moment only emboldened her. She pulled the woman to her, kissed her fully on the lips, and Mrs. Curtis tasted of grief.

Their kisses grew more demanding, and Jodie matched Sarah's experience with her own eagerness. Their desires meshed and earlier fears of awkwardness melted with their shared arousal. Jodie welcomed her pent-up desires, and when they were spent, they lay back in each other's arms. Jodie shed quiet, shameless tears of relief.

"Just now you called me Katherine." She hadn't minded at the time, but now was different.

"I did? Oh, I'm so sorry." She pulled from Jodie's arms and sat upright on the edge of the bed.

"No, it's okay. But you can't keep calling me Katherine. My name is …."

Sarah pressed a finger to Jodie's lips, and their scent was strong on her skin. "No, please. They do things—horrible things—to make me tell."

"I'm Jodie Taylor. And I'm not afraid."

"Oh, but you should be afraid."

Jodie didn't want to consider Sarah's warning. She reached, taking Sarah into her arms. But she pulled out of Jodie's embrace, stood, and began to hurriedly dress. She ran a quick comb through her hair and reapplied lipstick, growing more anxious, urging Jodie to hurry.


Monday night, Jodie clocked in and walked into the break room where three gossipy women huddled in a corner. At her approach, their circle of hushed talk drew tighter. Jodie stashed her supper pail and walked out in search of Bitsy while working at tamping down her sudden spike of anxiety.

She was still baffled over Sarah's hasty retreat from the cabin and her even stranger departure from the clearing without as much as a good-bye. Jodie had sat on the steps much of Sunday, near enough to hear the phone, and listened for sounds of the big Oldsmobile. Then, Sarah's Sundays, like those of Miss Ruth, were lost to God.

Among her co-workers, Jodie practiced the art of invisibility, and she was damn good at it. The others spoke openly of their miserable lives: their family and kin's early and hard deaths due to random and intentional violence, their many lesser scrapes and narrow escapes. They even shared their most intimate sexual fantasies, while cursing the trifling men they swore to love and hate with equal fervor.

Over time, a consensus had emerged, one that portrayed her as owning no stories, at least ones that mattered in the ways theirs did. Her fear reflex drove her denial, and in that way she bore part of the blame for her seeming lack of humanity. It was the price she paid to hold on to the small part of her that was honest.

Bitsy stood in a side door, sucking nicotine into her lungs, and Jodie called to her. "Hey, gal, what's up with that mug? Some guy slipped the vice of those great thighs?" Jodie forced a smile, but Bitsy was in no mood for jokes.

"No, it ain't like that." Bitsy was fighting mad, and if not about some guy, Jodie was at a loss to know.

"You remember that woman we joked about wanting a job here? The preacher's wife?"

Jodie shrugged. "So, what about her?" She was certain no one had seen them together, yet her blood surged.

"I'll tell you what. She put a gun to her temple and blew her pretty face away. That's what."

Jodie's fingertips remembered the sensation of the rough patches at Sarah's temples. She felt the round coolness of the gun barrel pressed into her own flesh, and she turned away from Bitsy, her heart pounding so hard against her ribs she imagined them splintering.

"Bess just now said the poor thing was to have had the choir's solo part in church yesterday."

With her back still to Bitsy, she managed, "There's stage fright, but damned if that don't take the prize." She closed her eyes, cursing herself for the cowardice of her words.

"Good God, Jodie. You're one cold-hearted bitch. And you don't even care what's being talked around?"

Jodie turned and Bitsy was staring at her in disbelief. "Christ, it's not like I knew her." Talk, what talk? Fear displaced her grief, shutting her down to all but self-preservation.

Bitsy stomped away, passing among the rows of idle machines.

Jodie called to her, "Bitsy, please, wait up."

Bitsy stopped and turned, glaring.

"I'm sorry. I'm … I didn't mean what I said. Please. Did you learn her name?"

"Name? You said yourself she's just another dead woman. Now you're telling me you're planning on sending flowers?"

"I never said she didn't matter. But what I did say was stupid. And I feel like ripping my tongue out."

"Her name was Sarah. Sarah Curtis." Bitsy wiped tears away with the back of her hand. "And don't it scare you? A pretty, smart woman like her? And me with this ape-ugly mug, barely hanging on. What do you think I might do?"

"Bitsy, listen to me. You're feeling ugly … and all alone. But you're not."

"Yeah, well, if you're figuring on those flowers, you'd better get a wiggle on. Deputy Lloyd cut short our tryst last night over some story about making arrangements to escort her body out of town. Her prick husband refused to have the undertaker fix that poor woman's face. He's sending her home to her family looking like that." She turned and walked away.

Outside the building, Jodie leaned, clutching her middle. Did Reverend Curtis mean to return Sarah's body to her family the way he might a broken appliance? After all, he was promised a whole woman, not some freak of nature. Jodie bit into her bottom lip and tasted her own blood. She wiped at her lip, and when strength returned to her legs, she walked back onto the floor, taking her place on the line.

Eight hours later, Jodie clocked out, called a tentative good-bye to a still brooding Bitsy, and headed for her truck. The open field between the parking lot and the highway lay blanketed in a heavy frost, and a stiff north wind blew loose gravel across her path. It was a damn poor day for a funeral.

Driving onto the highway, she considered a detour that would take her away from the converted plantation mansion with its huge white columns, serving bereaved whites only, but instead her grief drove her on in its direction. Across from the funeral home, she pulled the truck onto the shoulder of the highway and sat hunched and shivering. The warmth from the clattering heater couldn't touch the cold gripping her heart.

A polished black Cadillac hearse sat at a side door, flanked by four men dressed in dark suits. The men slid a plain wooden box into the hearse, and Jodie had a sickening sense that the box held Sarah's remains. The oldest of the men stepped to the driver's side door, looked back at the three men still standing, and laughed at some shared joke before sliding behind the wheel. He eased the hearse along the gravel driveway and onto the highway without the customary police escort. But there was no need for such; not a single car followed bearing grieving family or friends.

Jodie floored the old truck, sped onto the highway, and wedged the truck into the space between the hearse and the car that had pulled up directly behind it. The driver raised a fist, and she read profanity on his lips. Her careless action forced, if nothing else, the appearance of a slow-moving funeral cortege—one comprised of a jagged line of disgruntled strangers—until Jodie broke rank and turned back.

She stopped the truck in front of the pink trailer and shut down the engine. As heavy silence reclaimed the tiny clearing, she feared the weight of her own despair. She stepped onto the narrow path of trampled star thistles and moved unsteadily toward the single light hanging above the door.

## Thirty-Three

At the sound of Jodie's voice, the stray paced back and forth, keeping its customary distance. She lifted her glass in mock salute before putting it to her lips. The cat sat back on its haunches and watched her from the pile of dirty laundry, as though it needed time to make up its mind. Teddy had warned that she needed something steady. Sarah Curtis was everything, but nothing, that Teddy had imagined for her.

"What do you think, cat? Should I call Silas?" If she were to call him, there was nothing she could tell him about Sarah Curtis and her recurring bouts of guilt.

She drained the glass and headed straight into the drunk that promised to blunt her memories and bend her reality into a version she might bear. But first, she'd make that long overdue call.

She squeezed her eyes tight against her dread, counting the long, empty rings. She had started to believe Silas had opened the shop and gone next door to the Flamingo Café, where he would tolerate weak coffee for a chance at flirting with a willing waitress, when he finally answered.

"Hey, Silas, it's me." Her mouth flooded with words and there was no holding back. "I was damn stupid to leave the way I did. And I'm sorry for not calling back before now. But it was nothing like what you think. And you've got to agree to never again ask me about Roy Dale or why I left. You do, and I'm hanging up for good." Her outburst left her winded.

The phone line crackled, and she thought about all the wrongs her words would need to heal. And it was too much to expect that time, alone, had done more than scab over the deeper wounds.

"All right, Jodie. If that's what it takes to know your crazy ass is still in this fucked up world."

"That's good. Real good. I'm glad." Until her avalanche of tears for Sarah Curtis, Jodie hadn't known how much she'd missed him.

"If I'd known where, I would've called two weeks ago." His tone carried the full weight of tragedy.

"God, is it Red?"

"No, it's that Miss Ruth passed. Sudden-like. And Maggie's run off." His voice was barely audible.

Denial pressed so hard on her vocal cords she was speechless.

"Jodie?"

"She wasn't sick."

"Heart attack—a big one. Took her while she and Maggie sat peacefully on their back porch. No warning … nothing. One minute fine. The next not."

Jodie remembered—although she had not fully understood at the time—Maggie speaking of her and Miss Ruth's shared moments on their back porch as their sitting with their backs to the world's meanness. Moments when sheer pleasure rose as naturally as cream to the top, she'd chuckled.

"And what do you mean, Maggie ran off?"

"Don't know for sure. It's just that she hasn't come back." His voice grew weepy, and he cleared his throat. "Mr. Samuel and me followed her home after the funeral and helped her load her boat and gear. "After a day or so I got worried and went looking for her. Found her truck parked where we always cooked. But there was no sign of her."

"Where's Red? He'd know where to look."

"He's off on one of his damn whoring trips." His flash of anger surprised her. He'd always defended Red.

"Silas, Maggie can take care of herself. She knows that river like her own mind." She sought to quash her own fears as much as his.

Jodie pictured Maggie camped near the ancient bald cypress, her favorite spot on the river. The tree rose forty feet against the sky, its woody, right-angled knees sprouting out of the water, and she'd sworn that if it were not for its knees, the cypress couldn't breathe. The knees were anchors, she'd claimed, and instead of blowing over in the worst winds, it held strong. Jodie now believed that Maggie had meant to make a point about family.

"God, girl, we're all she's got. Why won't she let me help her?"

Jodie had no answer other than *She's Maggie*. Silas couldn't hear that. He needed to believe he could fix whatever she needed. Still, she'd say as much as he could hear.

"Silas, she'll be back when she's ready. And then she'll need you more than ever."

Jodie hung up the phone, Silas still pleading for her to come home to help look for Maggie, and although she knew neither could fix Maggie's pain, she could not manage as much as *when she comes home, please tell her I love her.*

Jodie drank whiskey and slept, woke and drank more, until the whiskey made her too sick to drink. She dragged herself out of bed, hugged the toilet, and puked until she was too weak to stand. She lay curled on the shower floor, her loss so acute she felt as though her mind separated from her lifeless body, and that it wandered in search of her mama, Miss Ruth, everyone she'd loved. She did not care if she drowned.

For two weeks, the gossipers had crowded into the break room, never tiring of chewing and regurgitating the smallest morsels surrounding Sarah Curtis's death—so much so that Jodie started taking her supper break sitting on the tailgate of her truck, beneath the glow of a security light.

The sudden crunching of loose gravel from the direction of the side door startled her, and she turned toward the sound. Bitsy walked into the circle of light carrying a covered plate.

"Hey, gal, you got something stuck in your craw that you can't eat with me no more?" Bitsy glared as though prepared to do an about-face should Jodie's response not suit her.

"Naw, I like the clean smell of frost." She pulled her jacket tighter, the air as cold as it got on average.

"Do believe news of the second coming would go unnoticed by that crowd." Bitsy took a seat next to Jodie on the tailgate. "The poor woman's dead and in her grave, cold as their hearts. You'd think they'd let up."

"I hear hate's got a long lifeline." Jodie wadded the uneaten half of her PB&J in waxed paper and tossed it into the bed of the truck.

Bitsy handed Jodie the slice of cake she'd been holding.

"If you're worried about losing friends among that bunch, you can forget it. Then, my junkyard dog could use a friend. He's 'bout to get shot for screwing a neighbor's fancy bitch." She smiled one of her twisted smiles that could leave Jodie confused as to her meaning.

"That's too bad. I end up being liked by most dogs I meet."

"Speaking of curs, my baby turned seven yesterday. And that asshole daddy of hers didn't as much as call and make up one of his lame excuses."

"Damn, that kid deserves better. You deserve better."

"Aw, don't we all." Her laugh was like a razor cut. "He never claimed her. Tried telling the damn fool I was fifty-one percent sure."

"That's not exactly what you'd call good odds." Jodie playfully bumped Bitsy's shoulder.

Bitsy raked a finger through the frosting, making a big show of licking the creamy chocolate icing away. "Maybe I'll try me a man darker than that chocolate smeared on your shocked face."

"I take it you're tired of living." Jodie worried that Bitsy was crazy enough to do such a thing. Then, that was no crazier than queer sex with a preacher's wife.

Bitsy jammed her hands between her knees and gazed into the cold darkness beyond the glow of the security light.

"You're fooling about smelling frost, right?"

Jodie shook her head. "Hell no, can't you tell? It's the clean smell covering all the stench in this shitty world.

## Thirty-Four

Jodie stayed away from the Hide and Seek, straight through spring and into early summer. Although she believed Teddy knew more than she let on, Jodie admitted to nothing, not even having known of Sarah Curtis's death. During the long days and weeks, she'd slept restlessly, ate little, shot baskets, and ran the five-mile distance of the dirt road until time to make her shift at the jean factory.

When her physical exertion could no long vanquish her most basic urges, she drove out of the clearing, headed for the one place she felt truly welcome. She backed her truck into the underbrush, respecting Crystal Ann's notion that doing so upped her chances should she take a sudden notion to leave. Shutting down the engine, she pulled the bottle of Jim Beam from beneath the seat and took a slow pull, the warmth of the liquor stoking her determination.

A faint breeze played catch-me-if-you-can among the tops of the tallest pines while sultry air hung at ground-level like a damp dishrag. From somewhere deeper in the woods, the frenzied baying of a pack of hounds charged the upper air currents with a certainty of death. She paused at the edge of the tree cover and stared back in the direction of the empty road that shimmered in the moonlight like a free-floating kite's tail.

She announced herself to the door person, and with her best butch leading, she strolled into the bar. Gabby looked up from fishing beers from the tub of ice.

"Damn, gal. How long has it been?" Gabby pushed a cold Pabst into Jodie's hand, and although she sensed an unfamiliar restraint pass between them, Jodie checked her anxiety.

"Too long, but I'm back. And I've brought along my urgency." She sat at the bar and took a long pull on the beer, sending bubbles up her nose.

"It's a mite slow, but it's early." Gabby paused. "Then your type will be along." The dark skin beneath her right eye quivered. "We get 'em all in here. Sunday school teachers to those working both ways. Reckon we'll be here as long as I grease the right palms."

Gabby loaded a tray with beers from the tub. "Watch the store? I'm going out back and carve meat for you carnivores." She walked away, the tray resting on her forearm.

Jodie watched her maneuver her way among tables of jovial women, exchanging cold beers for empties as she made her way to the rear door. Jodie looked for the slightest indication that what she'd just heard wasn't intended as a warning, and that there were no rumors that might connect her to Sarah Curtis. Women who threatened to bring trouble were dealt with swiftly, and not always in ways that were friendly.

Jodie stepped around the bar, helped herself to another Blue Ribbon, and placed a pencil mark on the tally pad next to her name. She retook her seat and sat with her hands wrapped around the icy bottle, considering all that hadn't passed between her and Gabby. The fact she was here, was that in itself proof enough?

The loud, playful bantering of the others, their whispered promises, and the heat rising from their bodies, steadied her. Her pulse rate leveled out, and the beer had begun to dull her raw edges. She wouldn't borrow trouble. It arrived often enough of its own volition.

The big, rough hand pounding Jodie's shoulder belonged to Ted, not Teddy.

"What the hell? What'd you do to Teddy?"

"Murdered the bitch." Teddy laughed. "No, that would be Maxine's mama."

"Why Ted, here?"

"Long story around my not getting done with a brake job on Maxine's sorry-ass car. We're on my machine." She pulled two beers from the tub, tossed two quarters into the cigar box, and took the stool next to Jodie.

"Got to ask."

"Aw, that one?"

"Yeah, complicated."

"All right."

"Am I in trouble here?"

"No, but a tighter rein can't hurt."

Jodie understood Teddy's caution was about class, and those with power to make wide-spread trouble.

Maxine came through the back door and, spotting them, she smiled. Hers was a smile that in any given moment could cause a skeptic to believe that life was void of limitations and held only possibilities.

Jodie stood, and she and Maxine hugged. Maxine asked how she'd been, and she lied, putting forth her best face. Pity showed in Maxine's eyes, and Jodie looked away, out onto the dance floor. Maxine squeezed Jodie's hand. "I'm sorry, Jodie. I just hate when someone I love is unhappy."

"Yeah, I know."

"What do you hear from Crystal Ann?"

"She's mostly good, I think." She'd had a scenic beach postcard from Pensacola, making her answer only a white lie.

"I know you two agree that Brenda's wrong for her. But I hope this time it works for them. Oddly enough, we perfectly sensible women do fall in love with those who seem wrong for us."

"And that would include every one of us lucky enough to figure we've found true love." Teddy reached and pulled Maxine close, burying her face in the curve of Maxine's neck. Maxine mussed Teddy's bristled crew cut with the tenderness Jodie had seen her show with her kids.

Teddy winked at Jodie, and with her arm around Maxine's slim waist, they moved toward the crowded dance floor.

Even though Jodie found it hard to believe in a kind of love that stayed, she envied the familiar way Teddy and Maxine moved in each other's arms. They fit the dream that all wanted to believe.

Jodie took a table and surveyed the room, but there was no one who caught her eye. It was the second time she'd heard of Brenda and Crystal Ann's multiple breakups. The possibility of Crystal Ann's old

218 • Pat Spears

Rambler rattling into the clearing and a chance for her and Crystal Ann at getting it right drove her lack of interest.

"Hey, Jodie, is it all right if I sit?"

Jodie pulled over a second chair, and Shirley sat, sniffling for a while before she could speak. Her eyes were beet red, and her bright, overdone orange makeup was streaked.

She leaned across the table and whispered, "Lou's at it again." She took a long swig from the glass of beer Jodie had poured. "And I've started thinking turnabout is fair play."

Jodie nodded. "Maybe, but it's got its downside."

"You wouldn't be interested in going home with me, now would you?"

"You know I can't do that. You two are bound to patch things up, and I'd land my ass in the middle of something neither of us intended."

"You're right. But would you at least walk me out? Please, I hate walking out alone."

"Sure, I was thinking to leave myself." There would be gossip to set straight, but there always was.

Outside the bar, Shirley called good-night and Jodie watched her drive away. She looked back toward the bar, the mournful voice of Kitty Wells pleading on behalf of honky-tonk angels.

Through the dark stand of trees, Jodie sighted headlights flickering, and at first she thought Shirley had changed her mind. Then more lights and the roar of engines. Vehicles approached, and they were coming hard.

She raced to the truck and sounded the horn three quick blasts—the agreed upon signal. Within minutes the clearing would explode in the roar of engines, the nightmarish shrill of sirens, flashing lights, and the screams of women.

## Thirty-Five

J odie ran full speed into the woods, underbrush tearing at her face and arms. At a distance of thirty yards or so into the cover of the trees, she dropped onto the ground and crawled beneath a large, uprooted pine. She pulled fallen branches to cover her and tried catching her breath. She was soaked to the skin in sweat, her scent that of pure fear.

She listened to the screams of panicked women as they pushed through the two doors and scattered in search of hiding places. Through the darkness, she thought she recognized Teddy moving in her direction. But she didn't see Maxine, and Teddy would never leave her behind.

In the harsh glow of spotlights, Jodie searched the faces of those pushed to their knees and pinned into a tight circle by swarming men wielding nightsticks. Jodie gasped as she watched Miss Doris's futile attempt to crawl beneath a nearby car. Kicking and cursing, she was dragged back into the circle by a burly man twice her size and half her age. Neither Teddy nor Maxine was in the circle of women.

At the flat, metallic thuds of batons slamming into soft tissue and the desperate cries of the pinned women, together with fits of male taunting, Jodie pushed further under the pine. The sound of someone moving through the trees in her direction drew closer, and she realized that the first runner was being chased by a second.

She peered into the gray void, struggling to figure her next move. She patted the ground in search of anything with enough heft to become a weapon. She grasped a fallen limb with the thickness of a bat, and tears of relief swelled in her throat.

Less than ten yards away, she recognized Teddy's slow, clumsy gait and Jodie risked calling out to her. But Teddy stopped and turned back into the path of her pursuer. She and her stalker faced off, and the cop shouted, "Goddamn you. I'll fucking kill you."

Teddy swore and lunged, striking the bigger man a blow to his face. He retaliated, catching her with a glancing shot to her right temple. She moaned, staggered backward, tripped, and fell to the ground.

The enraged cop was on her before she could regain her feet, and he raised his baton time and time again, pounding her. She covered her head, drew her body into a fetal position, and never made another sound. The cop landed a heavy boot into Teddy's ribs, and Jodie heard a low whistle as air rushed from her lungs.

Jodie screamed, her rage propelling her forward, her fear tasting metallic in her mouth. Tightening her grip on the limb, she covered the distance with fury fueled by all the wrongs she'd known. Before the cop could fully turn, she swung with all her strength, landing a glancing blow across his lower back but missing his kidney, her intended target. His body stiffened but he somehow kept his feet. She drew back and struck him a second blow across his shoulders. He buckled and crashed facedown onto the ground.

Back in the direction of the clearing, she heard a second set of heavy footsteps coming in their direction.

"Oh God, Teddy, I'm so sorry. Can you stand?" Jodie whispered. "We've got to hide."

Teddy struggled, but dropped back onto her knees.

"Go on, Jodie. I've got to go back. Find Maxine. She was right behind me. I don't know what happened." Teddy sobbed.

"You can't help her now. You've got to get to your feet." Jodie helped her stand, and Teddy stood doubled over, clutching her ribs.

There was no time to get deeper into the woods. They crouched behind the pine, watching as a second cop approached. The man on the ground struggled onto his knees.

"Shit, man. What the hell happened to you?"

"Don't make sense ... I know I downed ... a man. And then out of nowhere a second slugged me from behind. Never saw that one."

"You're crazy." The second cop snorted. "What you had was one them bull dykes. Can't tell them from the real thing." He laughed. "Unless you grab for their balls."

"You ain't one damn bit funny." His pride scorched, he fired his revolver blindly four times, screaming profanities. Bullets sprayed leaves, snapping limbs overhead, and Jodie slipped a hand over Teddy's mouth, struggling to hold her down.

"Damnit, man, quit that crazy cowboy shit. Boss don't want the kin of no dead woman on his hands. Don't matter if she is queer. We've got plenty beat down, loaded in the paddy wagon. Boss wants them jailed in time to make the Sunday paper. We're here to win an election.

The two retreated and Jodie helped Teddy to her feet, but they waited until the last of the vehicles had sped away amid an array of loud laughter, insults, threats, and blaring horns before stumbling into the clearing. From all directions, shaken women emerged from hiding. They gathered in the clearing, asking about the gunshots, and when reassured no one had been shot, they set about accounting for those missing. A deeper despair settled over the women when it was determined that Miss Doris was among those on their way to jail.

"They'll be lucky if she don't capsize that wagon and beat the hell out of them brutes," someone called, and their hollow laughter moved like a wave around the circle.

While two nurses among them attended to those who had suffered lacerations and bruises, those they feared suffered more serious injuries— concussions, cuts needing stitches, and broken bones—were driven to a known sympathetic doctor in a neighboring county. Veterans of raids sought to comfort the first-timers, especially those whose lovers were among the women taken away. Then there were no guarantees that their worst fate was behind them.

While Jodie and Teddy were reassured that Maxine wasn't among those taken, she was unaccounted for, and they feared that she lay too hurt to move or even call out. Others joined their search, but Jodie was first to spot Maxine crawling from beneath a pile of discarded lumber located beyond the perimeter of the clearing.

"There, Teddy." Jodie's relief was so complete her words came hoarse to her lips.

Teddy called to Maxine, and gripping her left side, she ran to embrace her.

"Easy, baby, easy. I think I might have a busted rib or two."

"Oh, Teddy," Maxine began to sob. "I was so afraid."

Teddy held her and whispered, "I know, baby. I know."

"There were rats. And you know how I hate those little bastards."

Jodie stood back from Teddy and Maxine, deeply shamed by her cowardice in having failed to react sooner, sparing Teddy at least part of the brutal beating she suffered.

Over the top of Maxine's head, Teddy looked at Jodie, and said, "Damned if Jodie didn't lay one of them bastards out flat. Saved my ass for sure." Teddy reached and drew Jodie into her and Maxine's embrace. They held each other, and not trusting words they might have spoken, they laughed uncontrollably until they cried.

## Thirty-Six

Sunday morning, Jodie drove into Selma, paid a quarter for the Sunday edition of the local newspaper that served the tri-county areas, and drove directly to Teddy's place: two rented rooms over a neighborhood liquor store. Parking next to Teddy's tarp-covered motorcycle, she rushed up the outdoor stairway and rapped on Teddy's door. She glanced about for unusual movement along the now empty street. The echo of Teddy's hurried footsteps, followed by the metallic whoosh of the deadbolt sliding and the door swinging open were the only sounds.

Teddy stood in the doorway, clutching her rib cage, her eyes the color of tomato paste, and it was clear she had suffered through a long night.

"Hey, what'd the paper say?" Teddy's breath was strong with the scent of chicory and bourbon.

Jodie handed Teddy the paper and followed her into the tiny alley kitchen. Teddy nodded toward the coffee pot heating on the stove and took a seat at the small table wedged against the wall.

Jodie poured coffee, then sat across from Teddy.

"Jesus God," Teddy moaned. "They're totally screwed."

Jodie sipped the strong coffee, remembering Jewel's warning that if she was to stay alive, she'd need to live small in this world. The women's photos appearing above the paper's top fold meant their carefully constructed, secretive worlds were flung open to ridicule, hatred, and the evil acts of those who didn't know them, but were sure they despised them. Jodie focused on Miss Doris's photo, her face haggard, but with a deeply defiant, hard set to her jaw, and she worried that Miss Doris might not have time enough to rebuild her shattered world. Then the passing of her beloved may have ended the life she'd most cherished, and there was nothing more others might attempt to take from her.

"Is there nothing we can do?"

"Damn, Jodie, sometimes your ignorance of how things work amazes me." Teddy retrieved a half-empty bottle of bourbon from the cabinet under the sink, poured a hefty slug of liquor into her coffee cup, and looked to Jodie. Teddy had spoken of the convenience of living above a liquor store, teasing it saved her plenty of shoe leather.

"No, it's early for me." She knew better than to hope for a magical fix, and forgave Teddy's harshness as an eruption of their shared anguish.

"It's later than you think."

The newspaper reporter praised the sheriff's diligence in ridding the county of the moral corruption of these female freaks of nature, calling their presence a blight on communities of God-fearing citizens, their sexual deviancy a threat to every woman and child.

"Paper says they're charged with 'illegal assembly with the intent to commit sodomy.' What exactly does that mean?"

Teddy shook her head, and smiled. "Like I said, darling, they're screwed. That is unless you've got the judge on your payroll."

Jodie nodded, and reached for the bottle.

The following Tuesday, the incumbent sheriff was reelected in a landslide victory, and the raid had served its purpose. From local gossip Jodie learned that Gabby, under considerable pressure, had agreed to sell the building that had housed the Hide and Seek and its eighty acres to the sheriff's brother-in-law: the first step in converting the property into a private, gentlemen's only, hunting club, with gambling and prostitution as its featured attractions.

After five days of incarceration, public interest had waned, and with Gabby further agreeing to pay the women's inflated fines, charges were reduced, requiring no additional jail time. The women were escorted from the jail at midnight through a side door.

The local newspaper didn't report their releases, but the personal damage had been done. The exposure resulted in painful losses: parents and extended families disowning their daughters, lesbian couples splitting for the sake of protecting the unidentified partner, loss of employment, housing, and, in the case of two mothers, the loss of parental rights to their children. They were easy targets, subjected to unrestrained righteous rants, and easy prey for the ruthlessness of men. They had no choice but to scatter like rats facing extermination.

In the six months following the raid, Gabby had moved to Birmingham where it was rumored she opened a pizza parlor. The front half of the building sold pizza to families. After closing, a separate clientele entered through an alleyway to the back half of the building, arriving with only a secondary interest in pizza. Gabby was reported to have spoken of the comfort to be found in the normalcy of corruption.


Jodie drove from the jean factory into yet another empty sunrise. She clasped a cigarette between her lips, lit it from the one pinched between her finger and thumb, and considered the storm that had been building inside of her for some time now. One that left her jittery, inside and out; a deep unsettling she'd come to know as her fear of surrender: capitulation to the deadly undertow of complacency.

She wasn't sure why today, ordinary in every way, sent her rushing into the trailer and going directly to the telephone. She pulled the worn card from her wallet, the number barely discernible, and placed a call to the number in Dallas. Her breathing came in hot puffs of air squeezed between her dry lips, and she counted seven rings.

"Anybody here know a Jodie ... what'd you say your name was?" The male voice was younger than before, abrupt, but not dismissive.

She answered and worked at deep breathing while the line spit static back at her for much too long to mean anything good. She imagined a black phone hanging from some dingy wall, the receiver dangling from its cord, swinging back and forth, seeking equilibrium,

226 • Pat Spears

and then hanging limp. She took a firmer grip, her palm sweaty, and wished she'd first made herself an Irish.

"Hold on, gal. She's coming."

Who was coming? She had no idea, unless it was the person charged with talking to fools like her. Talk aimed at easing the directive that she take a hike. Marry that shoe salesman and have babies.

"Hey, Jodie, you grown up some?"

She nearly strangled on her dry spit. She'd heard the same voice in her head every day since the sweet swish of the ball through the net.

"Jodie, you there?"

"Oh, yes, ma'am. I truly have. Grown up, I mean."

Her soft laugh was sheer joy to Jodie's ear.

"I called before, but they said you quit."

"So, that's what they told you?" There was a long pause that could only mean the truth would go unspoken.

"I kept your card. And I've tried every day since to get there. But one thing, and then another."

"Look, Jodie, I know life can be a bitch. But I'm real busy here. What can I do for you?"

"Trials. I mean to come there for the next round."

"You're still thinking about taking a shot?" Jodie imagined a nod so slight it was barely an acknowledgment, and clearly not encouragement.

"It's all I think about. I want it more than anything." She hungered for the exhilaration that came with pushing her body to exhaustion, the triumph she knew when dominating an opponent. She'd only known its match when the woman she was with came under her touch.

"The girls who come are younger. The competition's fierce. And the coach only wants a certain type of woman." She hesitated. "If you have a job, you might not want to give it up."

"You saying I'm not good enough?" She twisted the tangled cord and clamped her jaw. She'd heard "certain type of woman" but chose to bury it right along with all her other doubts.

"No, I'm saying home-town talents don't always measure up. But, all right, I'm pretty sure I can get you on the list. Trials are in four months. Be at the address on the card. And Jodie, be in the best shape of your life or I promise you'll die trying."

"Oh, God, thank you. I'll be there. And you won't be sorry."

Jodie placed a call to Teddy's workplace and asked to speak to Ted. She sat through the profane boss's rant about Ted getting too many calls from his girlfriend.

"Hey, make it snappy. I'm working here." Teddy's voice was gruff and Jodie smiled.

"It's me. I gotta talk right away. Can I come by your place tonight before my shift?"

"Yeah, yeah, right. That it?" Jodie was certain the boss hovered nearby.

Convinced she would not sleep, Jodie slipped on a pair of old shorts and a tee shirt. After a handful of food eaten standing before the open fridge, she laced up her tennis shoes and stepped into the bright sunlight.

Teddy swung open the door. "Hey, girl, come on in. Tell me who's got your cheeks all rosy. Do I know her?" Teddy was still dressed as Ted and smelled every bit the role. She claimed she didn't use deodorant on the job. Doing so would mean heavy teasing, and even the risk of suspicion among a few of her co-workers.

"Way better than any woman." Jodie laughed, her cheeks flushing hotter with her rush of excitement.

Teddy squinted. "Oh, yeah, and what could that be?"

"I called Dallas. And the woman I told you about, the one I scored on, she's back on the team."

"Okay, I guess I should be happy for her."

"Teddy, you don't get it. She's getting me on the list."

"That's not news. You were on the list before. And pissed it away."

"I know, but this time is different. With her backing, I've got a real chance. And by God, nothing short of a bullet to the brain is stopping me." Jodie paced the room, banging a fist into her palm.

Teddy slammed the fridge door. "Damn, now you're talking. That's what I've been waiting to hear. Let's celebrate." She grabbed two beers.

Jodie glanced at her watch. The super wouldn't notice a single beer.

"Take these and let me go unbind the girls. Morning since I've had a deep breath. I'm on my own tonight. Little Cindy's got a school thing." Her features pinched into what Jodie knew as an expression of painful regret. The kids begged Ted to come to their school events, but she dared not risk setting off an explosive bout with their grandma.

Teddy continued talking through the open bedroom door. "What's it going to take to get your ass there and keep you till your first paycheck?"

"Don't know." What she had wouldn't get her out of sight of Selma.

Teddy came from the bedroom wearing faded jeans, a stained tee shirt without a bra, and scuffed cowboy boots rather than the heavy, steel-toed boots Ted wore on the job. She grabbed a beer from Jodie's hand, took a slug, and wiped her mouth on her sleeve.

"Don't matter. I'll get you what you need." Teddy wore her banker's face. "But, know it's a loan. I don't do charity work."

"Hell, no, I'm good for it. That's if we both live long enough." She liked that Teddy had spoken first, sparing her the humiliation of asking.

"Hell, woman, I figure you'll owe me a long time before you'll beat me out of it." Teddy took another deep swallow of beer. "But you've got to promise me one thing."

"Name it and you've got it."

"You'll send me a signed photo of you in one of them skimpy little uniforms. Figure to hang it in my work locker alongside Liz and Marilyn. Charge the boys a quarter to look. Win back some of what I've lost to your pitiful game."

"Shut your mouth, you damn fool." Their laughter likely turned heads on the sidewalk below.

## Thirty-Seven

The ring shattered Jodie's deepest sleep. In her fog, she grabbed for the phone, expecting to hear Silas. He'd taken to calling on Saturday nights, after he'd screwed some woman other than his wife and needed time to lose some of his guilt before dealing his way back between matrimonial sheets.

She swung her feet onto the floor and glanced at the clock. Three-thirty, and even Silas never called this late. Beyond the tiny bedroom window the moonless night was black, thick as wet tar.

She growled into the phone, her nerves fully awake.

"Jodie, it's me. You've got to come, and you've got to come right now."

"All right, but slow down. What the hell's going on? Come where?"

"Jodie, I can't come to you. It's not safe. I think they're watching me." Teddy panted like a cornered animal.

"Wait. Who's watching?"

"Can't talk now. You've got to come before it's too late."

Jodie crossed over the Alabama River on the Edmund Pettus Bridge, careful to drive at a legal speed, heading out of downtown Selma. Twenty-five minutes east on Highway 84, she spotted the wooden hull of what she believed was the abandoned fruit stand Teddy had described. She slowed the truck and approached. There was no sign or sound of Teddy's machine. Then, she hadn't said how far out she was, only that she'd meet her there.

Under the glow of a single outdoor light, the freshly plowed field adjacent to the dilapidated row of stalls shone like weak moonlight on a shallow lake. Jodie drove to the back side of the stalls and cut the engine, wishing she'd stopped at the all-night diner and bought a cup of its strong coffee. She glanced at her watch. It had been two hours since Teddy's frantic call.

Headlights from the sporadic approach of vehicles cast eerie bursts of light across the walls of the fruit stand, and Jodie worried that drivers might detect the shape of the truck. She listened to their sounds as they faded into the distance, welcoming the returned chorus of katydids and crickets and the call of an owl from so close she was sure it was watching her.

She sat for what seemed an eternity, staring in the direction of Selma, listening for the sound of Teddy's machine, and fighting off fearful notions of why she hadn't shown.

Behind her, Jodie heard approaching footsteps, and she reached toward the glove compartment. At the sound of Teddy whispering her name, she snapped the lid shut.

"What the hell's the matter with you, slipping up on me like that?" Jodie's voice went hoarse around the tightness in her throat. Teddy was on foot, and she carried her saddlebags over her shoulder.

"Sorry, but I'm riding bare-assed in a shit storm. I can't get in touch with Maxine." Her outburst went the way of a punctured tire, and what Teddy had left was no more than a weak whimper. "And I'm about fucking crazy."

"Whoa down, big gal. You're going to need to breathe."

"Damn, but this time I've ripped it for sure."

"All right, maybe, but get in. Start from the top." A number of rips came to mind, all bad, but the story would need to unfold coherently if she was to find a way to cut through Teddy's panic.

Teddy got into the truck and eased the door shut. "Jodie, I've got to leave town. And fast."

"All right, but why?"

"It's a long story. And I'll be okay when I know Maxine and those babies haven't been dragged into my mess."

"What mess?"

"Remember that sonofabitch cop we tussled with the night of the bar raid?" Leave it to Teddy to call their fight a tussle.

"Sure, what about him?"

"Today, before dinner break, he drives up to the shop, claiming his car engine's overheating. But he don't bother raising the hood. Just slow walks around my Harley. And I don't think much about it. Lots of guys do. Next thing I know, the boss is pointing my ass out to him. He struts over to where I'm knocking out a routine tune-up, starts in friendly enough, talking about my machine. Then he shifts into pig talk, saying he's pretty sure he's seen my Harley over in his county. And I tell him me and my gal ride over his way every now and then."

"Okay, there's no law against that." But a bested, brooding cop on a personal vendetta didn't need the law on his side. He *was* the law.

"Right, but he asked about the night of the raid. Didn't mention it outright, but I know it was the same night. Asked my gal's name."

"You didn't ...."

"Shit, no. I laughed. Asked which one."

"Okay, who did he think he was talking to?"

"Ted, I'm still thinking. And that's what's got me puzzled. He didn't come at it like a blown cover. If he had, I'd be stripped naked, plugged, and what was left of my ass floating in the Alabama River."

Jodie nodded. "What, then?"

"That's just it. I don't know. But he sounded pretty sure about where he saw my motorcycle. It's not easily missed."

"Jesus ...." Jodie remembered a numbers runner called Sammy the Snake showing up at the factory loading dock every week, perfectly timed for the supper break, and the hordes of women who'd swarmed him, dollar bills wadded in their callused hands.

"What?"

"I remember you and Maxine rode your Harley to the bar the night of the raid. You came as Ted. And remember that cop said to the other that he thought one of us was a man?"

Teddy's brow gathered, and she stared.

"What if there's a dealer he's paid to protect, and he thought you were there encroaching on his territory—selling to the women at the bar? A rural territory could be as big as the entire county." The reality of a personal vendetta tied to graft was starting to take shape. She'd figured the shots he'd fired were motivated by his rage, but maybe it was calculated.

"Shit, I'm history." Teddy's voice broke, and neither spoke of the horrific thoughts they likely shared.

"No, not if you leave now."

"I can't go till I know Maxine and those kids are okay. I've called her momma's five times, but she's not about to let me through."

"Give me the number. And the name of someone she works with."

"Betsy Wright. She sleeps with their boss." Teddy scratched the number on a scrap of paper and gave it to Jodie. Then she pulled out an envelope and handed that to her as well.

"Get this to Maxine when you can. It's the balance of my stash. She'll need it for rent and utilities on that house." Teddy paused. "I'm sorry, but I'm tapped out now. It don't leave anything for you and Dallas."

Jodie nodded. "That's all right. I'll get there. Don't worry. How can Maxine get in touch with you?"

"On that same paper I wrote the number of a phone booth at a filling station I'll hit in about three hours. I'll wait there for her call."

Jodie squinted at the number and back at Teddy.

"Living the way I do leaves little time for proper good-byes. I've always got a plan for a fast getaway."

Jodie had thought she understood the high price of Teddy and Maxine's love, but not so. Fighting back her fears, Jodie embraced Teddy, and she felt Teddy's splintered heart floating in her heaving chest. Neither spoke of the unfairness of the situation. What was the point? Saving Teddy was all that could matter just now. There would be time for the other later.

"Drop me will you? About a quarter of a mile back. Stashed my machine in the woods and walked here. Quieter that way."

Jodie reached into the glove compartment and withdrew her gun and a box of cartridges, and handed both to Teddy. She nodded her thanks and placed both in her saddlebag.

Jodie drove Teddy to her Harley and watched as she mounted the machine and kicked it into start, its familiar roar splitting the silence. Without a backward glance, Ted sped onto the highway and disappeared into a veil of obscurity, heading away from the life she, Maxine, and their kids had created. Their love had not been enough to save them.

Maxine's mama answered on the first ring. Jodie explained that she was a work friend, and their boss had asked her to call.

"What did you say your name is?"

"Betsy. Betsy Wright. And it's urgent."

"Maxine, it's me. Don't talk, just listen."

On the strength of a lie that a co-worker had taken ill, and that she was called in to finish out what was left of the night shift, Maxine met Jodie at the city park where she and Teddy had played Sunday afternoon basketball. She handed Maxine a coffee and explained what she and Teddy had figured out, then gave Maxine the envelope of money and the telephone number she was to call.

"Jodie, I don't think I can make it without Teddy. If it was just me I'd follow her to the ends of the earth. But if I take my kids and run, what kind of life would that mean for them? In time we'd be discovered, and I'd surely lose my babies."

Maxine sobbed, and the truth of her choice burned in Jodie's belly. Maxine could be either Teddy's lover or her children's mother, but she couldn't be both. Maxine could never risk losing her kids. And Teddy loved the three too much to ever ask Maxine to make such a choice.

"Hon, something's bound to turn up. You'll see." Jodie forced herself to speak the lie she imagined Maxine needed to hear but neither believed.

Yet she felt Maxine struggling to hold on to any part of the future she'd once imagined with Teddy and her kids. She stared out at the empty street, fresh fear building in her eyes, before pulling Jodie to her, each drawing strength from the other. Maxine forced back her tears, and in a weakened voice, she whispered, "I think it's best we don't see each other for a while. That's until the cop stops coming around."

Maxine squeezed Jodie's hand. Then she turned and walked to her car, got in, and slowly drove away.


Jodie poured a second cup of coffee and returned to her seat on the trailer steps. It was early evening, hours before she'd start to ready herself for work, and the day's humid air still hung heavy. The sun-parched cornstalks in the field surrounding the clearing had begun to smell scorched. A slight movement in the broom sage at the edge of the field drew Jodie's attention to the nearly imperceptible approach of the stray cat. It hesitated and glanced cautiously about, its long black tail stiffened with alertness, its tip flicking back and forth like a periscope, before it emerged into the clearing and approached.

A limp field mouse dangled from its clamped jaws, blood showing in the corners of its velvet lips. At what the cat must have judged as a safe distance, it dropped the dead mouse onto the ground, sat back on its haunches, and watched her in the distant self-containment she'd come to expect before it disappeared beneath the trailer.

## Thirty-Eight

Jodie tossed a pair of inspected jeans into the hamper and glanced up at the clock on the wall. Two hours and ten minutes into her shift, she was off her best pace by two bundles, digging herself a big hole. At this rate, she'd be lucky to turn even the required bundles by quitting time, and the super would be leveling accusations of slacking.

Two months of rigorous conditioning meant she survived on four to five hours of sleep, leaving her little for the job. Eight hours, five nights a week, standing on a bare cement floor with her head throbbing at the roar of machines, had taught her all she needed to know about the full cost of her dream. Yet she was more determined than ever.

She glanced along the line to the inseam machines to better gauge the black eye and busted lip Bitsy would lay off to a drunken fall. Those who knew the truth would nod, add stories of their own clumsiness, meaning to make lying easier than the harsh truth for all their sakes. Why not grab up her kids and run, the so-called footloose ones were bound to question. Running was never that easy, the fearful would reply, declaring their kids were better off with no-account daddies than without them.

If bruised faces were their worst pain, Jodie believed they would surely run. But most had stopped thinking about ways out. They stayed, wanting to believe that the beatings would stop when they learned to please their men. But Bitsy wasn't like these women, and Jodie feared that her beating had a different story.

"Jodie, the super wants you," a wide-hipped woman sewing belt loops onto waistbands called with a quick jerk of her head. Her hands

236 • Pat Spears

were blood-red with the rash she kept, though it never slowed her frantic feed of denim under the pressure foot.

Jodie cupped a hand to her ear, bracing for a bitching, the supervisor's words scattering in the swirl of blue dust like a flock of blackbirds in a hail of buckshot.

"Long distance," the woman relayed, her eyes bearing the dread that such a message might hold. She nodded toward the narrow hallway where the telephone hung on the wall.

"Take it and it'll mean your break," the super called. "It's company policy. You girls get one emergency a year put back here."

Jodie turned and faced the super. "Yes ma'am. And I'm most grateful for a policy that holds my shitty luck down to one mishap a year."

She left the super glaring while likely struggling with a proper punishment. Walking along the hallway, Jodie wondered who was about to become her emergency.

"Yes, ma'am, operator. I'm Jodie Taylor." She wiped sweat from her face onto the sleeve of her shirt, and more ran along her spine, soaking into the waistband of her jeans.

"Hey, gal, how you doing?" There was no warning in his voice.

She loosened her grip on the telephone and exhaled. "Silas, you damn fool. You mean to put my ass in a sling worse than it is?"

"Hell, woman, if it'll get you fired and back to God's country, I'll call every Tuesday."

"Cut the romance. What the hell's this about?"

"Jodie, Red's had a bad stroke."

His words ground their way into her brain while she watched Sammie the Snake approach the break room. A once-in-a-blue-moon roll of dollar bills tucked between the breasts of a co-worker was the honey that kept them buzzing whenever he showed. Bitsy was a regular numbers player, but she played on credit, and that was likely the sorry story behind her battered face.

"Jodie? You still there?"

"How bad?"

"Happened yesterday. In that overgrown field back of the house." His tone was such that he could have been talking about a local fender bender. He paused, sucking air as though he was having trouble talking and breathing at the same time. "From the looks of the scuff marks on the ground, he was down for some time. Hadn't been for old Buster, they might've missed him altogether."

"None of that's what I asked you."

"Shit, Jodie, I'm no doctor and I'm sure as hell not God. But I believe he's knocking on death's door." He paused, then added, "Jodie, there's no one but me and Maggie to look after him. And we can't be with him all the time."

"What about Miss Mary?"

"Her? Hell, I was sure I told you. She's staying here in town with Hazel and William. The old bitch flatly refuses to step foot back in that house." It was as if he believed he'd made her going back easier, but there was still the harder part: facing Red.

"If you need a little extra, I'll wire you what you need."

She knew he'd drive forty miles to the next town to avoid the local Western Union operator, his wife's gossipy cousin. He had the strange practice of straddling fences while nibbling around the edges where he claimed the honey was the sweetest.

"That's all right. I got it." She hung up, Silas still talking about duty.

Jodie walked back along the hallway to the production floor in search of the super. She was up in the face of a new hire, reaming her for having stiff fingers connected to a brain too easily scattered.

"Ma'am, about that call?" The super paused and the terrified girl wiped at her face, grateful for the distraction.

"Taylor, I told you. No break. You're way off pace as it is."

"Yeah, I know. But what I've got to say isn't about that." The super's scowl signaled that whatever Jodie might say was already suspect.

"Red ... the man who took me in after my mama died ... what I mean is, he's had a bad stroke. I need time off to go down home."

"Time off? There's no time off for family mishaps." Her tone was absolute, as if she quoted scripture, chapter and verse.

Jodie stared out across the floor at women harnessed to indifferent machines, her tangled tongue betraying her. If she'd been smart, she would've warmed things up, promising to catch up her production before the shift ended. It was too late for that, and now good sense dictated that she cut her losses and move on. But a small part of her still wanted to believe in the notion of fairness in circumstances that seemed to demand the setting aside of rules.

"A week's all. And if he's as bad as …." The thought of Red dying hit her hard, and she took a step back, bumping into the hunched shoulder of a startled ticket-tacker.

"Taylor, the manager depends on me to hold you girls' feet to the fire. I got production quotas. I know you understand."

"No, I don't. At my slowest, I'm still faster than any new hire could be in a week." Before she started training, her claim would have been justified. Now she wasn't sure.

"Taylor, I'm done here. Now get back to work."

"Hell no. I'll do you one better. Screw your precious job. I quit."

The break whistle sounded, followed by the shuffling feet of those who would be first in line to use one of the two toilets. To reach the exit, Jodie would need to walk the gauntlet of questioning women.

"Hey, Jodie, wait the hell up." Bitsy's husky voice sounded over the low chatter, but Jodie kept moving toward the door.

The night air felt damp on Jodie's face, and in the direction of the trailer, heavy clouds built toward her. Her anger now cooled, she dared to consider the enormity of her decision. A bout of anxiety fired through her nerves, and in spite of her effort at slowing her habit; she reached for the bottle beneath the truck seat.

"Damn, girl, I guess you got cause to piss off your job?" Bitsy huffed to a stop, and an up-close look at her battered face flipped Jodie's stomach.

"Yeah, I do. Taking a little time off to go back down home." Jodie tilted the bottle but didn't offer it to Bitsy. They took a seat on the tailgate.

"Thought you were on the wagon." Bitsy grinned.

"I am."

"Uh-huh, I can see that."

"You going to tell me what happened to your face?"

"Bad happened. That ain't nothing special."

"That's all you got to say?"

"What the hell does it look like? I got the business end from a brute who don't cotton to holding debt."

"Snake?"

She nodded. "Crusades come and go, but bad habits stick around. Same as with that damn bitch, Lady Luck. Now I owe two hundred dollars I don't have a snowball's chance of whoring up."

"You got anybody?" It would take most of what she had to get her back to Florida.

"By that you would mean my round-heeled mama, or one of my several lovin' *uncles*? Damn, Jodie, take a hard look at my face and answer your own dumb-ass question." Bitsy slid off the tailgate and stood next to the truck.

"I'll get the money, but it'll take a while."

"Sweetie, I thank you. But it's what I said. He took what I had and still beat the crap out me, right in front of my child. Guess I ain't the two-hundred-dollar trick I'd figured would settle my debt."

"Here, take my keys. Truck's worth that, maybe more." She knew it to be a wall-eyed stretch.

"And just how the hell do you mean to get down to Florida?"

"I'm taking the bus. I'll come back with money. Buy back my truck."

"How do you know he won't take your money and keep your truck?"

"I don't. But you got a better plan?"

Bitsy looked up into the night sky, as though answers hid there if only she knew which star to wish upon. "Jodie, I'm bad scared. This thing's got holes we could both get buried in."

"You want your little girl to become a ward of the state?" She didn't have the heart to mention the worst that might happen. "Can you come to my place when you knock off in the morning? I'll need a ride to the bus."

"Me and my kids just might decide to leave town with you." They hugged under the glow of the security light.

Jodie emptied the glove box and put the half-pint into her hip pocket. Parting with her truck felt a little like losing a faithful dog. She set out walking the mile to the main highway. There she hoped to flag a ride to the trailer. If not, she'd walk the remaining five miles.

## Thirty-Nine

Beyond the car, darkness, like a tight fist, relaxed its grip, and slivers of light escaped from between its fingers, turning the sky from pewter gray to watermelon red. Jodie and Bitsy drank black coffee and ate the jelly-filled donuts Bitsy had brought from the all-night diner. The car smelled of decades of neglect, the strong scent of chicory, and the sweetness of sugar.

"How'd it go with Snake?" Maybe it was enough to know that Bitsy's black eye had turned a second-day green and there were no new bruises or worse.

"Ain't that he was happy. But he did send one of his lackeys to get your truck." The resolve stenciled into the lines of her face said all there was to say about her uncertain future. "You do know you're out your truck."

Jodie nodded. "It's okay. Don't worry." Its engine likely didn't have enough left to take her where she needed to go.

"You don't mean to come back, do you?"

"No, when I'm done in Catawba I've got business elsewhere."

"I was afraid of that." Bitsy stared out the window, then back at her. "You do know you're the best friend I've ever had."

"You ain't going sentimental on me now, are you?" Jodie forced a smile.

Bitsy laughed. "Shit, girl, it ain't that it's much of a contest. You're my only friend." Her throaty laugh had a sogginess neither wanted

242 • Pat Spears

exposed. She rested a hand lightly on Jodie's forearm. "And about that mean shit that got talked behind your back—I never cared about any of that."

Her hand on the door handle, Jodie again considered that Bitsy's gratitude had gone overboard. Yet under her level gaze, Bitsy didn't as much as blink.

Jodie nodded, "Still, if I was you, I wouldn't take on over my leaving. Big-mouth Sybil might try changing your mind on the meaning of friendship."

"I ain't afraid of that foul-mouthed bucket of lard." Bitsy flexed her scrawny arm muscle and giggled, the size of their honesty fogging the windshield.

They turned to watch two barefoot boys who had suddenly appeared. One boy was the color of buttermilk and the other of burnt coal. They waded through rain puddles coated with heavy oil and scampered onto a pile of scrapped auto tires. A long-legged dog with ribs that showed through matted brown fur chased around the mound. A broken chain hung from the dog's neck.

"Wish my boy could go back to being their age. Maybe we could start over." Bitsy paused. "You believe in starting over?"

"Not sure." She hoped something so unlikely was possible. If not with Red, then maybe she'd have a decent chance with Maggie and Silas.

"Figures you didn't leave under the best of good-byes. And you've got to wonder, after all this time, about … you know, fitting in."

"Never did. Fit in, I mean. But at least I knew what to expect."

"I get that." Bitsy nodded.

The bus pulled into the station and they reached across the space that no longer divided them. Friends hugging—their first—and one they each knew would be their last. Jodie retrieved her suitcase from the back seat, leaned through the open window, and handed Bitsy the scrap of paper where she had written the number to Silas's station.

"Hang on to this. It's for just in case. Speak only to Silas, and he'll get me a message." Jodie straightened, turned, and walked toward the bus. She'd left the same with Maxine, although doing so had the familiar uncertainty of scattered bread crumbs. Time and distance had a way of fostering disconnects, even among those she'd considered her family.

At the sound of squealing tires, Jodie spun about and watched as Bitsy leaned to say something to the boys. They both shook their heads and continued on toward the approaching bus, wet jeans riding low on their spare hips, lapping at their skinny ankles. They waved and shouted at the solemn passengers framed in the bus windows with dull expressions fixed, not one lifting a hand to return their waves.

Jodie watched as Bitsy lured the stray dog into the car with the donuts she'd meant for her kids. She looked in Jodie's direction and waved before driving away. The last thing Bitsy needed was another mouth to feed, but she was a woman with an impulse for seizing the sorriest of moments.

The crowded bus was short on fresh air and long on sour bodies. The door wheezed shut, sealing Jodie inside, and the finality of her decision hit hard.

Behind her, in a place she hadn't chosen, she'd left those Crystal Ann had called her "outlaw" family: women she'd trusted with her very life. It was a family she had not known to hope for when she left Catawba, and although she felt her life reeling in reverse, she'd hold tightly to the person she'd become.

Her dream of playing with the Cowgirls would need to sustain her—and move her forward once again when her stay in Catawba ended. She wiped a quick hand across her unexpectedly damp cheeks and forced her attention elsewhere.

## Catawba, Florida - 1963

## Forty

The bus slowed, and ahead through the bug-spattered windshield, Catawba, Florida, appeared like a recurring bad dream—a time and place Jodie had desperately attempted to outrun. She made her slow way along the aisle, her ankles swollen over the tops of her work oxfords, and her right knee a pulsating war zone. Her body ached as though she had been tossed from the top of the town's water tower.

Outside the bus, the air carried the familiar stench of the paper mill. The afternoon heat hung thick as tupelo honey, the kind of heat that set her to shallow breathing. She picked up her suitcase and started in the direction of Silas's station, her nerves spitting dread along her spine.

Silas's boyhood ambition of turning his dead uncle's shade-tree auto repair into a source of pride was evidenced by the addition of two new work bays, bringing the cluster of squatty concrete buildings to a total of three, all sandwiched between the Sheriff's Office and the Flamingo Café. A collection of discarded vehicles and motor parts were scattered about the sand and gravel lot like the junk yards he'd combed for treasures.

Silas knelt next to a mill car, its paint peeled, exposing a frame eaten thin by the chemical exhaust from the paper mill. He looked up, and a wide smile spread across his tanned face. The knot in her stomach, put there by years of uncertainty as to how this moment would go, loosened a bit. She raised a slow hand in response, and he dropped the tire iron, hurrying to meet her. His quickness was still that of the boy who'd forever chased the devil's tail.

"Hey, gal. I was about to think I'd never see you again." Color rushed like a slow-burning fire along the broad bridge of his nose to his yellow-blonde hairline. She credited their recent late night phone conversations for having doused the worst of the resentment he'd once harbored.

Standing as they were in full view of the curious, he approached and gave her a brief shoulder bump. His public restraint would carry little weight when news of her arrival heated the party lines between an idle store clerk and Silas's jealous wife. Coolness was bound to greet him at his front door, stay through a silent supper, and follow him into bed.

He put her suitcase in his pickup parked in the shade of the huge live oak, and from inside the station he brought her an icy RC Cola and a package of Tom's roasted peanuts. He'd run her out to Red's place as soon as he put another patch on a recapped tire. She took a seat on the tailgate and poured the peanuts into the soda, shook it, and with a touch of childhood glee, watched it fizz.

Along Main Street, stray dogs sprawled against the building fronts, garnering as much shade as possible. Storekeepers stayed put, unwilling to come out into the heat to chase them away. She rubbed the cold pop bottle along the insides of her arms and worked at finding calm.

Miss Bell, her English teacher through four years of high school, drove an ancient Ford away from the gas pumps with the deliberate speed of a crippled turtle, craning her neck, with a blank stare on her face. Jodie lifted her hand in a hesitant wave, but the old woman drove on in her rapt confusion. Admittedly, she had been an unremarkable student. Still, she felt slighted.

A young woman, near her age, approached carrying a whimpering baby astride her boney hip, while an unsteady toddler wobbled along behind her. Nearing Jodie, the woman turned away in an attempt at shielding a busted lip. She stopped, her back to Jodie, and yelled back at the boy who had squatted to pick up a shiny object from the ground. She shuddered at the thought of what staying and marrying Silas, or any other man, would have meant for her.

Two towhead boys, about five or six, each mirroring the other, came onto the sidewalk from what had once been Gaskin's Drugs. The boys bickered over the bike they yanked back and forth between them, and they seemed familiar to her in ways she couldn't say.

A pulpwooder, hauling slash pines to feed the voracious appetite of the paper mill's giant chippers, stared out at her from his overloaded log truck. He nodded and raised two fingers in greeting, revealing a faded American eagle tattooed on his muscled upper arm. Soldiers and sailors had returned after the war wearing this tattoo. When she looked back to where she'd seen the boys, a stooped woman with stringy gray hair was hurrying them along.

Silas walked toward the truck, wiping his greasy hands on a rag, and he too looked in the direction of the boys, grimacing, she thought.

"With all the damn kickbacks their crooked grandpa gets from local graft, you'd think he'd spring for decent bikes they wouldn't need to tussle over."

"Uh, Judge Walker's?"

"Yep, they're Clara Lee's boys." He didn't look at her, his words drifting, absorbed in the noises of the street. Jodie turned and hurried toward the truck. Silas followed, and she felt it odd that he seemed to share her sense of relief at not encountering Clara Lee.

He opened the truck door and several books slid from beneath the seat onto the ground. He stooped to gather them, stashing them back behind the seat. He was the one person Jodie knew who read as though a teacher's threats still rang in his ears.

There was a comfortable familiarity about the smell of the truck: sweat, grease, engine oil, gasoline, cigarettes, peppermint, and Mennen aftershave. Silas slipped the key into the ignition and the engine turned, purring like a well-tuned Cadillac. He looked over at her, a prideful glint in his eyes. He believed repairing broken-down vehicles and befriending those women he referred to as shaky ladies were his special gifts. They drove onto the highway in the direction of Red's.

"Saw Miss Bell, just now. She didn't know me from Adam's house cat."

"Yeah, that poor old soul can't remember which car she drove up in, and her sitting in it. But she can recite Shakespeare right on. Remember how she answered our fool questions with quotes from Shakespeare?"

"And how we kids tried stumping her, but never could?"

"Thirty-seven years and no one ever got her goat. And we read a lot more Shakespeare than we would have otherwise. That is, some of us did." He winked at her.

It was clear neither wanted to talk about Red's illness. Their laughter went a ways to relieve Jodie's full-blown case of nerves, and she took a measure of comfort in the thought that perhaps Silas hadn't changed all that much. Then, he wasn't Red.

"Wouldn't you know, Red's still got that old Dodge he's so crazy about? Had me go so far as to block it and sell off the tires. Took me the better part of a morning to hack it free of the kudzu." He paused. "Still can't figure why he held on to it. Engine is good right on. Figure I could've got him a little for it." He looked over at her as if he sought an answer to a deeper riddle.

Jodie shrugged. It would seem Red found it easier to hang onto old cars and blind dogs than to family. Then, admittedly it was she who'd done the last of the leaving.

"Like I said, Maggie's done the staying overnight. But your sanctified sister is pitching a damn hissy fit, threatening to pack Red off to her house. And if going without whiskey didn't kill him, leaving Buster behind would."

"She's bluffing, and that's half-sister, and only maybe."

"Yeah, I get that you two aren't exactly the Lennon Sisters. Still, she's determined. Says it's her Christian duty and, even stranger, William's backing her on it."

He rubbed a hand along his bearded chin and got that same troubled look he used to get when he believed Jodie's wellbeing was somehow his responsibility. It seemed he still liked all things broken and a bit off balance. How much so, she'd know before leaving again.

"What happened between you and the bus company?"

He sighed, pushed back his cap, laying bare a white strip of forehead.

"What'd you hear from that blabbermouth driver?"

"I'm asking you."

"The bus company pulled out on the deal struck between them and my uncle before he died."

"Why was that?"

"Some government bullshit over the bathrooms. Said *colored* had to get painted over. Just like that. Me having nothing to say about it. You'd think those doors belonged to Uncle Sam."

"They stopped using your station as a depot because you were too damned cheap to buy a little paint?"

"That's not what I said. Likely the Kennedy boys just discovered Negroes, but around here they're no oddity."

"But needing a public place to pee is?"

"No, I reckon not. Then, it's not about that. I nailed the door shut, and now we all pee in a pile of old tires back of the station. If we need to take a shit we go down to the new bus stop and use theirs."

"You'd rather squeeze off your dick in a pile of tires than give up a little Dixie?" Sally had denied Arthur and Bo the use of the Wing's public bathroom. The two had peed in the alley. Sally was weak, maybe even mean, but the Silas she'd known was neither.

"I see you haven't lost any of your ladylike manners." He sounded confused, and he looked wounded, the way she remembered from when they were kids. He fired up a Lucky Strike and passed it to her. "Bet you've even gone to smoking those funny cigarettes."

"Only when the whiskey can't cut it." She meant to let him know she wasn't the same girl he had believed he wanted.

He studied her, his bafflement giving way to a slow grin—one that likely dismissed her version of herself in favor of what he wanted to believe.

"I'm guessing prospects for women around here haven't changed for the better." Waitressing and piecework weren't exactly certain paths to prosperity, but it was a damn sight better than complete dependence on some abusive man.

"Nothing that has most thinking beyond marrying a mill hand or pulpwooder. Too bad how the things they claim to love and grow to hate can turn out to be the same." His voice had a hint of sadness, and she wondered if his remark included his wife.

They reached Red's, and Silas stopped the truck at the lane. He pulled his grease-stained cap off, tapped it against the steering wheel, settled it back into the red indentation on his sweaty forehead.

"You all right, Jodie?" He reached and touched her on the knee, as if he believed part of her coming back meant she'd welcome their taking up where he alone believed they left off.

"Bad case of nerves, that's all." She patted his rough hand and guided it away from her knee. Whatever trouble she faced was her own doing, nothing he should decide he needed to fix.

"I'd go in with you, but I'm running late for a family gathering at the in-laws'. Can you make it from here with that little suitcase?" He frowned as if he'd already calculated the cost of staying.

"You bet. I thank you for the lift."

"If everything goes as planned, Maggie should be along about dark. She went to Tallahassee, swore the trip was too important to put off." He glanced toward the house and back at her. "After all these years, I just can't figure her sometimes."

What he didn't know about either her or Maggie could fill a book. She stepped away from the truck and waved him on his way, his parting words lost to her over the roar of the engine.

## Forty-One

On the county road, a single headlight bounced toward her, and Jodie dragged a foot, bringing the swing to a stop. The palms of her hands tingled, and she wished that she'd left off her last drink.

The shrill chirping of katydids and crickets gave way to the clatter of Maggie's truck. The engine sputtered to a stop, and Jodie called a greeting into the stillness.

"It's me all right, shug." Maggie's voice was deeper and raspier, more and more like a lifetime smoker, although she'd claimed to have never smoked. She'd sworn that her voice box was smuttier than a stovepipe after years of inhaling Miss Ruth's closet smoking, while Ruth's sweet voice remained as clear as a tuning fork.

Jodie swung open the gate, and the night critters took up their chorus as though the squeaking hinges signaled a new beginning. Maggie wrapped her arms around Jodie and held her close, and in that moment she was once again the unwanted child made to feel safe. Maggie stepped back, cocked her head to one side, and gave Jodie a long look.

"Damn if you haven't nearly gone to skin and bones. But my, you're pretty as ever." She smiled broadly.

"It's the poor light. And pretty was never real pretty, now was it? But don't worry. You'll have plenty of time to fatten me up." Maggie still smelled of gardenia talcum and, tonight, of raw onions.

Jodie slipped her arm around Maggie's waist, and together they walked toward the light streaming through the door. There had been no one who'd called her pretty. Jewel had made it clear that life would have been easier for both had she been small like Ginger and had Ginger's soft curls and sweetness rather than big as a mule with a head full of bushy hair and what she'd called the disposition of a ground rattler.

"Come on in the kitchen. I got a fresh pot going."

"Coffee's good, I'd say." Maggie wrinkled her nose, pretending shock at Jodie's whiskey-flavored breath. "But first you'll need to get that box off the front seat of the truck while I squat and check on Red."

In the kitchen, Jodie put a match to the burner, and the quick burst of flame singed the hair across her knuckles. She broke a spiny-toothed leaf from the aloe on the windowsill and peeled back the outer skin, rubbing gel on the burn. Facing Maggie with her many regrets was even harder than she'd imagined.

"Could you tell if he'd eaten anything?" Maggie's words rolled hard into the kitchen ahead of her heavy steps.

"Nothing much, judging from what was left on the plate." She left out the swarming flies and empty water pitcher.

"I was afraid of that. Hazel was supposed to stay with him, and I swear I don't see the first sign that she did diddly-squat except scatter about them old records over the Victrola, unless you've had time to play music."

"No, ma'am, I didn't bother those old records."

"All those bedclothes piled back there … is that how you found him?" Maggie stood in the doorway, her hands riding her broad hips. Spit collected in the corners of her mouth.

Jodie nodded.

Maggie's face flushed red. "Damnit, I knew better than to leave that nice-nasty gal in charge. You'd think she'd never seen a man's pecker." Maggie flipped her hand to her face and squealed, mocking Hazel.

They laughed and Maggie's irritation lessened a notch.

"Just how bad is he?"

Jodie watched Maggie's face grow thoughtful as she took a seat at the table, appearing to choose her words carefully.

"At first, Doc figured him a goner." She swallowed hard. "He misjudged the healing powers of pure stubbornness." Her voice stronger, she added, "Hell, I remember a time when Red stumbled onto our front porch, soaked in blood from a knife wound that took a hundred stitches or better to close. A normal man would've bled to death."

Maggie paused, leaving space; her way of asking without asking, Jodie sensed. But she had no answers beyond that of why she came. Maggie nodded ever so slightly. "For now, I believe we can leave off covering the mirrors. You're here, and he's bound to rally."

"He hasn't spoken a word."

"Oh, hon, that's the stroke. He'll get some of his speech back, but his public speaking days are behind him." They shared a weak smile.

"Calling me was Silas's idea, right?" She hoped Maggie would tell her differently.

"If you're asking, Red's still got his drawers in a wad. You've got to know your way of leaving was hard on him." Her voice dropped off, and it spoke of pain to others.

"Yes'm," was all she could say.

"You may want to cut him a little slack. God knows he's slow to face up to his own wrongs."

Jodie nodded. Maggie had always been good at reading her mind.

"Now, if you're done with that, open up that box, and let's have ourselves a whopping piece of blueberry cheesecake. We need to celebrate your homecoming."

"Blueberry cheesecake? Where'd it come from?"

"Tallahassee. Got it from a bakery across the street from what was the girls' college. Ruth took me there to get cheesecake and coffee before I shipped out from Jacksonville with the WAC in '42. It's still the best there is this side of Paris, France."

Maggie spoke of times and places that spanned decades and distances halfway around the globe in the matter-of-fact way Jodie had spoken of trips between the pink trailer and the blue jean factory.

Jodie brought the cheesecake to the table, and while Maggie cut two wedges, she poured coffee. Maggie ate and drank as if the house was on fire, pushing her cup forward for a refill.

"Now days I'm greedier than Patty's pig. Ruth always said my foul temper would make me a fat corpse." She leaned back in the chair and patted her belly. "Put on thirty pounds. And, Lord God, just take a look at these babies." She boosted a heavy breast in each hand and lifted, bounced, and laughed.

"Ah, Maggie, you're not about to be fat. You're a big woman who runs best on a full tank." Jodie wiped a grin away with the back of her hand.

"Hell, fat's not all. I'm slower than molasses on a cold morning. Most days I wake feeling like a petrified turd. Can't do half of what I used to. Gone to letting Silas work on my truck, and damned if he hasn't just about junked it."

With broad fingers, Maggie twisted the coffee cup in tight circles and stared into the dark liquid as if she sorted through layers of pain. When she lifted her face to Jodie, her rheumy blue eyes held back little on the matter of her and Miss Ruth's shared lives, their full truth etched on her pained face.

"Maggie … I've been trying to figure how to say just how ashamed I am that I never as much as called when Silas told me Miss Ruth had died. You have every right to hold it against me." She wasn't sure what good her calling would have served. Here and now, sitting across the table from Maggie, her words felt stiff, forced, unworthy.

"Aw, child, burying my Ruth was the easy part. It's been the living afterward that's nearly killed me." Maggie shook her head as if in disbelief.

"Miss Ruth was an angel." Jodie hated the triteness that seemed to spring blood-blisters on her useless tongue. She'd once thought of Ginger Sutton that way, and she'd known nothing of angels and even less about loving a woman.

"Angel? She was no damn angel. Lord, whenever that woman took a notion, she could be meaner than a two-headed snake on a July tar road."

"I just meant … she was an angel to me. Silas, too."

"That she was. She loved you kids the way she would've loved her own." Maggie paused, her chest rising and falling with her grief. "Would you believe I still make coffee for two? And I'm ashamed that I go weeks without refilling her hummingbird feeders. I break my back trying, but I don't have her way with roses." Her voice was thin, watery.

"She had a special knack all right." Jodie knew something of the aloneness of which Maggie spoke.

"Hell, child, you know me. I've spit in the face of meanness my whole life, but how was I to ass-whip God?" She drained the cup and poured another, adding a generous shot of whiskey. "Death's a heartless bitch. She steals the future you thought you'd earned."

The house fell silent, enfolding each in the finality of their loss. The only sound was Buster gnawing at fleas, and when their silence had grown unbearable, Jodie leaped to her feet. Chasing a palmetto bug the size of a hot dog bun across the kitchen floor, she crushed it under the toe of her shoe, then picked up the roach by a quivering leg and threw it outdoors.

"Damn, girl. You got a future in the bug killing business," Maggie said with a straight face.

"Heard the pay's pitiful. And if the chemicals don't kill you, the steel-toed boots cripple your feet." Maybe she'd tell Maggie about the roach palace and the welcome home game she'd invented.

Maggie brushed cheesecake crumbs from her natural shelf, leaned back in the chair, her arms tightly wrapped across her breasts, and a wicked smile reshaped her sadness.

"When those undertaker boys took her away, I couldn't bear being alone in our little house. So, I sat in my truck till Silas came. We kept right on sitting until I felt I could face the truth, and he drove me to the funeral home. Dick Dawkins tried turning me away in favor of getting in touch with her nearest kin. Claimed the law was on his side. Like the law or that little shit had a side. Through my wrangling with Dawkins, Silas never uttered a word. Then all of a sudden, he grabbed that fat boy by the collar, hauled him into the back room, and flipped him butthole-upward onto a gurney. And in the calmest of voices, he threatened to pump him full of embalming fluid and hand me a lighted cigarette. Needless to say, mister go-by-the-book got busy making arrangements, right down to roses or gladiolas."

Their laughter pushed their pain into the deeper cavities of their bellies where it would reside, making the moment bearable. Maggie pushed up from the table and Jodie followed her to the truck.

"Give me another one of those big hugs I've been missing."

Jodie wanted to believe that setting wrongs right between her and Maggie was possible. But her part in the terrible wrong done Mr. Samuel would need to wait for a moment of greater courage.

## Forty-Two

The morning Jodie picked to clean away years of accumulated filth, the radio announcer promised a temperature in the mid-nineties with humidity that could grow mildew on hens' teeth. Still, she stripped the beds and dragged lumpy cotton mattresses into the yard, laying them to sun on a makeshift scaffold fashioned from sawhorses and scrap lumber. She mopped heart of pine floors with Murphy's Oil Soap, polished every stick of furniture, and scrubbed green growth from the bathtub and sink until her knuckles bled. Starting up the wringer washing machine, she sorted and washed faded curtains, bed linen, tablecloths and throw rugs—every rag in the place that could stand up to a hard bleaching—and burned what couldn't.

When the bed linens had dried in the sun, she propped Red on fresh pillows covered in pillowslips bleached white, scented with lemon juice, and smooth-ironed. He listened to the play-by-play of a Dodgers game on the radio through her changing of the bed. She commented on the national pennant race to help cover the awkwardness that had stayed between them like a bad case of mumps.

After supper dishes, she slumped, exhausted, on the couch in front of the snowy television screen, put her head back, closed her eyes, and drifted into a light sleep, only to be startled awake by scuffing noises coming from Red's bedroom. She expected to see Buster letting himself out for his nightly prowl.

Red slumped against the doorframe, weaving on knocked-out legs, wheezing hard with his effort. His pajama pants rode low, his hip joints like wall pegs.

She went to him and slipped an arm around his waist, steadying him. He leaned hard against her shoulder, his frailness mocking the strapping man she'd known. She wanted the Red who'd walked onto the porch where she and Silas played checkers—the man who'd driven them to Gaskin's for strawberry cream, and the man who had put a stop to the beatings.

Yet she had nothing more honest than, "I hate they closed Gaskin's."

He nodded, his bristled chin scratching the top of her head.

He motioned toward the front door, and together they shuffled across the clean floor. His movements were spastic, like those of a child's puppet with tangled strings.

Reaching the edge of the porch, he pulled away, and struggling to stand, he leaned against a porch post. His back to her, he peed off the edge of the porch, and when he was done, he lifted his chin and took a deep breath.

Together, they retraced his arduous steps, and he dropped onto the bed, wheezing so that she feared he'd die. With his good hand, he lifted the lifeless one to rest across his knees and began rubbing it, as if by sheer will he could make it work again. Dry skin flaked under the force of his hand, his arm raw and bleeding.

She sat down beside him and took his hand between hers. He strained against her strength, his cheeks draining of color with his futile exertion. He slumped, his head resting against her shoulder, and began to whimper. Buster licked Red's dangling hand and whined.

Putting an arm around his frail shoulders, she whispered, "You ready to get back down under the covers? Rest a little before heading off to a frolic?"

He lifted his face to hers and nodded. She took his scaly heels in her palms and lifted his legs onto the bed. She straightened her back, her hands pinching into her waist, relieving the pain in her lower back the way Crystal Ann had. Red was scarecrow thin, but still heavy. She turned off the overhead light, took a seat in the rocker at the foot of his bed, and waited for his breathing to return to its normal hoarseness.

It had taken a full week to make the old house once again livable, and Jodie was surprised that she still had energy enough to pull weeds from among the few surviving perennials that grew in the beds along the edges of the front porch. Miss Mary had prided herself in growing summer flowers—lavender-blue flax; white, pink and red sweet pea; golden buttons; scarlet sage; nasturtiums and dahlias—most blooming from early spring until first frost.

Jodie favored the scarlet peony with its double bloom and dark green leaves. Miss Mary had said the peony could bloom for decades with little care; its hardy traits carried over from its days as a simple wildflower, when the tiny flower had required only the help of birds and gentle winds to spread its beauty. Miss Mary's flowers had been the only things Jodie had known her to treat tenderly.

With the last of the weeds pulled and tossed into the chicken yard, Jodie sat in the porch swing enjoying a glass of iced tea, admiring the results of her labors. At the putt-putt clamor of a diesel engine, she squinted in the direction of the road.

Silas approached on his prized inheritance: a 1937 International Harvester. He had repeated his old man's claim that no tractor could be both good and cheap. Before the bank employee had arrived to repossess the tractor, his daddy had hidden it deep in the woods, swearing in court before an obliging judge that it was stolen. Silas had laughed and said, "You can bet your sweet ass it was stolen. My daddy never lied."

Shutting down the engine, Silas removed his cap, wiped sweat from his face onto the sleeve of his shirt, and grinned at her in that special way he had of inviting fun.

"Afternoon, Miss Jodie. You notice Ole' Trucker, just now? Damned if he didn't crawl out of his tunnel to let me know I was trespassing."

"Thought by now he would've followed some pretty lady gopher off." They'd first spotted the giant gopher tortoise the summer she arrived and had thought of Trucker as their shared pet.

"Hell, woman, the ladies come to him." He cocked his head to one side and smiled. "I'd say he's got all the luck there is."

She warmed to his foolishness.

He looked at the freshly weeded beds, his mischievousness replaced by a more pensive expression.

"Thought you might consider a patch of ground turned. Start from scratch with something new." He ran his hands up and down his thighs.

She wiped at the sweat rolling between her breasts, speculating that Silas hadn't bothered telling his wife about his renewed urge to farm.

"Got flowers aplenty, but you might fix a patch to sow a few turnip seeds."

Ground prepared, seed sown, they stood admiring their work. Jodie offered, "Late start, but maybe they'll make before first frost."

"Damn right. Who said you and me can't be out of step with *The Farmer's Almanac*?" He took off his cap and slapped her across her rear.

"Whoa now, you forgot who used to whip your skinny-boy ass?"

Grabbing the water bucket, he splashed her and ran with boyish devilment. She gave chase, but he was still the better sprinter. Rounding the corner of the house, he suddenly pulled up, taking her by surprise. He pivoted, pulling her to his chest. She drove a quick knee upward, stopping short of his crotch, and he backed off, his face flushed crimson.

"Aw, shit, gal. Tell me you didn't really intend sidelining God's gift to Catawba's lonely ladies?"

"Would that include your wife among the satisfied?" Although she knew his bravado was an awkward attempt at recovery, her belly anger, trigger-ready, had driven her response. His action had become every male's uninvited advance.

"Damn, Jodie. I believe you'd still rather stomp balls than screw." He slumped down on the porch steps. It would seem Silas had his own reservoir of pain.

"Guess I get my firey temper from my half-squaw mama."

He squinted at her, as if he needed a moment to spin her meaning into something he could accept.

"Yeah, well, you oughtn't to talk about your dead mama like that." He took a pack of smokes from his pocket, lit two, passed one to her. "You do smoke, right?" His question had its own sharp edge.

"When I'm not in training." She took the cigarette.

His broad forehead wrinkled. "Guess old Father Time's robbed you of any chance you had of catching on with that wild bunch of women."

"Not true. Hear they're recruiting older gals. Only problem I'm likely to have is holding my own in the bars." She wasn't sure why she didn't tell him of her plan. Maybe it was that she'd just arrived, and right now, after what just happened between them, she didn't want to argue.

"Wait, listen. There's a covey of quail right about there." He pointed in the direction of a clump of sumac beyond the freshly plowed ground.

"They're not exactly a rarity. They're after those scattered seed."

"There you go again. No imagination." He sat back, a slow smile gathering.

"Hmm, that so?" She'd never cared which part was the truth and which part was his need to spin a good story.

"Read where some smart cracker boys are raising domesticated quail on big-ass plantations. They bring rich Yankees down on luxury trains to shoot them little confused birds."

"That's sporting. Use Tommy guns, do they?" She spit on the ground.

"Now wait. I think we could get into the bird business. Put a little local twist on it. Bring fat cats into the port at Apalach'. From there we'd ride their soft asses up the river on a houseboat loaded with liquor and obliging ladies."

"Well, now, that's a fine plan, with one exception."

He squinted at her, a laugh behind his mock innocence.

"I hear prostitution's illegal, even here in Florida. And overall, I just don't have the stomach for buckshot wars with tiny, hand-fed birds."

"Now did I say a word about prostitutes?" His tone carried a false dismay. "Friendly ladies, that's all." He laughed, and maybe he did sometimes wish that his heart was in line with his ambition to become more than Catawba's best shade-tree mechanic.

They continued to sit, shoulders separated by a mere sliver of fading light, and talked about childhood feats of recklessness.

"Now days, I fret about things I never knew needed worrying over. A kid changes how a man looks at everything."

There was a tinge of regret in his voice, and she thought it odd that he didn't speak of his wife, only his little girl.

"I'd like to meet your girl. Does she look like you?"

He rubbed grease-stained knuckles against his palm. "No, not exactly, but it's early yet." A deeper stirring moved inside him, although there was little outward effect. Then, she knew him in ways he didn't know himself.

"Guess you won't stay for a piece of lemon pie. Baked it myself, fresh this morning." It felt strange that another had first dibs on his time, her jealousy even stranger.

"Damn, I do believe I'm seeing a softer side of you. Figured you to come and go wearing the same jeans."

"Don't look so surprised. I learned to like cooking better than doing without."

He shrugged. "What the hell. She's blistered aplenty already. Nothing gained by foregoing pie."

He leaned against the kitchen counter, his cheeks stuffed, and when he'd finished, he set the empty dish on the counter. He crossed his arms, his big hands tucked inside his armpits, and his eyes narrowed.

She felt his mood shift, his heat building, and the air in the tiny kitchen swirled with the inevitable, swollen like a festering boil.

"What about Roy Dale Pitts? Did you like cooking for him? Then, maybe he liked café eating, did he?"

"Thought we'd agreed never to talk about that again."

"Right, screw it. I hate liars worse than fools." His blue eyes seethed with anger at whatever he imagined.

"Jesus, Silas, I never stayed with him. I split the first chance I got." She lit a cigarette from the pack he'd tossed onto the table. What was so hard about accepting that she and Roy Dale were two naïve kids who'd wished to cash in their shitty birth hand for a chance at something better?

His eyes brimmed in tears, and he lowered his head.

"Silas, you've got to know I was headed away from here the day I set foot in this house. He was a ride. It started that way and it ended the same."

He raised his head, stared at her, his eyes searching hers. "Why didn't you at least tell me you were leaving?" He paused, seeming to gather himself. "Red expected me to know where you were. Shit, everyone did. I don't think he's ever believed me. And I've never lied to him."

"Silas, there were no promises between us. If there had been, then explain your wife and baby." She dropped the cigarette butt into the cooled coffee. "God, that's screwed. I didn't mean it the way it sounded."

"That whole thing with her … it just happened. She got herself knocked up. And I couldn't be sure. The other guy already had a pregnant wife and two rug rats. And you'd taken off the way you did."

"Oh, God. That's the best you've got?" An abrupt laugh escaped her tight lips like a churchhouse fart.

"Hell, I know it sounds lame. But nothing turned out the way I'd expected. Everything got flipped upside down."

"Look, I get it. And for the last time, my leaving was all about what I needed. I loved you. I still do, but not in the way you wanted." She feared he'd guess the truth about her.

"Damnit, Jodie, you sound like Maggie. But I never signed on to be your brother." He walked through the door and off the porch.

She couldn't bear the thought of losing him, but before moving on, she'd tell him about the trucker and Buddy Highway, about her friends Teddy and Maxine, and about the woman she loves. Maybe he'd understand that she'd have died before surrendering to Roy Dale Pitts or any man, even him.

Forty-Three

Jodie and Red had eaten breakfast in a comfortable silence, and she cleared the table while he fed Buster bits of table scraps. His movements were slow and clumsy, but he succeeded in moving bits of food from his plate to within the dog's reach.

"You figure to try that freeloader on peaches?" she sniped in jest, picking up the bowl and crossing to the fridge. Buster followed and sat at her feet, drooling.

"Cobbler," Red held out a biscuit, his tongue pushed forward from the left side of his slack mouth, his hoarse laughter escaping his throat in spurts of saliva, and he motioned her toward Buster's dish.

"Peach cobbler, your specialty." Jodie joined in laughter, awed by the sound of his voice; his first words since her arrival. The old dog spun in slow motion and they laughed at his antics. Their distraction likely explained neither having heard the approach of the vehicle before the hard slamming of its doors. Wiping tears from her cheeks, Jodie peered through the kitchen window, expecting to welcome either Maggie or Silas.

"Holy shit, Red, it's them. They're here."

Jodie's alarm stemmed from her dread that Miss Mary would emerge from the back seat. But only Hazel and a bull-like man Jodie took to be Hazel's husband, William, stepped from the bat-winged '59 Chevy sedan, and Jodie's anxiety throttled down a notch.

William bent, tugged at his wedged trousers; Hazel squinted toward the house, and maybe she puzzled over the unexpected merriment she could have heard. William took a firm grip on Hazel's elbow in the manner of dominance and steered her toward the house.

Jodie's instinct was to distrust a man of his bearing, to carefully judge his intent. They had taken their own sweet time getting here, and she pondered what exactly had finally delivered them. She wiped Red's face and brushed food crumbs from the front of his stained shirt. If there had been time, she would have changed his shirt and considered getting out of her cut-offs and Red's cast-off white shirt and into jeans and a shirt of her own. There was no time to even look for her shoes.

She helped Red stand, and together they walked into the front room, Buster trailing. Jodie was certain a snapshot would have shown that she, Red, and the dog wore expressions of dread.

Hazel came through the door and glanced about the room as if she inventoried the drab furniture. Jodie decided that she'd remained her mother's compliant spy. The fair-skinned man with rolls of pink flesh riding his tight collar stood in the doorway. He had the somber yet gleeful demeanor of an undertaker, appearing to silently measure Red for a coffin. Hazel wore a navy crepe dress with a stiff white sailor's collar that jutted out from her heavy bosom like a mantelpiece. Her feet were thrust into fire engine red pumps, and her heavy legs, encased in nylons, were the color of peanut oil.

"Afternoon, Daddy. I do believe you're looking some better."

How would she know? She didn't look at Red, but kept her eyes averted. William offered Red a wooden nod and he, like his wife, had the sanctimonious bearing of a hard-ass.

"My, my, Jodie. William and I heard you'd come back." Her high-pitched tone betrayed her strained civility.

"Back isn't exactly the case. But I'm here now." Local gossip being what it was, Jodie knew Hazel had known within an hour of her arrival.

"William, dear, this is Jodie *Taylor*." Hazel encased her name in layers of scorn.

Jodie exchanged a quick nod with William. She sat, her bare feet tucked beneath the chair, and picked at the frayed edges of her shorts.

Hazel took her mother's platform rocker nearest the oscillating fan that did little more than circulate the heat rising from decades of shared resentment.

"My gracious, but I must say I'm surprised at how you've spruced up the place. Don't you agree, William?"

"Found some near-rotted material and Maggie had it sewed into slipcovers. Never did like the prickly feel of that couch."

At the mention of Maggie's name, Hazel's mask of courtesy slid into the folds of her double chin and she blurted, "*You* are not to make decisions about my mother's home."

William grunted his impatience, and walking his round butt to the front of the chair, he drew a hard bead on Jodie. He wasn't here about sprucing up, but rather some yet undeclared mission of consequence.

"I'll come straight to the point. The old man requires a steadying influence. And as a loose woman, you must need to get back to wherever you've come from … doing whatever it is you do."

Jodie's hackles bristled at William's slander, but for now she'd hear *loose* to mean *unmarried*. To a man like William, there was no difference. She looked to Red but he sat, pulling on Buster's torn ear, as if he had nothing at stake in what was said.

Hazel's body had stiffened, a nervous giggle escaping her lips, and she stammered, "My gracious, dear." She glared at William, and Jodie took her displeasure to mean William had either deviated from the agreed upon script or that he'd simply spoken the truth too bluntly.

"William meant that it's only proper that I should be the one to handle Daddy's affairs. After all, he is *my* father. Decisions he's influenced to make could hurt my mother's interests."

"Affairs? I don't know about any affairs. What I do know is that he needs looking after till he's back on his feet." She remembered the sorry state she'd found him in on her arrival. If Hazel couldn't look Red in the face and Miss Mary had refused him as much as a visit, how did either expect to take care of him? Neither claim made sense.

"Are you forgetting his stash of money? Miss Mary's his wife and Hazel his lawful child. They're entitled. Certainly not you." William scoffed, his thin upper lip pulled over his teeth, and he wiped sweat from his face bright as a baboon's ass.

It was Jodie's turn at outrage and she shouted, "Money? What money? Everything he owns could be hauled away in a damn goat cart." Since her arrival Maggie had delivered every bite of food. When she'd asked, Maggie made it perfectly clear that she wasn't to stick her nose in what didn't concern her.

"Don't play innocent." Hazel smirked as if she'd gained some moral high ground Jodie knew nothing about.

Red tugged on Buster's collar and struggled to gain his feet. His body swayed and a grating sound ripped from his throat. "Get from here." He raised his good arm and pointed toward the door. His eyes flashed with anger, leaving no doubt as to his meaning. He displayed more fight than Jodie had seen until now.

William leaped to his feet, a chair leg tangling in the worn rug, and declared, "He's done things. We have proof. You'll see. My wife's God's servant in this. Her mother's interests will be protected." He turned and stomped out of the house, Hazel following him down the rickety porch steps. They got into the Chevy and sped away.

Jodie turned to Red. "What the hell was that all about?"

Red waved her off, turned his back to her scrutiny, and made his labored way toward the bedroom. "Damnit, Red. Why won't you tell me?"

She replayed the parting scene over and over in her mind, deciding that Red may have believed the scrimmage had gone his way. But the sharp echo of Hazel's red pumps rang in Jodie's ears as a warning to what surely lay ahead.

## Forty-Four

Maxine's letter arrived in the rusted mailbox on the road, and although she continued to lament the loss of Teddy and the family they'd had, she admitted that in Teddy's absence, she and her kids were settling into a difficult new normal. Jodie worried that news of Teddy was certain to become even more scarce.

The letter also included a newspaper clipping, dated two weeks earlier. Jodie read through tears of grief and anger the blurred account of Elizabeth Stover, an employee at the jeans factory, who was reported to have fallen from her employer's loading dock. Her substantial injuries required hospitalization. The plant's spokesman claimed Stover had received prior warnings about her on-the-job drinking, declaring the unfortunate incident was her fault. The article further reported that there were no witnesses to the accident.

Jodie knew the accusation against Bitsy was a lie. She'd drunk her share of days and weekends, but never on company time. That miserable job was the one thing that stood between her and returning to the cotton fields. She'd never jeopardize that. A more likely story was that Bitsy had continued to gamble, and to lose.

Maxine wrote that local gossip held that after the woman checked out of the hospital, there was neither word of her whereabouts nor that of her young daughter, but that her son was serving time in a juvenile detention center for robbery and assault on an arresting officer. The plight of a drunkard and failed mother held little interest beyond finger-pointing, and her story had predictably given way to fresher gossip. Jodie didn't want to think about how much Bitsy likely owed Snake, or where her daughter was if she'd run without her. If Bitsy had kept Silas's number, she might call. Then, what good could she do for a desperate woman on the run? She had no vehicle, no cash, nothing. Bitsy came into this fucked world alone, and she was destined to go out the same.

Jodie laced up her high-tops, sprinted down the lane and onto the county road. She ran blindly, her rage driving her legs until they turned rubbery and her lungs burned. She dropped onto the shoulder of the road, among intermittent patches of sandspurs, and wept openly, ignoring the curious who slowed their vehicles to stare.

A week with no word from either William or Hazel, and Jodie had begun to consider that her earlier estimate of threat may have been overblown. Although Red's speech was improving, he had grown quieter. He sat long hours, slumped in his porch rocker while he sipped whiskey, doing well to count the number of crows perched along the electrical wire. He stared in the direction of the road as if he awaited the arrival of an unwelcome messenger.

Concerned that Red's health had taken a turn for the worse, Jodie flagged Silas, asking that he call Maggie about her worries.

Midmorning, Maggie's truck pulled into the yard. She stopped on the porch and took the rocker next to Red. She leaned in close, and he whispered.

Maggie came into the house, walked straight to the phonograph, and began searching among the old record jackets. When she was done, she asked, "That first day you were here, I noticed these old records scattered about. Do you remember me asking you if you'd messed with them?"

"And you remember I told you I found them that way."

"Is that still your story?" Maggie's tone was firm, her gaze steady.

"Why would I need to change what I said?"

"You wouldn't. But somebody did."

"What does any of that mean?"

"Can't say exactly. But I can tell you it's not good." Maggie walked back onto the porch. Red listened and slowly nodded, his weak arm resting on the rocker, his hand trembling.

Jodie overheard Maggie say, "Yeah, of course, I'll look into it. But how many times did I try telling you?"

Red raised a hand, hushing her.

"Damn, Red Dozier, you're one stubborn fool." Maggie walked off the porch, got into her truck, and sped away.

Jodie went onto the porch and Red looked up at her.

"I worry … she got me cornered … this go 'round."

"Is this about you and me?" She tasted the bitterness of righteous anger between her teeth.

Red struggled to come to his feet. "Was always about that … and more. What it'll take this time …." His body swayed, and he caught to a porch post.

"Damn you, Red. Maybe you thought bringing me here settled any debt you felt you owed my mama. But even before that time with the comic books, you knew what went on in your absence. Did you ever care?"

He clung to the post and said, "I'm tired. Think … I'll lie down." He made his clumsy way across the porch and upon reaching the door, he turned back, her name on his lips, but he said no more.

Jodie borrowed Maggie's truck and drove to Silas's station. She parked beneath the oak and walked to where he leaned into the hood of a '56 Ford Falcon. Tapping him on the shoulder, she whispered her question.

He straightened, and without as much as a greeting, he guided her away from the piqued interest of his helper.

"That's got to be the second dumbest thing I've ever heard out of your mouth." He took an oily rag from his back pocket and wiped his hands; she knew him to be stalling.

"I'm not playing, Silas. Tell me what you know."

He looked at the ground between his boots. The skin at his temples furrowed, and he said, "You're asking me what I know about Red breaking the law in some of his political shenanigans."

"Screw you. I'm wasting my damn time." She turned to leave.

"Hold up there, will you?" He closed the distance. "What's got you so fired up?"

"Maggie came straight over like I asked. The two talked out of earshot, and whatever passed between them had both plenty stirred up."

"That's nothing. They've got decades of secrets between them." A duplicitous smile broke across his face as if he meant to dismiss her concerns, until she told him about Maggie's questioning.

He stared in the direction of the empty street, and when he looked back, he was clearly worried.

"Hell, Jodie, as far as I know, backstabbing and double-crossing among politicians aren't crimes unless weapons are involved."

She continued on toward the truck.

Silas jogged alongside. "Why's trying to talk sense to you got to be like butting a damn stump?"

She slid behind the steering wheel and started the engine.

"Wait." He placed his hand on the door frame. "With all your damn rearing, I nearly forgot about that gal friend's call."

"What call? What gal friend?"

"I've got it here. Somewhere." He patted down his coverall pockets and came up empty. "Must've left it in the wrecker. Was headed out just before I took the call." He trotted to the wrecker, sorted through a stack of papers on the dash, and returned, handing her a name and number scratched on a Dixie cup.

"You sure you got this right?"

"Yeah, I'm sure. She wasn't the sweetest woman I've ever talked to, still she kept saying 'urgent.'" He paused, tilting his head to one side. "Then, she didn't really seem all that upset. Whispered through most of what was a one-sided conversation."

Jodie shifted the truck into gear and he stepped back a ways.

"Don't you want to use the phone?" He motioned toward the office.

"You still keep the key behind the kerosene tank?"

He nodded, his confusion obvious.

"I'll come back later, if that's all right."

She didn't wait for his answer, but pulled the truck onto the street, working through the gears and trying to come up with any explanation for Teddy's urgency—anything that blunted her memory of Teddy's last narrow escape.

Jodie parked the truck behind the shop, shut off the headlights, and ran a zigzag pattern across the lot, avoiding rain puddles, thunder shaking the ground beneath her feet. Reaching the station's overhang, she was drenched, and she stomped her feet, shedding water soaked into her shoes and jeans. She retrieved the key and let herself into the office. It felt no bigger than a Buster Brown shoebox and smelled like an old toolbox. The pay phone hung on a back wall.

She shivered, her gut cramping, and she wished for easier, but there was no preparing for what she might hear. There was only doing it or giving up. She gave the operator the number, dropped six dimes into the slot, and asked to know when three minutes were up.

Teddy answered on the third ring, and she was sucking air as though she'd been running.

"Teddy, what's the urgency? Are you all right?"

"Jodie girl, you're gonna want to come here to Mobile." Her voice was excited, in the way she'd spoken of Maxine's boy's base hits.

"Mobile? What the hell are you talking about?" Maxine had written that Teddy was renting an extra room from Crystal Ann. Or maybe it was a couch.

"Something good here. Real good." Teddy gulped, and Jodie figured Teddy was drinking. But she'd never known Teddy to drink heavily. It was too risky for her. "That bat-brained bitch Brenda pulled out of here three days ago. And damned if she didn't steal Crystal Ann's car. She won't make it to Kentucky in that piece of junk. Hope her whoring ass is stranded on some mountain road in the company of half-wits with their dicks out."

Jodie's throat had seized, and whatever else she'd thought to say stuck in her throat. She eased her butt along the wall and sat on the floor with its decades of ground-in boot filth.

"Jodie, did you hear what I said?"

"I did, and how's this different from all the other times?"

"Trust me. Crystal Ann is done with Brenda."

"And you know this how?" She'd need to hear it from Crystal Ann, and she'd still hold her suspicions. She wasn't about to set herself up for that kind of emotional tumble.

"Okay, so maybe she does need a bit more time to figure her next move. But that's where you come in." Teddy took another big swig from whatever she was drinking.

Jodie teetered back and forth, struggling to stay on top of all that pulled her down. She only needed to remember how her time since the morning Crystal Ann drove from the clearing had done little more than drag—empty time. She stayed half-crazy with loneliness and was so horny Maggie had teased she'd likely be blind by the time she left Catawba.

"Jodie, trust me."

"Go to hell, Teddy."

Jodie sat, her forehead resting against her forearms She trusted no emotion that made her feel so excruciatingly vulnerable.

## Forty-Five

The silence between Jodie and Red stayed, neither seeming to know how to open a door to the other, and Jodie wasn't surprised when Maggie set about her remedy for what both she and Maggie knew to be much more than a family squabble. Still, she called Silas, and on the following Saturday they gathered for the conciliatory supper Maggie had fussed over.

Silas stepped through the door smelling of his familiar splash of aftershave and wearing pressed jeans and a blue dress shirt with the sleeves turned back two neat turns. He hugged Jodie and followed her into the kitchen. He stepped to the table where Red had stationed himself and took Red's hand in a two-hand grip.

Maggie looked up from chipping ice and smiled. Silas leaned and kissed her on the cheek, and she blushed, popping him a quick one on his behind. He took the ice pick and finished chipping ice for tea.

"All right, we're not strangers, here. Everyone get to the table. Food won't be good cold."

Her optimism rang a bit hollow, but it was clear Maggie meant to take aim at the awkward silence that hovered over the table. She set about picking bones from the fried catfish on Red's plate, coaxing him to eat the way she might a picky child.

They were well into the meal, a fragile ease displacing their earlier discomfort, when Silas turned to Maggie. "I do believe you've outdone yourself." His praise was genuine enough, but his tone carried a tinge of some disagreeable matter yet unspoken. He took a deep breath, his features pinched, and still he hesitated.

Jodie laid her fork down and braced for whatever she was about to hear; it wasn't going to be one of Silas's funny stories. Red leaned in, but since the stroke, reading his facial expressions wasn't easy.

"Boy, damned if you ain't wearing me out."

"Scuttlebutt about town is that William and Hazel have hired that new lawyer friend of Walker Junior's. Something to do with Red needing their help managing his affairs."

Quick, weighted glances passed between Red and Maggie.

"Then we know Tubby Slatmore favors idle gossip over the dull truth any day of the week," Silas quickly countered.

"Yeah, but his gossipy mama's right there in the thick of it," Maggie quipped.

Red's face flashed with color, his spastic hand flinging about, overturning his tea glass. His garbled words spit from his slack mouth.

"'Damn her rotten heart' is right," Maggie repeated, coming to her feet. "But hold still, before your rearing brings on another stroke." She reached for a dishtowel and soaked up the spill. Red's rant made him visibly weaker, and he leaned against Maggie's hip.

Silas fussed with righting the tipped salt shaker and scraping spilled salt into his hand. He seemed confused as to what he should do but then tossed the salt over his shoulder.

Maggie's hard gaze fixed on Silas. "It's not that we don't know the law can go contrary to everything that's right."

"Aw, come on, Maggie. Why don't we finish this fine meal and leave lawyering to lawyers? It's likely no more than loose talk."

"Silas, you of all people should know any chance of Red tangling with Judge Walker can't be taken lightly. He'll be on Red like a buzzard on road kill."

"What the hell are you three not telling me?" Jodie felt they were playing a game of blind man's bluff. She'd watched Silas's anguished face, and was convinced he wouldn't have risked upsetting Red on the strength of gossip alone, but something had backed him off.

Red nodded toward Silas, demanding that he tell what it was they alone shared.

"Hell, Mr. Red. Why stir an old stink?" He looked to Maggie against Red's insistence.

Maggie's chin jutted forward and she, too, pinned Silas to the truth. Cornered, he looked toward the door as if he suddenly remembered a hundred places he'd rather be.

"All right. Clara Lee and me messed around some after she married Walker Junior. But it sure didn't seem to matter to her."

Now it was Jodie's turn to wish she was someplace other than sitting across the table from the eyes that watched her chest rise and fall, her shock nearly taking her wind.

"Sheriff Walker was in a tight reelection primary, and everything turned to shit when his opponent paid the motel clerk a couple of bills to rat us out."

Once again he looked to Maggie, but she pressed him for more.

"Walker had Junior rush Clara Lee out of town before she could decide to tell the truth. Then the sonofabitch threw my surprised ass in jail." He blushed deeply, bowed his head, avoiding eye contact.

"Sonofabitch is right," Maggie echoed. "And would you believe on charges of kidnapping and rape?"

Jodie gasped. "No, no, how could he?" Had Clara Lee been forced to give a statement accusing Silas? Against all she knew, she still didn't want to believe Clara Lee was capable of such a selfish act.

"You're forgetting Walker is the law." The sound of Maggie gritting her teeth against such an injustice was audible.

The very thought of Silas as a rapist left a foul taste in Jodie's mouth, and while she knew him to be a habitually unfaithful husband, she was just as certain he could never be a rapist. He'd pressed her for sex after she turned fourteen, but he'd never attempted to force her.

Maggie glanced at Silas, and maybe out of pity she took up the story.

"Walker figured less damage if voters believed his daughter-in-law was raped. Lucky for Silas, Walker's race for reelection heated up, forcing him to bargain dropping charges against Silas if Red agreed to double-cross his opponent. Deliver votes to him instead.

278 • Pat Spears

"Red didn't trust Walker. Instead he took Walker's money and double-crossed him. To this day, he holds a fierce grudge."

Jodie winced.

Red didn't speak, only nodded, conceding his guilt.

A heavier silence engulfed the small kitchen, and William's angry threat that Red had done things and that he had proof resounded in Jodie's head. She could only hope that Red's shrewdness meant he still had leverage: he knew too much dirt on Walker.

Silas helped a visibly weakened Red to his bed while Jodie set about putting leftovers away, and Maggie poured heated water from the kettle into the dishpan and began to wash their dishes.

"God knows, Silas got bad hurt in all that mess. And as much as I love the boy, the truth is what he made it. He's never been one to holster his pistol, and it was bound to catch up to him." She straightened, turning to face Jodie.

"And for what it's worth, I do believe the Walkers meant to see Silas in prison. The law ignored the fact that she'd checked in a half-hour before Silas. And that it had not been the first such meeting between them."

"What about Clara Lee in all of this?"

"Don't know if she had a part in framing Silas. But I know firsthand that she got herself knocked up and expelled from the university. Her blubbering mama went to Doc and he flatly refused. Doc limits his work to making some devil's evil go away, claiming life's too hard on bastards of any color born straddling the tracks. Me, I figure, it's the mama's decision whether or not she wants to bring her baby into the cruelty she and it are bound to suffer. Lord knows, Doc and I have had our differences. Now we mostly stay out of each other's way."

Maggie walked onto the back porch and pitched dishwater into the yard.

Jodie felt Maggie's words in the pit of her stomach, and she leaned on the counter, considering a mama's choice. She wanted to know if Jewel had considered Maggie's kind of help. Since she could never know, she chose to believe that her presence in the world was answer enough.

Maggie walked back through the kitchen door. She took one look at Jodie, gave the dishrag a hard pop, and hung it on the stove handle to dry.

"You're gonna need to get some decent-looking dishrags in this house."

"I never knew about you and ... any of that."

"Child, you don't want to know any part of what I know. The truth of it has ground my few remaining teeth to the gums. Right along with breaking my old heart."

They each turned at the sound of Silas coming into the kitchen. He wrapped his arm around Maggie's shoulders, drew her close, and whispered in her ear, and whatever he said caused her blue eyes to water, her haggard face to brighten.

"Guess I'll be moving on. My baby girl expects her daddy home for story time. I'm damned determined she'll not grow up without knowing the pleasure of a few good books." His demeanor shifted, and he shoved his big, calloused hands deep into his pockets, his body swaying.

"Good for you, son. It ain't like we couldn't use a lot less ignorance around here." Maggie chuckled, handing Silas a waxed paper–wrapped dish. "See our boy out while I look in on Red."

Silas stopped on the porch and turned to Jodie. "About that mess with Clara Lee ... I never meant for it to hurt you."

"No, just surprised, I think." If he worried that she felt betrayed, he had it all wrong. But, why wouldn't he? He deserved the truth, but the thought of losing him terrified her.

"Whatever happened to her at the university messed her up real bad."

"What about your part in what happened?"

"I've thought about that a lot, and it's pretty much a mystery, right on. Maybe it was a revisit of whatever hit me that night at the fair when we were kids. I guess I still wanted to punish Stuart's privileged ass. Maybe hers too. They had what I wanted—a chance at something better."

She nodded. "Yeah, I get that."

He turned and walked off the porch. His stooped shoulders said all she needed to know about his regrets. She called goodnight, but he had moved beyond the sound of her voice.

Maggie came onto the porch. "I'd like your company in the morning. That is, if you don't have something better to do." She smiled.

They settled on a six-thirty start, plenty of time to go and get back before Red would want breakfast.

Jodie undressed and got into bed, her back pressed against a pillow, her longing big enough for both her and Maggie. She squeezed her eyes closed; tiny pinpoints of light danced against the backs of her eyelids, and she worked at setting aside her worries for Red and her tangled thoughts of Clara Lee. Come morning, she was to learn Maggie's newest secret, but tonight sleep would be a stranger to her.

## Forty-Six

Jodie stood at the end of the lane, watching the truck's fast approach. The bald tires slid to a jerky stop twenty feet beyond her. Jodie approached, watching Maggie's hard frown reflected in the side mirror. Maybe Maggie also worried now that she was alone, she might have slipped a cog or two.

Maggie gave her a groggy nod and spun the truck around in the road, driving back in the direction she'd come. Jodie settled onto the ragged wool blanket covering the ripped seat, her hands wedged under her bare thighs. For all the time she'd known Maggie, she'd referred to the blanket as her severance on behalf of an ungrateful nation. Even nosey Silas hadn't learned the story behind the blanket.

Maggie handed Jodie the battered thermos, a veteran of many nameless journeys. "Pour me another while you're at it. After all that mess last evening, I decided we'd need a little Irish to neutralize the red." Maggie's eyes were puffy, evidence that she too hadn't slept.

Jodie poured expertly to the cup's circled stain; the mark Maggie had long called the rough road mark. The strong scent of chicory and bourbon filled the cab.

"Can you handle one of those biscuits with ham and Ruth's strawberry jam there in that sack?"

Jodie bit into the warm biscuit, jam oozing from its crispy brown edges, the sound of Arthur's big laughter echoing in her memory. Someday she would tell Maggie about him, his biscuits, and their shared pilfering.

At a familiar crossroads, Maggie turned the truck eastward into the blood-red birth of what felt oddly enough like a stronger day. The noisy clatter of the truck scattered a flutter of sparrows and the tiny birds rose like a dark wave above the wet, grassy shoulder of the road.

"Those birds put me in mind of what Ruth once said about quails scattering widely when threatened, in the hope that at least a few survive." Maggie paused. "Then I've come to know surviving alone as a damn hard way to go." Her tone was one of deep sadness, her memories filling the cab like a bittersweet vapor, and Jodie believed Maggie's heart looked backward. She now spoke of more good days behind her than ahead.

Maggie steered the truck onto Old Church Road, and as Jodie had suspected, she was here with Maggie to visit Miss Ruth's grave. Ahead less than two hundred yards, a simple, rectangular-shaped church stood on a slight rise in an otherwise flat terrain. The narrow steeple held no bell to summon its faithful, and its rough spire made of shaved pine saplings spoke to the impoverishment of its congregation.

"Why she was so set on coming here to this church remains a mystery." Maggie drained the last of the coffee and stepped out of the truck.

Jodie had given little thought to Miss Ruth's faithfulness beyond its selfish meaning that Maggie had taken Sundays for her and Silas. Yet Miss Ruth had seemed better suited to a church Jodie had seen pictured in *Life Magazine*, a pretty vine-covered building constructed of huge gray stones with a steeple so tall it appeared a stairway to the pearly gates. Miss Ruth would have likely needed to travel as far as Mobile or New Orleans to find such a church.

Angie Otterman approached on arthritic knees along a worn path that ran between her family's failed farm and the church grounds. Her stomach and breasts sagged under the coarse cotton print dress sown from feed bags. Jodie remembered her daughter, Katie, a tiny, nearly mute schoolmate, had worn dresses sown from similar material. A pregnant Katie had dropped out of school in the eighth grade to harsh rumors. Jodie hadn't seen Katie after that, and believed she'd been sent away.

"Morning, Miss Maggie. Is it our Lord and Savior Jesus Christ who brings you to His Father's house?" Her smile included Jodie, and she tugged at her short cut-offs, looking to Maggie for an appropriate response. Miss Angie clutched a fist of freshly picked wildflowers, likely intended for the church altar.

"Not today, Angie. It would appear I'm good for a while longer on my own."

Miss Angie's brow gathered, her focus now on the approach of a man Jodie took to be her husband. While not as much as looking at Maggie or her, he glared at his wife, his hard eyes burning with reprisal. Having done so, he walked on, entering through what Jodie imagined as the church's narrowest of doors.

"Forgive my husband. He doesn't require love. Only obedience." Miss Angie stepped closer and spoke directly to Maggie. "I know our sweet Miss Ruth favored her roses." Her voice seemed to gather strength. "Just the same, I think she'd like these pretties." She handed Maggie the bouquet, turned and followed her husband.

Maggie took Jodie's hand in hers, and together they walked beneath a rusted metal archway with three rotund cherubs poised atop, grasping harps in their plump hands. Morning dew beaded on the teardrop-shaped leaves of the sweet-smelling vines entwining the arch, sunlight turning each droplet into a prism of rainbow colors.

"I like the idea of those chunky boys as backup to Ole Gabe should he mislay his trumpet. Reckon they know any Ruth Brown?" Maggie's wry smile fixed oddly on her otherwise sad face, and her hand in Jodie's was moist.

They walked among row after row of simple tombstones of porous lime rock, blackened with age; Catawba's pioneer families—Irish, Scottish, German, and English—human chains stretching back six generations, buried so close Jodie imagined their spirits whispering back and forth on the darkest nights. Among the poorer there were bread loaf-shaped indentations marked by simple, decaying wooden crosses. At one such grave, bearing the name of Katie Otterman, Jodie slowed.

"I was called too late to save her." Maggie glared back along the path, vengeance burning in her eyes. "If there's justice in the hereafter, it's surely meant for the likes of Jacob Otterman."

They walked on a ways, stopping at the foot of a newly erected double gravestone cut from solid granite, its silver-gray face polished to a smooth brilliance.

### RUTH ANN O'RILEY
### BELOVED COMPANION OF MARGARET E. FRANKLIN
### BORN OCTOBER 5, 1910 — DIED JANUARY 9, 1961

Jodie pressed her trembling finger tips to her quivering lips, and she whispered, "God, Maggie, it's fine. Real fine."

Maggie nodded. "Yes, it is. Isn't it?"

She knelt next to the grave, and in what Jodie believed was a defiant act of love, she traced with her fingertip the letters C-O-M-P-A-N-I-O-N chiseled deep into the stone. No longer a whisper between lovers, but a shout for all eternity. She placed the wildflowers on the grave and pushed to her feet with the aid of the stone.

When each was ready, they walked back along the path to where they'd left the truck. An off-key rendition of *Onward Christian Soldiers* rose from the congregation and echoed across the ridge.

Jodie turned to Maggie. "Do you think Miss Ruth's safe here?" She understood that she wished to be reassured that hatred and its violence stopped at the grave.

While Maggie's smile was gentle, her tone was pensive. "I can't know that, but I can tell you that men, women, and children openly wept at her funeral, yet not one spoke our names in the same breath."

Jodie nodded, and in the absence of knowing, she'd choose to set aside the evil she'd seen in the eyes of Jacob Otterman and accept that a gift of simple wildflowers was a lasting act of compassion.

Upon reaching the crossroads, Maggie pulled the truck to a full stop and looked in both directions, a hesitation Jodie believed had nothing to do with a sudden obedience to the rules of the road, but rather a momentary loss of the emotional compass Miss Ruth had been.

"Maggie, what would you say to our riding over to the beach? Checking out our old haunts?" Red would expect breakfast about now, but he'd soon need to get by on cereal. The practice of managing on his own would do him good.

Maggie looked at her, as though surprised by her presence, and she took a moment to recover.

"I'd like that." Maggie smiled. "We'll stop off at Samuel's and pick us up a hobo picnic."

"Mr. Samuel?" Jodie nearly choked on her deceit.

Maggie took a firmer grip on the steering wheel and stared straight ahead. "After that no-account Roy Dale Pitts robbed the store, Golden got the wrongheaded notion that if the mess ever got out, white customers would stop buying groceries from a Jew harboring a Negro thief. Hellfire, after twenty years, Samuel knew as much about the business as Golden. He opened his own store."

Maggie appeared to wait for whatever she might say, but Jodie only nodded.

"Wholesalers refused to sell to him, until Samuel persuaded Golden to over-order and to sell the overage to him at a markup of two cents on the dollar. Greedy men looked the other way, happy enough with bigger orders, and Golden got a little extra." Maggie grunted her irritation. "Money has a way of whistling Dixie where common decency fails."

"Maggie, I was with Roy Dale Pitts when he robbed Golden and pistol-whipped Mr. Samuel." Her words gushed from her mouth in a torrent. "But I wasn't in on any of his meanness."

"Jodie, you knew damn well that boy didn't break into the store for that mess of candy and gum he took."

"I was wrong the very moment Roy Dale took that tire iron to the door. But I didn't know Mr. Samuel was there, and I swear I didn't know about the gun and the beating until later. Still, I was a dirty coward not to come back and face up to my part."

Maggie glanced at Jodie and nodded.

"How bad was it?"

"He took a nasty bruise all right, but he called me at home more worried he'd be blamed for the missing money."

"Did you know right off that I was with Roy Dale?"

"Not at first, but I squeezed enough of the truth out of Clara Lee about your big fight. I knew for sure when one of my fishing buddies told me he'd seen you with Roy Dale at the boat landing."

"It all happened so fast. All I could think about was getting away. I was headed to Dallas. But that didn't work out."

"I accepted that you were desperate enough to leave the way you did. Roy Dale's meanness was his own doing. And I'd venture to say you've learned a hard lesson on the company you keep."

Her web of wrong was more intricate than she'd first imagined, and Maggie had made it clear that her next move was hers alone.

## Forty-Seven

Maggie pulled the truck to a stop at Silas's station. Jodie retrieved the key from behind the kerosene tank and pumped a tank of gas. A surprised Silas came from a work bay to lean on the truck, wiping grease from his hands.

"Where do you two delinquents think you're off to on stolen gas?"

"Hell, today's the Sabbath. Quit whatever you're doing and come with us. We have food and drink enough for Cox's Army."

"Oh, yeah, just what ya'll got in that sack?" Silas tilted his head to one side with interest.

"What's it matter, boy? Come on. It'll be like old times." Maggie chuckled and Silas was hooked.

"You still got those old crab nets? We mean to catch us a mess of soft shells." Jodie winked.

He broke into a boyish grin, the special one Jodie loved. "Nobody's used them since us. They're likely rotted."

Maggie started up the truck. "Does that mean you're coming?"

"You bet. Wait while I lock up the place." He went at a trot, yelling back at Jodie, "And put my damn key right back where you found it."

Silas returned with nets and a bucket of chilled Pabst Blue Ribbon. He offered to drive, but Maggie waved him in next to Jodie. He opened three beers, passing two over.

By the time they reached the beach, they'd finished the beers and Silas had Maggie pull over at a closed Gulf station. He walked around behind the building as if he intended to use the restroom. In less than five minutes he returned, a brown bag under his arm.

"Since when did filling stations start selling beer on Sundays? That's not exactly keeping the Sabbath."

"On the beach, sin's for sale any day of the week. Otherwise it *is* a blue Sunday." Silas grinned at Maggie and opened three more cold ones.

Maggie parked the truck on the edge of an oyster shell road, careful to keep the passenger's side wheels out of a sand bog. Placing the remaining beers on ice, Silas carried the sack, crab nets, and bucket. Jodie lifted the food box onto her shoulder, leaving Maggie to bring the army blanket.

They trudged a quarter of a mile through palmetto clumps and twisted scrub oaks to a secluded strip of white sand lying between a high-tide lagoon and the blue-green waters of St. Joseph Bay. On the shore's edge, a flock of seagulls rose from the surf, flapping their noisy retreat. Ahead, toward St. Joe, billowing clouds of heavy white smoke poured from the pulp mill, spewing its chemical stench against an otherwise clear sky.

Silas pointed out a shortleaf pine, its growth stunted, branches gnarled by constant salt spray and gulf wind. An anhinga perched on a lower limb, spread its bluish-black wings to dry, and beyond, in the lagoon, the silver backs of mullet flashed in the sunlight. Jodie breathed in the salt air, embracing it as an old friend.

Silas squinted across the wide expanse of water and shook his head in amazement, leaving her and Maggie behind. Still, she winked at Maggie, the two silently agreeing to give Silas the audience he craved.

"Florida tilts, you know. Standing here, it's easy to imagine its wide continental shelf righting itself by some geological event, and land pushing up out of the Gulf. We'd be standing east of what would be the center of the state."

It was as though he'd stepped out of heavy work boots and jeans into penny loafers and a corduroy jacket, making it easy to imagine him standing in front of a classroom. He'd read more books than the lifetime total of those whose old cars and trucks he kept running.

They slipped off their shoes, rolled up their jeans, and waded into the foaming surf. They each tossed a chicken neck, secured to a piece of twine, into the breakers, baiting crabs, the midday sun warming their backs. Silas pulled his shirt off and tied it around his waist.

"No fair you can do that and I can't."

"Go ahead. I double-dog dare and eat the hair." Splashing ahead, he turned back, repeating his boyish dare. It wasn't his challenge but a new voice that pushed to be heard. She pulled her shirt over her head, removed her bra, and tied both around her waist.

"Damn, Jodie, you are crazy." He looked back at her across the unrestrained blue waters and began to laugh.

"What's so damn funny? They're breasts, not too big, not too small, just right, I've been told." She waded into deeper water, her breasts floating freely.

He stopped laughing. "No, no, it's not that. For sure you aren't Sandra Dee, but you're not half bad."

Jodie looked toward Maggie, who stood with her feet spread wide, surf and sand swirling around her ankles.

"Forget me, gal. I'm not getting in y'all's mess." Maggie waded on, slinging the crab bait into the surf and retrieving soft-shelled crabs clinging to the raw chicken.

"After all these years of me in hot pursuit, and it's down to this." He shook his head. "But I'm more than happy to love your crazy ass right on." He turned and ran toward Maggie.

Jodie remembered Maggie had said Silas thought he knew what he wanted, but he was wrong. She believed that his laughter hadn't been ridicule but sudden awareness that the love they shared was indeed of a different nature. Then, he'd never stopped surprising her, and that was what she loved most about him.

Jodie walked out of the surf, struggled back into her clothes, and ran to join Maggie and Silas.

Their bucket filled with crabs, the three walked back along the beach to where they'd stashed the food and drink. Sitting on the sand beneath the rustle of a cabbage palm, Maggie made fold-overs from the bologna and bread. When they'd eaten their fill, Maggie slipped off behind a clump of palmetto while Jodie and Silas packed away the remaining food and drink. Maggie returned and spread the army blanket, settling onto the warm sand for a nap.

Silas stripped down to his boxers and waded into the water. His body had retained its youthful leanness. He plunged into the surf, his strokes strong and even, a man at ease in the water. He swam seventy yards or more into the bay before flipping onto his back, raising his arm in a quick wave while bobbing like a fisherman's cork.

Jodie walked back in the direction of the lagoon, gathering dry driftwood, downed palm fronds, and pine cones for the fire they'd need for steaming crabs.

Silas walked out of the surf, tugging at the front of his shorts. He pulled on his jeans and sat beside her, glancing over his shoulder at Maggie sleeping.

"Guess we've gained a step or two on her." The love on his face could have melted ice.

Jodie smiled. "Best you don't let her hear you."

She looked out across the blue-green expanse to where water and sky became one, and the gentle wave motion added to her newfound calm.

"What brings you such a peaceful look?" It was a treacherous question, but one that deserved an honest answer.

"I was thinking about what it might feel like to be in love." She didn't look at him, but at the tide inching its way onto the sand.

"Guess I'm willing to work on that being a good thing. And this man is back where you came from?" He slipped his arm around her shoulders and drew her to him in the way he might Maggie.

She stroked the rough, red skin over his knuckles, cleaned and softened by the salty water.

"Silas, I won't ever feel that way with a man." The lapping sound of the surf was suddenly magnified a hundred fold.

"But, just now, I thought you …." He got to his feet and his body grew stiff with his recognition.

"If it's the last thing I do, I promise you I'll hunt down Roy Dale Pitts. And I'll kill that mean sonofabitch."

"No, no, Silas. There's no one to blame. Trust me, I'm not broken. I don't need fixing."

"Good God, Jodie. Then stop your damn fooling around." He turned his face away from her, but not before she saw it twist into pain, her meaning slowly taking hold.

He stumbled backward, tears in his eyes. "Why'd you have to tell me? Why not go on lying? I could live with that."

He turned and ran, faster and faster, until he became a dark speck against the waning day. She wanted to believe that he had stopped running and stood bent, panting, searching for a way back.

The taste of salt spray on her lips, Jodie breathed more deeply, considering all the times she'd heard the word *queer* and felt fear, and had known anger and not pride. Scooping a handful of warm sand, she caressed it between her palms, her heart beating to a different rhythm, her resolve flowing through her veins warm as her blood.

She wasn't sure how long she sat before Maggie struggled to her feet, the tattered army blanket tightly wrapped around her shoulders.

"Girl, you're going to need to build us a fire. We've got crabs to steam."

When the crabs were ready, Jodie and Maggie sat on the blanket and picked sweet meat from the soft shells, washing their food down with RC Colas. While they ate, a full moon rose over the water, turning the sand to a wide slivery path as far as Jodie could see. She and Maggie were alone.

"Should we look for him?"

"No, shug. He means to get back on his own."

"Will he stop loving me?"

Maggie shook her head, sighed softly, "Lord, child, sometimes you amaze me at what you don't get out of living."

"Please, tell me. I can't bear the thought of losing him."

"He'd just begun to work out his feelings about giving you up to some other man. Now you've asked him to figure out how he's going to keep on loving you after hearing the truth. He'll need time."

She'd rarely heard such tenderness in Maggie's voice, and she seemed to struggle with her thoughts before deciding to leave something unsaid. Jodie stoked the embers with the remaining twigs and palm branches. Flames flickered, built, and rose skyward in the way of rebirth, and they leaned in, drawn to the fire's primordial powers to comfort.

"How'd you know Miss Ruth's was the love you could trust?" Love remained a mystery to her, and what little she knew defied the shape of words.

"I remembered watching my grandpa work iron. He never hurried. Heated and cooled the iron, content to pound it into shape a little at a time, believing a good piece of iron would need shaping and reshaping with considerable care if it is to hold its core strength. Don't know if he was right or not, but I took his point."

"For a moment back there with Miss Ruth, I thought I knew all I needed to know. But now, I'm not as sure." She looked into the wider world she'd come to distrust, and spoke to what she couldn't know. Still, she said, "There's a woman I think I loved, but I let her get away without ever telling her as much."

"Ah, and who is it you don't trust?"

Jodie felt her facial muscles relax, and she slowly nodded. She now believed she knew more fully why she'd run, but she'd need to understand the harder part of what she was willing to leave behind. She still had wrongs to settle.

"What's to be done about your half? The tombstone, I mean?"

"Uh, that …." Maggie paused, and maybe they each avoided the inevitability of her death. "Silas has yet to see it. But whatever he feels, he'll do what's needed when the time comes." She laughed. "What that sweet boy knows and denies about Ruth and me could fill one of those poetry books he keeps hidden behind the seat of his truck."

"Why him?" Her sense of betrayal was more real than she meant to expose, and maybe her childhood jealousy drove her response.

"He'll stay and you won't." Maggie smiled, and Jodie believed that Maggie wanted her to know that she, too, believed her leaving could be a good thing. They sat a moment longer, neither talking. When thick, black-velvet darkness enfolded them, they stood, gathered the remainder of the day, and walked the moonlit trail back to where they'd left the truck.

Maggie handed Jodie the keys, and they drove back along the mostly deserted highway, Maggie balancing two perfectly matched conch shells in her lap.

"My Ruth would have loved today."

"Except for the part where Silas ran away." For good, she thought, but could not bear saying it aloud.

"No, she would've liked that part best. Me waiting until her death was wrong. I should have never asked that of her. Thought I was sparing her pain, but she knew we weren't fooling anybody who really mattered."

Jodie leaned across the space and kissed Maggie on the cheek.

"Figure I must taste like a salt lick."

"No, ma'am. You taste good, like warm butter."

"Felt good. I miss kisses."

## Forty-Eight

Jodie and Maggie sat bent over a wobbly card table, the results of their meager start at assembling the fifteen-hundred-piece puzzle of the Grand Canyon spread before them. A thunderstorm rolled toward the ridge, its outer edges beginning to pound rain onto the tin roof, muting the sounds of Maggie's labored breathing, their cycling sighs, and the familiar voice of Walter Cronkite.

At the barely audible mention of Selma, Alabama, Jodie looked up from the puzzle. She came to her feet, crossed the room, and stood staring at the snowy television screen.

Maggie stood at Jodie's elbow. "What on earth, child? You're trembling."

"Just now, I may've seen someone."

Although the huge black man's features had appeared fuzzy on the screen, Jodie believed him to be Arthur Washington. But there was nothing more to learn. Cronkite had moved on from the bloody confrontation between police and protesters to an announcement from the White House on plans for a presidential visit to Dallas in mid-November.

"If Mother Nature keeps up her fury, those catch pans I set out all over this sorry excuse for a house will need emptying. Wouldn't hurt to check the one I set in the middle of your bed while I brew us a fresh pot of Irish."

Jodie emptied the rainwater into the bathtub, reset the pan, and worked at convincing herself that the man she saw wasn't Arthur. He was too smart to return to Selma. But with him, it was never a matter of smarts.

Maggie poured two steaming cups, stiffened both with a double shot of bourbon, and took a seat opposite Jodie. She sipped the spiked coffee in an attempt to wash her fears from the twisted knot her gut had become. Still, she felt Arthur's presence as real as if he, too, sat across the table from her.

Maggie placed a warm hand on her balled fist and squeezed. She looked away and then back into Maggie's warm gaze, realizing that the bigger part of being who she was wasn't her many lies but all the silences she'd kept.

"This man I knew back in Selma. Cooked at the café where I worked."

Maggie leaned forward, her torso perfectly square to Jodie's. Her expression, while expectant, spoke of patience.

"Wish you could have known him. He made biscuits nearly as good as yours." She glanced at Maggie, gauging her take.

A flash of irritation set Maggie's jaw hard and she scoffed. "And you're telling me that this man's biscuits are reason enough for me to want to know him?" She leaned back in the chair, her intolerance for anything less than the whole truth barefaced.

"No, I'm telling you … he was my friend." She paused. "Arthur. Arthur Washington. I think he was the man I saw just now, being jailed along with others I know nothing about. He's deep into all that civil rights business."

Maggie leaned forward, setting the cup back onto the table. Her open expression invited more.

"Before I left Selma, a bunch of night riders nearly beat him to death. He barely escaped Selma ahead of their finishing their meanness."

"And you had a hand in his escape."

She nodded. "Yes'm, I did. He could still die."

"Yeah, he could. It's a damn sorry thing, but more times than not suffering and dying is the horse change rides in on."

Jodie's breath caught, and her eyes filled with tears. She was likely to never cross paths with Arthur again, but he would forever be a part of how she knew courage.

"But darling, you and Arthur are the friends we all crave. And it's rare aplenty if we get one or two in a lifetime. And it doesn't hurt one whit that they can turn out a pan of good biscuits. Brew a jug of moonshine. Or steal from crooked politicians."

They sat for a time, listening to the last of the rainwater dripping from the eaves. Maggie appeared to sift through her own memories, a story gathering behind her furrowed brow. She poured bourbon into her empty cup.

"After the war, a bunch of us got booted out of the service."

"Booted? How so?"

"Army paid shrinks to say all of us queers who were serving were crazy. We were all scared, some of us more than others—them enough to tattle, thinking to save their own hides, I figured. Army handed those of us accused dishonorable discharges." Maggie's face grew harsh, her belly-stored pain boiling its way to the surface. "No one stood up for us. Not even those whose lives we nurses saved. I think that's what hurt me the most."

"What'd you do?"

"Let it beat me down. Drank too damn much. Then it was never more than I needed. Stayed depressed over missing out on all the hoopla for returning vets. Parades and celebrations popped up in every little chicken-shit town across the country. I was a proud soldier. I wanted to wear my uniform. March with the others in just one of those home-grown parades."

Jodie nodded.

"But all wasn't lost." A smile brightened Maggie's worn face. "My Ruth threw me a private homecoming. I dressed in my uniform, stripped of its insignia, and she pinned handmade insignia and medals on my jacket. Escorted me to a candlelight dinner in our own tiny kitchen. Afterwards, we danced until two in the morning to Benny Goodman's band."

"I fared better than those poor souls who suffered such fear and loneliness they took their own lives to escape it." Maggie hugged her arms tightly across her breasts, and Jodie believed she saw in Maggie's eyes the same despair she'd often felt, and had seen in Sarah's eyes.

## Forty-Nine

Jodie looked up from the line of wash she was hanging and spotted a county sheriff's vehicle turning onto the lane. Bad memories flooded back, and dropping the wet pillowcase into the basket, she hurried back inside to the rattling of the screen door. Red faked deafness to the deputy's persistent calls.

"Afternoon, Miss Jodie."

"If you're here to deliver bad news, then you can stick that hat back on your head and get the hell away from here."

They faced off, the screen door between them, while she more calmly measured his intent, and he surely did the same with her.

"Oh, no ma'am, it's nothing like that. You might say it's more of a special favor to Mrs. Hazel than anything official. That would be checking on her ailing daddy … that is, Mr. Red." He took great pains to explain that nobody wanted any more trouble.

"Uh-huh, and I'd be the reason she can't do her own checking?" Until now, she'd thought of Hazel as an unfortunate pawn.

"I'm still going to need to talk to Mr. Red." He stepped back, knocking over a potted geranium. "Shit … sorry about that." He stooped and righted the pot, pushing spilled dirt over the porch edge.

"Hell, come on in. Satisfy yourself that I've got the poor, pitiful cripple hog-tied there on the couch, flat on his back, forcing him to sip whiskey and listen to Alabama football."

The deputy, blushing under her scaling, stepped into the room. Red lifted himself onto an elbow, looked first at the officer and then back at her.

"Deputy Green's here to see your bedsores. So cooperate with his investigation by flipping yourself ass-side up."

Buster lifted his head and growled.

"It's the uniform, sonny. He hates meddling lawmen." Red dropped back onto the sofa and turned up the volume. Buster took up where he'd left off chewing the Bart Starr exercise ball Silas had given Red, believing it would strengthen his right hand. Jodie decided the near toothless dog was grateful nothing more was required of him.

The befuddled deputy looked to her for help. Although Red's speech was still slurred, his intent was clear. She walked out of the room, leaving the deputy to do Hazel's bidding.

Deputy Green drove away before the water for a fresh pitcher of tea had boiled. Jodie returned to the front room and Red waved an envelope addressed to Charles E. Dozier from Gregory K. Anders, Attorney at Law.

"That polecat boy left it. His duty, he said. Tell me what it says." The pink in Red's cheeks had gone white as a lye-boiled sheet.

She read the letter and explained that it summoned him to appear day after tomorrow at Anders's office.

"You don't have to go. It's not like the judge sent for you." Jodie tossed the letter onto the table. Red looked at her as if he weighed the merits of her argument.

"Maybe, but I'm tired. Want this mess settled." He turned back to the excited voices on the radio, but she thought he'd lost interest.

Maggie had warned that this fight wouldn't be settled in the old ways of sweeter bribes or, that failing, with fists, knives, and guns. Red was up against a vengeful wife, an ambitious lawyer, and, if called upon, a judge who'd easily use the blunt end of the law to settle an old score.

Sunday afternoon, Jodie left Red sulking and walked along the road until she spotted a neighbor's house with a telephone line running overhead. Once inside, the neighbor proudly pointed her to the brand new olive green telephone hanging from a wall in the kitchen.

Maggie answered Jodie's call, and in the background Jodie heard loud barking.

"You got a dog?"

"God, no. It's Lassie tearing off after the bad guys." Maggie had a long-standing infatuation with June Lockhart.

Jodie's remarks were brief, and Maggie kept her fuming down to a single burst of profanity, agreeing to drive them to the appointment.

Jodie walked back along the road, and at the familiar sound of Silas's truck approaching, she stepped onto the shoulder, allowing for regret should he choose to pass her by.

The truck slowed and he leaned, his face weary behind a week-old beard. "Where you headed?" The words were his, but his tone carried a strained distance.

"Nowhere." She looked into the sun's glare, his features lost to her.

"What'd you say we go there together? Throw back a few cold ones. Maybe get a thing or two settled. I'm not much good at this new way of ours."

"Beer sounds good." She got into the truck and he smelled, not of his usual Mennen and gas fumes, but oddly of turpentine.

"Want to take a run over to our tree house? See if she's still hanging?" His mischievous grin wasn't there, but she felt him working at it.

They drove the short distance and sat staring up at the tree house they'd built her first summer in Catawba with a ceremonial exchange of blood, pledging to its secrecy. The tree house took a full summer given to pilfering and hauling boards, roofing tin, nails, rope, and tools to the site.

"I remembered it a lot bigger," she said. It was a mere four-foot-square platform with three walls and a lean-to roof resting precariously across two flanking limbs of a giant live oak. A sheet of twice-used rusted roofing tin lay on the ground beneath the tree.

"That old ladder's apt to be rotted. You willing to try it?" His playfulness held only a faint slice of boyish challenge.

"Why not? Can't amount to more than a broken neck."

"You go first. If it holds, I'll follow." He winked.

They sat on the platform, legs dangling over the open side, neither finding words they trusted to talk about what had brought each there. When they had polished off the beers, he turned to her.

"I guess you want to know how it was I happened along on a Sunday afternoon when I'd otherwise be watching Bears football."

"If you've brought me here to try and argue me out of what I said ... it won't do any good. It's not like that—something to be fixed or taken back."

"It's true I don't like what I heard. Understand it even less, but it's not about that."

"What then?"

"I wanted you to know I pulled those boards off the bathroom doors and painted them over. I'm guessing those who don't like peeing together will pump their gas elsewhere." Maybe it was his failed play on words, but his eyes bled a bolder conviction.

"What changed your mind?"

"Those little girls." His voice broke.

"Not your girl?"

"Oh God, no. She's okay for now." He looked to where the tree line met the horizon and shuddered. "Those four little colored girls. Murdered by some twisted sonsofbitches who figured they could put a stop to history by killing kids." He spit into the air and wiped his mouth on his shirt sleeve. "News made it sound as if they'd just turned out Sunday school." He paused, catching his breath. "Goddamn, Jodie. Sunday school. Picture those four crowded together in a bathroom, primping and giggling over boys. Younger than me and you the summer we built this tree house."

Bitter bile had pushed upward from her stomach and Jodie felt dizzy. She moved back from the edge of the platform.

"That bomb blast blew out the walls, brought down the upper floor, and crushed those girls beneath the rubble."

When Jodie trusted herself to speak without gagging, she asked, "Where was this?" Not that place mattered.

"Birmingham," he answered, then more silence before he said, "If Kennedy, King, and the Klan mean to make this an all-out war using kid fodder, then it doesn't leave much wiggle room for us 'go along, get along' folk." He rubbed his paint-smeared knuckles and looked at her. It was the second time she'd seen such hurt in his eyes. She took his hand in hers and he leaned into her shoulder, whispering, "Jodie, this evil is way bigger than politics and the damn politicians who drive it. Don't know how many generations will need to die off before this meanness can right itself. You and me, we may not live to see it."

"I sure hope you're wrong. About how bad and how long."

He nodded, but she knew hope to be a sorry excuse for almost anything.

In the grip of a human world gone mad, they sat silently, breathing in the evil aftermath, its bitterness staying on their tongues.

Overhead, against a sky so pure, leaves danced to the musical whisper of a gentle breeze, and a chorus of unaware songbirds chirped. It was as though Mother Nature turned her face away in shame, damning all of mankind. What was perception without action but evil?

# Fifty

Maggie parked the truck near Catawba's only bank and pointed out the '59 Chevy. She waited until Jodie had helped Red to stand on the sidewalk before declaring she didn't have the stomach for the upcoming travesty. She drove away, promising to return in an hour.

Jodie tightened her grip on Red's razor-sharp elbow and they walked toward a side entrance of the bank building. The lawyer's name on the glass was freshly painted in bold lettering that spoke of his recent arrival and his intent to make good.

The shabby carpet and secondhand furniture bore out local rumors that Anders had not arrived with buckets of family money, but that he had taken advantage of his college friendship with Walker Junior, acquiring a generous, co-signed loan from the bank. Jodie understood that Anders's indebtedness likely explained his willingness to take a case against Red, a man of some reputation, if mostly scandalous.

Sadie Slatmore sat behind a secretarial desk, expertly stroking the keys of a Royal electric typewriter. She wore an orange and white striped tent dress, and when she stood, it unfolded to a size sufficient to house a three-ring circus. She looked up and gave Jodie a smile that worked only her mouth, directing her office-friendly manner to Red. He took her hand and inquired about her husband and their three adult boys. She led him to a side chair, and Jodie detected what she thought was genuine concern. But it was Sadie that Maggie blamed for the gossip that had reached Silas.

A slender man with blond curls, dressed in a worn, dark blue suit and maroon tie, came from the office labeled *private*. He spoke politely, introducing himself. He helped Red stand while apologizing for bringing him out under the circumstances of poor health, declaring the matter before them could be resolved in short order. His tone was sincere enough, but Jodie was certain lawyers were trained to sound that way. Red and Anders disappeared into the office, and Jodie caught a glimpse of Miss Mary, tugging at her dress hem.

The office door had no more than closed before Jodie headed out. She was unwilling to chance coming eyeball to eyeball with Miss Mary. She crossed the street, cut through the weedy vacant lot next to Silas's station, and headed for the Flamingo Café.

The door opened to the dull jingle of three tarnished bells held together by a faded red ribbon, remnants from a Christmas long past. Two locals stopped talking and watched her. The blurry-eyed man at the counter was apt to be the driver of the big rig parked in the vacant lot. He didn't bother looking up from his pursuit of the young waitress who stood close. A beefy man wearing grease-stained coveralls stared; his curled lip spoke of his disdain for any woman who wasn't home changing diapers. Jodie matched his cold stare and he looked away.

The young waitress approached, the scent of her cheap Evening in Paris perfume preceding her. Jodie flipped the turned down cup and nodded toward the steaming pot in the waitress's hand.

"You going to want something more?" Her words slipped between her painted lips, and the powder blotched on her face failed to cover a rash of pimples. Her legs were bound in nylons, and she wore scuffed oxfords.

"A couple of plain doughnuts if you've got 'em."

"They're yesterday's." She spoke with a take-it-or-leave-it shrug, her weight shifted onto one leg, and Jodie remembered Crystal Ann had said women who lasted in the café trade learned to wear out one leg at a time.

"They'll do." Jodie pulled a Lucky from the pack at her elbow.

"Can you spare one? Ran out an hour ago. And I can't leave out of here to get more." She nodded toward Silas's station. "Boss hates women smokers worse than he hates women in general."

Jodie pushed the pack across the table. "Take two. They burn fast."

The girl slipped the smokes into her apron pocket, left, and returned with the donuts. She lingered, as though she waited for a verdict.

"Not half bad."

The girl poured a refill, and she still remained. "You're the one ran off with that shiftless boy, way back, ain't you?"

"Where'd you hear that?" Jodie was careful to keep her surprise to herself. The girl would have been in elementary school.

"From bigmouth Deputy Green. Claimed he was out your way on business." She leaned closer. "Knowing him, I'd bet it was an excuse to snoop."

"Yeah, well, I'm still that fool. Why?"

The girl shrugged. "No reason. Just wondered, that's all."

At the sound of the bells over the door, both Jodie and the waitress looked up.

Clara Lee Walker stood haloed against the sunlight pouring through the open door. She surveyed the café's patrons before moving in Jodie's direction. Her willow-thin body turned heads, and pride erupted from somewhere in the recesses of Jodie's younger brain.

The steaming pot poised, the waitress whispered, "Do you know her? She's the closest we got to a Peyton Place woman." There was admiration in the girl's excitement. "I'm writing her story someday."

"I did once … know her. Then, that was a long time ago." Jodie wondered if the girl would dare to write her side of Clara Lee's story.

"Hello, Jodie. May I sit?" Clara Lee's voice caressed, and her smile still had the power to take Jodie's breath.

"Yes, but I can't stay long. Got business across the street." Jodie glanced toward the front door, but her mind and body betrayed her words.

"Patty, bring me a clean cup, please."

The rustle of Clara Lee's clothing and the swishing sound her silk-clad legs made, smoothly gliding one over the other, roared in Jodie's ears, and the familiar flexing of her ankle as she gently swung her right foot was hypnotic.

Jodie glanced in the direction of the departing waitress and worked at pulling herself together, attempting a casual tone. "Has it really been seven years?" She knew right down to the day, but would Clara Lee?

"Time best measured in roads not taken. But yes, it has been. I was away most of the summer, only heard last evening you were back. I hoped I'd see you before I left again."

"I'm not exactly back. I'm leaving as soon as Red's better."

"Yes, I understand that he's quite ill. I'm sorry."

"He was, but he's better now." Clara Lee wasn't here to talk about Red's illness, but Jodie needed more time to sort her jumbled thoughts. "The day I arrived I saw them. Your twins, I mean. They're fine looking boys."

"Yes, they are. But I'm sure you've heard, I'm a terrible mother." There was a resigned sadness about her, the kind that took time to gather, and Jodie understood that a painful price had been extracted from Clara Lee.

The waitress brought a clean cup, poured a round, and looked quizzically at Clara Lee.

"No, thank you, Patty, I'm fine." When the reluctant girl had moved on, trailing steam from the hot pot of coffee, Clara Lee leaned and said, "I've thought about you often. Where you might have actually gone." She twisted a loose strand of hair that she now wore shorter. "Are you with someone special?"

Jodie removed the cup from her lips and set it back down, sloshing coffee. She glanced about the café, but it was nearly empty.

"I'm sorry. I didn't mean to pry, make you uncomfortable. I apologize."

"No. I mean, I'm fine. And yes, I am ... with someone, you might say. She's smart and pretty. Lives in Mobile, Alabama, but she's coming with me to Dallas. I'm leaving tomorrow." It wasn't a lie, but a decision she'd only just made.

Clara Lee looked down at her folded hands, but not before Jodie noticed that her eyes flashed a familiar, warm liquid gold.

"I've known for some time that I should have gone with you."

In the moment, Jodie's body ached with the memory of how it had felt to touch Clara Lee. She needed her not to get so close to where her feelings could get tangled.

"At least tell me we weren't just a couple of misguided girls."

"No, Clara Lee. We were much more."

Clara Lee smiled, but it wasn't the one Jodie had cherished. "I'm sorry, but I must go. I promised my boys a rare trip to Panama City Beach. They love the kiddy rides."

She reached across the table and squeezed Jodie's hand. "Will you remember me?"

"Yes, I will."

Clara Lee stood, crossed the café, and stepped into the waning heat of an Indian summer.

Jodie signaled the waitress. "What's the damage?"

The waitress answered sixty cents, and Jodie slipped her hand into her pocket for three quarters.

"Gee, thanks. I'm saving for junior college." She leaned closer and whispered, "I'm going to be a writer someday." The girl blushed under the weight of what Jodie had known as a Jewel sentiment: don't go wishing for what you can't have. Life's kicks in the teeth hurt less that way.

"That's good." Jodie stood. "Can't hurt to have a plan."

She left the café and crossed the vacant lot. It had been a long time coming, but she too had a plan working its way through her brain, its clarity as pure as the brilliant sunlight.

## Fifty-One

The return trip was made in strained silence, and now Red sat, hunched in defeat, Maggie occupying the rocker across from him. Their steady gazes made Jodie prickly, and she wished he'd get on with whatever he'd insisted needed settling. He'd handed Maggie a set of pages bound in a blue cover, titled Last Will and Testament of Charles E. Dozier. When she'd finished reading the document, she came up out of the chair, her round face red with anger.

"I knew all along Hazel had plundered those old records. How many times did I plead with you to put that savings passbook in Silas's safe?"

"Spilt milk," he muttered.

"Damn you, Red Dozier. That's all you got to say?"

"Hush now, Maggie. If I'd got to that lawyer boy first, I could've turned this thing around." He rubbed his hand across his grizzly face, the roughness of his whiskers audible in the closeness of the room.

"You're a bigger damn fool than I thought. This was no pool hall brawl you could bleed and get up from. It had the stench of revenge from its onset."

"Don't you think I knew that?"

"I don't care that it hangs you with a stingy living that'll barely keep you in food and whiskey. Or that when you're pushing up daisies, what money's left, along with this worthless place, goes to Miss Mary. God knows the woman earned every cent."

"Maggie …," he pleaded, but Jodie felt his eyes on her.

"Shut the hell up. I ain't had my full say."

Red nodded, his shoulders slumped.

"Why not leave Jodie that old dog you're so crazy about? Anything at all to have put her name alongside yours. Although why she even cares beats the hell out of me." Maggie pitched the papers at Red and walked out, the air scorched.

Red lay back on the bed, his hands folded across his chest. "She's just riled. Things will die down and she'll see I ain't holding to this paper."

He closed his eyes, and maybe his raspy breathing returned to normal, but Jodie didn't wait around to know. Red seemed to have missed Maggie's finer point, but she hadn't.

She'd walked a third of the way to the creek before noticing that Buster followed. He veered off the main path, flushing a covey of quail. The birds lifted on silver wings, ably outdistancing the old dog. While she wished the tiny birds' pursuers were all slow, she was glad that the dog had retained his will to hunt.

After an empty chase, Buster drank his fill at the creek and flopped down next to her, panting. His wet tongue wallowed to one side of his pink mouth, and she stroked his broad head.

Sometime later, she heard footsteps approaching, and Maggie stumbled into the clearing, dropping onto the ground next to her.

"I thought you'd left."

"I did. Had too. Worried that I might smother him in his sleep. Came back looking for you. Figured I'd find you here."

"Was he always …?"

"Crooked? Let me tell you a story, and you decide."

Jodie nodded.

"The summer Red turned a strapping sixteen, he already had a smile to pick life's pocket. He left here, his head full of fanciful notions, and went down south with his mama's no-account kin. He got a job in one of those big Miami Beach hotels, sucking up to rich tourists. He charmed more money out of those fools than he ever knew existed. Came home with his pockets jingling, wearing city duds, and the local girls swarmed him like bees to honeysuckle. He was a sight." Maggie chuckled. "A time or two he even made me wish I was different."

"Did he ever go back?"

"Nah, he was already poolhall–wise and rattlesnake-quick. Turned to running bootleg whiskey over on the beaches in a brand new Buick roadster. He left honest work and never looked back. He once joked that what he did was akin to Roosevelt's WPA for rascals."

"Did he ever try farming this worthless patch of dirt?"

"No, but he liked talking about it. I think it made him think about someday living respectable."

"About what happened today—whether he ever says it or not, I know he's my daddy. I do think he went into that meeting believing he could turn things his way."

Maggie sighed. "He bargained everything for the chance to be done with that woman. And finish out his last days here on this godforsaken place."

From the direction of the house, the long blast of an automobile horn sounded, and Buster set out in a stiff trot. Jodie pulled Maggie to her feet, and they hurried back along the trail. Maggie stopped after a ways, bent forward, her hands resting on her knees, and motioned Jodie on.

Reaching the back stoop, Jodie caught sight of Silas's truck pulling onto the road. Red sat at the kitchen table slurping Rice Krispies. There were two other bowls on the table with spoons placed beside each; a jug of milk and the box of cereal sat in the center of the table.

"Good of you to fix dinner. But we weren't in that big a hurry," Maggie quipped as she came into the kitchen, panting like a dying fish.

Milk dribbled down Red's chin, but he appeared as smug as if he'd grabbed the good life by the tail.

Maggie shot him a look to kill. "You pathetic old fool." She turned to leave.

Red pushed up from the table and called, "Maggie, hold up. I'll need a favor."

"Forget it. I'm not the least bit interested in doing you any favors."

Red followed her onto the porch, and after a mostly one-sided conversation, Maggie got into her truck and drove away. Red slapped his hand against his leg in what appeared a celebratory shot, and whatever was said between them worked on him like a spring tonic. He scuffed off to bed and slept like a drunken man until time for supper.

Jodie woke after a restless night, dressed, and went into the kitchen to start breakfast. She'd decided to tell Red of her plan to leave over their meal. When he didn't answer her calls, she went to his door.

Buster, sleeping next to Red's empty bed, looked up as if he was surprised to see her and not Red. She worried, since man and dog had taken up their old habit of early morning wanderings in the woods behind the house. He would not have gone without the dog. Nor would Buster have left his side if he'd fallen and lay hurt.

In the distance, Jodie heard the deep roar of Silas's wrecker, and she hurried onto the front porch. Diesel smoke billowed from its stack as Silas drove into the side yard, Maggie and Red following in her truck. Jodie hurried off the steps to the sound of heavy chains slipping along a hoist.

"Morning, Miss Jodie." Silas dropped two mounted tires onto the ground at the rear of the old Dodge and grabbed two more from the wrecker.

"She's all yours, Jodie," Red called as he got out of Maggie's truck and shuffled toward her. He stopped and leaned on the Dodge, wheezing, as if a single shot of adrenalin had delivered more juice than his weak body could handle.

"Jesus, Red, I thank you. But I've got hundreds of miles ahead of me. Got to be in Dallas for tryouts on the twenty-second, and that's less than a week.

Red showed no surprise at her decision.

Silas squinted up at her from where he squatted next to the Dodge.

"If it's a long bus ride you favor, or Red working a trade with William, then I'll go on back to the station."

"Screw any trade. I'd walk first."

"Okay, so back off. Trust me to work my magic wrench on this old gal. She's a bit neglected, but I'll have her purring like a ruby-red Corvette. First, I got to get her off these blocks and back in high heels. Engine's solid. She needs hoses replaced, radiator flushed, carburetor cleaned, engine serviced, wiper blades, and whatever else I find to do between now and tomorrow morning." He pushed a tire onto the wheel mount and reached back for the iron. "When I'm done, this old gal will take you any place you point her."

"All right, but don't get my ass stranded someplace between here and Dallas." She was going for broke, and this time nothing would stop her.

Red waved off Jodie's help, and with considerable effort, he climbed the porch steps and made his way toward the bedroom.

"He held up good this morning. He's going to be fine."

It was just like Maggie to say as much. Silas sat back on his heels, lit up a Lucky and asked, "You gals got something like a secret handshake?"

"Shit, Silas, we're not the Eastern Star, you know."

"No, I don't. And what little I do, I don't like. But for now, I've settled on thinking of you as just plain weird. That way it's not such a stretch."

"That's handy thinking." She thought her heart would burst and she believed she better understood Maggie's peculiar love for Red.

"If you two are done with that piece of romance, Jodie may want to get that bird's nest out of the back seat and buff up the hood ornament." Maggie's voice was tender, her round cheeks flushed.

Silas hooked the Dodge behind the wrecker, tied down its steering wheel, and hauled it away.

"Guess I'm done here." Maggie turned toward her truck, stopped, and looked back at Jodie. "Hell, in all this commotion I nearly forgot." Her face broke into a smile. "I'm to tell you that a Crystal Ann called the station wanting to get up with you."

"You sure it wasn't Teddy who called?" Her distrust of hope bubbled up from her gut, but she felt her heart countering with a new rhythm.

"You heard right." Maggie shook her head and made a small sound of impatience. "Hell, girl, you can always come home with your tail between your legs, and I'll throw you a party."

Maggie pulled Jodie to her bosom and held her firmly, as if she intended to imprint the feel of her onto her own skin; her embrace carried the feel of a forever good-bye. The scent of gardenia and the slightest tinge of sweat would forever remind Jodie of Maggie. Had she known how unprepared she was to face the loss of Maggie, she might have reconsidered.


From Red's room, she heard, "That you, Jodie?"

A wedge of sunlight played across the bedcovers, and he pointed her to the rocker. The closeness of the room squeezed like a warm fist.

"Jodie, your mama … Jewel wanted to go off with them band boys in the worst way. Me, I didn't want her to and I told her so." He swallowed hard. "But the truth was, I had nothing to offer the two of you."

"Was there ever any truth to the two of you planning to run off together?"

"No, there was never such plan as that."

"When she left me at Aunt Pearl's, I don't think she ever meant to come back."

"About that, I can't say. But I do know your mama loved you. You were never the reason she left."

"Why did you? Come for me, I mean."

"You were innocent—and I never meant a stranger should raise you. You don't look like her. Too much like me …." He drifted a bit. "… had that smooth skin the color of fool's gold, that hair blacker than chimney soot. A pureness with a song that put larks to shame."

His voice held a dreamlike quality, barely audible. "Then, you've got gumption neither of us had. You'll be fine."

"I'm sorry about all those cards I never sent. I was too ashamed of the way I left."

"Never missed cards."

"Red, there's something else."

"No, Jodie. I know everything I need to know." He raised his hand and pointed toward the dresser. "You might want to take those papers with you when you go." His hand dropped back onto his chest.

She picked up four sheets of paper and a padded folder. Written in his hand were her complete game statistics for four seasons of high school basketball. The folder held her high school diploma. She turned to thank him, but he either slept or pretended. She straightened the tangled covers for the last time, and when she was ready, she pulled the door closed behind her.

She went to bed early, determined to get the sleep she'd need for a long drive, only to be awakened by the roar of the wrecker on the road. She dressed and went to stand on the porch, listening as Silas dropped the Dodge. Leaving the wrecker at the far end of the lane, he drove the Dodge into the yard. She stepped off the porch and went to meet him.

"Didn't plan on waking you. But now that you're up ..." He grinned.

He climbed onto the car and sat on its roof, his feet dangling. He pulled a bottle from his back pocket, and after she'd settled next to him, he passed it to her.

He rapped the roof with his knuckles. "You don't have to worry about getting stranded. This old gal's solid."

"I'm not worried. With any luck at all I'll drive her back in one of those little skimpy uniforms."

"You just might at that." He passed the bottle, and after they'd downed nearly half, she asked if he was drunk.

"Not yet. How 'bout you?"

"About the same." She moved closer to him.

He reached and gently pulled her down to lie next to him, and they each studied the starlit sky.

"Remember the summer we counted fourteen shooting stars and decided it had to be a world's record?" He smiled at what she believed was his memory of their shared innocence, the ease of it.

"Yep, and you were so sure, you wrote it up and sent it off to the *Grit* newspaper."

"I was naïve enough to think it would result in a miracle and I'd get a free ride to the university."

He'd gone to the mailbox every day that summer.

"Got little time for stargazing now days. But I think about it. The closest I come is the bits of poetry I read now and again. A lady poet wrote that love is love, and it doesn't need to make sense. What do you think?"

"A good woman once told me as much. If she's not altogether right, then she's real close." Tears ran along her temples, and she didn't feel to hide them.

"The woman I talked to yesterday? Crystal Ann, I think she said." He didn't look at her, and while his question was awkward, it was all right that he asked. They'd both need practice at honesty.

"Yeah. In Mobile. Think I'll start there. But first I'll make a quick stop at Mr. Samuel's place. Settle one last thing before heading out."

"Can't hurt."

He climbed down from the rooftop and pulled her to her feet. They held each other for all the right reasons, and then he let go.

She understood that he wished they could go back to the way he'd believed things were. But Jodie Taylor was right where she lived and breathed, and welcomed her tomorrows.

At dawn, after only a few more hours of sleep, Jodie took her suitcase in hand and stopped at Red's door. She listened to the sound of his steady breathing, and Buster raised his head, blinked, and resettled. She was content, believing that Red and Buster were to live out the remainder of their days together in this place.

On the passenger seat of the Dodge, Silas had left ten twenties stuffed into an envelope, along with a brief note that wished her a good life. On the dash, he'd placed a fistful of wildflowers.

Turning west, Jodie glanced back at the old house, awash in the radiant colors of the new day, and somewhere Jewel Taylor was smiling.

## ABOUT THE AUTHOR

Pat Spears's debut novel, *Dream Chaser*, was released in August 2014 by Twisted Road Publications. She has been nominated for a United States Artist Grant, and her short stories have appeared in numerous journals, including the *North American Review, Appalachian Heritage, Seven Hills Review,* and anthologies titled *Law and Disorder* from Main Street Rag, *Bridges and Borders* from Jane's Stories Press and *Saints and Sinners: New Fiction from the Festival 2012.* Her short story "Stranger At My Door" received honorable mention in the 2013 Lorian Hemingway Short Story competition and "Whelping" was a finalist for the Rash Award and appears in the 2014 issue of *Broad River Review.*

Pat is a sixth generation Floridian who lives in Tallahassee, Florida. For more about Pat and her work, visit her website: www.patspears.com, or find her on Facebook at www.facebook.com/pfspears

# Acknowledgements

I wish to thank my first readers for their astute insights and invaluable feedback on the manuscript: Sally Bellerose, Tricia Booker, Margie Craig, Connie May Fowler, Darlyn Finch Kuhn, Gale Massey, Donna Meredith, Lorin Oberweger, Amanda Silva, and Vickie Weaver. Each of you embraced the novel's protagonist, Jodie Taylor, and her sometimes dark, but always hopeful journey to self-discovery, thus encouraging me to tell her story from the heart.

A deeply felt thank you to Connie May Fowler, author and teacher extraordinaire, and to a special community of fellow writers for their gracious and enthusiastic support: Alex Dunlop, Karen K Becker, Debra Exum, Victor Hess, Bonnie Omer Johnson, Nancy Levine, John Macilroy, Diane Marshall, Rosemary Porto, Sheila Stuewe and Emily Webber.

Thanks to Dorothy Allison for her gift of friendship and encouragement over the long years it has taken to breathe life into this novel and a special thank you to Joan Leggitt, for her unyielding faith in this story and my ability to tell it honestly.

Praise for *Dream Chaser* by Pat Spears

"Fine, damn fine. And at times simply stunning !" - **Dorothy Allison**, author of National Book Award finalist *Bastard Out of Carolina*

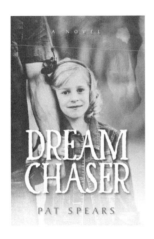

"An extraordinarily well written and original novel, "Dream Chaser" clearly documents author Pat Spears as a talented and imaginative wordsmith. With its deftly crafted characters and a riveting storyline from beginning to end, "Dream Chaser" is highly recommended." – *Midwest Book Review*

"Spears' ability to endear us to such flawed characters speaks to a rare, gifted view of humanity." – **Tricia Booker**, *My Left Hook*

"… a real accomplishment … [Dream Chaser] is a powerful and beautiful book." - **Sean Carswell**, author of *Madhouse Fog*

"Spears has a remarkable gift of taking the kind of rundown man we'd shake our heads over … and painting his humanity with such tenderness we want to rush up to the next down-on-his-luck stranger we see and offer a hug and assistance." – *Southern Literary Review*

"… readers will cheer Jesse's misguided efforts to salvage his life and win over his children. Pat Spears has created a realistic and hopeful story of a father's love and a family's hard-won salvation. *Dream Chaser* is a novel to relish and ponder, and the characters will stick with a reader long after the final pages." - *Tallahassee Democrat*